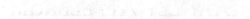

MEDIEVAL TALES AND STORIES

108 Prose Narratives of the Middle Ages

Selected and Translated by
STANLEY APPELBAUM

DOVER PUBLICATIONS, INC.
Mineola, New York

Dedicated to the memory of
my employer, publisher, friend,
HAYWARD CIRKER
(1917–2000)

Bibliographical Note

Medieval Tales and Stories: 108 Prose Narratives of the Middle Ages is a new work, first published by Dover Publications, Inc., in 2000. The work consists of new translations by Stanley Appelbaum of stories newly selected from the sources listed on pages xv and xvi, with introductory matter and notes supplied by the translator.

International Standard Book Number: 0-486-41407-8

Manufactured in the United States of America
Dover Publications, Inc., 31 East 2nd Street, Mineola, N.Y. 11501

PREFACE

This new anthology of 108 medieval stories has a twofold purpose. Its chief aim is to open up an unfamiliar field of pleasure for lovers of short stories; almost all the pieces included here are hard to find in any language, and only a handful have been translated into English previously. A narrower, more abstract aim is to try to establish within medieval studies a clearer notion of the short-story genre.

Both "medieval" and "story" are vaguely used, and both terms need defining for the purposes of this volume. The material included here was written in western Europe (France, Spain, Italy, Germany, and perhaps England—if the *Gesta Romanorum* was actually compiled there) between roughly 1100 and 1500. For precocious Italy the cutoff date was 1400; for tradition-bound Germany, a story collection published as late as 1515 (still before the Reformation) has been included. The original languages were medieval Latin, 13th- and 14th-century Italian, 14th-century Spanish, 15th-century French, and early-16th-century German.

So much for "medieval." As for "story": these are brief prose stories, fictional or legendary, intended for entertainment and/or moral instruction—in short, the exact medieval equivalents of the modern short story. Unfortunately, most anthologies of medieval literature in translation (not only into English), and even manuals of medieval literature, use "story" indiscriminately in place of "narrative," to include material from novels, biographies, histories, and many forms of narrative poetry.[1] It is just as if a historian of mid-19th-century American literature were to give the blanket name of "story" to Poe's "The Fall of the House of Usher," Hawthorne's *The Scarlet Letter*, Longfellow's "Paul Revere's Ride," the same poet's *Evangeline*, and excerpts from George Bancroft's *History of the United States*.

In the belief that tiny snippets of literature are uninstructive and unsatisfying even in a brief anthology, I have chosen stories from only ten medieval collections (major ones well known to medievalists), selecting enough from each to exemplify the true flavor and character of each collection. Not only are four centuries and several countries represented: the subjects cover the full medieval range from sacred to bawdy.

All the stories have been freshly translated into current colloquial English, directly from the original languages in their original forms. The stories have not been retold, abridged, adapted, conflated, reinterpreted, expurgated, bowdlerized, modernized, or processed in any other way to deprive them of their pristine form or

---

[1] It is chiefly the editors of actual medieval short-story collections who seem to have a firmer notion of genre in this area. Some histories of literature fail to indicate at all whether certain major works are in verse or in prose!

their documentary value for students of literature.[2] Modern original-language editions with some commentary (ranging from very skimpy to very full) were available to the translator in most cases; but only for stories Nos. 37–43, 49–61, 63, 73, and 91–99 was it possible to consult prior English translations (for Nos. 1–17, translations from the original Latin into medieval Spanish and medieval English were consulted).

In this volume, students of comparative literature will find stories that directly influenced such later writers as Boccaccio, Shakespeare, Cervantes, and Flaubert. Folklorists will find early treatments (in some cases, the earliest) of themes and motifs that were still being collected orally in the late 20th century. The numerous readers fascinated by medieval culture will find firsthand accounts of, or allusions to, such elements as: pacts with the Devil, witchcraft, magic, astrology, and alchemy; warfare, Crusaders, chivalry, martial priests, blood brotherhood, and prisoners captured for ransoming; trial by combat and judicial torture; Church councils; mercantile life and crafts councils; guile and deceit of all kinds; famous men, such as Abelard, Dante, and Giotto; and the obsession with Fortune as a rival to Providence in the governing of human life.

The major sequence within the volume is chronological by the ten major collections, insofar as their dates can be established. Within each collection, the sequence of stories follows that in the original collection (this was impossible to determine for *Il Pecorone*).

Although the collections included here sometimes borrowed stories from one another, only one plot has been included twice in this volume, because of the great interest attaching to the sources of *The Merchant of Venice* (see Nos. 20 and 73).

All the story titles in this volume were supplied by the translator as brief, convenient tags. Not all the original stories had titles, and when titles existed, they were usually cumbersome or misleading, or gave away too much of the plot.

For convenience of reference, the stories have been given one sequence of numbers, from 1 to 108. Except for a very few clearly indicated instances, the numbering referred to in the volume is always this numbering from 1 to 108.

The apparatus supplied by the editor has intentionally been kept brief and nontechnical. The general Introduction is meant only as a cursory survey of medieval story literature, intended basically to place the anthologized stories in perspective. The footnotes have been kept to a bare minimum, to avoid the appearance of a forbidding tome; the reader may still want to consult one or two good reference works for geographical and historical terms (such as "quintain"). The introductory comments to the ten individual story collections offer a few more explanations, provide basic information about the works and their authors (where the author is known), and suggest a few randomly chosen parallels in world literature. The original-language editions on which these translations were based are listed in the section "Sources of the Stories," which follows the general Introduction.

---

[2]There are two minor reservations to this declaration: (1) a number of the stories have been removed from the moralizing framework in which they were originally embedded (see the introductory comments to the individual collections); and (2) occasionally a technical term has been explained directly within the translation to avoid overburdening the page with footnotes (this occurs mainly in the Sacchetti section), since the volume is intended for the general reader.

CONTENTS

INTRODUCTION

The Medieval Short Story in Its Context

It was in the Middle Ages that the western European short story (defined as a brief fictional narrative[1] in prose) seems to have emerged as a viable literary genre destined for an unbroken line of development. The following is a cursory sketch of the context from which it issued, beginning with antecedent and collateral phenomena.

The Ancient Mediterranean World. Full-fledged short stories are known to us from the Middle Kingdom of Egypt, ca. 1800 B.C.[2] In Greece, story material was included in generous amounts in such works as the *Histories* of Herodotus (5th century B.C.), but, aside from the very brief Aesopic fables, there is no collection of brief prose fiction. In the early centuries A.D., Greek prose was used for a number of novels of romantic adventure, and some of the pieces by, or attributed to, the satirical writer Lucian (2nd century A.D.) could be classified as stories, but no such genre was firmly established. Ancient Rome produced novels such as the *Satyricon* by Petronius (1st century A.D.) and *The Golden Ass* by Apuleius (2nd century), both of which have stories inserted in them; but again: no genre.

Asia. The world's greatest prose storytelling area appears to be India, whose influence spread in all directions. The early centuries A.D. produced both purely secular story collections, like the *Panchatantra*, and the Buddhist *Jātaka* stories, which ostensibly narrate experiences of the Buddha in previous incarnations but are not intrinsically religious. A matchless pinnacle of interweaving of time-honored story material is to be found in the *Ocean of the Streams of Story* by Somadeva (late 11th century). By at least 600 A.D. a strong storytelling tradition had been established in China, which in turn soon influenced Japan. Meanwhile, stories

---

[1]Fictional, or legendary, from our current point of view, though some of these stories may have been believed in implicitly when they were written. (Drama is excluded from this survey.) [2]Here, as elsewhere in this Introduction, works are mentioned that, for one reason or another, could not have been known directly by medieval Europeans; no such direct knowledge is implied, but a tradition of storytelling is affirmed, as is the strong possibility of oral transmission of fictional themes and motifs.

from India were already being translated into the languages of Persia. After the Arab conquest they were translated into the newest world-class language, Arabic, in which form they reached Europe through direct contact with Arabic-speaking conquerors of Spain and Sicily and, later, via the Crusaders. The *Arabian Nights* collection was compiled from many sources during the period covered by this volume.

Medieval Latin. The use of Latin as a universal European language throughout the Middle Ages, and beyond, was a legacy of the ancient Roman Empire and the ecumenical organization of the Church. (Education was primarily intended for men who planned to enter the clergy and it was conducted in Latin; only gradually did such privileged characters begin to compose or transcribe literature in the vernacular— that is, in the individual national or regional languages.) Medieval Latin differs in certain basic ways from the classical Latin of Cicero and Horace (partly through natural development, partly through some writers' faulty education), but it is not intrinsically ludicrous or debased, and in the best hands it has a glory and beauty all its own.

Medieval Latin fictional narrative literature, taken as a whole (poetry dominates quantitatively, as in all medieval literatures), is too vast even for the concisest summary. Suffice it to say that a surprisingly wide range of narrative genres, subjects, and forms better known to the general reader from the vernacular literatures actually made their first appearance in Latin. Thus, for example, both the heroic epic (e.g., the *Chanson de Roland*) and the "beast epic" (e.g., the *Roman de Renart*) are already prefigured by Latin poems of the 10th century; while a full life of King Arthur first appears in the (prose) *History of the Kings of Britain* by Geoffrey of Monmouth, ca. 1135.[3]

Latin fictional narrative prose rarely attained the length of a novel (one example is the *Destruction of Troy* by Guido delle Colonne, of the late 13th century), but shorter pieces capable of being regarded as stories are abundant. There are many collections of fables.[4] One genre, which surely served as entertainment as well as edification, was saints' lives, which begin as early as the 4th century and become omnipresent in the 12th and 13th.[5] Closely related thematically to saints' lives are the numerous collections of Christian miracles.[6]

In addition, occasional stories are to be found embedded in chronicles and histories, travel accounts, and prose miscellanies, but the richest source of recognizable short stories is the so-called *exempla* literature. An *exemplum* ("example") is an illustrative story either occurring in the course

[3]Because Arthurian material is so widely available in translation today, it has been intentionally omitted in this anthology, except for one marginally Arthurian story from Italy (No. 40). [4]Fables of the Aesopic type occur in several medieval languages besides Latin; the only such fables included here, from general story collections, are Nos. 15, 24, and 62. [5]Incidental examples in this volume are Nos. 50 and 51. [6]The miracle story is represented in this volume by Nos. 32 and 34.

of a preacher's sermon or in the course of a didactic moral or ethical work. *Exempla* are found in sermons as early as the 10th century, and collections of separate *exempla* intended as a storehouse for sermon writers are found as early as the 13th. Didactic works that are fundamentally story collections begin early in the 12th century.

Four Latin *exempla* collections have been tapped for this anthology: the very first European-language short-story collection, the *Disciplina clericalis*; the earliest European version of the universally known Seven Sages story complex, the *Dolopathos*; stories from the sermons of the most highly regarded writer of such material, Jacques de Vitry; and selections from the best-known Latin story collection, the *Gesta Romanorum*.

French. Many of the chief fictional narrative genres, in verse and prose, appeared in French before they did in any other vernacular literature, though the prose short story was slow in arriving. In verse, French had saints' lives as early as the 9th century, heroic epics (*chansons de geste*) by about 1100, epics on Greco-Roman subjects (e.g., the fall of Troy) by the mid-12th century, Arthurian romances and "Breton *lais*" (brief narrative poems based on Celtic lore) by the second half of the 12th century, "beast epics" and *fabliaux* (humorous, often bawdy, brief narrative poems about commoners' foibles) by the 12th century.

The very end of the 12th century and the first half of the 13th witnessed the prose explosion of the magnificent (and sometimes unbelievably lengthy) Arthurian novels. French prose now became the instrument of other narrative genres (e.g., miracles) as well. Novel-length works continued into the 14th and 15th centuries, but it was only at the end of the medieval period that the short story began to flourish (it was to thrive in the 16th century). The first important French collection, the *Cent nouvelles nouvelles*, is represented in this volume.

Provençal. The other major language in the area that is now France (the southern part) was Provençal, most famous as the medium of troubadour lyric poetry. In the realm of fictional narrative, there are: a heroic epic poem (late 12th century), two major verse romances (one Arthurian) from the 13th century, and a number of brief narrative poems called *novas*.

Prose fiction is chiefly exemplified by the 13th-century *vidas* and *razos* written to accompany collections of older troubadour poetry. The *vidas* are highly fanciful brief biographies of the poets, and the *razos* are legends and tales meant to elucidate the content of specific poems. Both *vidas* and *razos* are full of floating folklore motifs and were highly influential on later European literature, especially Italian.

Spanish. Fictional narrative in verse includes heroic epics (*Poema de mio Cid*, ca. 1150) and a wide variety of long works in the 13th century: subjects from Spanish and from ancient history, saints' lives, and miracles. In prose, novels of chivalry begin shortly before 1300, with both

Arthurian and Crusades material extensively represented for the rest of the medieval period. In the 15th century a famous novel about love, the *Cárcel de amor* (Prison of Love), was written by Diego de San Pedro. Material resembling short stories appears in various prose chronicles. But the most typical medieval Spanish form of the short story is to be found in such didactic collections as *Calila e Dimna* (adapted from Arabic, ultimately from the Sanskrit *Panchatantra*), the *Libro de los enxiemplos* (Book of Exempla), and the *Libro de los gatos* (Book of the Cats; animal fables), all of the 13th century. The glorious culmination of this tradition is the work represented in this anthology, *El Conde Lucanor*, by Juan Manuel.

Catalan and Portuguese. Although they could not provide material for this book, the two other medieval Iberian literatures deserve mention here for the sake of completeness. Catalan narrative prose includes excellent chronicles of the 13th and 14th centuries, and several outstanding novels, including *Blanquerna* by Ramón Lull (Llull; late 13th century) and *Tirant lo Blanc*, by Joanot Martorell (mid-15th century).

Medieval Portuguese is known chiefly for lyric poetry, verse drama, and exceptionally fine chronicles. There is no separate short-story tradition.

Italian. Italian literature was a very late starter, about 1200, but Italy soon took the lead in European storytelling. The principal literary monuments of the 13th century are lyric poems (Dante, 1265–1321, was predominantly a lyric poet before undertaking the majestic *Divine Comedy*), but at least one major prose work appeared before the end of that century, *Il Novellino*, the first major Italian story collection, from which a dozen items have been selected for this book. The 14th century produced even greater prose, two very high points being *The Little Flowers of Saint Francis* and, in mid-century, the most famous and influential of all short-story collections, Boccaccio's *Decameron* (too readily available in English to be included here). Among the later 14th-century Italian story collections inspired by Boccaccio, two are represented in this volume, the *Pecorone* of Giovanni Fiorentino and the *Trecentonovelle* of Franco Sacchetti. In the 15th and 16th centuries, Italy continued to be the European leader in short stories, and the genre has continued to be a major one in Italian literature to the present day.

German. In the German lands, prose fiction developed late. Verse was the medium not only for such long, substantial works as the *Nibelungenlied*, Wolfram's *Parzival*, and Gottfried's *Tristan* (all early 13th century), but also for briefer, humorous narratives (*Schwänke*) in the *fabliau* tradition (13th through 16th centuries). Only in the 15th century did humorous prose stories make their appearance, culminating in the Till Eulenspiegel collection represented in this anthology (earliest extant publication 1515, but the material is earlier). In the later 16th century the floodgates were opened, releasing a wealth of prose stories and novelettes in the form of *Schwänke* (singular: *Schwank*) and *Volksbücher* (popular tales, chapbooks). **Dutch/Flemish.** All significant fictional narrative was in verse, including epic poetry on Greco-Roman subjects, French-inspired heroic epic and romance, saints' lives and miracles, and an important contribution to the literature of Reynard the Fox (everything mentioned dates from the 12th and 13th centuries). **English.** In the Middle English, post–Norman Conquest period, verse was the preferred medium for fictional narrative, with the rarest exceptions. One need only call to mind the numerous verse romances (in rhymed couplets, like *Sir Orfeo*; in stanzas, like Thomas Chestre's *Sir Launfal*; or neo-alliterative, like *Sir Gawain and the Green Knight* — all three of the 14th century), the briefer ballads of the type collected by Child (beginning in the 15th century?), and such longer works as Gower's *Confessio amantis* and Chaucer's *Canterbury Tales* (both from the end of the 14th century). (Of course, the Canterbury "Tale of Melibeus" and "Parson's Tale" are in prose, but Chaucer is so easily available in the original and in translation that there was no need to include those stories here.)

The 15th century produced that long prose masterpiece, Malory's *Le Morte Darthur*, but no significant prose short story, except for some direct translations by Caxton and others. That genre was to flourish, along with the short novel, in the 16th century, thanks to French and Italian influence.

*

To complete the survey, two literary traditions must be briefly mentioned, though they are not represented here, as they lie largely or altogether out of the translator's sphere of competence: the Nordic and the Celtic. **Scandinavian languages.** In Old Norse/Icelandic, we possess major monuments of western European prose narrative (not precisely fiction) in the mythological *Prose Edda* (early 13th century) and in the sagas (generally novel-length, mainly from the 13th century), which concern family history, regional history, the lives of important local individuals, the colonization of Iceland, and further explorations in Greenland and Vinland.

In Danish and Swedish, the most vital medieval fictional narrative takes the form of ballads. **Celtic languages.** In Irish, we have the earliest corpus of western European prose storytelling, all preceding the period to which this volume is devoted: the *Cattle Raid at Cooley* and the plentiful stories about Cuchulain, Finn, Ossian, and others. Fortunately, more and more of this material is becoming available in translation all the time. Its absence here may be regrettable, but: (1) it is from an older period, and (2) it is difficult to demonstrate that this material had a direct influence on subsequent mainstream European storytelling until the late rediscovery of this tradition.

In Welsh, the chief monument is the 12th-century story collection known as the *Mabinogion*, with partly mythological, partly Arthurian material. In this instance, a strong case has been made by some for direct influence on the early French-language writers of Arthuriana, particularly Chrétien de Troyes (ca. 1130–ca. 1190). When one gets beyond the question of very specific influences, there is little doubt that the entire Arthurian tradition is deeply indebted to Celtic sources.

Anyone who reads this volume through in its chronological sequence will undoubtedly observe the growth in both intricacy and flavor apparent in the medieval prose short story in the course of these four centuries. The changeover from Latin to the individual native languages of the writers made a big difference, adding to the coziness and the conversational flow, to the range of subject matter, and to the liberation of the story from its didactic and pedagogical utilitarianism. It is almost as if we were seeing the primitive mammals emerging from the shadow of the omnipotent dinosaurs and beginning to claim their place in the sun. At the close of the 20th century, prose is the medium of preference for fiction, but it was not always so. This present volume is devoted to these honorable ancestors.

SOURCES OF THE STORIES

Stories 1–17: *Die "Disciplina Clericalis" des Petrus Alfonsi (das älteste Novellenbuch des Mittelalters) (Kleine Ausgabe)*, edd. Alfons Hilka & Werner Söderhjelm, Heidelberg, Carl Winter's Universitätsbuchhandlung, 1911 (Sammlung mittellateinischer Texte, 1). [Story 1 = original exempla 1 & 2; Nos. 2–17 = exempla 6, 7, 9, 10, 11, 12, 14, 15, 16, 17, 19, 20, 22, 23, 24, 27, respectively.]

Stories 18–23: *Historia Septem Sapientum II. Johannis de Alta Silva Dolopathos sive De rege et septem sapientibus*, ed. Alfons Hilka, Heidelberg, Carl Winter's Universitätsbuchhandlung, 1913 (Sammlung mittellateinischer Texte, 5). [= the stories told in the original by Wise Men 1, 2, 4, 5, 6, 7.]

Stories 24–36: *Die Exempla aus den "Sermones feriales et communes" des Jakob von Vitry*, ed. Joseph Greven, Heidelberg, Carl Winter's Universitätsbuchhandlung, 1914 (Sammlung mittellateinischer Texte, 9). [= exempla 2, 3, 4, 20, 25, 39, 44, 53, 61, 74, 87, 98, 102 in the 1914 edition.]

Stories 37–43: *Le cento novelle antiche secondo l'edizione del MDXXV*, ed. Paolo Antonio Tosi, Milan, 1825. (Original 1525 edition: Bologna, Girolamo Benedetti.) [= stories 2, 3, 8, 63, 75, 96, 99 in the 1525 edition.]

Stories 44–48: *Tesoro dei novellieri italiani scelti dal decimoterzo al decimonono secolo*, ed. Giuseppe Zirardini, Paris, Baudry, Libreria Europea, 1847. [= stories 6, 54, 65, 68, 100 in the 1572 edition; see commentary to Nos. 37–48 in the main text for details.]

Stories 49–61: [*Gesta Romanorum:*] *Institutiones Catholicae (vulgo Gesta Romanorum) ex probatissimis Historiis excerptae, accuratius & elimatius, quam antea usquam castigatae*, Lyons, Heirs of "Jacobus Junta," printed by Jacques Faure, 1555. [Editions and numbering vary. The selections in this volume = stories 5, 15, 18, 28, 56, 59, 63, 66, 67, 74, 80, 120, 141 in the 1555 edition.]

Stories 62–72: *Libro de Patronio [El Conde Lucanor]*, in *Escritores en prosa anteriores al siglo XV*, ed. Pascual de Gayangos, Madrid, M. Rivadeneyra, ca. 1860 (Biblioteca de autores españoles, 51). [= original exempla 2, 11, 15, 20, 21, 24, 36, 41, 42, 44, 45.]

Stories 73–77: Same source as for Nos. 44–48. [Story 73 = Book IV, No. 1 of the *Pecorone;* other original numbering not available.]

Stories 78–90: *Delle novelle di Franco Sacchetti cittadino fiorentino Tomo primo/secondo/terzo.* Milan, Società Tipografica de' Classici Italiani, 3 vols., 1804, 1804, 1805. [= original stories 3, 17, 63, 83, 84, 86, 114, 159, 161, 163, 164, 191, 208.]

Stories 91–99: *Les cent nouvelles nouvelles / Publiées d'après le seul manuscrit connu,* ed. Thomas Wright, Paris, P. Jannet, 2 vols., 1858 & 1857. [= original stories 3, 5, 20, 28, 72, 75, 79, 96, 98.]

Stories 100–108: *Till Eulenspiegel. Abdruck der Ausgabe vom Jahre 1515,* Halle a/S., Max Niemeyer, 1884. (Original 1515 edition: Strassburg (Strasbourg), Johannes Grieninger.) [= original stories 13, 17, 27, 31, 34, 38, 50, 67, 71.]

STORIES 1–17

From *Disciplina clericalis*
by Pedro Alfonso

First place in this anthology naturally goes to the oldest collection of Oriental tales translated into a European language, which is at the same time the oldest European short-story collection of the Middle Ages (and just possibly: in all of history).

Painfully brief as the biographical references to its author are, they are nonetheless often contradictory, speculative, and suspect. The following brief sketch appears to be safe: He was born in 1062 in Huesca, Aragon, and was a Jew named Moshe. He was probably an intellectual (a physician? an astronomer?) at the court of Alfonso VI, king of León and Castile (1030–1109), who is most famous for having exiled the Cid and for having conquered Toledo from the Moors in 1085. That city became a center of the celebrated Spanish *convivencia* (cooperation between Moors, Jews, and Christians), a leading element of which was the translation, and transmittal to Europe, of much ancient and medieval thought previously accessible only to readers of Arabic.

On Peter and Paul's Day, June 29, of 1106, Moshe became a Christian and was thereafter called Petrus Alfonsi ("Peter of Alphonse"; the Latin version occurs in a wide variety of forms) in honor of St. Peter and of his godfather: the king himself. Some time afterward he wrote two works in Latin; one was a refutation of Judaism (almost an obligatory task for such a conspicuous convert), the other was *Disciplina clericalis* (Ethical Instruction for the Clergy).

In his preface to the *Disciplina*, the author claims to have both compiled the work and translated it from Arabic. Part of the vast tradition of "wisdom literature" going back to ancient Egypt, Mesopotamia, and India, it consists of ethical instruction, imparted in the form of philosophical disquisitions, maxims, and illustrative stories (*exempla*). The (very loose) framework is that of an old man (father, teacher, sage) proffering wisdom to a young man (his son, pupil, disciple). Many Eastern sources have been recognized by scholars, but intrinsically European narrative material may also have been included.

Prominent among the Eastern sages mentioned specifically by Pedro/Petrus/ Peter is Lukman (in the first sentence of the first selection). Lukman (Luqmān al-Hakīm) is a legendary sage referred to in the Koran; he is sometimes, as here, equated with the Old Testament prophet Balaam, whose utterances were looked on as oracles (it has been suggested that "Lukman" is actually an Arabic translation of the Hebrew "Balaam"; both names may possibly be connected with verbs meaning "to swallow up").

1

Because the *Disciplina* is so early and so fundamental, and because it visibly influenced so many other works in various languages for so many centuries, a generous selection of its stories has been made here: 18 out of the original 34 (our No. 1 corresponds to the first *two* original stories, including the prefatory and transitional text). The author's style is plain and unadorned, but not awkward; scholars have professed to find this Latin very peculiar and unidiomatic, but that aspect is much too readily exaggerated.

No. 1, as just stated, provides the reader with an opportunity to sample the sort of "gangue" in which the narrative "ore" is embedded. It seemed unwise to break up the first two *exempla* of the *Disciplina* artificially; and to strip them of the prefatory and transitional text seemed like an unwarranted falsification of the author's intentions. The story of the "half-friend," like Nos. 2, 9, 10, 12, and 14, was very widely imitated in medieval literature (the plots of Nos. 2, 9, and 12 reappear in the *Gesta Romanorum*).

Nos. 4, 5, 6, and 8 comprise a mini-cycle devoted to women's wiles, a major theme in both East and West. No. 8 is particularly important as the direct inspiration for the fourth story of the Seventh Day in Boccaccio's *Decameron* (ca. 1350), which hardly differs, apart from the Italian writer's infinitely greater verve.

No. 7 is the apparent inspiration for the "endless" story that Sancho Panza tells Don Quixote as they impatiently await daylight during their fulling-mill adventure (Part One, Chapter 20).

No. 15 is in the Aesopic tradition or mode.

No. 16 is closely connected to the versions of the subject in *Kalilah and Dimnah* (an 8th-century Arabic adaptation, via Persian, of the Sanskrit *Panchatantra* [ca. 300 A.D.]) and the Hebrew *Mishle Sendebar* (Tales of Sendebar; the earliest references to this work date from around 1300, but the material may well be much older).

No. 17, which, like No. 1, includes some bits of the "frame story," contains material (the slave's slowly unfolding, reluctantly disclosed, catalog of calamities) that had a long future ahead of it. In adapted forms, it became a routine in 19th-century American minstrel shows, and made an appearance in Broadway musical comedy early in the 20th century, when it was recorded by the comedian who delivered it.

1. Half-Friends and Whole Friends

Balaam, who is called Lukman in Arabic, said to his son: "My son, don't be inferior in wisdom to the ant, who gathers in summer what she will live on in winter. My son, don't be inferior in alertness to the rooster, who is wakeful in the morning while you sleep. My son, don't be inferior in spirit to the rooster, who governs ten wives while you are unable to discipline only one. My son, don't be inferior in nobility of heart to the dog, who never forgets his benefactors while you forget yours. My son, don't think that having a single enemy is a small thing or that a thousand friends are too many. I say to you:

"An Arab, feeling death drawing near, summoned his son and said to him: 'Son, tell me how many friends you've acquired during your lifetime.'

"The son said in reply: 'I've acquired a hundred friends, as it seems to me.'

"His father said: 'A philosopher has stated that a friend is not to be praised until he's been tested. I, for example, am older than you, and I have barely won half a friend. So how have you won a hundred? Therefore, go and test all of them in order to learn if any of them will be a perfect friend to you.'

"The son said: 'How do you advise me to test them?'

"The father said: 'Kill a calf, cut it into small pieces, and put it in a sack, so that the outside of the sack is stained with blood. Then, when you visit your friend, say to him: "Comrade, I've accidentally killed a man; I beg you to bury him secretly. No one will suspect you, and in that way you'll be saving me."'

"The son carried out his father's instructions. But the first friend he visited said to him: 'Carry the dead man away on your back! Undergo the penalty that fits your crime! You're not setting foot in my house!'

"And when he made the same request of each one, they all gave him the same answer. So he returned to his father and reported what he had done. His father said: 'What happened to you is what the philosopher stated: "You can count *up* many friends, but you can count *on* very few in times of need." Now go to that half-friend of mine and see what he tells you.'

"He went and told this man what he had told the others. This man said: 'Come inside. This is a secret that's not to be divulged to the neighbors.' He sent out his wife and all his servants, and dug a grave. When the young man saw everything in readiness, he revealed the true facts of the case and thanked him. Then he reported his doings to his father.

"His father said: 'The philosopher speaks about such a friend when he says: "That man is truly a friend who aids you when the world fails you."'

"The son said to his father: 'Have you ever seen anyone who had acquired a whole friend?'

"Then his father replied: 'No, I've never seen anyone, but I've heard of someone.'

"Then the son said: 'Tell me about him, in case I ever win such a friend.'

"And the father said: 'I have been told about two merchants, one of whom lived in Egypt and the other in Baghdad. They had never met in person, but would send messengers to transact their business. Now, it once came about that the resident of Baghdad was going to Egypt on business. When the Egyptian heard he had arrived, he went out to meet him, welcomed him heartily to his home, and served him in every way, as friends do, for a week, showing him all that he had in his home, in every nook and cranny. At the end of the week the guest became ill. His host, very worried about his friend, called in all the Egyptian doctors to examine his friend and guest. The doctors took his pulse and repeatedly looked at his urine, but failed to diagnose any disease. Since they thus ascertained that he had no physical ailment, they knew he must be lovesick.

"'Learning this, his host came to him and asked him whether there was any woman in the house that he loved. The sick man replied: "Show me all the women here, and if I happen to see her among them, I'll point her out to you."

"'Hearing this, he showed him his singing girls and his maids, but none of them was the woman he loved. Next he showed him all his daughters, but them, like the earlier women, he totally refused and ignored. Now, his host had a certain highborn maiden in his home whom he had long raised in hopes of making her his wife, and he showed her to his guest as well. When the sick man saw her, he said: "From her my death comes, and in her my life lies!"

"'Hearing this, his host gave him the highborn maiden as a bride, along with all the property he would have gained when marrying her. In addition he gave him the property he had intended to make over to the maiden upon their marriage. When all this was done, the guest took his bride and all that he had acquired along with his bride, transacted his local business, and returned home.

"'Now, it later came to pass that in a variety of ways the Egyptian lost all his property. Having become a pauper, he determined to visit his friend in Baghdad to ask him for assistance. And so, bare and hungry, he undertook the journey, arriving at Baghdad in the dead of night. Shame kept him from approaching his friend's home, lest they should fail to recognize him at that hour and should throw him out of the house. And so he entered a certain old mosque to spend the night there. But while he lay awake there in great anxiety, two men encountered each other on a street near the mosque. One of them killed the other and ran away secretly. The noise brought many townspeople running. They found the dead man and, wondering who had committed the murder, they entered the mosque in hopes of finding the killer there.

"'They found the Egyptian there, and when they asked him who had killed the man, he told them that he himself had done it, lying because he had such a strong desire to put an end to his poverty by death. And so he was arrested and jailed. In the morning he was brought before the judges, sentenced to death, and led to the cross. As usual, many came to watch, among them the friend he had come to Baghdad to see. When this man took a closer look at him, he realized he was the friend he had left behind in Egypt. Recalling the kindness he had shown him in Egypt, and reflecting that he couldn't return that kindness if his friend died, he decided to suffer death in his place. And so he called out loudly: "Why are you condemning an innocent man, and where are you taking him? He's done nothing to deserve death. I'm the one who killed the man."

"'They laid hands on him, tied him up, dragged him to the cross, and freed the other man from the death penalty. But the real killer, who was walking about in the crowd and watching, said to himself: "I did the killing, and this man is condemned! This man, who is innocent, is being led to execution, while I, the guilty party, enjoy my freedom! What is the cause of this injustice? I don't know, unless it's merely God's long-suffering. But God, the righteous judge, leaves no crime unpunished. And so, lest He take more severe vengeance on me at some later date, let me reveal myself as the perpetrator of this crime! Thus, by saving them from death I shall atone for the sin I committed."

"'And so he exposed himself to danger, saying: "I'm the one who did it! Release this innocent man!" And the judges, in no little amazement, saved the other man from death and bound this one. By now they were unsure about their verdict, and they brought the killer and the men they had released before the king. Telling him everything just as it had happened, they made even the king waver. And so, on everyone's advice, the king told the two friends that they would be absolved of every crime they had charged themselves with, if only they explained why they had done so. And they told him the truth of the matter. By common consent they were set free, and the local man who had decided to die in place of his friend brought him home with him.

"'Honoring him in every customary way, he said: "If you agree to stay here with me, we will share and share alike, as is only right. But if you wish to return home, let's divide all my property into two equal parts." The Egyptian, longing for the pleasures of his native land, accepted the same amount that he had formerly offered to his friend, and returned home.'

"When the father had finished the story, his son said: 'A friend like that can hardly ever be found.'"

2. Paying Duties on Defects

A certain poet made some verses and presented them to the king. The king praised his talent and ordered him to request a gift in exchange. The poet's request was that he be made the keeper of the city gate for a month, receiving a dinar from every hunchback, a dinar from everyone afflicted with scaly skin, a dinar from every one-eyed person, a dinar from everyone with a rash, and a dinar from everyone with a hernia. The king granted this and confirmed it with his seal.

The poet, taking up his post, sat down by the gate to fulfill his duties. One day, a certain hunchback, well wrapped up in a cloak and carrying a staff, came in. The poet came up to him and demanded a dinar. The hunchback refused. The poet, using force, lifted the hood from his head and saw that the hunchback had only one eye. He thus demanded two dinars, whereas he had asked for only one earlier. The hunchback, refusing, was detained. Being defenseless, he tried to run away, but was held back by his hood; his head was thus bared, and he was seen to have scaly skin. The poet immediately asked him for three dinars. The hunchback saw that he couldn't escape and that no one was coming to his aid, so he started to fight back. While doing so, he uncovered his arms and was seen to have a rash on them; and so the poet demanded a fourth dinar. He whipped the cloak off the struggling man, who fell to the ground, revealing that he had a hernia. And so the poet wrung the fifth dinar from him.

Thus it came about that the man, who refused to give one dinar freely, had to give five against his will.

3. Guilt by Association

It has been said that two clerics left town one evening for a stroll. They came to a place where people had gathered together to drink. One said to his comrade: "Let's go off in another direction, because a philosopher has said that one should not visit the haunts of evil people."

His friend replied: "Just passing through won't hurt us if we don't do anything else."

They continued passing through and heard singing in one house. One of the two men was detained there by the sweetness of the song. His friend warned him to leave, but he refused. His friend departed and he was left alone. Lured by the song, he entered the house. He was greeted on all sides, he sat down, and, sitting there, drank with the others. Just then, a constable who had been pursuing a runaway enemy spy, entered the very same tavern. The spy was found there, and everyone, including the cleric, was arrested. "This was the spy's lair," the constable said. "He came out of here and returned here. You were all aware of it and you were his confederates."

They were all led to the gallows. Among them was the cleric, who preached to everyone in a loud voice: "Whoever consorts with evil people will surely earn the penalty of undeserved death."

4. The Injured Eye

A certain man went out to harvest his grapes. Seeing this, his wife realized he would stay in the vineyard a long time, so she sent a messenger to invite her lover over, and she prepared a feast. But, as things turned out, her husband was hit in the eye by a vine branch and returned home quickly, with no sight in his injured eye. Arriving at his doorway, he knocked on the door.

Hearing this, his wife became very upset. She hid her amorous guest in the bedroom, and then ran to open the door for her husband. He came in, his eye causing him great grief and pain. He ordered her to prepare the bedroom and make the bed so he could lie down. His wife was afraid that when he entered the bedroom he would see her lover hiding there. She said to him: "Why are you hurrying off so to bed? First tell me what's wrong with you."

He told her everything that had happened. "Husband dear," she said, "let me strengthen your sound eye with medicine and a charm, so I don't suffer on account of your sound eye what I have suffered from your injured one—because I share in all harm to you." And, placing her mouth on his sound eye, she kissed it for the time it took for her hidden lover to leave his hiding place without her husband's knowledge. Finally she arose and said: "Now, husband dear, I'm sure that this eye won't be hurt the way the other one was. Now, if you like, you can go to bed."

5. The Sheet Ruse

The story is told of a man who, setting out on a journey, entrusted his wife to the care of her mother. But his wife fell in love with another man and told her mother about it. Her mother sympathized with her daughter and fostered her liaison. She invited the lover to their home and began to dine with him and her daughter. In the middle of the meal the husband showed up and knocked at the door. His wife got up and hid her lover, then opened the door for her husband. When he was inside, he ordered his bed made; he wanted to lie down because he was tired. His wife was upset and at a loss what to do. Seeing this, her mother said: "Daughter, don't rush to make the bed until we show your husband the sheet we've made."

Stretching out the sheet as much as she could, the old woman held up one corner of it and gave her daughter another corner to raise. And so, when the sheet was spread out, the husband was fooled, and the hidden lover had time to get away. Then the woman said to her daughter: "Spread this sheet, which was woven by your hands and mine, over your husband's bed."

The husband said: "Mother-in-law, are you, too, able to prepare a sheet like this?"

And she replied. "Son-in-law, I've prepared many a one of this sort."

6. The Sword Ruse

There's another story about a man setting out on a journey who left his wife in the care of her mother. The wife was secretly in love with some young man, and immediately told her mother about it. Her mother consented to the affair, prepared a feast, and invited the young man. While they were eating, the husband came home and knocked at the door. So his wife got up and let her husband in. But her mother and her lover remained where they were, because there was no place to hide him, and at first she didn't know what to do. But while her daughter was opening the door for her husband, the old woman got hold of an unsheathed sword, handed it to the lover, and ordered him to stand with drawn sword in front of the door where her daughter's husband was coming in. If the husband said anything to him, he was to make no reply.

He did as she ordered. When the door was open and the husband saw him standing there, he stopped short and asked: "Who are you?" When the man failed to reply, the husband, who at first had been surprised, now was more frightened. From inside, the old woman said: "Son-in-law dear, keep quiet so no one will hear you!"

This amazed him more, and he said: "Mother-in-law dear, what's going on?"

Then the woman said: "My good son, three men came here pursuing this man, and we opened the door and let him in with his sword until the people who wanted to kill him went away. Now, out of fear that you're one of them, he's lost his voice and can't answer you."

And the husband said: "Bravo, mother-in-law, for saving this man from death that way." And, going in, he called over his wife's lover and asked him to sit down. And so, around nightfall he sent him on his way soothed with encouraging words.

7. The Endless Story

A certain king had a storyteller who was accustomed to tell him five stories every night. It came about on one occasion that the king couldn't sleep because he had certain worries on his mind, and he asked to hear more stories than usual. The storyteller told three additional ones, but short ones. The king asked for even more. The man refused firmly, saying that he had already told plenty, as it seemed to him. The king replied: "Yes, you've told a lot, but very short ones. I'd like you to tell one that goes on and on, and after that I'll let you get to bed."

The storyteller consented and began thus: "There was a peasant whose cash amounted to a thousand *solidi*. He set out on a business venture and bought two thousand sheep at six dinars apiece. When he was returning home, the river happened to be extremely high. Finding himself unable to cross by either bridge or ford, he wandered about worriedly in search of some means to get over with his sheep. He finally found a tiny boat that was only big enough to carry two sheep along with himself. Finally, compelled by necessity, he put two sheep in the boat and crossed the river."

At this point the storyteller fell asleep. The king roused him and ordered him to finish the story he had begun. The storyteller said: "The river is wide, the boat extremely small, and the flock of sheep beyond counting. And so, allow this peasant to carry his sheep over, and I'll finish the story I began." And in that way the storyteller pacified the king who was yearning to hear long stories.

8. The Ruse with the Well

There was a young man who devoted all his efforts, all his wits, and all his time to learning every wile of women. His intention was not to take a wife before he had done so. But first he set out to obtain advice. Approaching a very wise man of that country, he asked him how to guard the woman he wanted to marry. Hearing this, the wise man advised him to build a house with high stone walls, to put his wife inside it, to give her enough to eat and only a moderate amount of clothing, and to fashion the house in such a way that it had only a single door and a single window to look out of, and that it was so high and of such construction that no one could go in or out any other way.

Hearing the wise man's advice, the young man carried out his instructions. Every morning, on leaving home, the young man locked the door, and he did the same after returning. When he slept, he hid the house keys under his pillow. He did this for a long time. But one day, when the young man went to the market, his wife went up to the window, as she was accustomed to do, and watched the passers-by intently. While she was standing by the window that day, she saw a young man who was handsome in both body and face. On seeing him she was immediately inflamed with love for him. Inflamed with love for the young man, but guarded as has been described, she began pondering on ways and wiles that would enable her to speak with the object of her affections. Highly resourceful and full of guile, she hit on the plan of stealing her husband's keys while he was sleeping. And she did so.

Now she became accustomed to getting her husband drunk with wine every night, so that she could more safely go out to join her lover and satisfy her lust. But her husband, already instructed by the warnings of philosophers that none of women's actions are free of guile, began wondering what his wife was up to with those numerous daily cups of wine. In order to observe for himself, he pretended to be drunk. Unaware of this, his wife got out of bed at night, walked to the house door, opened it, and went out to join her lover. But her husband, getting up quietly in the silence of the night, went to the door. Finding it open, he shut and locked it and went back up to the window, where he stood until he saw his wife returning, clad only in her nightgown.

Arriving home, she found the door shut. Greatly grieved by this, she nonetheless knocked at the door. Though the man heard and saw his wife, he pretended not to know her and asked who was there. She requested forgiveness for her fault and promised she would never do it again, but it was no use. Rather, her angry husband said he wouldn't let her in, but would tell her parents about her doings. Yelling louder and louder, she said that if he didn't open the house door, she would jump into the well that was next to the house and would thus put an end to her life. Then he would have to give an accounting of her death to her friends and relatives. Scorning his wife's threats, the man refused to let her in.

But the woman, full of guile and cunning, picked up a stone and threw it into the well, so that her husband, hearing the sound of the stone hurtling into the well, would think that she had fallen into it. After doing this, the woman hid behind the well. The man, naïve and foolish, heard the sound of the stone hurtling into the well, and immediately ran out of the house and up to the well swiftly, thinking he had really heard his wife fall in. The woman, seeing the house door open, and not forgetful of her guile, went inside, locked the door, and went up to the window.

He, seeing that he had been deceived, said: "You lying woman, full of the Devil's guile, let me in, and I swear I'll forgive you for anything you did to me outside!"

But she, insulting him, refusing him entry no matter what, and taking an oath to keep him out, called: "You seducer, I'll tell your parents about your doings and your crimes, how every night you habitually sneak out and visit harlots." And she did so. When his parents heard this, they believed it was true and they berated him. And so, that woman, set free by her guile, brought upon her husband the punishment *she* had deserved. It was no advantage, but a disadvantage to him, to have guarded his wife, because he received the additional grief of having most people believe *he* was guilty of what *she* made him suffer. And so, shunned by many good people, shorn of his honors, and stained in reputation because of his wife's slanders, he was legally condemned for lewdness.

9. The Ten Coffers

I have been told that a certain resident of Spain was on his way to Mecca when he arrived in Egypt. About to enter and cross the desert, he planned to put his money in safekeeping in Egypt. Before doing so, he inquired as to whether there was any trustworthy man in that region with whom he could leave his money. He was directed to an elderly man renowned for his trustworthiness. He entrusted him with a thousand talents of his money, then he proceeded. When his journey was done, he returned to the man to whom he had entrusted his money, and asked to have it back. But that man, full of iniquity, said he had never seen him before.

Cheated in that manner, he went to the honest men of that region and reported to them how the man to whom he had entrusted his money had treated him. Hearing such a report about him, his neighbors refused to believe it, and said that no such thing had happened. But the man who had lost his money went daily to the home of the man who was holding back his money dishonestly, beseeching him with soft words to return the money. The deceiver, hearing this, berated him, telling him not to go on saying such things about him or coming to see him; otherwise, he would suffer the penalty he deserved.

Hearing the threats uttered by the man who had cheated him, he began to return home sadly. On his way he came across an old woman dressed in hermit's garb. Supporting her weak limbs with a staff, she was removing stones from the road so that passers-by wouldn't hurt their feet; she praised God as she did so. Seeing the man crying, and recognizing that he was a foreigner, she was moved to pity. Calling him aside into a narrow lane, she asked him what had befallen him. He told her everything from start to finish.

When the woman had heard the man's report, she said: "My friend, if what you have told me is true, I shall help you out of your trouble."

He said: "How can you do it, handmaiden of God?"

And she replied: "Bring me a man from your country whose words and deeds you can trust." And he did so. Then she instructed the cheated man's associate to buy ten coffers painted on the outside with costly colors, bound with silvered iron bands, and provided with good locks. He was to take them to the house where he was staying and fill them with crushed stones. He did so. When the woman saw that all her instructions had been carried out, she said to the first Spaniard: "Now find ten men to bear the coffers to the home of the man who cheated you, along with me and your associate; they are to arrive one at a time in a long procession. As soon as the first one comes to the home of the man who cheated you and takes a rest there, you are to come and ask for your money. And I trust in God that your money will be returned to you."

He did exactly what the old woman had told him. She didn't forget the plan she had outlined, and she set out. With the associate of the cheated man she came to the home of the cheater and said: "A certain man from Spain has taken lodgings with me and wishes to go to Mecca; but first he wants to entrust his money, which is stored in ten coffers, to some good man for safekeeping until he returns. So I beg you to keep it in your house for my sake. Because I've heard, and I know, that you are a good, loyal man, I don't want anyone but you alone to be present while this money is being handed over."

While she was speaking, the first coffer bearer arrived; others could already be seen in the distance. Meanwhile, the cheated man, mindful of the old woman's instructions, arrived after the first coffer as he had been told. The man who had hidden his money was full of iniquity and evil guile, and as soon as he saw the man coming whose money he had hidden, he began to fear that, if that man should claim his money, this new man who was just bringing his money wouldn't go through with the deal. And so he went to greet him, saying: "My friend, where have you been, and where have you spent all this time? Come and receive the money you entrusted to my care so long ago, now that I've found you and I'm so tired of keeping it!"

The man from Spain received his money gladly and joyfully and expressed his gratitude. But when the old woman saw the man in possession of his money, she stood up and said: "My companion and I will go to meet those coffer bearers and tell them to hurry. Please wait till we're back and keep a good watch over what we've already brought."

The Egyptian, glad at heart, guarded what he had received and awaited their return—which is still pending. And so the sum of money was restored to the man through the sharp wits of the old woman.

10. The Ten Casks of Oil

A certain man, upon dying, left nothing to his son except his house. The son, though working hard, barely earned enough for his bodily necessities, but, hungry as he was, he refused to sell his house. Now, that lad had an extremely rich neighbor who was eager to buy his house in order to enlarge his own. But the lad wouldn't sell for love or money. Once the rich man was certain of this, he pondered over wiles and guiles to do the lad out of his house. But the young man avoided his company as much as he could.

Finally the rich man, vexed at his failure to acquire the house and deceive the lad, visited him one day and said: "My boy, lease a small portion of your courtyard to me, because I wish to bury ten casks of oil there for safekeeping. They won't be in your way, and you'll gain a little money for food."

Compelled by need, the lad assented and gave him the keys to the house. Meanwhile, as was his wont, the young man went out to earn his bread by working freely for free men. When the rich man received the keys, he dug up the young man's courtyard and buried there five casks that were filled with oil and five that were only half-full. Then he called the young man and handed back the keys to him, saying: "Young man, I entrust my oil to you and leave it in your keeping."

The naïve young man took charge of the casks, believing they were all full. It came about long afterward that the price of oil rose in that district. Seeing this, the rich man said to the lad: "My friend, come help me dig up my oil, which I left in your care long ago, and you'll be repaid for your labor and for keeping it."

When the young man heard that request accompanied by a proffer of money, he agreed to help the rich man to the best of his ability. The rich man, mindful of his unspeakable deception, brought men to buy the oil. When they arrived, they dug up the ground and discovered that five casks were full and five half-full. On seeing this, the rich man called over the lad and said: "My friend, through your improper keeping I have lost oil.

What's more, you have stolen by fraud what I entrusted to you. And so I want you to restore my property."

Saying this, he seized him and haled him into court against his will. When the judge saw him, he condemned him. The young man didn't know what to say in refutation, but requested a day's delay. The judge found that request legally proper and granted it.

Now, in that city there dwelt a certain philosopher who had been dubbed Helper of the Needy, a good, pious man. Hearing a report of his kindness, the young man went to see him and asked for his advice, saying: "If what many people have told me about you is true, lend me your customary aid, for I am unjustly accused."

Hearing the young man's request, the philosopher asked him whether the accusation against him was true or false. The young man took an oath that it was false. Discerning the accused man's sincerity, the philosopher was moved to pity and said: "With God's aid I shall help you. Since the judge has granted you a postponement until tomorrow, don't fail to show up at the trial, and I shall be there ready to aid your true cause and defeat your enemy's wickedness."

The young man carried out the philosopher's instructions. The next morning, the philosopher came to court. When the judge caught sight of him, he greeted him as a sage and a philosopher and seated him next to himself. Then the judge called the plaintiffs and the defendant and ordered them to repeat their pleas, which they did. While they stood there in public, the judge asked the philosopher to hear their case and deliver a verdict.

Then the philosopher said: "Judge, now order clear oil to be measured out of the five full casks, so you know how much clear oil they contain; and likewise from the half-full casks, so you know how much clear oil was in them. Next, let the thickened oil in the five full casks be measured, so you know how much thickened oil they contain. If you find as much thickened oil in the half-filled casks as in the full ones, you can be sure the oil was stolen. But if you find in the half-filled casks an amount of thickened oil merely proportional to the amount of clear oil in them, gauging the proportion by the full casks, you can be sure the oil was not stolen."

Hearing this, the judge approved of the procedure and had it carried out. And in that manner the young man was rescued by the wisdom of the philosopher. After the trial the young man thanked the philosopher. Then the philosopher said to him: "Have you never heard the philosopher's advice about never buying a house before you're acquainted with your neighbor?"

The young man replied: "We owned the house before he moved next door."

And the philosopher said: "Sell your house rather than remaining next door to a bad neighbor."

11. The Golden Snake

A story tells of a rich man coming into a town with a sack filled with a thousand talents in money and a golden snake with eyes of jacinth. He lost the entire sack and a poor man found it on the road. Giving it to his wife, he told her how he had found it. Hearing this, the woman said: "What God has given us, let us keep!"

The next day a town crier passed along the street calling: "Whoever has found such-and-such a treasure should give it back, and he will receive a hundred talents without incurring any blame!"

The woman said: "If God had wanted him to have the treasure, he wouldn't have lost it. What God has given, let us keep!" The finder of the treasure urged her to let him return it, but she staunchly refused. Nonetheless, in spite of his wife's wishes, the husband returned the money and asked for what the town crier had promised. But the evil rich man said: "I want you to know that there was another snake, which is still missing." He said this with the wicked intention of depriving the poor man of the promised talents.

The poor man kept repeating that he hadn't found anything else. But the citizens of the town favored the rich man, rejected the poor man's claim, and, bearing an implacable hatred against him, haled him into court. The poor man loudly swore that he hadn't found anything else, as stated above.

The story spread so far abroad from mouth to mouth among poor and rich alike that the king's ministers referred to it and it finally reached his ears. As soon as he heard it, he ordered the rich man, the poor man, and the money to be brought before him. When all were assembled, the king summoned the philosopher called Helper of the Downtrodden together with other sages, and ordered them to listen to the words of accuser and accused, and untangle the knot.

Hearing this, the philosopher, moved to pity, called the poor man over and said to him in secret: "Brother, tell me whether you have held onto this man's property. If you haven't, with God's aid I shall try to free you."

The poor man replied: "God knows that I returned all I found!"

Then the philosopher said to the king: "If you are pleased to hear a just verdict on this case, I shall give it."

Hearing this, the king asked him to try the case. Then the philosopher said to the king: "This rich man is very good and trustworthy, and has a great reputation for telling the truth, so that it's unbelievable that he should be asking for something he hasn't really lost. On the other hand, I find it believable that this poor man found nothing beyond what he returned, because if he were a criminal he wouldn't have returned as much as he did, but would have concealed the whole thing."

Then the king said: "What, then, is your judgment, philosopher?"

The philosopher replied: "Your Majesty, take the treasure and give the poor man a hundred talents out of it. Then hold onto the rest until someone else comes asking for the treasure. Because this rich man isn't the owner of this particular treasure. Let him go to the town crier and have him announce the loss of a sack containing *two* snakes." This judgment pleased the king and all those present. But when the rich man who had lost the sack heard this, he said: "Good king, I tell you that this treasure was really mine, but because I wanted to deprive the poor man of what the town crier promised, I've said up to now that a second snake was missing. But now, Your Majesty, have pity on me and I will give the poor man the amount that the town crier promised."

Then the king gave the rich man's treasure back to him, and the rich man gave the poor man the reward, and so by wisdom and wit the philosopher saved the poor man.

12. The Three Dreams

There is a story of two townsmen and a peasant on their pilgrimage to Mecca who shared provisions until they were near Mecca. At that point their food ran out so thoroughly that all they had left was a little flour, just enough to make one small loaf of bread. Seeing this, the townsmen said to each other: "We don't have much bread, and our comrade eats a lot. So we need to have a plan whereby we can take away his share of the loaf, and just the two of us can eat up what is supposed to be shared among all three."

Then they agreed upon a plan whereby they would knead the loaf and bake it, and sleep while it was baking. Whoever had the most remarkable dream would eat the whole loaf by himself. They announced this deceitfully, because they thought the peasant was too simple to make up such things.

They kneaded the loaf and put it over the fire, then they lay down to sleep. But the peasant had seen through their plot. While his companions slept, he removed the half-baked loaf from the fire, ate it, and lay down again. But one of the townsmen woke up as if he had been startled by his dream, and called his companion. The second townsman said: "What's wrong?"

The first one said: "I had a wondrous dream. I thought two angels were opening the gates of Heaven, taking me, and leading me before God."

His companion said: "Yes, the dream you had was remarkable. But I dreamt that two angels were leading me to Hell, splitting open the earth."

The peasant was listening to all this while pretending to be asleep. But the townsmen, deceived while intending to deceive, called to the peasant to awaken him. Shrewdly the peasant replied, as if frightened: "Who is it that's calling me?"

They answered: "It's us, your companions."

The peasant said to them: "Are you back already?"

They countered: "Where have we gone, that we should be back from?"

The peasant said: "I've just dreamt that two angels were taking one of you, opening the gates of Heaven, and leading him before God. Then two other angels took the other one, opened the earth, and led him down to Hell. After those visions I figured neither one of you would come back anymore, so I got up and ate the bread."

13. The Royal Tailor's Apprentice

My teacher told me the story of a king who employed a tailor to cut out various garments for him to suit the various seasons. This tailor had apprentices, each of whom would sew together skillfully the pieces of cloth that their master, the royal tailor, cut. Among these apprentices was one named Nedui, who surpassed his fellows in sartorial skill.

Once, when a holiday was approaching, the king summoned the tailor who made his clothes and ordered him to prepare costly robes, befitting the festivity, for himself and his courtiers. So that this might be done more quickly and without obstacles, he assigned a eunuch from among his chamberlains (one who normally had such duties) as overseer of the tailors, ordering him to keep an eye on their filching fingers and to supply them with everything they needed.

On one working day the king's servants brought a meal of hot bread and honey, with other dishes, to the tailor and his apprentices. Those who were present began to eat. While they were dining, the eunuch said: "Master, why are you eating while Nedui is absent? Why don't you wait for him?"

The master tailor replied: "Because he wouldn't eat honey even if he were here." And they went on eating.

Then Nedui arrived and said: "Why did you eat with me away, without saving my share?"

The eunuch replied: "Your master said that you wouldn't eat honey even if you were here."

Nedui was silent, thinking about how to pay his master back for that. After hitting on a plan, he said to the eunuch in secret, while his master was away: "My lord, my master sometimes has fits of madness, loses his senses, and indiscriminately beats and kills those around him."

The eunuch said: "If I knew the time when that happened to him, to keep him from doing anything out of the way, I'd tie him up and whip him with thongs."

And Nedui said: "When you see him looking all around, tapping the floor with his hands, getting up from his stool and grabbing hold of it, then you can be sure that he's out of his mind, and that, if you don't look out for yourself and your people, he'll belabor your head with a club."

The eunuch replied: "Bless you for telling me. Now I'll look out for my people and myself."

On the day after that conversation Nedui hid his master's shears. The tailor, searching for his shears and not finding them, began to strike the floor with his hands. He looked all around, got up from his stool, and moved it around with his hand. Seeing this, the eunuch immediately summoned his aides and ordered them to tie up the tailor and give him a good beating to keep him from beating others. The tailor shouted: "What crime have I committed? Why are you beating me so hard?" But they went on beating him more severely without replying.

When they were tired of beating him, and he of being beaten, they released him more dead than alive. Catching his breath, after some time had gone by he asked the eunuch what he had done wrong. The eunuch said: "Your apprentice Nedui told me that you had occasional fits of madness and that you wouldn't stop unless you were restrained by being tied up and lashed. And so I tied you up and lashed you."

Hearing this, the tailor called over his apprentice and said: "My friend, when did you ever hear that I was crazy?"

The apprentice replied: "When did you ever hear that I don't eat honey?"

The eunuch and the other listeners laughed, and deemed that both of them had suffered their punishment deservedly.

14. The Peasant and the Bird

A certain man owned a park where the flowing streams made the grass green, and where the suitability of the spot attracted birds that sang varied songs in modulated strains. One day, while he was resting from his labors in his orchard, a bird alighted on a tree and sang delightfully. When the man saw it and heard its singing, he captured it in a deceptive snare.

The bird said to him: "Why did you take so much trouble to capture me, and what do you expect to gain by having done so?"

The man replied: "I merely want to be able to hear your singing."

The bird said: "In vain, because in captivity I won't sing for love or money."

The man said: "If you don't sing, I'll eat you."

The bird countered: "How will you eat me? If you boil me, what will you have from such a small bird? Besides, my flesh will be tough. And if I'm roasted, I'll become even smaller. But if you let me go, you'll gain a great advantage from me."

The man said: "What advantage?"

The bird replied: "I'll show you three types of wisdom which you'll prize more than the flesh of three calves."

The man, obtaining the bird's firm promise, released it.

Then the bird said: "Here's the first maxim I promised you: Don't believe everything you hear. The second is: Hold onto what you possess. The third is: Don't grieve over things you've lost." Saying this, the bird flew up into the tree and began to say, to a sweet melody: "Blessed be God, who blinded you and took away your good sense; because, if you had searched through my insides, you would have found a jacinth weighing an ounce."

When the man heard that, he began to weep and grieve and to beat his breast, because he believed what the bird said. But the bird said to him: "How soon you've forgotten the wisdom I taught you! Didn't I say that you shouldn't believe everything you hear? How can you believe that I have inside me a jacinth that weighs an ounce, when I don't weigh that much in my entirety? And didn't I say that you should hold onto what you possess? So, how could you acquire the gem if I'm flying around? And didn't I say that you shouldn't grieve over things you've lost? So, why are you grieving over the jacinth that's inside me?" After deriding the peasant with these words, the bird flew off into the impenetrable grove.

15. The Plowman, the Wolf, and the Fox

There is a story about a plowman whose oxen refused to proceed on a straight course. He said to them: "May the wolves eat you!" A wolf heard that and was pleased. When the sun was setting and the peasant released the oxen from the plow, the wolf came to him and said: "Give me the oxen you promised me!"

The plowman replied: "Even if I said that, still I didn't take an oath on it."

The wolf countered: "I must have them, because you granted them."

They solemnly agreed to take the matter to a judge. On their way they met a fox. Seeing them heading somewhere, the cunning fox said: "Where are you off to?" They told the fox what had occurred, and he said: "By no means seek another judge, because I will give you a just verdict. But before that, allow me to confer, first with one of you, then with the other. If I can reconcile you without a formal judgment, I won't state my verdict; otherwise, I'll state it to both of you together."

They agreed. First the fox took the plowman aside and said: "Give me a hen and my wife another, and you'll keep your oxen."

The plowman consented. Then the fox conferred with the wolf, saying: "Listen, my friend, because of your merit in the past, whatever eloquence I possess should be put to work on your behalf. I convinced the plowman to give you a cheese as big as a shield if you leave his oxen alone."

The wolf consented. Then the fox said to him: "Let the plowman take away his oxen, and I'll lead you to the place where his cheeses are made, so you can pick out the one you like best."

The wolf, deceived by the fox's shrewd words, let the peasant depart in peace. The fox, wandering randomly in every direction as long as he could, led the wolf astray. When it was getting very dark, he brought him to a deep well. As the wolf stood next to the well, the fox showed him the image of the half-moon reflected at the bottom of the well, and said: "Here is the cheese I promised you. Go down and eat it if you like."

The wolf said: "You go down first, and if you can't bring it up by yourself, I'll do whatever you tell me, to assist you." Then they saw a rope hanging down into the well. To the end of it a bucket was attached, and another bucket to the other end of the rope, hanging in such a way that when one rose the other descended.

When the fox saw this, he got into the bucket as if in compliance with the wolf's request, and sank to the bottom. The wolf, mightily pleased at that, said: "Why don't you bring me the cheese?"

The fox said: "I can't, it's too big. Get into the other bucket and come help me as you promised." The wolf got in, and his weight pulled the bucket swiftly down to the bottom, while the other bucket rose with the fox, who was much lighter. Reaching the rim of the well, the fox leaped out and left the wolf in the well. And so, because he had let go what was at hand in hopes of future gain, the wolf lost both the oxen and the cheese.

16. The Moonbeam

There is a story about a burglar visiting a rich man's home to rob it. Climbing onto the roof, he reached the opening through which the smoke escaped, and listened to hear if anyone was awake inside. The owner of the house became aware of this, and said softly to his wife: "Ask me out loud how I came by this great fortune I possess. Keep after me till I tell you."

Then she said aloud: "Husband, how did you acquire such a great fortune, since you were never a merchant?"

He replied: "Hold onto what God has given you, use it as you wish, and don't ask where I got all this money."

But she followed his orders and kept urging him to tell her. Finally, as if under the compulsion of his wife's entreaties, he said: "Be careful never to disclose our secrets to anyone. I was a burglar."

She said: "I find it strange that you could amass such a great fortune by burglary, because we've never heard any talk about it or any blame cast on you."

He said: "A certain instructor of mine taught me a charm to recite when I was climbing onto a roof. When I got to the skylight, I would seize a moonbeam in my hand and recite my charm, "*Saulem*," seven times. Then I would shinny down safely, gather up all the costly items I found in the house, and take them away. Next, I would return to the moonbeam, recite the same charm seven times, climb up along with everything I had stolen from the house, and carry my haul back to my lodgings. By that art I acquired this fortune of mine."

His wife said: "You did right to tell me all this, because when I have a son I'll teach him that charm to keep him from a life of poverty."

Her husband said: "Now let me sleep, because I'm dead tired and I want to rest." And in order to fool the burglar even more, he started to snore as if asleep.

When the burglar heard all this, he was overjoyed. He recited the charm seven times and grasped the moonbeam, loosing the firm hold of his hands and feet. He fell through the skylight into the house with a terrific crash and lay there moaning, a leg and an arm broken. The owner of the house, as if ignorant of the whole thing, asked: "Who are you that took such a fall?"

The burglar replied: "I'm the unfortunate burglar who believed your lying words."

17. Maimundus the Slave

The youth asked the old man:[1] "When I'm invited out to dinner, which should I do, eat too little or too much?"

The old man replied: "Too much! Because if you've been invited by a friend, he'll be very pleased; and if your host is your enemy, it will vex him." The boy laughed at those words, and the old man asked him why.

The boy said: "I recalled a story I heard about Maimundus the African slave. An old man asked him how much he could eat, and he replied: 'Whose food, mine or someone else's?' The man said, 'Yours,' and Maimundus said, 'As little as I can.' 'And someone else's?' 'All I can get.'"

The old man said: "You're now quoting remarks made by a lazy glutton, a foolish, talkative, frivolous man. Whatever people say about him is more than matched by the facts of the matter."

The youth said: "I greatly enjoy hearing about him, because every story about him is funny. If you remember anything he said or did, please tell it to me, and I'll consider it a great favor."

Then the old man told this story:

"One night his master ordered him to shut the house door. Overcome by sloth, he was unable to get up, and so he said the door was already shut. In the morning the master said to the slave: 'Maimundus, open the door!'

"The slave replied: 'Master, I knew you'd want it open today, so I didn't shut it last night.'

"Then his master realized that he had neglected to do so out of laziness,

---

[1]This youth and old man are the father-and-son interlocutors who supply the framework for the *Disciplina clericalis* as a whole.

and he said: 'Get up and do your work, because it's daytime and the sun is already high!'

"The slave replied: 'Master, if the sun is already high, give me food.'

"The master said: 'Miserable slave, do you want to eat at night?'

"The slave retorted: 'If it's nighttime, let me sleep!'

"On another occasion the master said to the slave at night: 'Maimundus, get up and see whether or not it's raining!'

"The slave called in the dog, who was lying outside the door. When the dog came, he felt its paws. Finding them dry, he said to his master: 'Master, it's not raining.'

"Another time the master asked the slave at night whether a fire was burning in the hearth. Maimundus called over the cat and felt it to see whether or not it was warm. Finding it cold, he said: 'No, master.'"

The youth said: "All right, I've heard about his laziness. Now I'd like to hear about his talkativeness."

The old man narrated: "The story goes that his master was returning from a business trip, happy over the very profitable deal he had made. The slave Maimundus went out to meet his master. Seeing him, the master was afraid that he might be hawking news as he was accustomed to do, and he said: 'Take care not to tell me any bad news!'

"Maimundus said: 'I won't tell you bad news, but our little dog Bispella is dead.'

"His master said: 'How did she die?'

"The slave said: 'Our mule got frightened and broke its halter; while it was running away, it trampled the dog to death.'

"The master said: 'What happened to the mule?'

"The slave said: 'It fell into the well and was killed.'

"The master said: 'How did the mule get frightened?'

"The slave said: 'Your son had a fatal fall from the balcony, and that frightened the mule.'

"The master said: 'What is his mother doing?'

"The slave said: 'She was so unhappy about her son that she died.'

"The master said: 'Who's watching the house?'

"The slave said: 'Nobody, because it's been burned to ashes along with everything that was in it.'

"The master said: 'How did it get burned?'

"The slave said: 'The same night that Mistress died, the maid who was sitting up with her body forgot the candle in the bedroom, so the whole house was burned.'

"The master said: 'Where is the maid?'

"The slave said: 'She was trying to put out the fire when a beam fell on her head and killed her.'

"The master said: 'How did you escape, lazy as you are?'

"The slave said: 'When I saw the maid was dead, I ran away.'

"Then the master, in great grief, went to his neighbors and begged them to receive him and put him up in one of their homes. Meanwhile he met a friend of his. Seeing him so sad, the friend asked the reason why. He told him all that his slave had reported to him. His friend quoted verses to the unhappy master to console him, and said: 'My friend, don't despair! A man is often called upon to bear such violent floods of calamity that he longs to put an end to them, even by a dishonorable death, but right away so many good things happen to him that he finds it actually pleasant to recall the calamities. Yet, this enormous fluctuation in worldly affairs is controlled by the will of the Supreme Ruler in accordance with our various merits. This is confirmed by the example of the prophet Job, whose courage was not vanquished by the loss of all he owned. Have you ever heard this saying of a philosopher? "Who can have anything permanent in this impermanent world, or who can have anything lasting in this life in which all things are fleeting?"'"

STORIES 18–23

From *Dolopathos*
by Jean de Haute-Seille

Dolopathos, sive De rege et septem sapientibus (Dolopathos, or Concerning the King and the Seven Sages) is part of the vast medieval and premedieval literary tradition of the Seven Sages, represented in dozens of texts in numerous languages, and generally divided by scholars into an Oriental (or Eastern) group and a European (or Western) group.*

Dolopathos, which is the earliest European version, has certain individual features that set it apart from the majority of Western versions: its frame story, in which the separate stories are embedded, is unusually long and complex (see details below); and it contains only half the average number of stories, since the evil woman is given no stories with which to refute or combat those of the sages. *Dolopathos* includes only eight inserted stories, one each narrated by the seven sages, and a final one by the philosopher Vergil.

The author, whose name in its Latin form is Johannes de Alta Silva, was a monk in the Cistercian abbey of Haute-Seille in the bishopric of Nancy (Lorraine). Using oral sources, according to his prefatory declarations, he wrote the book about 1184 (not later than 1200).

The basic situation in every Seven Sages version is that a young prince, under a temporary vow of silence, is falsely accused of unwanted attentions by the stepmother whose own advances he has spurned; he is saved from death by seven wise men who tell his royal father cautionary (and generally antifeminist) tales until the matter is finally cleared up.

In *Dolopathos,* the title character is the (fictitious) ruler of Sicily during the reign of Augustus, the first Roman emperor. From age eight to age fifteen, the king's son, Lucinius, is educated away from the court by the great poet and philosopher Vergil. Then Lucinius has a vision informing him that his father will remarry and recall him to court. When this comes true, Vergil instructs him not to speak for the duration. His stepmother duly attempts to seduce him, then accuses him falsely. On seven occasions his execution is halted by the arrival of a story-telling sage. The eighth and final story is told by Vergil, who sets everything straight. When Lucinius ascends the throne years later, he is converted to the new religion of Christianity.

---

*Readers desirous of further information on the entire Seven Sages complex will find an excellent conspectus in Appendices A and B of *Tales of Sendebar,* by Morris Epstein, The Jewish Publication Society of America, Philadelphia, 1967.

The author's Latin is very close to classical, and his style is lofty, almost pretentious, with many classical quotations and allusions.

Because the stories in *Dolopathos* are such early examples of their themes and plots, because they are so carefully told, and because they were so influential, six of the eight are included here. (The plots of the two not included, Vergil's and the third sage's, are very similar to those of Nos. 8 and 48, respectively, presented elsewhere in this anthology.)

The crucial plot element in No. 18, probably most familiar to readers of English as the fight between the greyhound Gellert (belonging to Llewellyn the Great, ca. 1200) and a wolf in the Welsh version, goes back to the *Panchatantra* (India, ca. 300 A.D.), in which the combatants are a mongoose and a snake. But in the *Dolopathos* the main emphasis is on the all-round fecklessness of the hound's master.

No. 19 has an extremely widespread folkloric plot, which the fifth-century B.C. Greek historian Herodotus heard in Egypt, where the king in the story was called Rhampsinitus (Book II of the *Histories*).

No. 20 is especially fascinating to English-speakers as a primitive version of *The Merchant of Venice* (see No. 73, and the commentary on *Il Pecorone*, for the later version that was the direct source for the main plot of the play). Here, in *Dolopathos*, the sanguinary contract is already associated with the folklore motif of the suitor whose virility is counteracted by a drug or a charm.

No. 21 is partially similar to the popular story of the Roman emperor Trajan's prompt attention to a widow whose son was killed (story 69 in the *Novellino*; not included in this anthology).

No. 22, rich in all sorts of folklore, includes a fairly detailed version of Odysseus's adventure with Polyphemus in the *Odyssey* (the giant is actually named in the post-story discussion in *Dolopathos*). This is unusual, because Homer was not yet widely read in Western Europe.

No. 23 is the gem of the collection. Not only is it an excellent, highly literary telling of what is essentially a fairy tale (*Märchen*), full of such folktale elements as the white deer that introduces the hero to fairyland, the mother accused of bearing nonhuman young, the "compassionate executioner," the children suckled by a doe (as in the story of St. Genevieve), the bird-children, etc. Not only does it reach narrative and descriptive heights in the idyllic sequence of the swans at their father's castle on the lake. It is also the earliest written record of the swan-knight (or, Lohengrin tale, which was to be retold variously in many languages, particularly in the French *Crusade Cycle* of epic poems, in which the swan-knight is the ancestor of Godfrey of Bouillon, historical hero of the First Crusade!

18. The Faithful Hound

O King, there once was a youth of noble birth, as mortal dignity goes. He wished to avoid avarice, lest it detract from his well-born nature, and desired to increase his reputation as widely as possible, equaling those of highest station. Thus he began to squander the fortune his parents had left him, more prodigally than generously. As is the custom of youth, he was "easy as wax to be molded into evil ways, harsh to his advisers, slow to provide for useful things, a spendthrift, prideful, greedy, and changeable in his likings."[1] He was eager to multiply the number of his soldiers and servants, to change his wardrobe regardless of the season, "to delight in new horses and weapons and the grass of the sunny field," and to give away his money recklessly to all who asked, especially actors and dancing girls skillful and diligent in the art of adulation.

Those friends and acquaintances who cared for him often tried to make him change his ways by reproaching and admonishing him, but he rejected their warnings and advice as if they envied his fame and glory. And so, by such a prodigal life, in a few years he went through his movable property and started to lose his landed property. Meanwhile, his reputation spread through the world and was on everyone's lips. Truly, if you always take and add nothing, you can drain the deepest well, and so this man, by constantly spending and acquiring nothing, was soon deprived of his fortune and his inherited lands, and had nothing more to give or take. Sad and ill, he was finally compelled to acknowledge his folly, though too late.

Thus, O King, in his desire to appear renowned and powerful beyond his measure, he lost both that measure and the glory he had excessively coveted. At the end he was left in direst poverty. And that crowd of flatterers, in whose praises he had formerly been raised to the stars, refrained from words of praise once their rewards were gone. He had no one to accompany him or show him any reverence. Even his friends and acquaintances, whose beneficial advice he had long scorned, couldn't abide to see him.

Seeing himself now placed on the lower rim of Fortune's wheel, a burden and laughingstock not only to strangers but even to friends, he decided to leave his homeland and travel to unknown regions, thinking that it was better and more blessed to be a pauper among foreigners than among familiar people, because, as the saying goes, "Lonely places make wretched people happy."

And so, O King, being ready to go wherever Fortune led, in the dead of night, with no one's knowledge, he left home, taking along only his wife, his baby boy in his cradle, his horse, his hound, and his hawk—all that was left of his possessions. Traversing lands, cities, and villages, he arrived at a city in an unfamiliar region. Having entered it while the sun was already setting, and not knowing where to turn, he stopped in one of the public squares. A townsman, seeing him and recognizing that he was a stranger, came up to him and asked who he was, where he had come from, and why he had come. He stated his rank and misfortune, adding that he'd like to stay in the city if he could find lodgings.

The townsman, moved to pity by his plight, said: "I have a stone house, but no one has lived in it for five years. If you like, I can let you have it for

[1]A quotation from Horace, *Epistles*, Book II, No. 3 ("Ars poetica").

as long as you wish to stay there." The nobleman thanked him. When they went together to the house, the stranger received the key from the townsman and brought in his family and belongings. Thus the knight remained in the city, hunting for food daily with either hound or hawk, because he had nothing else to live on. His noble birth precluded him from living in the manner of commoners, from ditch-digging, for instance, or begging. And so, as I said, he went out hunting every day, his wife remaining at home hungry until he returned with a hare, a crane, or some such quarry. If he came back empty-handed, they went hungry until the evening of the next day or whenever he caught something.

Now, it came about that one day he bagged nothing, and on the next morning, having eaten nothing for two days, he left his hound at home and went out in quest of his usual food with only his hawk and his horse. As he stayed away for some time, his wife, unable to tolerate her two days' hunger, was forced to leave the house and visit the home of another housewife to ask for food. In the meantime, while she was in the other woman's home and her husband was out hunting, an enormous snake left its hollow in the old stone wall and attacked the baby, who had been left at home, with an intent to kill him. When the hound saw this, he broke the chain by which he had been tied up and started to fight the snake. When the snake was defeated and killed, the hound dragged it with his teeth far away from the baby. But during their struggle the cradle had been upset, so that the baby's face was looking downward at the floor.

At once the knight, returning with some quarry, entered the house and saw the cradle overturned, the hound all bloody, and the whole floor blood-stained. And so, believing that the hound had been driven by hunger to devour the baby, and that his wife had run out in fear, the knight took his sword and slaughtered the horse and the hound in his impulsive anger and excessive excitement; then he tore the hawk into pieces. As he was about to kill himself as well with his sword, his wife returned, set the cradle right again, and nursed the baby. Then they found the dead snake and realized how faithful the hound had been. The knight regretted what he had done, but too late.

19. The Resourceful Burglars

In olden days there was a great and powerful king. Fully intent on amassing treasures, he had filled a very lofty and ample tower to the brim with gold, silver, and all sorts of precious things. Now, he had a knight whose fidelity he had tested in many matters, and to him he entrusted the keys to the treasure. But after the knight had undertaken the guarding of the treasure, he found that he was worn out by the labor of many years and by old age, and was unable to bear the hubbub and the cares of the court any longer. He pleaded with the king to have mercy finally on his weakness and age, to take back the keys to the treasure, and to allow him to return home and spend the rest of his life peacefully and happily with his children. The king, deeming his request reasonable and cogent, regretfully allowed him to depart, laden with many gifts. Taking back the keys and the treasure, he entrusted them to another man's keeping. When the knight returned home, all his anxious thoughts were for himself and his family. He had many sons, the eldest of whom already wore the military belt. His father, loving him too dearly, informed him of all his riches and ordered him to spend his wealth generously, thereby winning fame and friends. The son, with this permissiveness, spent his father's money too recklessly and lavishly, eagerly purchasing horses, weapons, clothing, and all the other things in which young men take special pride and pleasure. With gifts he bought many friends who were sure to desert him once the gifts gave out. And so, before long he diminished his father's coffers, and when the money was gone he went back to his father to say the money had run out.

Then his father finally took proper stock of the situation and regretted what he had done. "My son," he said, "since I foolishly loved you too well, I placed all I had in your hands. When you saw that your reins had been slackened, you forgot all moderation and spent everything until you've left me with only the roof over my head. What more can I do for you? I'm sorry indeed that your name and reputation have withered away in the flower of your youth, but I have nothing left to support you with. Only one bit of advice remains, but it's dangerous: If you want to live as extravagantly as before, let's go to the tower in which the king's treasure is stored, when the night is dark and silent."

Hearing this, his son said: "Father, I'm not afraid to face any danger with you, no matter how great, as long as our wealth doesn't vanish, lest, if it does, the glory of my name should disappear with it." And so the two of them set out at night, approached the tower, and made a hole in the wall with iron mallets. The father went in, removed as much of the treasure as he wanted, went out, and closed over the hole. They returned home laden with wealth that wasn't theirs, and the young man reverted to his spendthrift ways. Whenever they needed money again, they would return to the treasure they knew so well.

Now, it came about that the king wished to view the treasure. Summoning its custodian, he entered the tower and saw that a large part of the treasure was missing. Filled with anger, he nonetheless hid his feelings when he went out. He then visited a certain feeble old man in search of advice. This old man had once been an extremely notorious burglar. When he was caught, the king had had his eyes put out, but was still providing him with food daily from his own table. He often gave the king good and useful advice, since he had seen and heard many things and had learned much through his own experience.

The king told him of his losses, and asked him how he could recover his wealth. The old man gave the following advice: "O King, if you wish to know who did this, whether it was your keeper or someone else, order a bundle of green grass to be placed in the tower and a fire lit under it. Lock the door and keep walking around the tower, trying to spot any smoke issuing from a crack in the wall. After that, come back to me for advice on what to do next."

The king swiftly ordered the old man's instructions to be carried out. He shut the door and began walking around the tower in silence. A great amount of smoke, generated by the heat of the fire and the dampness of the green matter, filled the whole tower up to the roof. Having no other outlet, it issued through the place where the hole had been made, since it had been closed with a bare stone without mortar.

Seeing this, the king hurried over to the old man and reported what he had seen. Hearing the report, the old man said: "O King, know that the burglars stole your treasures through the place from which the smoke is issuing. Unless you catch them by some ruse, they'll remove what's left. They won't stop before they've taken the entire treasure, because they've been so successful up to now. And so my advice is to say nothing of your loss, but to bury it in silence, so news of it doesn't reach the ears of the public and make your efforts known to the burglars. Meanwhile, fill a wide, deep cask with hot pitch, resin, tar, and glue, and place it up against the hole on the inside. When the burglar, self-confident and suspecting no trap, returns to the familiar treasure as before, he will suddenly fall into the cask and, captured and held fast by the glue, he'll reveal himself to you the next day, whether he wants to or not."

The king, marveling at the old man's shrewd advice, immediately set the cask, filled with boiling glue, against the hole, locked the door, and left. The fate that no man, good or bad, can avoid finally led the wretched father and his son to the tower on the same night. Removing the stone from the hole, the father entered, with no suspicion of the trap set for him. While he hastened to leap to the floor as he had done the day before and the day before that, the incautious wretch jumped into the cask up to the chin, dressed and shod as he was, and, enveloped in the glue, was immediately bereft of his mobility, so that he could move neither hand nor foot nor any other member, except his tongue, which had just barely been saved from his misfortune.

And so, with groans the unhappy man called to his son, told him in what trap he had been caught, and begged him to cut off his head and depart quickly, before anyone arrived, so that his head wouldn't identify him, by chance, and bring eternal shame and loss upon his family. The son tried with all his might to pull his father out, but when he saw that his efforts were in vain, he began to be distressed and to waver between two courses of action. On the one hand, he loathed to bloody his hand with his father's death; on the other hand, he was afraid of being caught because of his father's face. Thus, while his love stayed his hand from murder, whereas his fear and his need urged him to it, and he didn't know which was a more opportune thing to do, he cut off his father's head with his knife and ran away with it.

At dawn the next day the king got out of bed, entered the tower, ran over to the cask, and found the wall broken, the entire surface of the pitch spattered with blood, and the thief himself, but minus his head. He dashed back to his adviser, the old man, and reported that the thief had been caught, but with his head gone. When the old man heard this, he smiled slightly and said: "I admire this burglar's cunning. Because he was of the nobility and didn't wish to give away himself and his family, he had his head cut off by his partner. So that I consider it hard for you to regain your treasure or identify the burglar."

Then the king fervently urged the old man to advise him, saying that he didn't care about the lost treasure, so long as he could learn who the burglar was. The old man said: "Have him taken out of the cask, tied to the tail of a very strong horse, and dragged through the squares and streets of the towns in your kingdom. Let armed soldiers follow him in order to arrest any men or women they see weeping at the sight of the corpse, and let them bring them before you. If his partner, wife, or children is present, they won't possibly be able to refrain from tears."

The king found the old man's advice good, and hastily ordered the headless body to be tied by the feet to a very strong horse and dragged through the next town, escorted by armed soldiers. While the wretch was being dragged, he happened to pass outside his own home. That eldest son of his, who had accompanied him on his burglaries, was standing right outside his door. When he saw his father being dragged so mercilessly, he didn't dare to weep but, unable to check his tears, he found the opportunity to seize a knife and a stick of wood, as if he were going to whittle, and he purposely cut off his left thumb. Then, with this thumb as a pretext, he called out in his grief and burst out weeping. His mother, brothers, and sisters came running and tore their clothes, faces, and hair with their hands, lamenting in the son the misfortune of the father.

At once soldiers rushed over to arrest them and lead them before the king. The king, overwhelmed by intense joy in hopes he could recover what he had lost, promised he would let them live and pardon them if they confessed their crime and returned his treasures. The young man, emboldened by fear and need, said: "O mighty King, my family and I didn't shed tears because that wretched body is any concern of ours, but because this unlucky day has robbed me of my left thumb. We shed tears, scratched our faces, and tore out our hair because today, though still young, I have been unfortunately bereft of such a useful member."

The king, seeing blood still flowing from the thumb, deemed it a firm indication of the man's truthfulness and, moved to pity at the youth's mis-fortune, said: "It isn't surprising if someone grieves when he's injured. Go in peace and in the future be especially cautious on this ill-omened date." Thus the youth saved himself and his family by his wits and returned home, while the king, deceived by this appearance of veracity, went back to the old man for advice.

The old man asserted that the king could hardly find what he sought, but nevertheless urged him to have the body dragged through the same town again. This was done. When the dead man arrived at his home as be-fore, his son, unable to bear the grief in his mind, secretly threw his baby boy into the well that was located in front of the house. Then, tearing his face with his nails, he called his neighbors tearfully, as if to save his son. Again his mother came running with her other children. They gathered around the well weeping. Some lowered themselves into the well to pull out the little boy, and others drew them up again.

What use are further words? Again the young burglar was arrested, this time alone, and led before the king. Meanwhile the corpse was dragged through other towns without any results; when it got back to the king, only bone and sinew held it together. The king, seeing the same man he had formerly let go arrested again, was greatly amazed and said: "What good are your cunning ruses to you? The gods above give you away, your thefts and crimes accuse you. Give back the treasure and I swear to you by my might and that of great Jupiter that I will not take away your life or any limb, but will release you safe and sound."

Whereupon the burglar, relying on his cunning, first sighed from the bottom of his heart, then spoke as follows: "I am the unhappiest of men, so persecuted by the gods' hatred that they won't let me get through a day without grief and torture in mind and body! Yesterday an unlucky day took away my thumb; today, a day unluckier still, my only son was drowned in a well, and here you are interrogating me about your treasure!" Then, bathed in tears that were deceptive but nonetheless very genuine, he con-tinued: "O King, you'll be doing an unhappy man a great service and favor if you remove me from this life, which strikes me as being more grievous than any torment or death."

The king, seeing the youth bathed in constant tears and requesting death as a favor, and learning that his report of losing his son that day and his thumb the day before was true, took pity and let the man go, giving him a hundred silver marks as consolation. Thus, fooled again, the king visited his adviser and told him that his efforts had been in vain.

The old man said to the king: "There is one more thing you can do, and if you don't catch the remaining burglar that way, you won't manage it any other way. Pick out forty very strong soldiers; let twenty of them be equipped with black armor and black horses, and the other twenty with white horses and armor of the same color. Have them hang the corpse from a post by its feet and guard it night and day, with the twenty white-clad soldiers on one side and the twenty black-clad on the other. If they really guard him vigilantly, they'll capture your burglar, because he won't be able to abide the sight of his partner hanging there any longer, even if he knows it means immediate death for himself."

The king ordered the black-armored and white-armored soldiers to guard the suspended corpse as the old man had advised. But the burglar, unable to endure that disgrace to himself and his father, and preferring to die once and for all rather than continuing a life of misery, determined to rescue his father from that shameful mockery or else to die along with him. And so, by a subtle ruse, he manufactured particolored armor, all white on one side and all black on the other. Dressed in that armor, he mounted a horse draped with a cloth that was white on one side and black on the other, and thus passed through the midst of the soldiers in the moonlight, so that the black side of his armor would deceive the twenty white-clad soldiers and the white side would deceive the black-clad ones, the black-clad soldiers thinking he was one of the white-clad ones and the white-clad soldiers thinking he was one of the black-clad ones.

Passing through them in that manner, he came to his father, took him down from the post, and carried him away. In the morning the soldiers saw that the dead burglar had been surreptitiously spirited away. In confusion they returned to the king and reported how a soldier had fooled them with his black-and-white particolored armor. Then the king despaired of ever being able to recover what he had lost, and he gave up the search for both burglar and treasure.

20. The Heartless Creditor

There was once a powerful nobleman who owned a well-fortified castle and many other possessions. His wife had died, leaving him one daughter. Having no other heir, he had her educated in the liberal arts so that, acquiring the best kind of wisdom from training in those arts and from the books of the philosophers, she would be able to hold onto the property she would inherit from her father, which her womanly weakness made it impossible to do by force of arms. Nor was he disappointed in this hope. She amassed so much knowledge and shrewdness from the arts that she even learned magic without a teacher.

Now, it came about afterward that her father was smitten by a severe fever and had to take to his bed. Realizing that he wouldn't recover from that illness, he made his daughter testamentary heir of all his property and, putting his affairs in order in this way, he died. Once in possession of her father's inheritance, the girl determined not to marry any man who wasn't her equal in wisdom and nobility of stock. Very many sons of the nobility, ensnared by her beauty or her abilities, came courting. Seeking her hand in marriage, they assailed her with entreaties, lured her with gifts; some offered a great deal and made many promises. In her prudence, she spurned no one, refused no one, and declared she would share her bed with any of them, provided that on the first night he paid her a hundred marks in silver before enjoying her and her embraces as much as he liked; then, in the morning, if they liked each other, they would be married more officially in the company of their friends.

When this condition became known, many young men arrived, as well as men of a more advanced age, offering the amount she had asked and twenty marks more, but they went home without either her love or their money. For by her magic she had enchanted the feather of a night owl. Whenever she placed it under her bedfellow's head, he was immediately overcome by sleep and remained motionless until the following dawn or until she removed the feather. In that way she took away many men's money, amassed a fortune, and increased her own holdings at the expense of others.

Now, among the men who were throwing their money down this well was a certain quite noble youth, without any special abilities, who borrowed a hundred marks with his property as collateral and offered the sum to the girl to meet her stipulation. She accepted it, and that day indulged herself in much food and drink. In the evening they both undressed and stretched out together on a soft bed, the owl feather having first been placed beneath the young man's pillow. The moment he laid his body on the bed and his head on the pillow, he fell asleep until daylight with never a thought of the maiden sleeping beside him. Then she got up, removed the feather, woke him up, and sent him on his way befuddled.

But the youth, complaining that he had been tricked, asked a rich servant, whose foot he had once cut off in a fit of anger, for the loan of another hundred marks of silver, intending either to lose this new sum or to win the maiden's maidenhood. The servant, mindful of the injury he had sustained, granted the youth the money with the condition that, if it wasn't repaid in a year, he could remove the weight of a hundred marks from the youth's flesh and bones. The carefree youth assented and, what's more, gave him a written note stamped with his seal.

After receiving the money he revisited the girl and offered it to her. She accepted it and they spent a cheerful day until evening. Then, when the bedroom was in readiness and the feather placed under the pillow as usual, she sent the youth ahead, promising to follow. Finding the same bed as on the previous night, and thinking that his disappointment had been due to the softness of the bed, he turned over that soft pillow, moving it from its place, thereby accidentally shaking away the owl feather. Then he laid his body on the bed, raised his eyelids, and struggled against sleep with all his might.

The girl, thinking that her magic had once more put the youth to sleep, undressed and lay down beside him confidently. But after he had pretended to be sound asleep for a while, he drew the girl over to him and claimed what was due him. Perplexed and filled with tremendous surprise, she was totally unable to change the terms of the agreement. What more is there to say? That night was spent in pleasure until daybreak. In the morning, agreeing mutually and gladly to wed, they were married in the presence of their friends and relations, and not without the amazement and envy of many.

These pleasant circumstances made the young man forget his creditor, and he didn't return the money by the stated time. Whereupon that lame man rejoiced in finding the opportunity to avenge his injury. He went to the king who was then ruling, preferred charges against the young man, with the note of the transaction as evidence, and demanded that justice be done in the matter. Although the king, a very fair man, abhorred the agreement, nevertheless he summoned the young man to appear before him to answer his accuser's charges.

Finally remembering his debt and frightened by the royal summons, the young man came to court with a crowd of friends and a large amount of gold and silver. The plaintiff exhibited the note, the young man acknowledged it, and by the king's orders the judges decreed that the lame man could either proceed according to the terms of the note, or else accept as much money as he wanted to release the young man. And so the king asked the lame man to spare the youth and accept twice the amount of the loan.

After the king had tried to bring this about for many days, the creditor always refusing, the young man's wife, dressed in man's clothing and her features and voice altered by her magical power, dismounted in front of the royal palace, came up to the king, and made obeisance to him. Asked who she was and where she had come from, she replied that she was a knight whose home was in the remotest part of the world, and that she was skilled in jurisprudence and a profound student of judicial proceedings. Overjoyed, the king asked the woman, whom he took for a knight, to sit down beside him, and he turned over the case between the lame man and the youth to her for her decision.

Calling both parties, she said: "O lame man, by the decree of the king and the judges you have the right to remove the weight of a hundred marks from this young man's flesh. But what will you gain by that, except his death if you happen to kill him? It's better for you to accept seven or ten times the amount of the loan instead."

The lame man said he wouldn't accept ten thousand marks. Then she ordered a pure white sheet to be brought in, and the young man to be stripped and stretched out on the sheet with his hands and feet tied. When that was done, she said to the lame man: "Cut off a weight equivalent to your marks with whatever instrument you choose. But if you remove as much as a pinpoint more or less than the legal amount, or if a single drop of blood stains the sheet, since the young man's blood is his property, you may be sure that you will immediately become subject to a thousand deaths. Torn into a thousand pieces, you will be food for the animals and birds; your whole family will suffer the same punishment; and your property will be confiscated."

Terrified by that horrible sentence, the lame man said: "Since no one but a god can control his hands so completely as to avoid removing a little more or less, I refuse to expose myself to that risk. I absolve the young man and renounce my debt, and I give him an additional thousand marks to make it all up to him." In that way the young man was freed by his wife's wisdom and gladly returned home.

21. The Widow's Son

While a king of the Romans was leading his army against the enemy, who had already occupied a large part of his kingdom, he happened to pass through a narrow street in a town where a poor widow occupied a small cottage with her only son. Of all that exists in the world she owned but a single hen. As the army was passing her house, the king's adolescent son, who was carrying a hawk, in the manner of the nobility, let it fly at the widow's hen.

When the hawk killed the unhappy fowl with its crooked talons, the widow's son ran over to help it and killed the hawk with a cudgel blow. The king's son, angered by this and worked up into a frenzy, avenged his hawk by running the widow's son through with his sword; then he went upon his way. What was the poor widow now to do, bereft of her only son and her paltry wealth?

In her excitement she ran after the king and, following him, asked him with tears, cries, and sobs to avenge her unjustly killed son. The king, who was gentle and compassionate by nature, halted and kindly and gently urged the woman to await his return from battle, saying: "Then I shall avenge your son in any way you like."

But she replied: "And what will happen if you're killed in the war? Who will avenge my son then?"

The king said: "I'll turn the matter over to my successor."

But she said: "What will be your reward if someone else avenges him, when he was killed while you were alive and reigning?"

"I won't have any," he said.

The widow said: "In that case, do yourself what you intend to turn over to others, in order to win praise from men and a reward from the gods."

Moved both by the widow's reasoning and by pity, the king postponed the battle and returned to the city. Learning that the slayer of the widow's son was his own son, he said: "I believe that the death of your hen has been sufficiently requited by the death of the hawk. As for the killing of your son, I give you the choice of one of two things. If you wish, I shall kill my son, or, if you deem it better for him to live, I give him to you in place of the dead boy; he will respect you as his mother, worship you as a queen, fear you as a mistress, and serve you all the days of your life."

Judging that she would have more benefit from the king's son alive than dead, she accepted him in place of her dead son, and she moved from her hovel to the palace, exchanging her rags and tatters for robes dyed in purple. Thereupon the king proceeded against his enemy.

22. The Highwayman's Sons

An extremely notorious highwayman, wishing to amass riches by theft, plunder, and murder, had formed a large gang of men who emulated his evil, wicked ways. Becoming their leader, he chose for his dwelling not walled towns or fortified castles, but the remote wilderness, rocky caves and caverns and hidden corners of dense forests. Ceaselessly, day and night, he and his men lay in ambush at the more difficult stretches of the royal roads and mercilessly robbed of life and goods anyone that Fortune sent their way, regardless of rank or sex.

After spending his whole life until old age on this criminal path, and growing rich on the immense stores of gold and silver he had wrongfully acquired, he realized that no bad deed remains unpunished, that no secret remains unrevealed, and that the man powerful in evil does not boast of his iniquity indefinitely. Thus he renounced his wicked ways, though belatedly, and spent his remaining days honestly, striving for virtue. It was amazing to everyone that the Ethiopian had so suddenly changed his skin, and that the multicolored leopard had rubbed away its multicolored spots.

When he reached extreme old age, he determined to instruct the three sons his wife had given him in more honest subjects than he himself had studied, and he suggested a variety of different professions to them, leaving each one the freedom to decide for himself, and promising each one an exact third of his property. They conferred together, and answered unanimously that they wanted no other profession than the one their father had lived by up to then. Their father said: "Well, since you have decided to set aside honesty and the safe path, and you all incline to the crooked path that leads to destruction, that danger-laden path from which hardly anyone is liable to return, do as you wish. Seek out new wealth by robbery at the peril of your life in the heat of the sun and the cold of the winter, because none of you will get a cent of the riches I possess. Let me tell you that Fortune has allowed very few followers of that path to come to a happy end."

But they scorned their father's warning, and on the following night they stole in the following manner the queen's riding horse, which was practically beyond all price: They gathered a bundle of that herb we call bitter vetch (for they had heard the horse was of such a nature that it rejected any sort of feed except that herb), hid the youngest brother in the bundle, and quietly brought it toward evening to the market square as if to sell it. That horse's groom came walking through the market as he usually did, and chanced upon the bundle containing the boy. Unaware of the hidden danger, he bought the herb, placed it on his shoulders, and carried it to the stable. There he put it in front of the horse, locked the door again, and went off to bed.

Around midnight, when all mortals are wont to lie in deep slumber, the "snake in the grass" got up, placed a golden bridle on the horse, spread a silk covering over it, saddled it, and tightened the saddle girth. The saddle and girth were of purest gold, with jingle bells of the same metal attached to them; to deaden the sound he blocked them with wax. Then he opened the door, mounted the horse, and rode swiftly to the place where he and his brothers had agreed to meet.

But this maiden attempt at robbery didn't turn out well for him, because he was sighted by town watchmen, who pursued him hotly as he fled. When he reached the place where his brothers were waiting, he was captured. In the morning all three were brought before the queen. On seeing their good looks and on hearing that they were the sons of that once very notorious highwayman (who was now an acquaintance of the queen), she threw them into prison. Meanwhile she ordered their father to come to her. When he arrived, the queen asked him whether he wanted to ransom his sons. When he said that he wouldn't give even a penny as ransom, the queen said: "In that case, now tell me about incidents or serious dangers that befell you in your career as a highwayman, and I'll release your sons to you."

He said, and I quote his exact words: "Since, as the poet says, 'It's easy to spend words, and they're a small loss,' I think it's much easier to gain something by words alone. Therefore," he said to the queen, "hear at your request the incidents that frightened me most.

"At one time we heard that a giant who owned many thousands in gold and silver was living in the wilderness about twenty miles from the haunts of men. And so, in a group of a hundred robbers, all attracted by the gold, we made our way to his home with great difficulty. Glad to discover his lair, we carried off all the gold and silver we could find. But while we were returning safely, that giant, accompanied by nine others, came across us unexpectedly, and, shame to tell, the hundred of us were captured by ten.

"They distributed us among themselves, and to my misfortune I and nine companions fell to the lot of the one whose treasures we had rifled. He tied our hands behind our backs and drove us to his cave like ten sheep. That monster was over thirteen cubits tall! We offered him a huge sum of money as ransom, but he insulted us, saying he would accept nothing but our flesh. At once he grabbed the fattest one among us, throttled him, tore him limb from limb, and threw him into a kettle to boil. "What more can I say? He killed, boiled, and devoured that man and all the rest but me, and—oh, the sin!—he forced me to eat a little of each one. When he was about to throttle me, too, I lied, saying I was a doctor, promising him that I'd cure his eyes, which gave him a lot of trouble, if he allowed me to live. He gladly assented to this in order to gain relief for his eyes, and he asked me to fulfill my promise right away.

"I placed a pint of oil on the fire, to which I added a large amount of lime, salt, sulphur, ink, and everything else that I knew was harmful to eyes. I made an ointment of all this and, when it was boiling on the fire, I suddenly poured it onto the patient's head. Badly scalded by the boiling oil all over his body, his skin all shriveled, and his sinews stiffening, he soon lost that little bit of eyesight he seemed to have. Then you could have seen that enormous hulk rolling on the ground like an epileptic, imitating now the roar of a lion, now the bellow of a bull, and putting on a ghastly show for me.

"After thrashing around for some time, but finding no relief from his pain that way, he furiously grasped his cudgel and, trying to hit me with it, made the walls and floor shake at times as if they were struck by a battering ram. But what was I to do, where was I to flee? His dwelling was enclosed all around by the solidest of walls, and there was no way out except through the front door, which was locked with iron bars. As he ran around the corners of his home in search of me, I, unable to do anything else, climbed a ladder to the ceiling, grabbed hold of a beam, and hung from it by my hands for a whole night and day.

"When I couldn't stand it any longer, I was forced to come down again, hiding myself now between the very giant's legs, now among his flock of sheep. For that giant had about a thousand sheep. He would count them every day, keep a fat one for himself, and let the others out to graze. Enchanted by some spell or black art, they would return on their own in the evening with none missing. While he was doing his daily count and sending them out, I, eager to escape, wrapped myself in the thick fleece of one ram, nestled my head against its horns, and thus mingled with the departing sheep.

"When I came under the hands of the giant, who was making his count, he fingered me and kept me back, finding me fat. 'On you,' he said, 'I shall fill my empty belly.' I came under his hands that way seven times, and seven times I was held back, but each time I escaped his hands. The last time I came under his hands, he felt me, but in great anger he drove me out the door, saying: 'Go! May the wolves eat you, because you've fooled your master so often!'

"When I was a stone's throw away from him, I derided him for having been fooled so often and letting me escape. Taking a gold ring from his finger, he said: 'Take this as a gift. You shouldn't leave a man like me without a present.' I put the proffered ring on my finger, and immediately bound by some spell, I was compelled to shout as I went: 'Here I am! Here I am!' Though blind, he ran constantly after the sound of my shouts, leaping over the lower bushes, and sometimes falling like a huge chunk of masonry when he tripped over something.

"When he was quite close to me, and I could neither stop shouting nor tear the ring from my finger, I was forced to bite off finger and ring, and throw them at him. And so, by losing one member, I saved my whole body from imminent death." After that story, the highwayman said to the queen: "There! I've recounted many dangers during a single incident in order to ransom one son, and now I'll add other occurrences on behalf of the two remaining.

"When I escaped from the giant, I started to roam far and wide in the trackless wilds, with no idea of where to go. I often climbed tall firs and lofty cedars, and I ascended mountain ridges, so that, from a commanding position, I could at least see in the distance land suitable for human habitation. But nothing met my eyes in any direction but forest and sky. I descended from the mountaintops to deep valleys, as if into an abyss, and again I rose out of them into mountains that seemed to touch the heavens. It still gives me a shudder to remember all the lions, bears, boars, panthers, and wolves I came across during that time, all the herds of buffalo and wild asses I met up with, all the satyrs and different kinds of monsters muttering some barbarous words against me, all the two- and three-headed snakes hissing at me.

"After wandering hungry, weary, and frightened over mountain ravines and valley hollows for two days, I finally arrived at a mountain peak while the sun was setting. Directing my gaze at a dark and terribly deep valley, I saw in the distance smoke that seemed to be rising from a pan. And so, making note of the spot, I quickly climbed down the mountain, and at its foot I found three robbers who had recently been hanged. Terror-stricken, I shuddered and began to falter and despair of my life, believing I had fallen into some giant's lair. But, emboldened by my plight, though nearly disgusted with life, I kept going until I found a cottage with its door open. Inside I saw a small woman with a young child sitting by the glowing coals.

"I went in and walked up to her, greeted her, and asked her what she was doing there all alone, whether she had a husband, and how far I was from human habitation. Declaring that I was thirty miles from human territory, she added tearfully that she and her son had been kidnapped from her husband's bosom the night before by those women who are known as witches, and transported into the wilderness. She had been ordered to cook her son and have him ready to serve to the witches that evening.

"Hearing this, I was moved to pity by the woman's misfortune, and I promised to rescue her and her son. Though I was suffering from great exhaustion and hunger, though I despaired of my own life, nevertheless I ran back to where I had found those three robbers hanging, took down the middle one, who was the plumpest, and brought him to the woman, instructing her to entrust her child to me and to cook the robber for the vampires. She agreed, handed me the child, cut the robber into pieces, and put him on the fire. I hid the child snugly in a hollow log, and I myself hid near the house, wishing to see the monsters when they came, and to help the woman if necessary.

"When the sun was already reddening the western ocean, I saw coming down from the mountains very noisily what looked like a multitude of apes carrying something blood-stained with them. Entering the house, they lit a huge fire, tore that blood-stained thing with their teeth, and devoured it. After awhile, they removed the unspeakable pot from the fire and, dividing the pieces of the cooked robber among them, they ate their Thyestean supper.

"After that, the one who seemed to be the most powerful among them asked the woman whether they had eaten her child or someone else. She replied that it was her child, but the vampire said: 'I'm inclined to believe that you've hidden your child and served us one of those three robbers. To prove this quickly,' she said to three of the witches, 'bring me a slice of flesh from each of the robbers.' Hearing this, I ran swiftly and hung myself up by the hands between the two robbers. Immediately afterward two witches came and cut two slices from the robbers' buttocks, and a third one from my thigh, as the scar and the hole still indicate. Then they returned to their leader."

Saying this, the highwayman said to the queen: "Believing that by the narration of this perilous event I have done enough to win my second son, I shall now add a third story to win the third.

"Badly wounded, I lowered myself from the gallows on which I had hung and, binding the wound in linen, I tried unsuccessfully to stem the blood, which was flowing onto the ground in a stream. But worried more about the woman whose defense I had promised to undertake than about myself, I returned to my hiding place, often feeling faint at heart because of great loss of blood, great hunger, lack of sleep, and weariness. The leader of the vampires sampled the individual slices from the robbers. When she tasted my flesh with her blood-stained mouth, she said: 'Go quickly and bring me the middle robber, because his flesh is fresh and the best of all.'

"Hearing this, I returned to the gallows and suspended myself between the robbers again. The servants of darkness returned, took me down from the gallows, and dragged me by my hands, feet, and hair over brambles and sharp stones all the way to the house. They were all whetting their fangs for me and gaping avidly to devour me, when, frightened by the awesomeness of some hidden power hostile to them, they gave a great shout and fled like a storm through the door, the roof, and other openings in the house, leaving me safe with the woman.

"Two or three hours later, radiant dawn arrived to drive away the darkness of the night and the servants of darkness. Taking along the woman and child, I crossed the wilderness. This took a full forty days, during which we survived on roots of grasses and leaves of trees. Arriving among mankind, I restored the woman and child to their family."

Telling these stories, the overjoyed highwayman got his three sons back from the queen along with gifts.

23. The Swan Children

A certain youth, a great man according to our common perceptions of greatness based on high birth and riches, was once hunting in a forest with his hounds, when on the hills he found a doe that was whiter than snow and had ten points on each antler. When it fled, he pursued it on his swift horse through the dense growth. Moving deeper into the forest, he came to a deep valley thick with trees. There, both the doe and his hounds lost, he wandered here and there blowing his horn and calling his hounds, until he came across a spring, in which he saw a maidenly nymph holding a golden chain and bathing her nude limbs. Immediately seized with love for her beauty, he ran up to her before she became aware of him, took away the chain, which was the source of the maiden's powers and abilities, and, naked as she was, suddenly drew her out of the spring in his arms.

Forgetting the doe and his hounds, he immediately claimed her for his wife and celebrated the nuptials that night outdoors next to the spring. In the silence of midnight, the nymph, having now lost the name of virgin, studied the movement of the stars and learned that she had conceived six sons and a daughter. Timidly and shyly she informed her husband of this. He comforted her with consoling embraces and words. In the morning he returned to his castle, bringing his wife with him.

The youth's mother, seeing the nymph and learning that her son had married her, realized that the girl would soon surpass her in power and honor. Grieved at heart and tortured by jealousy, she strove to find a way to make her son renounce his love and to sow discord between the pair. Finding herself unable to accomplish this, because her son not only disregarded her words but even got very angry with her, she turned to a different approach and conceived in her mind a frightful crime, terrible even in the hearing of it. Awaiting an opportune moment, she concealed her plan in the recesses of her heart. In order to carry out the crime more cautiously and easily, she hid her fierce hostility, concealed the grudge she bore within her, and presented a gentle exterior to her daughter-in-law, honoring her as her liege lady, and cherishing and instructing her like a daughter.

Her womb swelling daily, the nymph finally went into labor and—should I say happily or unhappily?—gave birth on her wicked mother-in-law's lap to six boys and a girl (as she had predicted long before), each of them wearing a golden chain around his neck like a necklace. Then her mother-in-law, finding that the time was ripe to carry out the crime she had long had in mind, stole the seven infants from their mother. In their place she put next to the sleeping woman's bed seven puppies born nine days earlier. She handed the infants to a faithful servant of hers, making him swear an oath that he would kill them and either bury them or plunge them into the river.

Promising prudently and faithfully that he would do so, he took the infants, carried them into the forest, and set them down under a tree. When about to strangle them, he was restrained either by pity or by the enormity of the crime, and he left them there alive, telling himself that he had kept his hands clean and had carried out his orders with adequate faithfulness.

But the god who founded and created the world, who sees, maintains, and governs all things, especially mankind, recognized that those infants, though puny creatures, were nevertheless his creations, and sent them a foster father in the very same hour in which the servant had departed, an old man who for the sake of practicing philosophy had preferred the forest to the city and was living in a cave. Finding them, he received them as his own children and brought them to his grotto, feeding them on the milk of a doe for seven years.

Meanwhile, as the infants were being carried into the forest by the aforesaid servant, the wicked old woman summoned her son and said: "Come, my son, see what beautiful and noble children your wife has given you." And she showed him the puppies, berating him for having hitherto scorned the words with which his mother had tried to make him give up a wife of that sort. Trusting his mother too much, he was appalled at his wife, though he had earlier been so wildly in love with her. Given over totally to hatred for her, he had the puppies drowned and, affording his wife no opportunity to speak for herself or deny the crime, he ordered her to be buried alive up to her breasts in the middle of his palace. He then instructed all his knights, servants, jesters, and dinner guests to wash their hands above his wife's head before dinner and supper, and to wipe them on her hair. She was to be given no other food to sustain her than what was prepared for the dogs.

She remained in that predicament for seven full years. Her white body was stripped bare after her clothing had rotted with age, and that snowy whiteness was turned to blackness. Her face was clouded, her eyes were sunken in, her brow was wrinkled, her hair turned dark, and as her flesh wasted away she was reduced to skin and bone.

But her children, after being well reared by that old philosopher on doe's milk during those seven years, were now eating the meat of birds and animals which they caught themselves by hunting. After this, by the dispensation of the all-seeing god, it came about that the children, wearing the golden chains around their necks, unexpectedly ran across their father, who was out hunting in the forest. Immediately smitten by natural affection, he began to follow the runaways, trying to catch them, but they suddenly disappeared before his eyes. Returning disappointed to his castle, he told his mother and the others what he had found. She, recalling her crime and agitated in her mind by what she had heard, immediately summoned her servant and asked him whether he had killed the infants or let them live. He confessed that he had left them under a tree, alive, to be sure, but certain to die soon. Then she said: "Without a doubt, they're the ones my son found today, and if you don't hasten to seek out the children and take away their chains somehow, both of us are lost!"

The servant, worried about both himself and his mistress, quickly entered the forest in search of the children. After seeking them one day, a second, and a third through the dense growth, he finally found them on the fourth day transformed into swans. They were playing on a river, while their sister guarded their chains on the bank. As they darted this way and that in their sport, and the girl was intently watching their games, the servant, walking cautiously and softly, suddenly came upon her and took away her brothers' chains. Only hers, which he was unable to seize, remained.

He returned joyfully to his mistress and presented the chains to her. She summoned a goldsmith and ordered him to make a goblet out of them. He took the chains and tried to melt them over the fire, but couldn't. He tried to break them with a hammer, but his efforts were in vain. They wouldn't yield to iron or fire, except for one link of one chain, which was slightly broken. Seeing that he was getting nowhere, he weighed the chains and put them away in his shop. Then taking an equivalent weight of his own gold, he made a goblet out of it, and when it was finished he brought it to the old woman. She immediately placed it in her strongbox, never drinking from it and never showing it to her son or anyone else.

Now, the boys who had been transformed into swans, as stated above, were unable to return to human form once their chains were lost. Then, like swans, they long lamented their misfortune in sweet song, now that they were changed as the supreme fates had ordained. Taking along their sister, also changed into a swan, they took to the skies on their wings in search of some lake or river suitable to live in. After flying for a long time through the empty skies, they espied a remarkably long and wide lake next to a castle. Charmed by its beauty, they alighted upon it, pleased to have found a proper place to stay.

This castle was their father's. It was so situated on a steep mountain crag, as the natural site demanded, that it was encircled by the lake on almost every side. The crag, protruding from the mountain, was so high that it seemed to cling to the clouds rather than to the earth. On the side facing the mountain it offered only an extremely difficult and narrow climb up to it; on the other side it projected completely into the lake, so that if you saw it hanging there from above, you'd think it was on the verge of collapsing into the gulf with all its buildings. It was on this side that the palace was built; its windows looked out onto the lake.

Just then the master of the castle, pondering over something or other, happened to be facing those windows when he caught sight out there of these avian specimens as yet unfamiliar to him. Charmed by their beauty and the sweetness of their singing, he ordered his whole household not to dare to frighten them away, but rather to throw them the leavings of the table every day, so that they would get used to this and gladly remain on the lake. After the servants had done this for a few days, the birds became tame so quickly that every day at dinner- and suppertime they would come to the shore, awaiting their usual food with great eagerness. It was pleasant and delightful to watch them chasing the half-eaten loaves or bits of fish over the waters of the lake.

But the girl, the swans' sister, had resumed her human form and climbed up to the castle. Every day she begged for her food like an orphan. Whatever scraps she received from her father's table she saved, offering part of it to the nymph, who, as narrated above, was kept buried to her breasts in the middle of the palace. She wept over her, spurred by natural affection, but unaware that it was her mother. The food that remained she brought to the lake shore for her brothers. When the swans saw her, they flew right over to her. Greeting their sister happily with wingbeats and melodious song, they picked the food she had brought right out of her lap. Then, after hugging and kissing them all, she would return to the castle, sleeping at night next to her mother, though, as I've said, she didn't recognize her.

Everyone saw her go down to the lake daily and distribute among the swans the food she had begged. They saw her cry over the buried nymph and were amazed, saying that her features were almost like those of the nymph in her happier days. But when the lord of the castle beheld her, natural love compelled him to stare at her frequently, until he summoned her and studied her diligently. He noted in her a likeness to his own family, and he observed the golden chain around her neck. Then, suddenly recalling his nymph, he said: "Tell me, little girl, who are you? Where are you from? Who are your parents? How do you make the swans come to you out of the lake?"

Sighing and bathing her face with tears, she replied: "My lord, I would say that I didn't know whether I ever had a father and mother—because I never saw them or ever heard that anyone else saw or knew them—if it weren't that nature doesn't allow anyone to be born and exist without them. As for the swans you ask me about, they're my brothers by birth." And she told him how they were found by the old philosopher and fed on doe's milk for seven years; how her brothers, bathing in a river, lost their chains and were then unable to return to human form; and for what reason they had settled down on that lake.

Also present was that old woman, fountainhead of all iniquity and chief of all wicked women, and so was the servant who had abetted her in that great crime. As the girl spoke, they kept exchanging glances as confederates in those evil doings, and couldn't hide their feelings sufficiently to keep from blushing, thus revealing the crime they had secretly committed. And since all good and bad things come to light at one time or another, the god who created and begot all things, whose eyes penetrate all secrets, whose knowledge reveals everything, who doesn't allow the innocent to perish or the wicked to boast too long of their evil ways, permitted the bloodthirsty thoughts of the old woman and her servant to be agitated to such a pitch that they attempted to kill the girl herself.

When she was going down to the lake as usual, the servant followed her. But when he pursued the fleeing girl with drawn sword, the lord of the castle, by chance returning from the fields, came up behind him and knocked the unsheathed sword out of his hand. Terrified by the fear of death, he immediately revealed the secret crime and reported it from beginning to end, declaring that he had acted on his mistress's orders.

Why prolong the story? The lord questioned his wicked mother about it and wrung the truth from her under torture. The golden goblet that she believed was made from the chains was taken out of its strongbox, and the goldsmith was summoned and asked whether he had converted the chains into the goblet. He confessed what he had done, and he returned the chains.

The girl, taking them joyfully, brought them down to the lake to her brothers and gave each one back his own. And so they all returned to human shape, except for the one whose chain had had a link broken by the goldsmith. He was totally unable to be transformed again, but remained a swan, entering the service of one of his brothers. This is the swan of everlasting fame that drew the armed knight in the boat by the golden chain.

And so the father acknowledged and welcomed his children, the children welcomed their father, and the nymph was brought back from her burial place and restored to her normal beauty by means of baths, ointments, and various poultices. And by the wise man's verdict the evil old woman who had conceived and hatched the wicked scheme fell into the pit she had dug for another, being forced to undergo the same punishment to which the nymph had been condemned.

STORIES 24–36

From *Sermones feriales et communes*
by Jacques de Vitry

The narratives in this group are a representative sampling of the vast number of *exempla*, or illustrative stories, that medieval preachers included in their sermons to make a point in an entertaining way. They have been selected from the Latin sermons of perhaps the greatest master of this genre, a great churchman and a born storyteller.

Jacques (James in English, Jacobus in Latin) "of Vitry" was born between 1160 and 1170 in an unidentified place (Vitry-sur-Seine, near Paris, is often given as his birthplace). His earlier career is associated with places that are now in northernmost France and adjacent parts of French-speaking Belgium. In 1208 he arrived in Oignies, near Namur, where he became a canon in the Augustine abbey. He preached in favor of the Albigensian Crusade against heretics in southern France (1208 ff.) and of the Fifth Crusade (1216–1221; chiefly directed against Egypt), in which he participated personally, arriving in the Holy Land in 1216 and becoming the bishop of Acre, the Crusaders' chief port. Between 1219 and 1226 (he spent parts of 1222 and 1223 in Italy), he wrote an *Oriental History*, which was both a history of the Crusades down to 1212 and a remarkably instructive guide to the daily life of the Crusaders in the Holy Land.

He returned to Europe in 1226, and from 1229 until his death in 1240 he served the papal Curia with the title of cardinal-bishop of Tusculum. During this period he composed over four hundred sermons for all sorts of occasions (Sundays, feasts, saints' days, etc.); perhaps the most famous group is the 74 *Sermones vulgares*, in which he addressed the various ranks and occupations of Christian society.

The 13 selections in this volume are all from the 107 *exempla* in the 36 *Sermones feriales et communes*, which Jacques may have intended as a special gift for his old friends in Oignies. The 11 *communes* sermons were suitable for any day whatsoever. The 25 *feriales* sermons were meant to be delivered on specific weekdays (*feriae*); more specifically, they refer to the six days of Creation. (For instance, it is clear from the remarks at the end of our stories 25 and 26 that they were included in sermons about the separation of light and darkness.)

Jacques's Latin is delightful, both very correct and very straightforward. His narrative style is unadorned but compelling. Some of his stories can be characterized as pious legends and miraculous tales.

No. 24 is a version of a famous fable by the 1st-century A.D. Latin writer

Phaedrus, a follower of the Aesopic tradition. La Fontaine offered a fine new version in his own *Fables* (Book IV, No. 21).

Nos. 27, 29, and 36 contain widespread narrative motifs.

No. 31 is typical of the way that legends quickly become attached to historical figures. The great French scholastic philosopher Peter Abelard (also famous for his romance with Heloise) had died in 1142.

Nos. 32 and 34 are typical medieval miracle stories.

No. 33 was most likely a story that the author had heard in the Holy Land—again, a humorous legend about a historical figure from the preceding century.

24. The Stag among the Oxen

The fire of wickedness among priests destroys their simple parishioners by its bad example. "Land" stands for these parishioners when Job says: "If my land cries out against me." This happens when the parishioners complain about the priests for not seeking the parishioners' benefit and neglecting the care of their souls. But the supreme Shepherd will not neglect their negligence, as shown in the story of the stag.

When the stag was fleeing from hunters, he entered a stable of oxen. Remaining there and eating the food placed in the manger for the oxen, he did considerable harm to their owner. The stable hand, or oxherd, out of negligence failed to notify his master or even to distinguish the stag from the oxen. Then the stag began to rejoice and feel safe.

One of the oxen said to him: "Now you're happy because of the oxherd's negligence, but your joy will soon be changed to grief. For our owner has eyes in front and in back of his head. He'll make a careful inspection of this stable, and you won't be hidden from his eyes." Right after that speech the owner arrived, saw the stag that was eating his property unprofitably, and ordered him to be skinned, cut up into bits, and placed in the infernal cauldrons. Then he had his negligent servant crucified and tortured in various ways.

A righteous judge is our Lord Jesus Christ, who lives and reigns eternally. Amen.

25. The Demon Abbey

It came to pass recently in France, as I've heard from trustworthy people, that when a certain abbot was returning from a general conference of Cistercians with his monks and servants, night came upon them and they lost their way and were unable to find a place to lodge. Demons, taking the shape of extremely pious monks to delude them (their habits and wide tonsures gave the outward illusion), began to urge them to spend the night with them in their abbey, which was nearby in the forest.

They consented and were honorably welcomed in a very beautiful monastery with suitable lodgings. A large fire and a meal befitting monks had been prepared. But before entering their lodgings they were led, as the rules of the order required, into the church to pray. When they sat down to eat, the monks assigned to that duty served them quite generously, but some of the servants of the Cistercian abbot, who had stayed in the stable to look after the horses, said in his ear: "Father, we have strong misgivings about these lodgings. You see, even though our horses have enough hay and fodder, they refuse to eat and they're breaking their halters because they're afraid of something, and we're having trouble restraining them. What's more, we've never heard that such a fine monastery as this one appears to be was ever founded in this place, and our spirits tremble and are troubled within us."

Hearing this, the abbot sent his people for some food he had taken along on the journey, and he didn't allow anyone to eat the food from that monastery. The monks serving them seemed to be grieved and saddened by that. After the guests' beds were made, they could hardly sleep all night long, because their minds gave them no rest, and they were terror-stricken.

In the morning, as they were about to depart, the abbot of that monastery came to them and started to beseech them to hear Mass first. Everything necessary for the service was ready. While at Mass, it seemed to them that one of the local monks was celebrating the divine service most piously. After Mass the abbot of that monastery and all his monks began to entreat the Cistercian abbot to preach a sermon in the chapter house for the edification of the brothers. When the abbot finally agreed, he ordered a certain well-educated and spiritual monk he had with him to proffer some edifying words.

That man, seeing over three hundred monks seated in the chapter house, all seemingly very pious, began to speak subtly and sublimely about the loftiest hierarchy and about the hierarchies and orders of the angels, indicating the special duties and glory of each class. He told how, when God was dividing the light from the darkness, some of the angels fell miserably, and how God had strengthened the others. The listening monks, unable to abide these words, began to bow their heads in embarrassment and shame and to go out, one after the other, as the preacher progressively spoke about the angelic orders from which the departing monks had fallen. When only the abbot of the monastery and a few others were left, the monk who was preaching thought that he had bored them, and brought his sermon to an end.

The Cistercian abbot, in his surprise, began to ask the local abbot why almost all the brothers had gone out. Then the local abbot said: "I'll tell you without concealing the truth. We are those angels who fell with Lucifer. There were some here with me from every order, and whenever their order was mentioned, they couldn't abide it, and left. Your monk had not yet got up to the order to which I and these few remaining monks belonged, and that's why the few of us stayed after the others were gone."

After those words the illusory spell was broken, and neither monks nor monastery were to be seen. The Cistercian monks found themselves beside a swamp, surrounded on all sides by mud and bog, so that they could hardly make their way out, especially because their horses were very weak, not having eaten all night, just as the abbot and his men had slept not at all, or very little, that night. Because they had been detained so long by the illusion of the Mass and by the sermon, they were scarcely able to reach any lodgings for the rest of that day.

Perhaps, if their monk had spoken on a different subject and the local monks had stayed put, they might have been led to places from which they were unable to escape without danger to their life, and they might not have found any town or food that entire day.

And so it is very important to separate light and darkness carefully and to test spirits to see whether they proceed from God.

26. Celestial Hospitality

Just the opposite happened to a pious and religious layman I saw and knew. While he was living in a village called Wambaix in the diocese of Cambrai,[1] and earning a modest living by the labor of his hands, he was touched by God and began to despise the world and perform severe penance at home, serving God day and night. Since he had no church that suited him, he began planning to build a secret chapel at home. He went to a village called Fontaine l'Evêque, about two days' journey from his home, where they make fine and elegant images of the Blessed Virgin. He bought one that was quite heavy, wrapped it in linen, and set it on his shoulders.

On arriving, very weary, at nightfall in the town called Binche, he found it very difficult to secure lodgings that suited him. A man in humble monk's garb appeared before him, calling himself Brother Peter, and said: "Hello, John!" (That was the layman's name.) "I take pity on your labors," he continued, "and it's not good for you to spend the night here among worldly people. Come with me a little way outside town, and I'll show you excellent lodgings."

When John agreed after much persuasion, they left town and entered a very beautiful forest. Before they had gone very far, Brother Peter showed him into an extremely beautiful dwelling. There, a large fire being lit and the table set, he was cheerfully welcomed by the owner of the house, who ordered Brother Peter to take care of all his needs. John was amazed because he had never seen or heard of such a forest or manor near Binche.

At the table he saw a perfectly clean tablecloth white as snow, but was unable to determine what it was made out of. He was served extremely white

---

[1]All the places in this story are located in what is now the northernmost part of France and adjacent parts of Belgium.

bread and a beverage so tasty that no other flavor can be compared with it or equal it. In addition, Brother Peter served him vegetables on a perfectly clean plate. When John tasted their wonderful flavor, he was afraid they had been prepared with meat, and he shied from eating them, because he abstained from meat and animal fat. But the owner of the house said: "Don't be afraid to eat them! No meat or animal fat has ever touched those vegetables." Finally he was served excellent pears. Refreshed by their taste and fragrance, John sat by the fire in the palace after dinner.

Now the lady of the house sat down next to the owner with two maids. She greeted John and asked him what he had there wrapped up in linen. He said: "It's a statue of the Blessed Virgin that I'm bringing home. I'll place it in the chapel I've built for myself."

Then the lady, unstitching the cloth, began gazing at the statue, and she said: "This statue is most beautiful, and it pleases me. Be sure to kneel before it frequently and say your Hail Mary, and she'll reward you for it." And, sewing up the linen much better than before, she returned the wrapped statue to John.

When Brother Peter showed him to bed to sleep, John asked him who the master of the house was, and who had shown him such hospitality. Brother Peter replied: "The master of this house is named Jesus, and the lady you saw is named Mary." When John saw the fine white sheets spread on the bed, he didn't want to get in, because he abstained from using linen apparel or sheets. But Brother Peter said: "Get in and have no fear. I'll have you know that these sheets aren't made of linen."

He lay down and slept so peacefully that he didn't awaken until daylight, though he usually got up every midnight and remained in prayer until day. When Brother Peter came and said it was time to be up and on his way, John was greatly surprised and he blushed. When he gratefully took leave of the master of the house, the Lord said to Brother Peter: "I know that this man has one shortcoming: he needs to eat at dawn. Give him this apple to eat, so that he isn't faint on his journey."

When he ate it, he acquired so much strength that forever afterward he was able to go without breakfast. After Brother Peter had escorted him for a way and they were now at the edge of the forest, Peter said: "My Lord Jesus and my lady, His Mother the Blessed Virgin, and I, the apostle Peter, observing your devotedness in carrying the statue on your own back with such fatigue, wished to visit you and comfort you. Be sure to continue in your good ways just as you've begun! Go to Master Jacques, a native of Reims and canon at Cambrai,[2] confess all your sins to him, live by his instructions, and tell him and anyone else you wish what the Lord did for you."

Saying this, Peter suddenly disappeared, and John, turning around, saw neither forest nor manor. He found that in that short time he had jour-

---

[2]Some scholars think that the author is referring to himself, and thus providing precious biographical details.

neyed fourteen miles from Binche and was near Le Cateau, not far from
his own village. Afterward, as I've heard him personally tell, every time he
was troubled or tempted during the day, Peter appeared in his dreams at
night and, reminding him of his host and lodgings, freed him from all
temptation and sorrow.

That is how, from various circumstances, we are able to divide the light
from the darkness and divide the night of temptation that befell the monks
in my previous story[3] from the morning of this poor man's comforting,
being instructed by our Lord Jesus Christ, for His is the honor and glory
forever. Amen.

27. The King and His Astrologer

In opposition to those who say the heavenly bodies are portents of the future and who believe in augury and divination, I have heard that when a
certain astrologer occasionally made true predictions—just as demons
sometimes foresee the future—the king he served began to trust him implicitly and believe in his divinations.

One day in the presence of the king he looked very sad. When the
king asked him why he was sad and gloomy, he refused to reply.
Finally, on being prodded, he told the king secretly in mournful and
sorrowful tones: "Sire, I have looked at my astrolabe and from the position of the stars I have ascertain beyond a doubt that you have only
six months to live."

The king believed what he heard, and day by day he grew more troubled
and wan, and always so sad that his knights marveled and grieved over him.
For the king, who used to greet them cheerfully and chat with them, no
longer did so. Finally, heeding the frequent entreaties and admonitions of
one man who was especially close to him, he confessed that his scholar,
that excellent astrologer, had predicted his imminent death.

Then that knight, fearing that the king might lapse into excessive grief,
get very ill, and die (for many people die from fear of dying), summoned
the astrologer to a general council and said: "How can you be sure about
the king's death?"

He replied: "I'm sure about his death because I learned of it through my
infallible art."

The knight said: "You ought to know about yourself better than about
anyone else. Do you know how long you have to live?"

He replied: "I know, and I'm certain, that I won't die for twenty years."

The knight said: "You've lied in your throat!" And, drawing his dagger,
he killed him in public view. Then the king, seeing that the astrologer's
predictions were wrong, was comforted, regained his strength, and lived for
many more years.

---

[3]No. 25

And so we shouldn't believe those who say that the heavenly bodies are portents of human life and death, but we should put our hope in God alone, who never deserts those who trust Him.

28. The Hermit Served by a Devil

I've heard about a hermit served by a devil who had assumed human guise. When the hermit found himself unable to say his prayers at the proper times of night, sometimes arising too early at the devil's instigation, and sometimes too late, that servant said to him: "Master, you should by all means buy yourself a rooster, so that you can get up at the right time of night when he crows."

Now, the hermit had firmly resolved not to own a rooster, hen, or any other creature, and yet he agreed to the suggestion after much prodding. For a while he got up on time when the rooster crowed, but then the devil saw to it that the rooster couldn't crow, and the hermit became very sad. His servant said to him: "Master, he fell ill and lost his voice because he doesn't have a hen, as his nature requires." And after further prodding he persuaded the man to buy a hen for his rooster. Then the devil made the rooster crow again.

It finally came about that the hermit was sorely tormented by a serious illness. The tempter approached him and said: "Master, didn't you see that the rooster was totally unable to regain his health until he had a hen? And so you can be sure that you won't get well unless you have a woman." The hermit kept refusing strenuously and his adversary continued to tempt him until, as his pain increased, he assented, and the devil brought him the daughter of a nobleman. After they had lain together, the servant informed that knight.

When the knight was near the hermit's cell, that evil one said: "Master, here comes the knight whose daughter you've slept with! You can be sure that if he finds his daughter here, he'll kill you on the spot, and you'll be unable to repent for your sin of fornication. You'd do better to kill her and hide the body." When the hermit did so, the devil derided him, vanished, and departed.

Then the hermit, regaining his original piety and sincerely repentant, prayed to God with many tears until He brought the girl back to life, and the hermit restored her to her father.

That is how that fallen star, accursed from the outset, would have brought that holy man to a miserable end under the guise of doing good, had not our Lord Jesus Christ, forever blessed, aided him in His mercy. Amen.

29. The Bishop's Horse

I've heard about a bishop in France who had an excellent horse. His brother, a knight, greatly desired to have it, to ride it in tournaments, but couldn't get it. Finally, after much pleading, he persuaded his brother to lend him the horse for three days. Visiting one of the bishop's chaplains, he made a point of asking what words his brother uttered most frequently while riding. The chaplain reflected and replied: "When my master rides, he says his hours, and I don't think he pronounces any words more frequently than those that occur at the beginning of each canonical hour: 'Make haste, O Lord, to deliver me!'"

Then the knight began riding the borrowed horse. He uttered the aforesaid words frequently and, every time he did so, he pricked the horse sharply with his spurs. Thus, in three days' time he had so trained the horse that whenever he said "Make haste, O Lord, to deliver me!" the horse, fearing the pain of the spurs, would give big leaps and gallop so violently that it could hardly be held in check.

Afterward, when the bishop intended to ride the horse, his brother accompanied him to see the result. When the bishop said, "Make haste, O Lord, to deliver me!" the horse started to give big leaps and to gallop so hard that it almost threw its rider. When it had done that several times, the knight said: "My lord, that horse doesn't suit you. You are a heavy man and if you happened to fall, you could be badly hurt."

Then the bishop said: "This horse used to carry me very gently at a moderate pace. Now I don't know how he got this way. I'm sorry to have lost such a good horse, but, as things stand, I make you a present of him! He's more suitable for a knight than for a bishop." And in that way the knight acquired the horse he had longed for.

How wretched are those who don't fear God's scourge, but are hardened against God's lashes and grumble, when even brute beasts fear the lash! When holy men are scourged, they are purified and give thanks to our Lord Jesus Christ, who is forever blessed. Amen.

30. Self-Crucifixion

I've heard about a simple layman who was very pious but had more religion than knowledge. While he was living in a town called Huy in the diocese of Liège, an evil spirit in the guise of an angel of light persuaded and admonished him that he ought to suffer for Christ's sake what Christ had suffered for *his* sake. He ordered the smith to make four very sharp nails, he made a cross out of two pieces of wood, and on Good Friday he went out alone to a hill not far from the aforesaid town.

Adjusting the cross to his body, with hammer in hand he nailed his two feet to the cross. Piercing both hands, with his right hand he nailed his left hand to the cross, and then, holding the nail with the fingers of his free hand, he put in through the hole he had made in that hand.

After hanging there awhile, when the moment of death was approaching, he was seen by shepherds, who took him down as he shouted and struggled, and then brought him to his house half-dead. But in a few days he had been so fully healed that only a few traces of his wounds were visible. And so, if the Lord hadn't come to his aid, he would have been eternally damned for committing suicide.

Therefore we mustn't give ready credence to visions, but the spirits must be tested to see if they proceed from God.

31. Abelard's Unusual Lectures

I've heard that the king of France was greatly angry and stirred up about the eminent professor Peter Abelard, who lectured in Paris. He forbade him to give any more lectures on French soil. So he climbed up a tall tree near the city of Paris, and all the students in Paris followed him to hear their master's lessons beneath the tree.

When the king looked out of his palace one day and saw the crowd of students seated beneath the tree, he asked what was going on, and was told that they were clerics listening to Master Peter. In a violent rage, he summoned the professor and said: "How could you be so bold as to give a lecture on French soil after I forbade it?"

Abelard replied: "Sire, after your prohibition I didn't lecture on French soil; I lectured in the air." Then the king forbade him to lecture on French soil or in French skies. So he got in a boat, and from the boat he instructed crowds of disciples.

When the king saw the students seated on the riverbank one day, he asked what was going on, and was told that Master Peter was giving lessons there. In high dudgeon he summoned him and said: "Didn't I forbid you to lecture on French soil or in French skies?"

Abelard replied: "I lectured neither on French soil nor in French skies, but on French water."

The king smiled. His anger was changed to mildness, and he said: "You've beaten me. In the future you can lecture wherever you like on my territory, on land, in the air, or on water!"

32. Saint Theobald and the Demon

The story is told of Saint Theobald[4] in the Champagne region that when some very fierce men were waging war and no one could make peace between them, the holy man was sent for, to appear on the day set for the peace negotiations. Since he was very old and feeble, he had a carriage prepared for himself. But while he was crossing a river, a devil, wishing to hinder his journey, removed a wheel from the carriage and threw it into the river. The saint ordered him to take the place of the wheel and perform

---

[4]Died 1066.

its function. Not daring to oppose him, the devil seized the axle and began to act as a wheel.

When the saint arrived at the meeting place with one wheel, a great crowd had gathered, and there was no more hope of peace. Seeing the carriage proceeding on one wheel, the demon being invisible, everyone was awed at such a great miracle and, in their fright, they immediately did everything the holy man requested. And so the devil, who thought he could obstruct the peace process, fostered it against his will, and fell into the pit he had dug.

When the holy man was back at the river, he ordered the devil to fetch the wheel, which had already drifted far downstream, and attach it to the carriage. When he had done so, he allowed him to depart.

33. The Pledged Beard

A beard and facial hair seem to be great adornments, especially among the Orientals, who consider a clean-shaven face to be the height of shame and label as effeminate those who are shorn of that sign of manhood. And so, when a noble knight, Count Joscelin,[5] came from France to reside in the district of Antioch, and asked for the hand of the daughter of some rich and powerful Armenian, the man absolutely refused unless he agreed not to shave his beard but let it grow.

He did so, and it came about later that this same count incurred many debts and was short of money, but was totally unable to squeeze any money out of his father-in-law. So in his anxiety he began to plot how he could get a sum of money from his father-in-law, who was rolling in it. Coming to see him one day, he pretended to be sad and to indicate a heartfelt sorrow with sighs and tears.

When the Armenian asked him what was wrong and he kept silent, as if he didn't dare tell, he finally replied after much coaxing: "My lord, under strong compulsion I've borrowed money amounting to a thousand marks, and I gave my beard as a pledge because I had nothing to pledge that was more valuable. I swore an oath that if I didn't return the money by a given date, my creditor would deprive me of my beard."

Hearing this, the Armenian was grieved and conferred with his friends. Unwilling to have his son-in-law lose his beard, to the shame and disgrace of his family, he gave him the money.

34. Too Much Olive Oil

To say something further about the virtue of abstinence: I've heard from those who were at the monastery of Saint Catherine on Mount Sinai that

---

[5] He became Count of Edessa in 1118 and was married to an Armenian princess.

when their food supplies gave out and they had nothing left but a little bread and raw herbs, they began to ask the Lord to aid them in their hunger. When their provisions continued to dwindle, they visited one of their monks who dwelt apart from the rest on the summit of the mountain, where he had long lived frugally on roots and certain herbs. They reported to him that the whole community of monks was on the point of perishing from famine and scarcity of food.

He began to pray to God on behalf of his brothers. While he was immersed in prayer, God sent olive oil in such abundance that the brothers filled all their containers to the brim. But the oil didn't give out but kept gushing up, filling not only the monastery building, but also the cloister and all the work buildings, so that the brothers almost drowned in that great flood.

And so they returned to that monk I mentioned and asked him to stop praying, or else they'd all perish, unless the oil gave out. He thus ceased praying and the oil ceased multiplying. After escaping that great flood, they sold the oil and bought provisions to last a long time. As a memorial of such a great miracle they have kept a jar full of that oil to the present day. They never use it except in times of famine, and then, they say, it never grows less, no matter how much they draw from it.

In addition, they have another oil, not edible but medicinal, which never ceases to ooze from the bones of Saint Catherine. And so the Saracens revere that place greatly, trusting in, and proclaiming with praise, the power of our Lord Jesus Christ, who is eternally blessed. Amen.

35. The Daughter of the Count of Toulouse

I also remember that when I was in the neighborhood of Toulouse, the daughter of the Count of Toulouse,[6] a noble lady devoted to God, though her mother and nearly all her kin were infected with the plague of heresy,[7] adhered staunchly to her Catholic faith all the same. She never consented to swerve from the true path at the urgings of the heretics, though they earnestly strove to destroy her with the poison of their perfidy.

Her mother happened to die, and on the same night, through the agency of an evil spirit, she appeared to her daughter, looking very beautiful, as it seemed to the young woman. She was clad in costly robes and wore on her head a crown of gold and precious gems. Looking at her daughter piercingly, she said: "Wretched girl who never wanted to believe me, see how much glory you have lost! By complying with good people and their teachings I have been crowned with glory and honor in heaven." With those words she vanished from her sight.

The noble lady began to be lost in wonder; she grew sad and was trou-

---

[6]Probably Raymond VI (1194–1222).   [7]Catharism.

bled by various temptations. Reporting her vision to some religious men, she begged them to pray for her. On the following day she had a Mass of the Holy Spirit sung. That night, after many tears and prayers, the evil spirit was compelled to bring before the daughter an accursed, stinking, vile old woman burning in hellfire from the soles of her feet to the top of her head. Weeping and howling, the old woman shouted: "Daughter, take care not to be seduced by those scoundrels who deceived me, but remain in the Catholic faith as you've done up to now!"

And so the noble lady, receiving comfort form the Holy Spirit, and with her faith and delight in God strengthened, later edified many people and propped up those who were wavering in their faith. And the evil spirit fell into the pit it had dug. Many wish to do harm but prove to be beneficial.

36. Stinking Money

Though heretics promise salvation, without the necessity of making restitution, to usurers and others who amass ill-gotten gains and entrap their fellow men, it pleased God to indicate the opposite to a man from Acre who was voyaging to Santiago de Compostela. Though that man had come by much of his money honestly by inheritance, he had also acquired some dishonestly, selling wine to pilgrims with false measures, and sometimes watered down.

While he was at sea, a monkey was on the same ship. Seeing that man occasionally open and shut the purse in which he kept his money, and watching him count it, the monkey lay in wait for the man, snatched his purse, and climbed up the mast. Opening the purse, it started to put some of the coins to its nose. In loathing of some of them, as if they stank, it threw them into the sea. The other coins it left in the purse. After it had been doing this for quite some time, sailors climbed up after it and brought it down along with the purse.

When the man opened the purse, he knew for a certainty that the monkey had left in it not one of the coins he had received from the pilgrims he had cheated when selling them wine; it had cast them into the deep as if they stank. Only those coins were left that had come to him honestly by inheritance. (He could tell because the coins carried by pilgrims differ from those issued by the city.)

Everyone on the ship marveled at that, believing the occurrence to be a miracle, in that Saint James didn't want dishonestly acquired money to be spent in his service. But heretics, in their envy and strife against the Catholic Church, preach all sorts of things—though they may have pangs of conscience, because their teachings are perverse.

STORIES 37-48

From *Il Novellino*

Il Novellino, written not earlier than 1281 and not later than ca. 1300 (the dates are based on internal evidence, references within the stories), is the oldest large story collection in the Italian language. Its original form, precise contents, title, and authorship are a mystery, because it has only come down to us in relatively late printed editions (not to mention a few stories scattered in medieval manuscripts). The title *Il Novellino* (The Book of Short Stories) was only given to the collection in the 19th century, though it may have cropped up as a suggestion as early as 1525 (perhaps in imitation of a well-known 15th-century collection by that name).

One hundred of the *Novellino* stories were edited by Carlo Gualteruzzi da Fano (a secretary of the great humanist cardinal Pietro Bembo) and published in Bologna by Girolamo Benedetti in 1525 with the title *Le ciento novelle antike* (*sic*; The Hundred Old Stories). This number of one hundred need not have represented the original work; Boccaccio's hundred stories in the *Decameron* (ca. 1350) had made that number sacrosanct in such collections.

Of the hundred stories in the next edition (edited by Vincenzo Borghini, published by the Giunti family in Florence in 1572), which was called *Libro di novelle e di bel parlar gentile* (Book of Stories and of Elegant Courtly Speech), eighteen were new additions (some of the 1525 edition's stories being omitted). Some modern editions of *Il Novellino* also include one story, from a manuscript, found in neither the 1525 nor the 1572 edition.

The original author(s) or compiler(s) are totally unknown, though there have been plenty of conjectures. The language is Florentine, but some scholars believe that the material was assembled in northeastern Italy and then subjected to a Florentine polishing. The sources of the stories are multifarious: ancient history, saints' lives, Italian historical anecdotes, Arthurian material, etc.

As the 1572 title and the 1525 preface indicate, there is a significant "self-help" aspect to the collection. It offers models and examples of clever sayings and appropriate actions that could be beneficial to the reader (or listener) in his social life and business transactions. Traces of this self-improvement philosophy are still clearly discernible in Boccaccio's *Decameron*, which is also indebted to *Il Novellino* for specific story plots. (It is also possible that the original *Novellino*, though it has no frame story, was organized into ten thematic groupings, like the ten Days of the *Decameron*.)

The style of the *Novellino* is plain and homespun, but not primitive or crude,

and many stories are told with zest and gusto. Most of the dozen stories in this selection are not obviously related thematically to stories in other collections, or to
other literary works, with the exception of Nos. 40 and 48.

No. 40 is marginally related to the vast pan-European Arthurian cycle (or Matter
of Britain), at least by the names of the characters.

No. 48 is one of an extremely widespread group of tales about the disadvantages
of eliminating the elderly. The theme already appears in the late 12th-century
Dolopathos (see the commentary preceding stories 18–23), and still shows up in
folktales collected in the 20th century. The explanation of dreams, near the end of
No. 48, is an especially engaging feature of the *Novellino* tale.

37. The Three Gems

Prester John, a most noble lord of India, sent a rich and noble embassy to
the noble and powerful emperor Frederick,[1] the man who was truly a mirror to the world in speech and in habits, who greatly loved eloquent
speech, and who strove to give wise responses. The nature and intention of
that embassy were merely twofold: to try to discover definitively whether
the emperor was wise in both speech and actions.

By the hands of the ambassadors Prester John sent him three precious
stones, instructing them: "Give them to the emperor and ask him on my
part to tell you what is the best thing in the world. Remember his words
and replies, and observe his court and its ways. You'll then tell me what you
have discovered, omitting no detail."

They went to the emperor, to whom they had been sent by their lord.
They greeted him in terms befitting his own majesty and their own lord.
They gave him the gems they had brought. He took them but didn't inquire as to their special powers. He had them stored away and praised their
great beauty. The ambassadors asked their question and observed the ways
of the court; then, after a few days, they begged to take their leave.

In reply the emperor said: "Tell your lord from me that the best thing in
this world is moderation." The ambassadors returned home and reported
and narrated what they had seen and heard, praising highly the emperor's
court, adorned with fine ways, and the character of his knights. When
Prester John heard his ambassadors' report, he praised the emperor, saying
that he was very wise in words but not in actions, because he hadn't inquired as to the properties of such costly gems.

He sent back the ambassadors to offer the emperor the post of seneschal
of his own court, if he liked. He had them recount their lord's wealth, the
various types of his subjects, and the nature of his country.

Not long afterward, Prester John, thinking that the gems he had given to
the emperor had lost their powers, since they hadn't been recognized by
the emperor, summoned a lapidary who was very dear to him and sent him

---

[1]Frederick II (1194–1250), Holy Roman Emperor and king of Sicily. He reappears in story No. 44.

secretly to the emperor's court, saying: "Use all your wits and get those gems back to me. Let no expense stand in your way!"

The lapidary set out, furnished with many gems of great beauty, and near the court began to put his gems in settings. The lords and knights came to see his handiwork. The man was very wise. Whenever he saw someone who was attached to the court, he didn't sell the stones, but gave them away. He made presents of many rings, so that praise of him reached the emperor's ears.

The emperor sent for him and showed him his own gems. The man praised them but said they had no particular powers, and asked whether he had more costly stones. Then the emperor had those three valuable gems brought, since the man wished to see them. The lapidary, rejoicing, took one of those gems, held it in his hand, and said: "Sire, this stone is as valuable as your richest city." Taking the second, he said: "Sire, this one is as valuable as your richest province." Then, taking the third, he said: "Sire, this one is worth more than your whole empire."

He closed his fist, with those three stones in it. The power of the first one made him invisible. He went back down the steps, returned to his lord Prester John, and in great glee gave him the gems.

38. The Imprisoned Philosopher

In the regions of Greece there was a lord who wore a royal crown. He had a large kingdom, and his name was Philip. He was keeping a Greek philosopher in prison for some misdeed. This man was so wise that in his mind he traveled beyond the stars.

It came about one day that this lord received from Spain a noble warhorse of great strength and beauty. The lord sent for his marshals to tell him the value of the horse. He was told that in his prison he had the greatest expert, one who understood all things. He had the horse led to the field and the Greek brought out of prison, and he said to him: "Master, observe this horse, because I've been told you're very wise."

The Greek observed the horse and said: "Sire, the horse looks beautiful, but I'll tell you this much: it was raised on asses' milk." The king sent to Spain to find out how it had been raised. His envoys learned that the horse's dam had died and that the colt was raised on asses' milk. The king was amazed at this, and ordered the wise man to be given half a loaf of bread every day at the court's expense.

It came about one day that the king gathered together all his precious stones, sent for that Greek prisoner, and said: "Master, you're very wise, and I believe you have understanding of all things. If you know about the properties of gems, tell me which one seems most valuable to you."

The Greek studied them and said: "Sire, which one do *you* find most valuable?"

The king picked up a gem, the most beautiful in appearance, and said: "Master, this one seems to me the most beautiful and the most valuable."

The Greek took it, put it in his fist, squeezed it, and put it to his ears, then said: "Sire, there's a worm in it." The king sent for jewelers and had it split open, and they found a worm in that stone. Then he praised the Greek for being miraculously wise, and ordered him given an entire loaf daily at the court's expense.

Many days later, the king got the idea that he was of illegitimate birth. The king sent for that Greek, led him to a private place, and began to speak as follows: "Master, I believe you are very learned, and I've seen it with my own eyes when I asked you about those other matters. I want you to tell me whose son I am."

The Greek replied: "Sire, what kind of question is that? You know very well that you're the son of So-and-So [naming Philip's father]."

But the king replied: "Don't try to please me. Tell me the whole truth. If not, I'll have you cruelly executed."

Then the Greek replied: "Sire, I tell you that you were the son of a baker."

The king said: "I want to hear about it from my mother." He sent for his mother and threatened her with dire punishments. His mother confessed the truth.

Then the king locked himself in a room with the Greek and said: "Master, I've had a great proof of your wisdom. Please tell me how you knew all these things."

Then the Greek replied: "Sire, I'll tell you. I knew that the horse had been raised on asses' milk because I saw he had drooping ears, which isn't natural to a horse. I knew the stone was wormy because stones are normally cold and I found that one warm. By nature it couldn't be warm unless it had a living creature in it."

"And about me, how did you know I was the son of a baker?"

The Greek replied: "Sire, when I told you such an unusual thing about the horse, you made me a gift of half a loaf of bread daily. Then, when I told you about the gem, you gave me an entire loaf. As you can imagine, it was then that I realized whose son you were. Because, if you had been a king's son, you wouldn't have thought it too much to give me a noble city. But your nature was satisfied with rewarding me with bread, just as your father would have."

Then the king, recognizing his own baseness, released the man from prison and rewarded him most nobly.

39. The Right Way to Spend Money

A lord of Greece, who possessed a very great kingdom and was named Aulix, had a young son. He had him raised and taught the seven liberal arts praise of education

and morality, that is: good habits. One day this king took a large amount of gold, gave it to his son, and said: "Spend it any way you like." He ordered his noblemen not to advise him how to spend it, but merely to observe his behavior and character.

The barons followed the youth's steps. One day they were with him at the windows of the palace. The youth was lost in thought. He saw passing along the road people who seemed quite noble, to judge by their attire and persons. The road ran right in front of the palace. The youth ordered all those people brought before him. His wish was obeyed, and the wayfarers came into his presence. One of them, whose heart was boldest and face most cheerful, said: "Sire, what do you wish of us?"

The youth replied: "I'd like to know where you're from and what your station in life is."

The man answered: "Sire, I'm from Italy and I'm a merchant. I'm very wealthy, and the wealth I have I didn't inherit, but earned it all by my efforts."

The youth called for the next man, whose features were noble but whose expression was timid. He stood further back than the first man, and wasn't as confident when he replied: "What do you wish of me, Sire?"

The youth replied: "I want to know your place of origin and your rank in life."

The man replied: "I'm from Syria, and I'm a king. I behaved in such a way that my subjects drove me out." Then the youth took all the gold and gave it to that exile. The news spread through the palace. The noblemen and knights held a great conference about it, and the whole court was buzzing with discussions as to how the money had been spent.

All of this was reported to the youth's father, both the questions and the answers, word for word. The king began to speak to his son, in the presence of many noblemen: "Why did you spend it that way? What was your motive? What reason can you show us for not giving the money to the man who had earned a fortune through his industry, but instead giving it all to a man who had lost his own through guilt and folly?"

The wise youth replied: "Sire, I refrained from giving it to a man who failed to instruct me. In fact, I didn't give it to anyone: what I did was to reward someone, not make him a gift. The merchant taught me nothing, and I felt no obligation to him. But the man who was of my rank, a king's son who had worn a king's crown, yet through his folly had made his subjects expel him, taught me so much that my own subjects won't expel me. For that I gave him a small gift for such a valuable lesson."

Hearing the young man's judgment, his father and the noblemen commended his great wisdom, saying that his youth gave great promise that in mature years he would be very capable. Letters on the subject were sent to lords and nobles all over the country, and great disputations were held on the matter by wise men.

40. Meliadus and the Fearless Knight

The good king Meliadus and the Fearless Knight[2] were mortal enemies on the field of battle. This Fearless Knight, riding out one day incognito as a knight-errant, met some of his very loyal servants, who failed to recognize him. They said: "Tell us, knight-errant, on your honor as a knight: Who is the better knight, the good Fearless Knight or the good king Meliadus?"

The knight replied: "As I hope God will give me good fortune, King Meliadus is the best knight that rides a horse!"

Then the servants, who bore a grudge against King Meliadus for their master's sake, captured their lord by a ruse, pulled him from his horse in his armor, and laid him across the back of a nag, all saying they would hang him. On their way they met King Meliadus, who was heading for a tournament, also in the guise of an unidentified knight-errant. He asked the vassals why they were treating that knight so shamefully. They replied: "Sir, it's because he has richly deserved to die. If you knew what he has done, you'd be the first to treat him this way. Ask him about his crime."

King Meliadus came forward and said: "Knight, what have you done to these men to make them treat you so disgracefully?"

The knight replied: "Nothing. I did them no harm, I merely wanted to tell the truth."

King Meliadus said: "That can't be. Tell me more about your misdeed."

And he replied: "Gladly, Sire. I was going my way as a knight-errant. I met these servants, who asked me, on my honor as a knight, to tell them which was the better knight, good king Meliadus or the Fearless Knight. I, to tell the unvarnished truth, as I said before, replied that King Meliadus was better. And I said so merely because it's true, even though King Meliadus is my mortal enemy, and I hate him extremely. I didn't want to lie. I did nothing else wrong, and yet they suddenly disgraced me."

Then King Meliadus started to beat the servants and had him released. He gave him a valuable horse, draped in a cloth that covered his own insignia on the saddle, and asked him not to remove the cloth before reaching his lodgings. They parted, each going his own way. That evening King Meliadus, the servants, and the knight arrived at that hostel. The knight removed the saddlecloth and found the coat-of-arms of King Meliadus, who had so generously freed him and given him that gift, though he was his mortal enemy!

---

[2]Meliadus is the name of Tristan's father in some versions of the legend, and a different relative in some others. The Fearless Knight belonged to the Round Table.

41. God and the Minstrel

God once went into partnership, incognito, with a minstrel. Now, one day they heard two announcements: one of a wedding party and one of a rich man's funeral. The minstrel said: "I'll go to the wedding, you go to the funeral." God went to the funeral, brought the man back to life, and was given a hundred besants. The minstrel went to the wedding and filled his paunch. Returning home, he found his partner, who had earned money. He paid his respects to Him.

His partner hadn't eaten. The minstrel took money from Him, bought a fat kid, and roasted it. While roasting it, he took out its kidneys and ate them. When the kid was set before his partner, He asked about the kidneys. The minstrel replied: "The goats in this area don't have kidneys."

Once again there were announcements of a wedding and a rich man's funeral. God said: "This time I want to go to the wedding. You go to the funeral, and I'll teach you how to bring the dead man back to life. Make the sign of the cross over him and command him to get up, and he will. But first make them promise you a reward." God ?

The minstrel said: "I certainly will!" He went and assured them he would bring the man back to life, but his making the sign didn't make the man get up. The dead man was the son of a great lord. His father got angry, thinking the minstrel was making a fool of him, and ordered him to be hanged by the neck. God appeared before him and said: "Don't be afraid, I'll bring him back to life. But tell Me honestly, who ate the kid's kidneys?"

The minstrel replied: "My friend, I swear, by the heaven I hope to go to, that it wasn't me!" God, seeing that He couldn't make him confess, felt sorry for him. He went and brought the dead man back to life. The minstrel was set free and was given the reward he had been promised. They returned home.

God said: "Friend, I want to part company with you, because I haven't found you as trustworthy as I thought."

The minstrel, seeing that he could do nothing to make his friend stay, said: "All right, divide up the money and I'll take my share." God divided the money into three parts. The minstrel said: "What are you doing? There are only two of us."

God said: "That's true, but the third part is for the person who ate the kidneys. One of the other parts is for you, and the other for Me."

Then the minstrel said: "On my honor, since you put it that way, I tell you that *I* ate them. At my age, I shouldn't tell lies anymore!"

And so we see people admitting things for money that they wouldn't admit to save their life!

42. A Bad Rate of Exchange

There was once a Florentine named Bito, a fine courtier who lived in San Giorgio across the Arno. There was also an old man named Master Frulli, who had a very fine farm above San Giorgio, and lived there with his family almost all year long. Every morning he sent his maid to sell fruit or vegetables at the market by the bridge. He was so stingy and untrusting that he tied up the bundles of vegetables, counted them out to the maid, and told her how much to ask for them.

The admonition he dwelt on most was not to loiter in San Giorgio because there were thieving women there. One morning that maid was passing through the village with a basket of cabbages. Bito, who had planned a prank, was wearing his costliest squirrel-fur robe and was seated on the bench in front of his house. He called to the maid, who came right over to him. A number of women had called her first, but she paid them no mind. "My good woman, what are you asking for those cabbages?"

"Two bundles for a farthing, sir."

"That's certainly a good price, but, I tell you, only I and one maid are living here now. The rest of my family are at our country house. And so two bundles would be too much for me, especially because I like my vegetables fresh each time." In those days there were coins current in Florence called "medals," two of which were worth one farthing. And so Bito said: "Give me one bundle now; give me a farthing and take a 'medal.' Another time I'll take the other bunch."

She thought he was requesting the correct change, and she gave him what he asked. Then she went to sell the rest at the price her master had set. Back home, she gave Master Frulli the money. He counted it over and over, but still found it a farthing short. He reported that to his maid, who replied: "That's impossible!"

He got annoyed with her and asked her whether she had loitered in San Giorgio. At first she denied it, but he kept after her until she said: "Yes, I stopped to talk to a fine gentleman, who paid me handsomely. And, I tell you, I still owe him one bundle of cabbages."

Master Frulli replied: "So, with all that, there's a farthing missing?" He thought the matter over, put his finger on the deception, bawled out his maid, and asked her where that man was located. She told him exactly where. He realized it was Bito, who had already played many a trick on him. Hot with anger, he got up early the following morning, hid a rusty sword under his furs, and walked to the bridgehead. There he found Bito sitting with many other gentlemen.

Master Frulli raised his sword and would have struck him if another man hadn't held his arm. People assembled there in amazement, wondering what was going on. And Bito was very frightened. Then, recalling the situation, he started to smile. The people surrounding Master Frulli asked him what he was after. He was in such distress that he could hardly get the words out.

Bito made the people calm down and said: "Master Frulli, I want to settle up with you. Let's have no more words. Give me back my farthing, and take back your 'medal.' And keep your bundle of cabbages with God's curse on them!"

Master Frulli said: "That's fine with me. If you had said that in the first place, none of this would have happened." And, unaware of the new trick, he gave him a farthing, took a 'medal,' and departed with his mind at ease. The laughter was enormous.

43. A Romantic Triangle

A young man in Florence was in love with a maiden of good family. She didn't care for him, but was madly in love with another young man, who loved her in return, but not nearly as much as the other man did. And this was evident, because that first man had given up everything else for her and suffered like a madman, especially on days when he couldn't see her.

A friend of his felt sorry for him, and finally persuaded him to come along to a beautiful country home of his, where they spent two peaceful weeks. Meanwhile the girl had a falling out with her mother. She sent her maid to speak with the man she loved and tell him she was ready to run away with him. He was overjoyed. The maid said: "She wants you to come on horseback when it's very dark. She'll pretend to go down to the cellar. You'll be ready at the house door, and she'll leap onto the horse behind you. She's light and a good rider."

He answered: "All right." Once this plan was made, he had one of his country houses made ready in grand style, assembled friends on horseback, and posted them by the city gate to see it didn't get locked. He mounted a fine horse and proceeded to her house. She hadn't been able to come down yet, because her mother was guarding her too carefully. He left and rejoined his companions.

But the lovesick man couldn't stand it in the country anymore. He mounted his horse, and his friend was unable to hold him back with his entreaties: he didn't desire his company. That evening he reached the city walls. All the gates were locked. But he kept circling the walls until he found the gate which those men were keeping open. He entered the city and headed for the girl's house. He didn't expect to find her or see her, but merely wanted to see the street where she lived. He stopped opposite her house not long after the other man had been there.

The girl unlocked the door and called to him quietly, telling him to ride over. He did so at great speed. She jumped on behind him, and they were off. When they reached the city gate, the other man's friends gave him no trouble, because they didn't recognize him: their own friend, whom they were awaiting, would have stopped to pick them up.

The two riders covered some ten miles, until they were in a beautiful meadow surrounded by very tall firs. They dismounted and tied the horse to a tree. The man started to kiss the girl and she recognized him. Aware of her mishap, she began to weep hard. But he began to console her, weeping himself, and to show her so much respect that she stopped crying and started to have tender feelings for him, seeing that he was the one that Fortune favored; and she embraced him.

The other man rode back and forth to her house several times, until he heard her parents making a noise in the latrine, and he learned from her maid the manner in which she had departed. He was alarmed. He returned to his friends and told them about it. They said: "We did see him pass by with her, but we didn't recognize him, and it's been so long that he may very well be at some distance, going down such-and-such a road."

They set out in pursuit at once. They rode until they found them sleeping in each other's arms that way, and looked at them in the light of the moon, which had risen. Then they were unwilling to disturb them, and said: "Let's wait till they wake up, and then we'll do what we have to do." And they remained there until slumber came upon them and they all fell asleep.

The two lovers awoke, meanwhile, and took stock of the situation. They were surprised, and the young man said: "These men have shown us such great courtesy that God forbid we should do them any harm!" He mounted his horse, she vaulted onto another, one of the best ones there, and they departed. The others awoke and wept bitterly because they could no longer go in search of them.

44. The Emperor's Face

In the days of Emperor Frederick there was a blacksmith who worked at his trade all the time, and didn't observe Sunday, Easter, or any other big holiday. Every day he worked for as long as it took him to earn four *soldi*, then for the rest of the day he was idle. No matter how much work remained, or how much more he might stand to earn, he did nothing else after earning the four *soldi*.

Now, it came about that people informed against the blacksmith to the emperor for working every day, even on Easter, Sundays, and other holidays, just as on normal weekdays. Hearing this, the emperor sent for him at once and asked him whether what he had been told was true. In his reply the blacksmith admitted everything. The emperor asked him: "Why do you act that way?"

"Sire, I've resolved to follow that plan every day of my life, to enjoy my freedom. Every day I earn four *soldi*, then I do no more work that day."

"What do you do with those four *soldi*?"

"Sire, one of them I give back, one I give away, one I throw away, and one I use."

"How is that?" the emperor asked.

He replied: "Sire, one I give away in charity. Another one I give back to my father for his expenses (since he's too old to earn money) because of all that he lent me when I was young and still unable to earn for myself. Another *soldo* I throw away; that is, I give it to my wife for *her* expenses; it seems to me like throwing it away, because all she knows how to do is eat and drink. The last *soldo* I use for my own expenses. And that's what I do with the four *soldi* in question."

Hearing this, the emperor didn't know what to say. He said to himself: "If I ordered him to behave otherwise, I'd cause him trouble and confusion. And so I'm going to lay a strong injunction on him, and if he doesn't follow it, I'll pay him back for anything he may have done in the past contrary to God's commandments and my own laws." He called over the blacksmith and said: "Go with God. I order you, subject to a fine of a thousand *libre*, not to tell what you replied to a soul who asks you before you've seen my face a hundred times." And he had his notary make a record of that command.

The blacksmith left and returned home to work. And I'd have you know that, for his station in life, he was a wise man. On another day, the emperor, wishing to test his own advisers on the subject of the blacksmith's reply (that is, what he meant when he said that, of his four daily *soldi*, he gave one away, gave one back, threw one away, and used one), sent for them and put the question to them abstractly. Hearing this, his wise men asked for a week's postponement, and it was granted.

Conferring, the wise men couldn't resolve the issue. Then they learned that the question had arisen from that particular blacksmith's interview with the emperor, but none of the wise men knew the answer. They found out where he lived and, visiting his home in secret, questioned him about the matter. He positively refused to give them the answer, and so they offered him money. Then he agreed, saying: "Since you insist on my telling you, go and, between you, bring me a hundred gold besants. Otherwise there's no way that you can find out."

When the wise men saw they had no other choice, and were afraid of missing their deadline, they gave him all the besants he had requested. At once the blacksmith picked up the coins, before giving his answer, and looked at each one. On one side they bore the emperor's face stamped in relief, and on the other his full figure, seated on his throne and in armor on horseback. After looking at them all one by one, where the emperor's face was depicted, he gave the wise men the same complete answer he had given to the emperor earlier.

The wise men departed and returned to their homes. When the week was up, the emperor sent for them again to give him the answer to the question he had put to them; and the wise men stated everything clearly. Whereupon the emperor wondered greatly how they could have found out. He sent at once for the blacksmith, saying to himself: "I'll make the fellow pay dearly for what he's done, for I'm sure they flattered or threatened him until he told. It can't be any other way, because they could never have found out by their skill alone. And so he'll regret having done this!"

The blacksmith came as ordered. The emperor said: "Master, I believe you have contravened my orders too outrageously, because you've disclosed what I commanded you to keep secret. And so I think you'll suffer for it."

The master said: "Sire, you are lord over not me alone, but the whole world, to do as you see fit. Therefore I'm at your orders, respecting you as my dear father and lord. But I'd have you know that I don't think I disobeyed your orders, because you told me not to reveal to anyone else what I said to you before I'd seen your face a hundred times. Now, when I was under compulsion to reply, I refused absolutely to do so before carrying out your orders. And that's what I did: before I gave them the answer, I made them give me a hundred gold besants, and on each one of them I saw your face stamped. After looking at each coin in their presence, I replied. And so, my lord, I don't think I've done that much harm to my soul in this matter. I gave them the answer in the way I've described, to get both them and me out of a difficulty."

Hearing this, the emperor started to laugh, and said: "Go, my good man, because you've outdone all my wise men! May God give you good fortune!" And so the blacksmith got out of the emperor's clutches as you've heard, and returned home safe and sound to do his work.

45. The Determined Widow

Long ago in Rome no woman dared to remarry after her first husband died. No matter how young a widower or a widow might be, the woman couldn't remarry or the man take a new wife. Now, it came about that an eminent gentlewoman, who had been widowed for some time (she had lived only briefly with her husband, and she was still very young and lusty), but was unwilling to bring blame on herself, her relatives, or her friends, pondered deeply and decided to marry again, no matter what. But she didn't know how to set about it without incurring severe disgrace.

She was of a very noble lineage and had inherited a great deal of money, so that many eminent knights and other unmarried Roman noblemen cast their eyes on her, as she did on them. What plan did this gentlewoman devise? She had a horse which she ordered her grooms to skin alive. Then she sent it roaming through the city with those two grooms. One of them led it, the other walked behind, and both listened to what people would say. Everyone assembled to look at it, all wondering at it greatly. The person who caught first sight of it anyplace considered himself superior. Everyone considered it a great novelty. The horse's attendants had tied a rope to its lower jaw. Many people asked them why the horse had been treated that way, and who owned it. They made no reply but just proceeded on their way, so that all the citizens were eagerly discussing such a great novelty as that was, and many longed to know who owned the horse. The grooms led it around until evening, when almost everyone had gone home. When they themselves arrived home, the lady asked them what had happened. They told her everything, how a great number of people had assembled to see the horse, as many as were able, and how they all found it a great novelty and asked who owned it, though the grooms had never replied.

The lady said: "Good! Now go and give him a good feed, and tomorrow go back outside and do the same thing. Then in the evening report to me what you've heard." The next morning they took the horse out again and walked him through the city. As soon as the people found out that it was the flayed horse, no one who had seen it once or twice before wanted to see it anymore, because everyone had already grown pretty tired of it. For you must know that, no matter how beautiful a thing is, the time will come when it gets tiresome. Practically no one wanted to see the horse anymore except for newcomers or strangers who had not yet seen it. Besides, it can't have been too fragrant, so that many people were as disgusted as possible, and many insulted the grooms, saying: "Take him to the moats, to the dogs, to the wolves!" And so the horse was shunned by most people, who practically didn't want to hear it mentioned as being a strange sight.

In the evening the grooms stabled the horse again and returned to the lady. She asked them to report what they had done. They replied, telling her the facts, how the people were sick of it, and didn't want to see it anymore, how a number of people had insulted them and everyone had had something to say. Hearing this, the lady said to herself: "Good! Because I know they'll do the same thing in my case—so, come what may!" To the grooms she said: "Go, give him food tonight, but never again. Tomorrow, walk him through the city a little more, then take him to the moats and leave him there for the wolves, dogs, and other animals. Then come back here and report on what happens."

The story tells that they carried out the lady's orders. The horse couldn't eat anything, feeling unable to do so after losing its skin, and started to stink terribly. Now the grooms wanted to obey their lady, but each of them said to himself: "I think that this time we'll be greeted with mud and vegetable stalks, because this horse stinks!"

In the morning, when the lady heard the grooms grumbling to each other, she promised them a good reward and they were satisfied. Now they led out the horse and started to walk through the city, as they had done on the two preceding days. The citizens of Rome, both nobles and common-ers, are highly irritable. As the grooms went through the city with the horse, which stank so badly that everyone got as far away from it as possi-ble, the people cursed them viciously. The boys, with the permission of their elders, began to insult them and throw mud at them, mocking them and playing tricks on them. They kept saying: "If you come back with him again, we'll throw stones at you, because you've stunk up the whole town!"

The grooms were now running through the city with the horse, fleeing the people to avoid being killed, and the butt of so much insult and injury that they didn't know what to do. But when the day was declining, and young and old, and men and women, were all tired of the whole thing, the grooms brought the horse to the moat. There it remained, half-dead, and the wolves, dogs, and other animals ate it.

Now they returned home and reported to the lady how that day they had been cursed, pelted with mud and vegetables, threatened, and subjected to enormous insult and highhandedness. Then the lady was overjoyed, gave the grooms the reward she had promised them for the services the two had rendered, and said to herself: "Now I can do whatever I like and carry out all my intentions. Because after everyone hears about it, the gossip will spread for a week or two, or a month, or even more, and after everyone is fed up with the subject, they'll mind their own business."

Now she proceeded with the plan she had undertaken. One day she in-vited her friends and relatives and told them the whole story, what she had done with the horse and what she had had in mind, and she asked them for their advice. Everyone considered it a great novelty, because no widow had ever remarried; everyone gave his opinion, and some agreed with her. The lady, hearing her relatives' advice, made many clever remarks and cited many good examples, like the very wise lady she was. Afterward, she summoned an eminent knight, very noble and wise, and said to him candidly:

"Sir Agapito, you are a good and eminent citizen of Rome and you are unmarried, like me. I know that you have long loved me, just as I have loved you. Therefore I want no broker or friendly go-between, but I state right out that, if it pleases you, I wish to become your wife and for you to be my lord husband."

When Sir Agapito heard that, he considered himself the luckiest man in the world. The lady said: "I'm ready to say and do what you like, whatever that may be. You may be sure that I'll make you lord of all my castles and possessions that I inherited from my father and from my first husband." And the knight consented.

The family and friends on both sides got together, and they were mar-ried. They both loved and respected each other for many years. And so, from then on, widows began to remarry, as you've heard, she being the first. The people in Rome and elsewhere had plenty to say about it, but then everyone minded his own business, and the couple enjoyed much love, honor, and distinction.

You ought to know that Sir Agapito was of the noble house of Colonna in the city of Rome, an eminent, high-placed citizen, of nearly the foremost lineage in that house. He had many children with that lady, all of whom achieved great rank and honor.

46. The Blind Men's Dispute

At the time when the king of France was waging a great war with the count of Flanders,[3] they had two big pitched battles, in which many brave knights and others were killed on both sides. Most of the time the king lost more men. In those days, two blind men were standing on the road begging for alms to live on, near the city of Paris. A great argument had arisen between those two blind men. All day long they did nothing but discuss the king of France and the count of Flanders. One said to the other: "What do you say? I say the king will win."

The other answered: "No, the count." Then he said: "It will be as God wishes," and the other one didn't respond. But he nagged him all day long, saying the king would win.

One of the king's knights, riding down that road with his company, stopped to listen to the argument of those two blind men. After doing so, he returned to the court and with great merriment reported to the king how those two blind men were arguing all day long about him and the count. The king started to laugh, and immediately sent one of his household to find out about the argument of those two blind men. He was to take care to tell them apart and to listen to their conversation attentively. The page went and learned everything, returned, and reported to the king on his mission.

Hearing this, the king then sent for his seneschal and ordered him to have two large, very white loaves baked. In one he was to put nothing; in the other, before baking, he was to put ten gold tournois coins, scattered through the loaf. After baking, the page was to bring them to those blind men and give them to them as charity. The loaf containing the money was to be given to the one who said the king would win, and the other one, with no money, to the man who said: "It will be as God wishes." The page carried out the king's orders.

Evening came. The blind men were in their homes, and the one who had received the loaf without money said to his wife: "Since God has been good to us, let's enjoy it." They ate the loaf and found it very tasty. The other blind man, who had received the other loaf, said to his wife that

[3]This particular war is hard to pinpoint historically because there were so many, but there was especially hard fighting in the very last years of the 13th century.

evening: "Wife, let's save this bread and not eat it. Instead, let's sell it to-morrow morning and get a few farthings for it. We can eat the other things we begged." In the morning they arose, and they all went to the places where they were accustomed to stand and beg.

The two blind men arrived at the road, and the blind man who had eaten his loaf said to his wife: "Wife, didn't this companion of ours, who begs like us, and with whom I argue all day long, also get a loaf from the king's servant, just like us?"

She replied: "Yes, he did."

"Now, why don't you go to his wife? If they haven't eaten it, buy it from them at any price they ask, because I found the one we got so tasty."

She replied: "Don't you think they ate theirs the way we did?"

He answered: "Maybe not. In fact, they may have saved it to get a few farthings for it, and didn't venture to eat it, the way we did, because it was so big, beautiful, and white!"

His wife, seeing that her husband was determined, went to the other woman and asked her whether she and her husband had eaten the loaf they had received the day before from the king's servant; if they still had it, would they sell it to her? The woman said: "Yes, we have it. Let me find out whether my husband still wants to sell it, as he said last night."

She asked him, and he told her to sell it, but for not less than four Parisian farthings, because it was well worth that amount. Now the other woman came and bought the loaf and brought it to her husband. When he learned this, he said: "Good! Tonight we'll have a good supper, like last night." Then the day went by. They went home and the man who had bought the loaf said: "Wife, let's have supper."

When she started to slice the bread with her knife, with the first slice a gold tournois fell onto the table. She continued slicing it, and a coin fell out with each slice. Hearing the sound, the blind man asked what it was he heard clinking, and she told him. He said: "Keep on slicing, since it's been this good so far."

The story tells that she sliced the loaf all up and searched it slice by slice, and so found the ten gold tournois that had been put inside it by the king's command. Then the story tells that he was the happiest man in the world, and said: "Wife, I stand by my true saying, that all will be as God wishes, nor can it be otherwise. Because look: our friend argues with me all day long, maintaining that the king will win, and I tell him it will be as God wills. This bread with these gold coins was meant to be ours, and all the people in the world couldn't take it away from us. It turned out as God willed."

Then they put the money away. In the morning they arose to go and tell the news to their companion. The king sent a messenger early in the morn-ing to find out who had wound up with the loaf from which the money had emerged; because, the day before, neither blind man had mentioned it, neither of them having eaten his loaf yet. Now, this servant of the king was hidden off to one side, so the blind men's wives wouldn't see him. Both blind men arrived where they were accustomed to stand during the day. The one who had bought the loaf started to talk to the other one, calling him by name:

"I say once again, it will be as God wishes. Yesterday I bought a loaf that cost me four Parisian farthings, and, when I had it cut open, I found ten good gold tournois in it. And so I had a good supper, and I'll have a good year."

Hearing this, his friend who had first received that loaf and wasn't smart enough to slice it, but was willing instead to take four Parisian farthings for it, was crushed and said he no longer wished to argue with him, because what he said was true: it will be as God wishes. When he had heard that, the king's servant immediately returned to court and reported his entire mission to his lord: what the two blind men had said to each other.

Then the king sent for the blind men and had them tell him the whole story, how each of them had received a loaf from his page, how one had sold his loaf to his friend, who had found the money inside it, how they had formerly argued with each other all day long, and how it was not the man who predicted the king's victory that got the money, but the other man, who always said: "It will be as God wishes."

When the king heard all this from the two blind men, he dismissed them. Then he made great merriment with his nobles and knights, saying: "Truly, this blind man speaks the truth: it will be as God wishes, and all the people in the world are powerless to change it."

47. The Maligned Youth

A wealthy nobleman had an only son. When the boy reached adolescence, he put him in the service of a king to learn chivalry and noble ways. He was much liked by the king, and some envious men were stirred up against him. They suborned one of the leading knights at the king's court, with entreaties and with money, to arrange for the boy's death. One day, this knight secretly summoned the lad and said that it was his great love for him that made him say the words he was about to speak. He continued as follows:

"My dear young man, His Majesty the King loves you more than anyone else in his household. But, from what he says, he can't stand your breath. And so, for God's sake, be careful and, when you serve him wine, cover your mouth and your nose with your hand, and turn your face away, so your breath doesn't bother the king."

The lad did this for some time and the king took great offense at it. He summoned the knight who had so instructed the boy, and ordered him to tell him the reason for it at once, if he knew it. While obeying the king, he twisted all the facts, saying that the boy could no longer stand the king's breath.

And so, through that nobleman's mischief, the king sent for a furnace owner and ordered him to throw the first man he sent his way into a blazing furnace. If he failed to do so, or if he revealed the matter to anyone, the king promised, and took an oath on it, that he'd cut off his head. The furnace man promised him to do it all gladly. He lit a fire in a large furnace and waited impatiently for the man who had deserved that penalty to come along.

The next morning, the innocent boy was sent by the king to the furnace man with the message that he should do what the king had ordered. When the boy was almost at the furnace, he heard the bells ringing for Mass. Dismounting, he tied up his horse in the cloister of the church and attended Mass devoutly. Then he went to the furnace and told the furnace man what the king had ordered him to say.

The furnace man replied that he had already done everything. This was because the knight, anxious in his malice for the deed to be done without delay, had gone there and had asked the furnace man whether he had carried out the orders. The furnace man said that he had not yet complied with the king's command, but would do so at once. He seized the knight and immediately threw him into the blazing furnace. Then he returned to the king and reported that his orders had been carried out.

Marveling at this, the king tried to learn through subtle means the whole state of affairs. Learning the truth, he had all the envious courtiers who had misrepresented the innocent boy hacked to pieces. To the boy himself he recounted what had occurred. Knighting him, he sent him back to his own land laden with riches.

48. The Massacre of the Elderly

On an island in the sea there was a young king, very strong and powerful, but too young to govern a realm properly. When his reign began, he married a young woman, crafty and subtle for evil rather than good. An elderly man, who had been the foster father and tutor of the young king, her husband, kept watch over the queen's doings. When she became aware of it, she made every effort to please the king. Once, when he was flushed with wine or food, she said:

"My lord, young as I am, if you're willing to trust me, I'll make you the greatest ruler in the world. But you'd rather trust someone else, and not me. It's wrong of you, and not sensible."

The king replied: "You can be sure I love you more than anyone else in the world, and I'm prepared to do whatever you like, and to have all your orders obeyed throughout my kingdom."

She said: "It will be for your honor and benefit. But now I beseech you to give me the gift I ask you for."

The king replied: "I will, and gladly."

The queen said: "If you consent, I'll have it done tomorrow," and he replied that he was very pleased to comply. That's where things stood until morning.

In the morning the queen issued a proclamation throughout the kingdom that no old man who had passed sixty should be left alive. They should all be killed without delay, because they did great harm in the kingdom. She did this because of her bitter hatred toward the elderly tutor of the king, observing that the king loved him and paid close attention to what he said. Women very frequently tend to hate those whom their husbands love.

The queen saw to it that her wishes and commands were put into execution. The king, seeing the death of his tutor and the other old men, was very upset, but the queen, by her cunning and eloquence, was soon reconciled with him.

Now, it came about that, while the king was sleeping alone without the queen, he had a significant and strange dream, in which he had been captured by many people who were pinning him to the ground on his back and heaping stones and earth on him; he was struggling to stand up and shout, but he was unable to. He remained in that torment for some time.

When he awoke, he was panting and covered with sweat. Recalling his dream and wondering what it might mean, he said to himself: "I think that the load I was bearing means that some people who hate me want to kill me." As soon as it was day, he arose, assembled his counselors, told them the dream he had had that night, and asked for their advice about it. But no one there was able to explain it to him. They said:

"Sire, we're all young and inexperienced. The elderly wise men, expert in counsel and instruction, are dead. But in the kingdom adjacent to ours there are some old sages. And so, write to them, that is to their king and lord, so that he can ask his old men the meaning of your dream."

The king accepted this advice, and immediately wrote to the king who lived closest to him. That king, receiving the letter from the messenger, assembled his wise men and presented the letter to them. Obtaining their response, he sent it to the young king, thanking him for the honor he had showed him. He stated further:

"It is established that you sent to my land for advice, though that does not redound to our honor as much as it does to your dishonor. You took foolish advice when you killed the old men of your kingdom. No one should trust his wife blindly. If the old men of your kingdom were alive, you would not now have sent to mine, or any other, for advice. Therefore, our advice to you is that, on a prearranged day, you have someone from your kingdom come to you, bringing along his friend, his enemy, and his jester. If you can find such a man, he will be able to interpret your dream for you. You can have no other reply from us."

Hearing this, the king was greatly troubled, but his nobles consoled him and ordered a proclamation to be made throughout his kingdom. Whoever, on a stated day, brought along his friend, his enemy, and his jester would receive the king's favor and a great treasure.

When the order had been issued to kill all old men, there was in the kingdom a young man who loved his father dearly, as nature and custom demand. He had hidden his elderly father in a secret chamber, where he clandestinely brought him what he needed to stay alive. He kept him there a long time before his wife found out. But, observing her husband's frequent comings and goings, she became aware of it and came to know the whole truth of the matter.

When this new proclamation circulated through the kingdom, the young man went to his father to tell him about it, and his father said: "I want you to go there, taking along your wife, your little boy, and your dog." Then he indicated that his wife was his enemy, his dog was his friend, and his little boy was his jester.

Many highborn and noble people came to the court, in various fashions, with jesters of different sorts and with friends and enemies. And the son of the concealed father came to court with his wife, son, and dog. The king asked him why he had come, and he replied: "In response to the proclamation you issued throughout your kingdom. And I've brought along my enemy, my friend, and my jester."

The king said: "How can that be?"

The young man said: "My lord, I've brought my dog, who is a great friend to me; he guards my house, threatens my enemies, and is a better friend than any other who's been brought here; because no one is such a good friend that he'd remain your friend if you cut off his foot. And I maintain that, if I were to cut off a paw from this dog of mine, and then call him over with a pleasant expression, he'd gladly follow me lovingly."

Then he indicated his little boy and said: "This is my jester, because he's an innocent child, and whatever he does pleases me, satisfies me, and amuses me."

Then he took his wife by the hand, and said: "Here is the worst enemy I have in the world, because I can guard against an outside enemy when I sense that he wants to injure me, but I'm sure that this woman won't be of any service to me if she can help it. Such is the nature of woman: she never does any good to the man who loves and honors her, unless she does it as a subterfuge; and I have no way of guarding myself against her. When I think I'm perfectly happy, she instigates things that upset and torment me; she assaults me with reproaches; she quarrels and fights. Whatever I want, she wants just the opposite; where no one else could vex me, she afflicts me and overcomes me, because truly she's my worst, my mortal enemy."

When the young man had finished speaking, his wife pulled away the hand he was holding and began to grow angry and turn red. She cast a baleful sidelong glance at her husband, and began to say in her fury: "You may consider me your enemy, but that's not why I thought I was being brought here. I've never shown you the hostility you speak of. On the contrary, I've saved and watched over your father, whom you've kept hidden so long, breaking the king's laws, for which you ought to be put to death!"

Then everyone at the court began to smile. And the young man said: "Gentlemen, I don't have to go out of my way to prove that she's my enemy."

Then the king stood up and said: "Because my order to kill old men was not based on wise advice (for which I'm very sorry), God forbid that you suffer any harm for that reason. But I want you to have the reward that was offered, and I command you to go fetch your father at once and bring him to me, because his advice has been good and useful."

The young man set out at once for the cellar where his father was hidden, and recounted what had happened word for word, how the king had ordered him to bring him into his presence. His father consented, and they came before the king at once. When they arrived in the great hall, the king honored and entertained the old man lavishly, seating him next to himself and telling him how sorry he was that he had been so uncomfortably confined for no good reason. Then he told him the dream he had had, and asked his help in explaining the dream.

The old man said: "My lord, experience is acquired in three ways: by memory, when we retain what we have seen; by instruction, when we retain what we've been told; and by long life, which allows a man to have seen so many things in the past that, when new things come to pass, he can recognize them and know them by his accumulated wisdom. And I tell you truly that old men are the perfect advisers. I don't say this on my own account, as if I were one of those self-important people, nor to save my life, because it's advantageous to old men to depart this life. No, I say this for your own good and honor As for dreams, I say that they originate from a number of causes. In one case, a man may love something with intense desire, so that, with his thoughts dwelling on it so much, it comes to his mind in his sleep. In another case, when a man has a good constitution and is healthy, he dreams that he's running or flying, because his spirit is so lively. The third case is due either to sanctity or to sinfulness, as when the angel announced the birth of Christ to the Magi; and as for sinfulness, when Nebuchadnezzar had *his* dream. Sometimes, when you sleep on your back, your blood gathers around your heart, and so you feel anguish and your spirits flag. Because of that illusion, you dream of being attacked by people, or weighted down, because you were lying on your back."

The young king realized that the old man had explained his dream, which no one else in his kingdom had been able to do. He issued an order that all the old men who had survived were to be left in peace, honored, and waited on. He openly acknowledged the folly he had been guilty of when he trusted his wife and complied with her evil desires.

STORIES 49-61

From *Gesta Romanorum*

The earliest known manuscript of this story collection dates from 1342, but all scholars agree that in its first form the *Gesta Romanorum* was written significantly earlier; for the purposes of this anthology, it has been placed in a time slot of ca. 1300. No one is sure where it was written, though England has been tentatively suggested for certain technical reasons.

The title, "Deeds (or Exploits) of the Romans," does not adequately cover all the contents, but it does indicate that some of the plot elements date from Greco-Roman antiquity, and that many of the stories have been artificially placed within the reigns of real or fictitious Roman emperors. The stories, however, come from all sorts of sources, some not much earlier than the collection itself.

No preface with a stated aim for the collection is extant, but the *Gesta* is usually considered to be a collection of *exempla* (illustrative stories) for use in sermons. A distinctive feature of the work is the presence at the end of almost every story of a *moralisacio*, or "application," giving a devoutly Christian allegorical interpretation of the characters and plot. Some of these moral tags are very long—longer than the stories they are attached to—and many are dragged in by the heels and strained beyond belief. No *moralisacio* has been included in this anthology.

The *Gesta Romanorum* is the medieval story collection best known (at least by name) to readers of English: because it contains so many stories, because an English translation has been available since 1824, and because it is always pointed out as a source in editions of Chaucer and Shakespeare. Nevertheless, it comes at the very end of Latin-language fictional creativity (before the Renaissance) and is extremely derivative. Therefore it seemed sufficient to include a mere 13 stories here. (The longest version contains 283 stories; the Latin edition available to the translator of this volume had 181; see "Sources of the Stories," following the Introduction.)

The style of the *Gesta* is notoriously awkward and repetitious, but very lucid.

In No. 49, one of the father's arguments against his son's marriage is strikingly reminiscent of the line in Shakespeare's *Othello*: "She has deceiv'd her father, and may thee" (Act I, Scene iii).

With regard to No. 50, the story of Saint Alexis was frequently told in the Middle Ages, most notably in the French narrative poem *La vie de Saint Alexis* of the mid-11th century, one of the earliest monuments of literature in Old French, written in the same verse form as the (later) *Chanson de Roland*.

No. 51 is taken almost verbatim from the *Legenda aurea* (Golden Legend) of

79

Jacobus de Voragine (second half of the 13th century). This story was the direct source of Gustave Flaubert's story "Saint Julien l'Hospitalier" in his *Trois contes* (Three Tales) of 1877.

The plot of No. 52 was widespread, occurring in the earlier *Disciplina clericalis* and the later *Conde Lucanor*.

No. 53 seems wildly improbable at first glance, but there is at least one historical record of kinsmen's corpses being kept at home as a reminder of the vendetta that was due!

The plot of No. 54 reappears in *El Conde Lucanor*.

In No. 55, the ball of thread in the labyrinth is a clear reminiscence of the story of Theseus and Ariadne, probably derived from Ovid's *Metamorphoses* or from some compendium of mythology.

No. 57 lent itself easily to an allegorical interpretation, because the entire story is one big allegory.

The motif of finding an extremely stupid person, which figures in No. 58, occurs universally in folktales, though individual plots differ.

The bizarre reasons given in No. 59 for an implicit trust in God's will may be found in the traditions of numerous world religions, which all have difficulty explaining away the apparent injustices of human existence.

No. 60 contains such universal folktale motifs as magical objects and a special legacy (often apparently worthless, but ultimately the most valuable) left to the youngest of three sons. A special feature of this version is the flying carpet, right out of the *Thousand and One Nights!*

49. The Pirates' Captive

In the realm of a certain king, a young man was captured by pirates and wrote to his father for ransom. His father refused to ransom him, and so the young man languished in prison for a long time. The man who kept him in chains had begotten a beautiful daughter, pleasing to people's eyes. She was raised at home until she reached the age of twenty. She often went to visit the prisoner and console him. But he felt so miserable that he was unable to receive any consolation; he continually uttered sighs and groans.

It came about one day that, during one of the girl's visits, the young man said to her: "Kind maiden, if only you wished to help set me free!"

She said: "How can I attempt that? The father who begot you refuses to ransom you, so why should I, a stranger, make such plans? If I set you free, I'd make my father angry, because he'd lose the money for your ransom. Nevertheless, grant me one request and I'll free you."

He said: "Kind maiden, ask whatever you like of me. If I can possibly grant your wish, I will."

She said: "All I ask in return for freeing you is that you marry me when the right moment comes."

He replied: "I promise you that solemnly."

At once the girl loosed his chains without her father's knowledge and ran away with him to his country. When they had reached his father's house, his father said to him: "My son, I'm happy to see you. But tell me, who is this girl you've brought with you?"

He said: "She's a king's daughter, whom I intend to marry."

His father said: "On pain of losing your inheritance I forbid you to marry her."

The young man said: "Father, what are you saying? I have a greater obligation to her than to you. When I fell into the hands of my enemy and was thrown into chains, I wrote to you for ransom and you refused to ransom me. But she freed me not only from prison, but also from mortal danger. Therefore I insist on marrying her."

His father said: "My son, I'll prove to you that you can't trust her and therefore must by no means marry her. She deceived her own father when she set you free from prison without his knowledge. By that action of hers her father lost the large sum he might have gained by your ransom. That makes it clear that you can't trust her and therefore must by no means marry her. But there's another reason as well. Though she freed you, it was out of her lust to have you for a husband, and because her lust was the reason for her freeing you, I don't think she'll make you a good wife."

When the girl heard that reasoning, she said: "First I'll answer your objection that I deceived my own father. It isn't true. A man is deceived when he suffers the loss of some good thing. But my father is so wealthy that he needs no further aid from anyone. With that in mind, I freed this young man from prison. If my father had received ransom for him, that wouldn't have made him much richer, but you would have been impoverished by paying the ransom. Therefore, by my actions I spared you from paying the ransom, while I did no harm to my father. To reply to your other argument, that I acted out of lust: that's altogether out of the question, because lust is aroused by either good looks, wealth, or strength. But your son had none of those qualities: his looks were destroyed by his imprisonment; he wasn't rich, not even having the money to ransom himself with; and he wasn't strong because he had lost his strength through languishing in prison. Therefore I acted solely out of goodness and pity when I set him free."

When his father heard those words, he was no longer able to dissuade his son. And so his son married the girl with all ceremony and lived the rest of his days in peace.

50. The Story of Saint Alexis

In the empire of a certain emperor there was a young man named Alexis. His father was Euphemianus, who was a man of the highest Roman nobility and the emperor's leading courtier, and was served by many slaves and attendants wearing golden belts and silk garments. Now, this Euphemianus was very charitable. Every day in his home, three tables were laid for poor folk, orphans, pilgrims, and widows, whom he served assiduously. At nones, about three in the afternoon, he ate a meal in the fear of the Lord in the company of pious men. His wife, Agaelis, was equally pious and charitable.

Long childless, they prayed to the Lord, who granted them this son, Alexis. Thereafter they determined to live in absolute chastity. The boy was handed over to teachers to be instructed in the liberal arts. When he had mastered all the arts of philosophy and had reached adolescence, a bride was chosen for him from the emperor's household and they were married. Night fell, and he remained with her in peaceful silence.

Then the holy young man began to instruct his bride in the fear of God and to urge her to preserve her maidenly modesty. Next, he gave her his gold ring, and the buckle of the belt he wore, for safekeeping, saying: "Take these and save them as long as it pleases God, and may the Lord be between us!"

Then he took a sum of his money, went down to the coast, and secretly boarded a ship bound for Laodicea. Proceeding from there, he arrived in Edessa, a city in Syria that boasted of an image of Our Lord Jesus Christ not made by human hands; it was kept wrapped in linen. When he got there, he distributed all his belongings among the poor. Putting on coarse garments, he began to sit with the other paupers in the porch of the church of Mary, Mother of God. He kept just enough of the alms he received to live on, and gave the rest to the other beggars.

His father, grieved at his son's disappearance, sent servants all over the world to inquire diligently after him. When some of them arrived in Edessa, Alexis recognized them, but they didn't recognize him at all. They bestowed alms on him along with the other beggars. Receiving them, he thanked God, saying: "God, I thank you for allowing me to receive alms from my own servants."

When the servants were back home, they reported that Alexis was nowhere to be found. But his mother, from the day he disappeared, had spread sackcloth on the floor of her bedroom. There she howled and uttered words of lamentation, saying: "I shall always remain in mourning here until I recover my son." And the youth's bride said to her father-in-law: "Until I receive word about my darling husband, I shall remain with you like a turtle-dove."

After Alexis had dwelt in that church porch, serving God, for seventeen years, finally the statue of the Blessed Virgin, which was in that church, said to the sacristan: "Bring in that godly man, because he has earned the kingdom of Heaven, and the spirit of God rests upon him; for his prayers rise to the sight of God like incense." Since the sacristan didn't know which man she meant, she said: "The one sitting outside in the porch." Then the sacristan went out hurriedly and brought him into the church.

When this event became generally known, and everyone began to venerate Alexis, he desired to shun human glory and departed for Laodicea, where he took ship for Tarsus in Cilicia. But, as God would have it, the ship was driven by winds until it arrived at the port of Rome. Seeing this, Alexis said to himself: "I shall remain incognito in my father's house, without being a burden to anyone."

He came across his father, who was returning from the palace surrounded by a multitude of retainers, and began to call to him: "Servant of God, have me, a pilgrim, received in your home and fed on the crumbs from your table, so that the Lord may deign to take pity on your own pilgrim as well." His father, hearing this, had him received for his son's sake, prepared him a place of his in the house, sent him food from his own table, and assigned him a personal servant. But the man remained immersed in prayer, and castigated his body with fasting. The household servants laughed at him, and frequently poured dishwater over his head, but he underwent everything with great patience. Alexis spent seventeen years incognito in his father's house.

Then, perceiving in his spirit that the end of his life was drawing near, he asked for paper and ink and, on the spot, wrote down the whole story of his life from start to finish. But on Sunday, after Mass had been sung in church, a voice from Heaven was heard to say: "Come to me, all who labor and are heavily burdened, ..." Hearing this, all those present fell on their faces. And, lo, the voice came again, saying: "Seek out the man of God, so he can pray for Rome!" When they sought him and failed to find him, the voice was heard again: "Seek in the house of Euphemianus!" When Euphemianus was asked, he said he knew nothing about it.

Then Emperors Arcadius and Honorius,[1] together with Pope Innocent, visited the designated man's house, and, lo, the voice of Alexis's servant reached his master's ears: "Master, see if they don't mean our pilgrim, who is a man of great patience!" And so Euphemianus came running, only to find him dead, his face shining like the face of an angel. He attempted to take the paper he held in his hand, but was unable to. He went out of the room and reported this to the emperors and the pope, who went in with him, saying: "Though we are sinners, we do govern the realm and oversee all ecclesiastical administration. So, give us the paper, so that we can learn what is written on it." The pope went over and grasped the paper that was in his hand, and the dead man released it at once. The pope had it read in the presence of the assembled populace and Alexis's father.

Hearing the contents of the paper, Euphemianus was deeply terror-stricken. He became mute, fainted, and fell helplessly to the ground. When he began to return to his senses, he ripped his clothes and began to tear out his gray hair, tug at his beard, and scratch himself bloody. Rushing over to his son, he stooped over him and cried: "Alas, my son, why did you

---

[1]Their joint reign began in the year 395; neither one resided in Rome. The papacy of Innocent I began in 401. Saint Alexis may have lived (in Edessa, not Rome) during these reigns, but certainly not in 327, the date given at the end of the story.

grieve me so, making me sorrow, groan, and sigh for so many years? Woe
is me, wretch that I am, seeing you, who should have protected me in my
old age, lying on your deathbed, unable to speak to me! Alas, what consolation can I ever have in the future?"

Alexis's mother, hearing this, was like a lioness bursting out of a hunter's
net. She tore her clothes, unbound her hair, and raised her eyes heavenward. Unable to approach the saintly body because of the great crowd, she
called out: "Let me through, so I can see the comfort of my soul, the child
that I nursed!"

When she arrived at the body, she stretched out on it, crying: "Alas, my
dearest son, light of my eyes, why did you do this to us? Why did you behave so cruelly to us? You saw your father and me weeping, and you didn't
make yourself known to us. Your own servants insulted you, and you put
up with it." Again and again she prostrated herself on the body, now
stretching out her arms over it, now feeling the angelic face with her
hands, kissing it, and shouting: "Weep with me, all of you here, because
for seventeen years I had him in my house and didn't recognize him,
though he was my only son. His own servants used to scold him and slap
him. Alas, who will give my eyes a whole fountain of tears, so I can weep
out the sorrow in my soul day and night?"

But his wife, dressed in mourning, ran over in tears and said: "Alas, for
today I am made desolate and it's certain that I'm a widow! Now I have no
one to gaze upon or turn my eyes to. Now my mirror is broken, my hopes
have perished. Now that sorrow has begun which has no end." Hearing
this, the populace, too, wept bitterly.

Then the pope and the emperors placed the body on an honorable bier
and led it into the center of the city, where it was announced to the people that the man of God, whom everyone in the city had been seeking, was
now found. Everyone ran to hail the saint. Whenever a sick person
touched that sacred body, he was instantly cured. The blind regained their
sight, those possessed by demons were freed from them, and all those suffering from any ailment whatsoever were cured by touching the body.
Seeing such great miracles, the emperors began to carry the bier themselves along with the pope in order to gain sanctity themselves from that
saintly body.

Then the emperors ordered a large quantity of gold and silver to be scattered abroad in the city squares, so that the crowds, distracted by love of
gain, might permit the holy body to be carried to the church. But the commoners set aside their love of money, and rushed in ever greater numbers
to touch that most holy body. Thus, with great efforts, they finally brought
it to the church of Saint Boniface Martyr. There they remained for seven
days praising God, and they constructed a monument of gold, gems, and
precious stones, in which they laid that most sacred body to rest with great
veneration. From that monument there issued such a sweet fragrance that

it seemed to everyone to be filled with incense. Alexis died about the year of our Lord 327.

51. The Story of Saint Julian the Hospitaler

A knight named Julian killed both his parents unwittingly. When that noble youth Julian was out hunting one day, and was pursuing a stag that he had sighted, the stag suddenly turned to him and said: "You, who are pursuing me, will be the slayer of your father and mother." When Julian heard that, he was sorely afraid that the stag's prediction might come true. He abandoned all his possessions, left home secretly, and traveled to a very far-off territory, where he entered the service of a prince.

He did such good service in every way, both on the battlefield and in the palace, that the prince knighted him, and gave him the widowed lady of a castle for his wife. He received her castle as a dowry. Then Julian's parents, grieving sorely for the loss of their son, roamed the world randomly, searching for him diligently. Finally they arrived at Julian's own castle. Julian's wife noticed them, in his absence, and asked them who they were. They told her everything that had befallen their son, and she realized that they were the parents of her husband, who had often chanced to speak about them.

Therefore she welcomed them heartily and, for her husband's sake, gave up her own bed to them. She made another bed for herself elsewhere. In the morning the lady of the castle went to church. And, lo, that very morning Julian returned and went into his wife's bedroom to awaken her. There he found a couple sleeping side by side. Suspecting that it was his wife with a lover, he quietly drew his sword and killed the two of them. But as he left the house, he saw his wife coming back from church. In his amazement he asked her who had been sleeping in their bed. She replied: "It's your parents, who searched for you for a long time, and whom I gave our room to sleep in."

Hearing this, he nearly fainted away and began to weep most bitterly, saying: "Woe is me! What am I to do? I've killed my beloved parents! Now the stag's prediction has come true! By attempting to avoid this, I brought it about, wretch that I am! And now good-bye, my darling wife, because from today on I shall know no rest until I am certain that God has accepted my repentance!"

She replied: "Darling husband, God forbid that you should desert me and go away without me! Just as I shared your joys, I shall also share your sorrows!" Then they both left home and founded a large hospice beside a broad river that was very dangerous to cross. There they intended to do penance, continually ferrying people who wished to cross the river, and giving hospitality to every poor person who came their way.

Long afterward, one midnight while Julian was resting from his labors, and there was a heavy frost, he heard a man calling him tearfully to ferry him across, and hailing him in mournful tones. Hearing this, he arose briskly and found the man nearly perishing with cold. He carried him into his house, lit a fire, and strove to get him warm. But he was unable to do so, and, to keep the man from dying on the spot, he carried him to his own bed and covered him up solicitously.

After a while the man who had looked so ill, almost like a leper, rose heavenward in radiance, and said to his host: "Julian, God sent me to you to announce that He has accepted your penance. Before long, both of you will rest in the Lord." Then he vanished. Not long afterward, Julian and his wife, full of good deeds and charity, rested in the Lord.

52. The Weeping Dog

In a certain empress's realm there was a knight whose wife was noble, chaste, and honorable. It came about that the knight had to go off on a journey, but first he told his wife: "I'm not leaving anyone to watch you, because I'm sure there's no need to." When his escort was ready, he set out, and his wife remained home, living chastely.

It befell at one time that, yielding to the entreaties of a female neighbor of hers, she went out to dine at her house. Afterward she returned home. But a young man had caught sight of her and fell deeply in love with her. He sent several envoys to her, hoping she could love him just as ardently. She spurned them all and shunned him altogether. Finding himself rejected, he became so depressed that he fell ill. He would often walk over to her house, but it did him no good, because the lady absolutely refused to see him.

It happened one day that this man was heading for church, sorrowful and downhearted, when he met an old woman who was reputed to live a saintly life. When she saw how sad the young man was, she asked him why he felt that way. He replied: "What good will it do me to tell you?"

But she said: "My dear boy, so long as a sick man conceals his illness from his doctor, he can't be cured. So tell me the reason you're so sad! With God's help I'll cure you." When the young man heard that, he revealed to her his love for that lady. The old woman said: "Go home quickly, because I'll cure you before very long." Hearing this, the young man went to his home, and the old woman to her own.

That old woman owned a little bitch, which she forced to remain hungry for two days. On the third day she fed the hungry dog bread baked with mustard. After the dog tasted it, her eyes teared all day long from the sharpness. Then the old woman, taking along her dog, went to the home of the lady so beloved by that young man. She was immediately welcomed with honor by the lady because of her reputation for sanctity.

When they sat down together, the lady saw the little dog weeping.

Greatly surprised, she asked why. The old woman said: "My dear friend, don't ask why she's weeping! She is bearing such great grief that it's scarcely possible to describe it to you."

When the lady kept insisting on hearing the reason, the old woman said: "This dog was my daughter, a very chaste and honorable girl. A young man once fell wildly in love with her, but she was so chaste that she completely rejected his love. As a result, the young man grieved so much that he died of his grief, and for her fault God changed my daughter into this little dog you see here." Then the old woman began to weep, saying: "Every time my daughter recalls what a beautiful girl she was, and finds herself now a dog, she weeps inconsolably and, in fact, makes everyone else weep because of her great sorrow."

Hearing this, the lady thought to herself: "Woe is me! That young man loves me in just the same way, and he's sick for love of me." And she told the whole story to the old woman. Hearing it, the old woman said: "Dearest lady, don't reject the young man's love, in case you may be changed into a dog, too, like my daughter, which would be a terrible punishment."

The lady said to the old woman: "My good woman, give me good advice, so I don't become a dog."

The woman said: "Send quickly for that young man and comply with his wishes with no further delay!"

The lady replied: "I ask you, holy woman, to fetch him and bring him with you. For it might give offense if anyone else went to him."

The old woman replied: "I feel for you and I'll gladly bring him to you." She went and brought along the young man, who slept with the lady. And in that way, through the agency of the old woman, the lady committed adultery.

53. Who Is Free from Cares?

There was a certain prince who took great delight in hunting. On one occasion he was out hunting when a merchant happened to come down the same road behind him. Seeing that the prince was handsome, graceful, and richly attired, the merchant said to himself: "O Lord God, this man must mean a lot to You: how handsome, vigorous, and graceful he is, and how well dressed everyone in his party is." With these thoughts in mind, he said to a member of the prince's party: "My dear fellow, tell me what sort of man your master is."

The man replied: "He's lord over many lands, and extremely wealthy in gold, silver, and servants."

The merchant said: "He's greatly beloved by God. He's the handsomest and wisest man I've ever seen."

The retainer, hearing this, secretly reported to his master everything the merchant had said. Toward evening, when the prince was heading back home, he asked the merchant to spend the night in his castle. The merchant didn't dare refuse. He accompanied the prince to the city, and, when he had entered his castle, he saw so many costly objects and beautiful rooms painted in gold that he was numb with amazement. When suppertime came around, the prince had the merchant seated next to the lady of the castle. Seeing the lady so beautiful and charming, the merchant was nearly beside himself, and thought: "My God, the prince has everything his heart desires: a beautiful wife, daughters, sons, and a tremendous flock of servants!"

While he was engaged in these reflections, food was served to the lady and him. Behold! excellent food was served up in a dead man's skull and set down before the two of them, whereas all the others in the family were given their food on silver plates. When the merchant saw the skull in front of him, he felt queasy inside, and he said to himself: "Woe is me! I'm afraid that I'll lose my head in this place!" But the lady strove to set his mind at ease.

That night, he was shown to a fine bedroom, where he found a curtained bed made. In one corner of the room there was a large lamp. When he had gone to bed, the servants closed the door and the merchant was left alone in the room. Looking at the corner with the lamp, he saw two dead men hanging by their arms. At that sight he was smitten with such unbearable terror that he couldn't sleep.

In the morning he arose and said: "Woe is me! I'm afraid that today I'll be hanging alongside those two!" But after the prince had arisen, he summoned the merchant and said:

"My good man, how did you like my home?"

He replied: "Everything was fine with me, except that, when I was served food in a skull, I was terrified more than words can say, so much so that I couldn't eat. Then, when I was shown to bed, I saw two young men hanging in a corner of the room, and I was so frightened that I couldn't sleep. And so, for the love of God, let me go my way!"

The prince said: "My good man, here is why you saw a skull placed before my extremely beautiful wife: The owner of the head was once a noble duke, who seduced my wife and slept with her. I caught them in the very act. I grasped my sword and cut off his head. And so, as a mark of her shame, I place that skull in front of her every day, to remind her of the sin she committed. Afterward the son of the slain duke killed those two young men, kinsmen of mine, who are hanging in the bedroom. And so I visit their bodies every day in order to increase my ardor to avenge them. When I recall my wife's adultery and bring to mind the young men's death, I am unable to taste any joys. So, go in peace, my dear man, and henceforth do not judge the life of any man until you have learned more of the facts."

The merchant took his leave and set forth on his business.

54. The Overbearing Emperor

Emperor Jovinian wielded great power in his reign. Once, while lying in bed, he became presumptuous beyond belief, and said to himself: "Is there another God besides me?" Thinking such thoughts, he fell asleep. When he got up in the morning, he summoned his knights and other retainers and said: "Men, let's eat, because I want to go hunting today." They were ready to carry out his orders. After eating they went hunting.

While the emperor was riding, an unbearable heat came over him, so that he thought he'd die if he couldn't bathe in cold water. Looking around, he saw a large lake in the distance. He said to his knights: "Stay here until I rejoin you!" He spurred his charger and galloped speedily to the lake. Dismounting, he shed all his clothes and waded into the lake, where he remained until he was completely refreshed.

While he was lingering there, a man came along who resembled him entirely in face and build. This man put on the emperor's clothes, mounted his charger, and rode over to the knights. He was welcomed by everyone as though he were the emperor, because they had no reason to believe it was anyone other than their lord, whom he resembled so completely. They hunted and then he rode to the palace with the knights.

Afterward Jovinian came out of the water, but found neither clothes nor horse. He was surprised and also very unhappy, because he was naked and there was no one in sight. He thought to himself: "What am I to do? This is an awful thing to happen to me!" Finally he took heart again and said: "A knight of mine, whom I myself dubbed, lives near here. I'll go to him and get clothes and a horse, and so I'll return to my palace and find out how, and by whom, I've been placed in this predicament."

Completely naked, Jovinian walked to the knight's castle and knocked at the door. The doorkeeper asked who was knocking, and why. The emperor replied: "Just open the door, and you'll see who I am!"

The man opened the door and, seeing him, asked: "Well, who are you?"

The emperor replied: "I'm Emperor Jovinian. Go to your master and tell him to send me clothes, because by some chance I've lost my clothes and my horse."

The man said: "You're lying, you scurvy drunk! A little before you got here, my lord Emperor Jovinian rode back to his palace with his knights, and my master accompanied him, returned, and is now at table. But, since you call yourself emperor, I'll tell my master you're here." The doorkeeper went in and reported to his master what that man had said. Hearing this, his master ordered him brought in, and it was done.

When the knight saw the emperor, he didn't recognize him at all, though the emperor knew *him* perfectly. The knight said: "Tell me who you are and what your name is."

He replied: "I'm the emperor, I'm called Jovinian, and I dubbed you knight on such-and-such a day at such-and-such a time."

The knight said: "You scurvy drunk, where do you get the nerve to call yourself the emperor? Well before you got here, my lord Emperor Jovinian rode back to his palace with his knights; I was with him on the way and then I came back here. You scurvy drunk! It's true that I was knighted by my lord the emperor on the day and at the hour you mentioned. Because you've reached such a pitch of presumptuousness that you call yourself the emperor, you won't leave here unpunished!" And at once he had him severely whipped and then thrown out.

Seeing himself scourged and ejected, Jovinian wept bitterly and said: "My God, how can it be that the knight I myself dubbed fails to recognize me and, on top of that, has me severely whipped? A duke who's one of my advisers lives near here. I'll go to him and show him my terrible situation. He'll help me find clothes and get back to my palace." Arriving at the duke's door, he knocked.

The doorkeeper, hearing the knock, opened the door. Surprised to find a naked man, he said: "Who are you, and why have you come completely naked?"

The emperor replied: "I beg you to tell the duke I'm here! I'm the emperor, and I accidentally lost my clothes and my horse. That's why I've come to him, so he can help me out in my adversity."

Hearing his words, the perplexed doorkeeper went in and told his master that a naked man was at the door claiming he was the emperor and seeking admittance. The duke said: "Show him in at once, so we can see who is presuming to call himself the emperor!" Then the doorkeeper opened the door and led him in. The emperor recognized the duke perfectly, but not the other way around. The duke asked: "Who are you?"

He replied: "I'm the emperor who promoted you to your honors and your dukedom, and made you a member of my council."

The duke said: "You miserable lunatic, a short while before you came, I escorted my lord the emperor back to the palace and then came home. Because you've arrogated such a rank to yourself, you won't leave here without a punishment." He had him imprisoned and fed only bread and water for several days. Then he let him out of prison and had him severely whipped until the blood flowed. Next, he ejected him from his property.

Finding himself so thoroughly rejected, he uttered groans and sighs, and said to himself: "Woe is me! What am I to do? I'm confused. I'm put to shame by men and hated by the people. I'd do better to return to my palace, where my courtiers will recognize me. And even if they don't, my lady wife will recognize me by certain secrets we share." He proceeded to the palace, completely naked, and knocked at the door. Hearing the knock, the doorkeeper opened the door. When he saw him, he said: "Tell me, who are you?"

He replied: "You really don't know me?"

The doorkeeper said: "Not at all."

The emperor said: "That amazes me, because you're wearing my livery."

The doorkeeper said: "You lie, because I'm wearing the livery of my lord the emperor."

The emperor said: "That's me! To prove it, I beg you, for the love of God, to go to the empress and tell her I've arrived, so she can send me clothes quickly, because I want to go to the great hall. If she doesn't believe what you say, tell her about such-and-such secrets, which only the two of us know, and then she'll believe you completely!"

The doorkeeper said: "I have no doubt that you're crazy, because my lord is already dining, and the empress is sitting next to him. But, since you say you're the emperor, I'll inform the empress, though I'm sure you'll be severely punished for this."

The doorkeeper went to the empress, knelt down, and reported the entire conversation. She was deeply saddened. Turning to her presumed lord, who was sitting beside her, she said: "My lord, listen to this amazing thing! Some drunk has made the doorkeeper recite secrets to me about things you and I have often done. He says he's the emperor and my husband."

When he heard that, he ordered the doorkeeper to lead the man into the sight of all assembled there. When the emperor was shown in, completely nude, a dog that used to love him dearly leaped at his throat to kill him, but some men kept it from hurting him. In addition, one of his hawks, which was on its perch there, broke its strap and flew out of the hall. The false emperor said to everyone in the hall, both those seated at table and those standing: "My good people, listen to what I say to this man. Fellow, tell me who you are and why you've come here."

Jovinian replied: "Sir, I'm the ruler of this empire and the master of this house, and so I've come here to speak with the empress."

The impostor said to everyone present: "Tell me, by the oath of allegiance you've sworn, which of us is your emperor and lord?"

They said: "My lord, that's a strange question. By the oath we swore, we've never laid eyes on this good-for-nothing, as far as we know. You have been our lord and emperor from your youth on. And so we beg you to punish him as an example to all to refrain from such presumptuousness."

The impostor turned to the empress and said: "Lady, tell me, on your obedience to me, do you know this man, who says he's the emperor and your husband?"

She said: "My dear lord, why do you ask me such things? Haven't I lived with you over thirty years and borne you children? But there's one thing that surprises me: how this drunk came to know the things we've kept secret between us."

The impostor said to Jovinian: "Since you were so bold as to call yourself the emperor, my sentence is that you be tied to a horse's tail today and be dragged by him. And if you persist in your shameless claims, I'll sentence you to the most disgraceful of deaths!" He called his guards and ordered them to have him dragged by a horse, but in such a way that he wouldn't be killed. This was done.

After that, Jovinian was sadder than words can tell. Close to despair, he said to himself: "Damn the day when I was born! My friends have abandoned me. My wife and children don't know me." As he said this, he thought: "A hermit who is my confessor lives near here. I'll go to him. Maybe he'll recognize me, because he's often heard my Confession." He went to the hermit and knocked at the window of his cell. The hermit said: "Who's knocking there?"

He said: "It's I, Emperor Jovinian. Open the window so I can talk to you."

When the hermit heard his voice, he opened the window. Seeing him, he immediately slammed it shut again, saying: "Leave my presence, accursed one! You're not the emperor, but a devil in human shape."

When the emperor heard that, he fell to the ground in his grief, pulled out hair from his head and beard, raised lamentations to the very skies, and said: "Woe is me! What am I to do? How miserable I am!" When he said that, he remembered how, lying in bed one night, he had presumptuously said: "Is there another God besides me?" Again he knocked at the hermit's window and said: "For the love of Him who hung on the Cross, hear my Confession! If you don't want to open the window, leave it shut, but at least hear me out till I've finished!"

The hermit said: "All right." Then the emperor delivered a Confession that covered his whole life, making special mention of the time he had defied God, saying that he thought there was no other God than himself.

After Confession and Absolution the hermit opened the window, immediately recognized him, and said: "Blessed be the Most High! Now I recognize you. I have a few clothes here. Put them on quickly and go to your palace! I expect that everyone will recognize you." The emperor got dressed and proceeded to the palace. When he knocked at the door, the doorkeeper opened it and greeted him reverently. The emperor said: "So you recognize me?"

The man said: "Perfectly, my lord. I only pause because I've been on duty here all day and I didn't see you leave." The emperor entered the great hall and everyone bowed. The impostor was with the empress in their bedroom. A knight left the bedroom, took a close look at the newcomer, went back into the room, and said: "Lord, there's a man in the great hall to whom everyone is bowing. He resembles you so much in every way that we're at a loss to say which of you is the emperor."

Hearing this, the impostor said to the empress: "Dear lady, go out there and tell me whether you recognize him when you report back." She went out and was dumbfounded when she saw him. She reentered the bedroom at once and said: "My lord, on the peril of my soul, I tell you one thing: I'm at a loss to say which of you is my husband!"

He replied: "If that's the case, I'll go out and investigate the truth." Entering the great hall, he took the emperor by the hand, made him stand next to him, called over all the noblemen then in the hall, as well as the empress, and said: "On the oath you've sworn, tell me: which of us is the emperor?"

The empress was the first to answer: "My lord, it is incumbent on me to answer first. God in Heaven is my witness that I'm at a loss to say which of you is my husband!" All the others made the same reply.

Then the man who had just come out of the bedroom said: "Listen to me! This man is your emperor and lord. At one time he defied God, so that no one could recognize him until he made satisfaction to God. I am one of God's angels, the emperor's personal guardian. I protected his empire during the time he performed penance. His penance is now complete and he has made satisfaction for his wrongdoings, because, as you saw, I had him tied to a horse's tail and dragged." After saying this, he added: "From now on, obey him! I commend you to God." He immediately disappeared from their sight.

The emperor gave thanks to God, lived peacefully for the rest of his days, and finally gave up his spirit to God.

55. Lady-of-Solace

King Vespasian had a very beautiful daughter named Aglaes. She was so lovely and beautiful in men's eyes that she surpassed all other women in beauty. It came about one day that, while the king's daughter was standing in front of him, he looked at her closely and said: "My dear, I'm going to change your name. Because of your physical beauty, let your name henceforth be Lady-of-Solace, as a sign that all those who come to you in grief will depart in joy."

Near his palace the king had a very beautiful garden in which he frequently walked for relaxation. He issued a proclamation throughout his kingdom that any man who wished to marry his daughter should come to his palace, stroll in the garden for three or four days, and return to the palace; then he would obtain his daughter's hand. When the proclamation was made, many men came to his palace, entered the garden, and were never seen again. No matter how many came, none of them escaped.

At that time there was a knight dwelling in a remote district. Hearing the rumor that anyone coming to the palace might win the king's daughter for a bride, he came to the palace door and knocked. The doorkeeper opened the door and showed him in. He came into the king's presence and said: "Sire, there's a general report that whoever enters your garden will obtain your daughter's hand, and so I've come."

The king said: "Go into the garden and, if you come out, she'll be yours."

The knight said: "Sire, grant me one thing. I beseech you to let me speak briefly with the girl before I enter the garden."

The king said: "All right." The knight went to the girl and said: "My dear, your name is Lady-of-Solace. It was given to you so that all who come to you in grief might depart in joy. Now I come to you in extreme grief and desolation. And so, give me some advice and aid, so that I can depart in joy. Many men preceded me here, entered the garden, and were never seen again. If the same thing happens to me, I'll say: 'Alas that I ever wanted to marry you!'"

She replied: "I'll tell you the truth and I'll change your grief to joy. In that garden there is a very ferocious lion that kills everyone who enters. It is that lion which has killed all the men who went in there in hopes of winning me. Clad your entire body in steel, from the soles of your feet to the top of your head, and see that all your armor is smeared with gum. When you enter the garden, the lion will attack you at once. Fight him manfully and, when he's tired, move away from him. He will hold you with his teeth by an arm or leg until his teeth are so jammed by the gum on your armor that he's incapable of doing you much harm. When you become aware of this, draw your sword and cut off his head. But there's still another danger in that garden. There's only one entrance, but many branching paths, so that anyone who goes in can scarcely find his way out. And so, I'll give you something that will save you from that danger. Here is a ball of thread. When you get to the door of the garden, tie one end of the thread to the door and keep reeling out the thread as you go farther into the garden. As you value your life, don't lose the ball of thread!"

The knight carried out the girl's instructions to the letter, and entered the garden in his armor. When the lion saw him, it attacked him with all its might. The knight defended himself manfully and, when the lion was tired, he leapt away from it. The lion held him by one arm until its teeth were full of gum. Seeing this, the knight drew his sword and cut off the lion's head. But in his great joy he lost the thread that he had unwound as he went in. In sadness and sorrow he walked around the garden for three days, seeking diligently for the thread. On the third night he found it, and thereupon in great glee he followed the thread until he reached the entrance. There he untied the thread, went to the king, and obtained the hand of his daughter, Lady-of-Solace. His joy was extreme.

56. The Memorial Suit of Armor

A certain king had a beautiful daughter whom he loved dearly. After his death she ascended the throne, as his sole heir. Hearing this, a tyrannical duke came to her and promised her many things if she would yield herself to him. She was seduced and deflowered by him. After losing her virginity she wept bitterly, but the tyrant deprived her of her own inheritance. Driven out, she uttered groans and sighs and sat every day by a public road begging alms of the passersby.

One day as she sat there weeping, a noble knight rode by her. At the sight of her, his eyes were ensnared by her beauty, and he said: "Dearest, who are you?"

She replied: "I'm the king's only daughter. After my father's death, the kingdom was mine by the laws of inheritance, but I was seduced and deflowered by a tyrant, who then stole my inheritance from me."

The knight said: "Would you like to become my wife?"

She replied: "Yes, my lord, I'd like that above all things."

He said: "Promise me that you will be faithful, and that you will have no other man but me, and I shall wage war on that tyrant and win back your kingdom. But, if I'm killed in the war though I win your inheritance, all I ask is that you keep my blood-stained armor with you as a sign of your love. If someone comes to marry you, go into your bedroom, where the armor is hanging, look at it closely, and remember how I lost my life for your sake."

She said: "My lord, I promise this solemnly. But God forbid that you should lose your life in the war!"

He put on his armor and set out against the tyrant. Hearing this, the duke opposed him with all his might and they fought each other. The knight won the victory and cut off the tyrant's head, but in the battle he received a mortal wound. He had recovered the girl's inheritance, but he died three days later. The girl wept over his death for many days. She hung up his blood-stained armor in her bedroom and often went to look at it. Whenever she did so, she cried bitterly.

Many noblemen visited her to ask her for her hand, making many promises. But before she replied to anyone, she went into her bedroom to take a close look at the armor, and she said: "Husband, you died for my sake, restoring my inheritance to me. God forbid that I should yield myself to another man!" Then she stepped out of the room and said: "I have made a vow to God never to be joined to another man." When they heard that, they departed, and so she spent her whole life in sexual abstinence.

57. The Rocky Path and the Level Path

In the reign of Maximian, a prudent king, there were two knights, one wise, the other foolish, who were close friends. The wise one said to the other: "Would you like to form a partnership with me? It will be beneficial to both of us."

The other said: "I'm willing."

His friend said: "Let's draw blood from our right arm. I'll drink your blood, and you mine, as a sign that neither one will abandon the other in good times or in bad, and, whatever one of us acquires, the other will have half."

The foolish knight said: "I'm perfectly willing." At once they drew blood, drank each other's blood, and from then on always shared one house.

The king had founded two cities. One was on a mountaintop, and he had commanded that everyone coming there should receive a substantial sum and stay there permanently. But the road to that city was narrow and stony. Three knights with a large army were stationed along it, and everyone taking the road had to fight them or lose his property and his life. In that same city the king appointed a governor to welcome whoever entered and to serve him as his rank and status demanded.

He founded another city in the valley below that mountain. The road to that city was broad and delightful to travel on. Three knights were posted on it to welcome all wayfarers cordially and serve them in every way. In that city he installed a governor who was to imprison all who entered or approached and turn them over to the judge when he was on circuit there. The judge was to spare no one.

The wise knight said to his partner: "My friend, let's go out into the world as the other knights do. We'll be able to acquire much wealth, on which we can live decently."

His friend said: "I'm willing." They both set out on a road.

The wise one said: "As you see, my friend, two roads branch off here. One leads to that very noble city. If we take it, we'll reach that city, where we'll get all that our hearts desire. The other one is the road leading to the other city, situated in the valley. If we take it, we'll be arrested, imprisoned, and haled before the judge, who'll hang us on the gallows. So my advice is to avoid the latter road and to follow the former one."

But the foolish knight said: "My friend, I've long heard about those two cities, but the road to the city on the mountain is very narrow and dangerous, because three knights are stationed there with an army to attack all wayfarers, killing them and stripping them. But the other road is quite broad and level; there are three knights there who greet all comers kindly, providing them with whatever they need. I see this clearly, and so I trust my eyes more than I trust you."

The wise knight said: "Even though one of the roads is easy to travel on, nevertheless it will lead us to eternal shame, because we'll be led to the gallows. If you're afraid to take the narrow road because it means a fight, and there are highwaymen on it, that's an everlasting disgrace for you, because you're a knight and knights are honor-bound to fight their enemies. If you agree to come with me on the narrow road, I give my solemn promise to be the first to join battle and to cut my way through any number of enemies, if you just help me."

But his friend said: "I've said my say. I refuse to take that road, and I prefer the other one."

The wise knight said: "Because I gave you my pledge and drank your blood as a sign of loyalty, I won't let you proceed alone, but will come with you." They both took the pleasant road. Along it they found as many comforts as one could wish, and finally arrived at the lodgings of the three knights, who welcomed them most honorably and ministered to their every need.

Every time they were refreshed, the foolish knight said to the wise one: "My friend, didn't I tell you so? Look at all the great comforts we're enjoying on this road. On the other one, we'd have been lacking all of them."

His friend replied: "If it ends well, it will all be well, but I doubt it." They remained with those knights for some time. The governor of the city, hearing that two knights were approaching the city in defiance of the king's orders, immediately sent his constables there to arrest them and bring them into town. When they were before him, the governor ordered the foolish knight to be bound hand and foot and cast into a pit; the other knight he imprisoned. When the judge came to town, all the criminals in the city were led into court, those two knights among them.

The wise knight addressed the judge: "My lord, I have a complaint against my partner, since he's the cause of my death. I warned him about the laws of this city and the dangers here, but he absolutely refused to believe my words, consent, or follow my advice. On the contrary, he replied to me: 'I trust my eyes more than your words.' Nevertheless, since we were bound together for good or for bad by a pledge and an oath, when I saw him setting out alone I remembered my oath and accompanied him. That's why he's the cause of my death. And so, pronounce a fair judgment."

The other knight said to the judge: "*He* is the cause of *my* death. The whole world is aware that he's the wise one, and I'm foolish by nature, so that in his wisdom he shouldn't have acceded so easily to my folly. When I set out alone, if he hadn't followed me, I would have turned back to the road that *he* wanted to follow, because of the oath I took to stick with him. And so, because he's wise and I'm foolish, he is the cause of my death."

The judge addressed both of them, the wise knight first: "You, the wise one, because you so readily fell in with his folly and accompanied him; and you, the fool, because you didn't trust your wise friend's words and committed your normal folly—I sentence you both to be hanged on the gallows today." And it was done.

58. The Golden Apple

A certain king had an only son, whom he loved dearly. That king had a golden apple made at great expense. When the apple was ready, the king fell mortally ill. Calling over his son, he said: "My dear son, I won't live through this illness. After I die, travel through kingdoms and domains with my blessing, and take along the golden apple that I made. Whenever you find someone matchlessly stupid, give him this apple from me."

His son promised to carry out his orders faithfully. The king turned to the wall and gave up the ghost, and his son gave him a splendid funeral. After the funeral he immediately took the apple and wandered through various kingdoms and domains. He found and saw many fools, but didn't give any of them the apple.

Then he went to a certain kingdom and arrived at the capital of that kingdom. He saw the king riding on horseback through the midst of the city with a large retinue, and he asked some of the local people what that kingdom was like. They said: "There's a custom in this kingdom that no king rules over us for more than a year. When the year is over, he's exiled and there he comes to a bad end."

Hearing this, the prince thought to himself: "Now I've found the man I've been looking for all this time!" He approached the king, knelt down, greeted him, and said: "Hail, O King! My father died and left you this golden apple in his will."

The king accepted the apple and said: "My friend, how can that be? The king, your father, never set eyes on me, nor did I ever render a service to him. So why did he give me such a costly toy?"

The prince replied: "My lord King, he didn't bequeath the apple to you specifically, but with his blessing he ordered me to give it to the biggest fool I could find. I assure you, I've made the rounds of many kingdoms and domains, but never found a fool and fathead to match you. That's why I followed my father's orders and gave you the apple."

The king said: "I wish you would tell me why you think I'm such a fool."

The prince replied: "Here goes, Sire: I'll make it clear to you. The custom in this kingdom is for the king to reign one year only. At the end of the year he is to be bereft of all honors and wealth and sent into exile to die an unhappy death. I tell you for a fact that in the whole world there's no one else as stupid as you, who are to enjoy such a brief reign and then end your life so wretchedly."

The king replied: "Everything you've told me is undoubtedly so. Therefore, while I'm still in power this year, I'll send a lot of wealth in advance to my place of exile, and, when I get there, I'll live off it for the rest of my days." And he did so.

At the end of the year he was deposed and exiled, but he lived off that wealth in exile for many years, and ended his life peacefully.

59. God's Mysterious Ways

There was a hermit who lived in a cave, where he served God devotedly day and night. Near his cell a shepherd grazed his flock of sheep. It came about one day that the shepherd was overcome by sleep. While he slept, a thief came and took away all the sheep. The owner of the sheep came by and asked the shepherd where the sheep were. He started to swear that he had lost the sheep, but had no idea how. Hearing this, his master flew into a rage and killed him.

The hermit, seeing this, said to himself: "O Lord, behold: this man cast blame on an innocent person and killed him. Since You permit such things to happen, I shall return to secular life and live as everyone else does." With these thoughts in mind, he deserted his hermitage and returned to secular life. But God didn't want to lose him, and sent an angel in the shape of a man to accompany him.

When the angel found him walking down the road, he said: "Friend, where are you heading?"

The hermit replied: "To the city I see in front of me."

The angel said: "I'll escort you on your way, because I am an angel of God, and I've come to you so that we can be companions in this life." They went together to the city. When they had entered the gates, they asked a local knight for charitable lodgings. The knight welcomed them most gladly and supplied all their wants honorably, generously, and zealously.

That knight had an only son, an infant in his cradle, whom he loved dearly. After supper a room was prepared and very fine beds were made for the angel and the hermit. At midnight the angel arose and strangled the baby boy in his cradle. Seeing this, the hermit thought to himself: "So this is what God's good angel is like? The knight, who charitably gave him everything he needed, had only this one innocent son, and he killed him!" Nonetheless, he didn't dare say anything to the angel.

In the morning they both got up and went to another city, where they were honorably welcomed and splendidly waited on in the home of one townsman. That man owned a golden goblet, which he was remarkably fond of. At midnight the angel arose and stole the goblet. Seeing this, the hermit thought to himself: "I believe this is an evil angel. This townsman treated us wonderfully, and he stole his goblet." But he said nothing to him because he was afraid of him.

In the morning they got up and continued their journey until they reached a river that was crossed by a bridge. They walked onto the bridge and a poor man came their way. The angel said to him: "My friend, show us the way to such-and-such a city." The poor man turned around and pointed out the way to the city. But, as he turned, the angel suddenly seized him by the shoulders and threw him off the bridge. The poor man drowned. Seeing this, the hermit said to himself: "Now I know he's a devil, not a good angel of God. What wrong did that poor man do? And yet he killed him." Beginning then, he planned to part company with him, but he was afraid and didn't say anything to him.

Arriving in the city toward evening, they approached a rich man's home and asked for lodgings in God's name. The rich man refused categorically. The angel of God said: "For the love of God, just let us sleep on the roof of the house, so we aren't eaten here by wolves or other evil beasts."

The rich man said: "Here is my pigsty. If you want to sleep with the pigs, you may. Otherwise, be on your way, because I won't give you anyplace else."

The angel said: "If it can't be any other way, we'll sleep with your pigs." And they did. In the morning, when they got up, the angel called their host and said: "My friend, let me give you this goblet." And he gave him the goblet he had stolen from that townsman. Seeing this, the hermit said to himself: "Now I'm positive he's a devil! He stole the goblet from a good man who welcomed us with all his heart, and he's given it to this scoundrel who denied us lodgings." He said to the angel: "I don't wish to tarry with you any longer. Go, and God be with you!"

The angel said: "Hear me out before you go. In the first place, while you were still in your hermitage, the owner of the sheep killed the shepherd unjustly. I want you to know that on that occasion the shepherd didn't deserve to die, but earlier he had committed a crime deserving of death. On the occasion you witnessed, he was sinless; therefore God allowed him to be killed, so that after his death he might escape punishment for the crime he had committed earlier, and for which he had never done penance. But the thief who made off with the sheep will suffer eternal punishment, and the owner of the sheep, who killed the shepherd, will redeem himself by giving generous alms and doing works of mercy.

"Next, I strangled during the night the son of that knight who showed us fine hospitality. I want you to know that, before that child was born, the knight was an excellent almsgiver and performed many works of mercy, but, after the child was born, he became stingy and greedy, amassing money to make the boy rich, so that the child was his ruination. That's why I killed the child. Now the knight has become the same good Christian he was before.

"Then I stole the goblet belonging to the townsman who welcomed us wholeheartedly. I want you to know that, before the goblet was crafted, there was no soberer man in the land, but he took such delight in the goblet after it was made that he drank from it daily, and so heavily that he got drunk two or three times every day. That's why I purloined the goblet. He has now become as sober as he used to be.

"Next, I threw the poor man into the river. I want you to know that that poor man was a good Christian, but if he had continued walking another half-mile, he would have killed another man, committing a mortal sin. As it is, he has been saved and is enjoying celestial glory.

"Finally, I gave that townsman's goblet to the man who denied us lodgings. I want you to know that nothing on earth happens without a reason. He let us sleep with the pigs, so I gave him the goblet, and after this life he'll lodge in Hell. And so, from now on watch what you say and don't censure God, because He knows all things."

Hearing this, the hermit fell at the angel's feet, asked his forgiveness, and returned to his hermitage, once again a good Christian.

60. The Three Valuable Gifts

King Darius, a prudent ruler, had three sons he loved dearly. On his deathbed he bequeathed all that he had inherited to his first-born. To his second son he left everything he had acquired during his lifetime; and to the third, who was still a minor, he handed three valuable objects: a gold ring, a neck chain, and a costly carpet. The ring possessed the power to win all people's favor for whoever wore it on his finger, so that they would give him anything he requested. The neck chain possessed the power to acquire for whoever wore it on his breast anything his heart desired within the realm of possibility. The special property of the carpet was that whoever sat on it and thought of a place he'd like to be in was suddenly there. The king gave his youngest son these objects with the command that he go to pursue his studies; his mother would keep them safe and give them to him at the proper time. Immediately after making this gift, the king gave up the ghost and received a splendid funeral.

The two older sons came into their legacies. The youngest son received the ring from his mother so he could set out to study. His mother said to him: "My son, gain knowledge and watch out for women, so you don't lose the ring." Jonathan took the ring, began his studies, and made progress in them.

One day not long afterward he met a very beautiful girl on a city square. Smitten with love for her, he took her along with him. He made constant use of the ring, enjoying everyone's favor and obtaining whatever he wanted from them. The girl, now his mistress, was surprised that he lived so lavishly though he had no money. One day, when he was in a good mood, she asked him how that was, saying that she loved him better than anything else in the world, and so he ought to tell her.

Suspecting no evil intentions, he described the magic power of the ring. She said: "You're in constant contact with people, and you might lose it. I'll guard it for you faithfully." He gave her the ring, but when his financial needs made him ask for it again, she shouted that burglars had stolen it. He was moved to bitter tears because he had nothing else to live on.

He immediately went back to his mother, the queen, and reported the loss of the ring. She said: "My son, I warned you to watch out for women! Now I'm giving you the neck chain, and I want you to guard it carefully. If you lose it, you'll always be deprived of honor and benefit." Jonathan took the neck chain and returned to where he was studying. His mistress met him at the city gates and welcomed him joyfully. Then, as in the past, he threw many parties and lived lavishly.

Because she saw that he had no gold or silver, his mistress was amazed. She wondered what other valuable object he had brought back with him, and she questioned him about it shrewdly. He showed her the neck chain and described its powers. She said: "You always wear that neck chain. In one hour you could wish for enough things to last you a year. So give it to me to keep."

But he responded: "I'm afraid that, just as you lost the ring, you might lose the neck chain, too, and I'd incur a crushing loss."

She replied: "My lord, because of the ring I've learned my lesson, and so I promise you faithfully that I'll guard the neck chain so well, no one could get it away from me." He trusted her and handed over the neck chain. After everything he owned had run out, he asked for the neck chain. As before, she swore that burglars had taken it.

Hearing this, Jonathan wept bitterly and said: "Wasn't I out of my senses to entrust the neck chain to you after the ring was lost?" He went home to his mother and told her everything that had happened. She was sorely grieved and said: "Dearest boy, why did you trust the woman? Once again she's deceived you, and everyone considers you a fool. This time, act wisely, because all I have left to give you is the costly carpet your father left you. If you lose that, it will do you no good to come back to me."

He took the carpet and returned to the city where he was studying; there his mistress met him joyfully, like the last time. He spread out the carpet and said: "Darling, this carpet was given to me by my father." Both of them sat down on the carpet. Jonathan thought to himself: "I wish we were in a place so remote that no human being was ever there before!" And it came to pass: they were at the edge of the world in a forest far away from the haunts of men.

She was unhappy, and Jonathan vowed to God that he would abandon her to be devoured by wild animals unless she returned the ring and the neck chain. She promised to do so if she could, and at his mistress's request Jonathan told her what powers the carpet possessed: whoever sat on it would immediately find himself in any place he wished. Then she sat down on the carpet, put his head in her lap, and, when he had fallen asleep, drew the part of the carpet on which he lay over to herself. Then she thought: "I wish I were where I was this morning!" She sped off, and Jonathan remained sleeping in the forest.

When he rose from sleep, and discovered that his mistress had made off with the carpet, he wept most bitterly and didn't know where to go. Standing up and crossing himself, he walked down a path that led him to a deep river, which he had to cross. Its waters were so acidic and hot that they burned his feet down to the bare bone. Saddened by this, he filled a container with that water and took it with him. As he continued on his way, he grew hungry. Seeing a tree, he ate of its fruit and immediately became a leper. He gathered some of the fruit and took it along. Then he came to another river. When he crossed it, the water restored the flesh to his feet. He filled a container with it and took it along. Growing hungry again as he proceeded, he saw another tree. Picking its fruit and eating it, he found that the second fruit cleansed him of his leprosy just as the first one had caused it. He gathered some of that fruit, too, and took it along.

After walking farther, he espied a castle. Two men met him and asked who he was. He said: "I'm an expert physician."

They said: "The king of this country lives in this castle. He's a leper. If you were able to cure him of his leprosy, he'd shower riches on you."

He said: "Let me try!" They led him to the king, to whom he gave some of the second fruit, which cured him of his leprosy. When he gave him some of the second water to drink, his flesh was restored. And so the king conferred many gifts on him. Then Jonathan boarded a ship that had come from his own city, and he sailed back there. The news spread through the whole city that a great doctor had arrived. His mistress, who had stolen his valuable objects, had fallen critically ill, and sent for that doctor.

Jonathan wasn't recognized by anyone, but he recognized her. He told her that his medicine wouldn't work unless she first confessed all her sins and had restored anything she had ever stolen. She confessed in a loud voice to cheating Jonathan out of his ring, neck chain, and carpet, and to abandoning him in the wilderness to be devoured by animals. Hearing that, he said: "My lady, tell me where those three valuable objects are."

She said: "In my trunk." She gave him the keys to her trunk and he found the objects. Jonathan gave her some of the fruit from the tree that had given him leprosy and some of the water from the first river, which had burnt the flesh off his feet. When she ate and drank, she immediately withered up. Seized by internal pains, she wept, shouted, and breathed her last.

Jonathan went home to his mother with his valuable objects. At his arrival the entire populace rejoiced. He told his mother from start to finish how God had rescued him from many grave dangers. He lived for a good many years and died in peace.

61. The Household Snake

In the reign of Emperor Fulgentius there lived a knight called Zedekiah, who married a woman who was beautiful but not clever. A snake lived in one room of his house. The knight participated in so many tournaments and jousts that he was plunged into dire poverty. Weeping bitterly and nearly desperate, he went here and there, not knowing what he should do. Seeing his grief, the snake (which was granted the power of speech by God, just like Balaam's ass in olden days) said to him: "Why are you crying? Follow my advice and you won't regret it! Feed me sweet milk every day, and I'll make you rich!"

Hearing this, the knight rejoiced and promised to comply with the snake's wishes faithfully. Before very long he became extremely wealthy, the father of beautiful children and the owner of many riches.

It came about one day that his wife said to him: "Husband, I think that that snake possesses a great fortune in the room it occupies. So I advise you to kill it, and we'll gain control of its belongings." Taking his wife's advice, he took along a hammer with which to kill the snake when he brought it its plate of milk. When the snake saw the plate of milk, it stuck its head out of its hole in the wall, to lap up the milk as usual. Seeing this, the knight reached out with the hammer, intending to hit the snake. The snake saw this at once and drew in its head, and the plate bore the brunt of the blow.

Immediately afterward the knight lost his children and all his possessions. His wife said: "Alas, I gave you bad advice, but now go to the snake's hole and humble yourself in every way, and maybe it will forgive you." The knight went to the snake's room and wept bitterly, asking its forgiveness, so it would make him rich again.

The snake said: "Now I see what a fool you are, and you'll remain a fool, because the memory of that great hammer blow will unavoidably come back to me again and again, and *you* will always remember that I killed your children and took away all your riches. So there can never be true peace between us."

Grieving sorely, the knight said: "I promise you solemnly that from now on I will never do you any harm, if you will only forgive me."

The snake replied: "My friend, a snake is cunning by nature. Let my venom-filled words be enough for you, because I am now recalling your hammer blow and your worthlessness. Get out if you don't want something worse to happen!"

The knight left the snake very sadly, and said to his wife: "Woe is me that I ever took your advice!" And so, ever afterward they lived in poverty.

STORIES 62–72

From *El Conde Lucanor*
by Juan Manuel

Of all the authors, known or unknown, represented in this anthology, Don Juan Manuel (1282–1348) was beyond a doubt the most highly born. He was a grandson of King Ferdinand III of Castile and León (1199–1252), who recaptured Córdoba, Jaén, and Seville from the Moors, and whose saintly life was the basis for his canonization in the 17th century; and he was a nephew of Ferdinand's successor Alfonso X (1221–1284), known as "El Sabio" (the Wise), who took Cádiz and who sponsored a vast program of scholarship, legislation, and literary activity.

Juan Manuel himself was a major landholder who became embroiled in the hostilities between Castile and Aragon (at times taking sides against his own cousins), in the course of which his inherited province of Murcia passed in and out of his hands repeatedly. Yet, for all his military and social involvement, he had enough time to write an impressive number of didactic works (not all preserved), including poetry, history, fiction, and treatises on such varied topics as ethics, religion, Spanish society, and hunting. He has been considered to be the first self-conscious Spanish author, concerned with refining and conserving his own catalog of works, as well as the best Spanish prose stylist of the 14th century.

His masterpiece, completed in 1335 (prologue, 1340), is the *Libro de los enxiemplos del Conde Lucanor e de Patronio* (Book of Exempla of Count Lucanor and Patronio), generally called *El Conde Lucanor* for short. In the main part of the work (often republished separately) Count Lucanor informs his privy counselor Patronio of specific real-life problems that confront him, and each time Patronio's response includes, embedded within it, an *exemplum*, or illustrative story. There are 51 such stories in all; the 11 selected here do not include the opening and closing discussions between count and counselor. The remaining parts of *El Conde Lucanor* consist of more abstract disquisitions, as well as lists of proverbs and maxims.

Thus, the work is part of a long-standing Spanish literary tradition of didactic storytelling (see Introduction). Some of the 51 stories are based on universal "floating" folklore themes, on Aesopic fables, Oriental tales, religious anecdotes, and the like, but some of the best of them are more distinctive, or even unique: those based on Spanish history, Moorish legend, and reminiscences of the Reconquista. The stories concerning magic and alchemy often, but not always, display a skeptical or rationalistic cast of mind.

The narrative is generally brisk and logical, but occasionally (as in No. 62) there are wearisome repetitions, perhaps because one of the author's professed purposes was to make his wisdom available to "simple minds."

No. 62 is a widespread fable in the Aesopic tradition. The most celebrated literary version is the one by La Fontaine (*Fables*, Book III, No. 1).

No. 63 is an outstandingly brilliant retelling of a universal folklore theme (there are significant East Asian versions) involving a time illusion, and sometimes, as here, also involving a question of ingratitude. The local color adds much flavor: Toledo was notorious for black magic in the Middle Ages, and roast partridge was a typical Toledan dish.

No. 68 contains motifs that are related, at some remove, to the bird's advice in No. 14 and to Julian's rashness in No. 51.

No. 70 is in the grand tradition of womanly-guile stories, and of stories in which the Devil is outdone by his human competitors; while in No. 72, one of the numerous medieval pact-with-the-Devil stories, the Father of Lies is successful in deluding his over-confident victim, who doesn't seem to notice that his patron's aid is arriving more and more slowly all the time. The second sentence of No. 72 is reminiscent of Francesca da Rimini's famous "No greater sorrow" speech in Dante's *Divine Comedy* ("Inferno," Canto V), written only decades before *El Conde Lucanor*.

62. Satisfying Public Opinion

My lord, it came about that some good man had a son, who, though young, was of quite sharp wits. Every time the father had some business afoot (and there are few matters in which some disappointment may not occur!), he told his son what he intended to do, seeing that there might be a hidden obstacle. In that way the boy kept him away from some transactions that might have turned to his advantage; because, believe me, youngsters with the sharpest wits are the most likely to make big mistakes in their dealings: they're smart enough to initiate the deal, but they don't know how it may end, and thus they commit great errors if there's no one to prevent them. And so, that boy, who was very clever but lacked the experience to foresee the full course of events, did his father harm in many transactions.

After many such experiences with his son, the father, recognizing the harm that had ensued from things the boy told him not to do, and the vexation he received from taking the boy's advice, became intent on giving him good counsel. To give him an example to follow in future matters, he chose the method I'm about to describe.

The good man and his son were rustics who lived near a village. One day when a market was being held there, the man told his son that they should both attend it in order to buy some things they needed, and they agreed to take along a pack horse to carry their purchases. As they made their way on foot to the market, leading their unburdened horse, they met some men who were coming from the village they were headed for.

After the two parties had greeted one another and separated, the men they had met began a conversation among themselves, saying that they didn't think that that father and son were very sensible, traveling on foot while the horse carried nothing. After the good man heard that, he asked his son for his opinion on their statement. His son said that they were right, and that with the horse carrying nothing, it made no sense for the two of them to be walking. Then the good man ordered his son to mount the horse.

As they proceeded in that manner, they came across other men, who, after the parties separated, began to say that the good man had made a big mistake going on foot, old and weary as he was, while the boy, who could endure hardships, rode the horse. Then the good man asked his son for his opinion on their statement. He said he thought they were right. So the man ordered his son to get off the horse, and he himself got on.

Before long they fell in with other people, who said that the man was be-having like a criminal letting the boy, who was delicate and unable to with-stand hardships, walk while he himself, accustomed as he was to face any hardship, rode. Then the good man asked his son for his opinion on their statement. The boy said that, as far as he could see, they were right. Then the good man ordered his son to get up on the horse behind him, so that neither of them would be walking.

Proceeding in that manner, they met still more men, who said that the horse they were riding was so weak that it could hardly keep going, and that therefore they were making a big mistake by both riding. The good man asked his son for his opinion on what those good people had said. The boy told his father that he found their words to be true.

Then the father replied to his son as follows: "My son, as you know, when we left home we were both walking and leading the unburdened horse, and you said it was the right thing to do. Later, we came across men on the road who told us it was wrong, and I told you to mount the horse while I kept walking. You said it was right. Then we met others who said it was wrong, and therefore you dismounted and I mounted the horse. You said that was the best way. But, because the next group we met said it was wrong, I told you to get up behind me, and you said it was bet-ter than having you walk and me ride. Now we've met these people who say that it's a mistake for us to be both riding, and your opinion is that they're correct.

"All this being the case, please tell me what we can possibly do that people won't object to. We were both walking, and they said it was wrong. I walked while you rode, and they said we were in error. I rode while you walked, and they said it was a mistake. And now we're both riding, and they say we're acting badly. Now, there's no way we can avoid doing one of these things, and by now, we've done them all and someone says each one is wrong.

"I did this to provide you with an example of things you may come across in business, for you may be sure that nothing you ever do will be approved by everyone. If it's something good, people who are bad or who don't profit from your action will say it's no good. If you do something bad, good people who delight in good things won't be able to call your bad action good. And so, if you want to do what is best and most advantageous to you, take care to do the best thing and the thing that you see will profit you most. So long as it isn't evil, don't abandon your plan out of fear of what people may say, because you can be sure that, in general, people always say whatever comes into their head and don't look after their own best advantage."

63. Partridges for Supper

My lord Count (Patronio said), in Santiago there was a dean[1] who was very eager to learn the art of black magic. Hearing that Don Yllán of Toledo knew more of it than anyone else at that time, he went to Toledo for lessons in that art. On the day he arrived in Toledo, he headed straight for Don Yllán's house and found him reading in a very remote room. As soon as he came in, Don Yllán welcomed him heartily, telling him not to say a word about why he had come until he had eaten something. He entertained him generously, had a good room prepared for him, furnished him with everything he needed, and gave him to understand that he was very pleased at his coming.

After they had eaten they withdrew to a private spot, and the dean stated why he had come, urging Don Yllán ardently to teach him the art he was so eager to learn. But Don Yllán said that he was a dean, a man of great style who might attain a high rank — and men of high rank, once they have everything their own way, are very quick to forget what others have done for them. And so, he said, he was afraid that, after the dean had learned from him all that he wanted to know, he wouldn't reward him as richly as he was now promising to do. But the dean promised and assured him that, no matter how well-to-do he became, he'd never fail to do what Don Yllán ordered.

They were engaged in this conversation from dinnertime at midday until nearly suppertime. After they had fully agreed on terms, Don Yllán told the dean that that art could only be learned in a very private place. He wished to show him that very evening what place they had to remain in until he learned what he wanted to know. Taking him by the hand, he led him to another room. Stepping away from the others present, he summoned one of his maids and told her that there were partridges for supper

---

[1] Head of the cathedral chapter.

that evening, but that no one should begin roasting them until he gave the order.

After giving these instructions, he called over the dean, and the two of them started walking down a staircase of finely dressed stone. They went down a long way, until they seemed to be so far down that the river Tagus flowed above their heads. Reaching the bottom of the stairs, they found a very fine apartment and, in it, a very neat room containing the books they needed to consult for their purpose. Sitting down, they began planning which books to start with. While they were thus engaged, two men came in and handed them a letter from the dean's uncle, the archbishop, saying that he was critically ill and that, if the dean wanted to see him alive once more, he should come at once.

The dean was greatly saddened by the news, not only because his uncle was ill, but also because he feared he'd have to abandon the studies he was just beginning. But he decided in his heart not to abandon those studies so soon. He wrote a letter in reply and sent it to his uncle, the archbishop.

Three or four days later, other men came on foot bearing another letter for the dean. This one informed him that the archbishop had died, that all the cathedral canons were engaged in electing his successor, and that, by God's mercy, he, the dean, was expected to be chosen. Therefore he should not hasten to the cathedral, because it was better for him to be elected while he was away from the cathedral.

Then, seven or eight days after that, two very well dressed and equipped squires arrived. When they came up to the dean, they kissed his hand and showed him a letter informing him that he had been elected archbishop. When Don Yllán heard this, he came up to the archbishop-elect, saying how grateful he was to God that this good news had reached him in *his* house. Since God had been so good to the dean, he added, he asked him as a favor to give the now vacant deanship to his, Don Yllán's, son.

The archbishop-elect begged Don Yllán to allow him to give the deanship to one of his own brothers. He would see to it, he said, that Don Yllán was well rewarded, and he invited him to accompany him to Santiago and bring his son along. Don Yllán said he would do so. They departed for Santiago. On their arrival they were welcomed warmly and ceremoniously. After being there for a time, one day the archbishop received envoys from the pope bearing a letter to the effect that he was giving him the bishopric of Tolosa, with permission to grant his own archbishopric to anyone he wished.

When Don Yllán heard this, he reminded him emphatically of what had already occurred between them and requested the position for his son. The archbishop begged him to allow him to give it to an uncle of his, his father's brother. Don Yllán replied that he was aware that the archbishop was acting very unjustly toward him, but that he consented this time, so he could be sure of having amends made to him in the future. The archbishop promised him up and down that it would be so, and asked him to accompany him to Tolosa along with his son.

Arriving in Tolosa, they were heartily welcomed by counts and all the other local noblemen. After they had been there about two years, papal envoys came with a letter stating that the pope was making the bishop a cardinal and granting him permission to bestow the bishopric of Tolosa on the man of his choice. Then Don Yllán went to him, saying that, after breaking his agreement with him so many times, he was now unable to find any other excuse, but must give his son one of these high positions.

The new cardinal begged him to allow him to give the bishopric to another uncle of his, his mother's brother, who was a worthy old man. Now that he was a cardinal, he added, Don Yllán should accompany him to the papal Curia, where there would be plenty of opportunities to reward him. Don Yllán complained about this bitterly, but agreed to the cardinal's request, and accompanied him to the Curia.

Arriving there, they were warmly welcomed by the cardinals and all the other members of the Curia, and they remained there a very long time. Every day Don Yllán nagged the cardinal to do something for his son, but received only excuses. While they were at the Curia, the pope died and all the cardinals elected the former dean as pope. Then Don Yllán went to him, saying he could no longer offer any excuse for not keeping his promise. The new pope asked him not to put so much pressure on him, saying he'd always find some opportunity to reward him properly.

Don Yllán began to complain violently, reminding the pope of all his promises, none of which he had kept. He said he had feared that very thing the first time he had spoken with him. Now that he had attained that highest rank and still wasn't keeping his promises, there was no more reason to expect any reward from him. The pope complained about the complaint, and began to treat Don Yllán badly, telling him that if he kept insisting, he'd have him thrown in jail, because he was a heretic and a sorcerer. He, the pope, was well aware that back home in Toledo he had had no other trade or profession, but had made his living solely by that art of black magic.

After Don Yllán saw how meanly the pope was rewarding him for what he had done for him, he took his leave, and the pope even refused to give him provisions for his journey. Then Don Yllán said to the pope that, since he had nothing else to eat, he'd have to have recourse to the partridges he had intended to have roasted that evening. He summoned the maid and told her to start roasting the partridges.

When Don Yllán said that, the pope found himself back in Toledo, still the dean of Santiago, as he had been when he arrived there. He was so ashamed that he didn't know what to say. Don Yllán told him to be on his way, because he had already sufficiently tested his character and would consider it a great waste if he were to eat his share of the partridges.

64. An Incident at the Siege of Seville

My lord Count (Patronio said), the saintly and blessed King Ferdinand[2] was besieging Seville. Among the many noblemen with him there, there were three knights who were considered the three best in the world at that time: Don Lorenzo Suárez Gallinato, Don García Pérez de Vargas, and a third whose name I don't recall. One day these three knights had an argument over which of them was best of all. Unable to reach an agreement in any other way, they all consented to put on good armor, ride right up to the gate of Seville, and strike the gate with their lances.

The next morning the three of them put on their armor and headed for the city. The Moors on the wall and towers, seeing that there were only three knights, thought they were coming as envoys, and no one sallied out. The three knights passed the moat and the barbican, reached the city gate, and struck it with their lancepoints. Having done so, they turned their horses' bridles and started back to camp.

When the Moors saw that they hadn't come to parley, they realized they had been mocked and set out after them. By the time they opened the city gate, the three knights, who were riding back at a level pace, were already some distance away. More than fifteen hundred horsemen sallied out in pursuit, along with twenty thousand infantrymen. Seeing them getting close, the three knights turned their horses' bridles to face them, and waited.

When the Moors were very close, the knight whose name I've forgotten attacked them and wounded some. Don Lorenzo Suárez and Don García Pérez stayed put, but when the Moors were even closer, Don García Pérez de Vargas attacked. Don Lorenzo Suárez stayed put, never advancing toward them but waiting until the Moors were upon him. When they attacked, he rode into their midst and started to perform remarkable feats of arms.

When those in the camp saw the knights among the Moors, they hastened to their aid. Even though they were hard pressed and wounded, God in His mercy saw to it that none of the three was killed. The battle between Christians and Moors was so great that King Ferdinand decided to join it personally. The Christians were very successful that day.

Back in his tent, the king ordered the three knights arrested, saying they deserved to be executed for venturing out so foolishly. For one thing, they had made the army enter battle without orders from the king; for another, they had put their own valuable lives at risk for nothing. After the leaders of the army pleaded with the king to pardon them, he ordered them released.

---

[2]Ferdinand III of Castile (1199–1252), grandfather of the author, took Seville from the Moors in 1249. His conquest of Córdoba in 1236 is mentioned in story No. 69. He was canonized in 1671.

When the king learned that they had done what they did as a result of their argument, he summoned all the noblemen in camp so they could give their opinion on which of them had acted best. After everyone was assembled, they disputed hotly: some said that the most valiant of the three was the one who had attacked first; others said it was the second; others, the third. Each contingent gave such good reasons that they all seemed to be right. And, in truth, the three knights' behavior in itself was so meritorious that anyone could find many good reasons to praise it.

But, when the discussion was over, the verdict was as follows: If the Moors pursuing them had been few enough to be overcome by the strength or valor possessed by those knights, then the first one who attacked was the best, because he was starting something that could be brought to a conclusion. But, since there were so many Moors that the knights couldn't possibly overcome them, the knight who attacked them didn't do so with a view to overcoming them; it was shame that kept him from fleeing; and, since fleeing was out of the question, the anguish in his heart (because he couldn't abide the fear) caused him to attack them. The second man, who attacked but waited longer than the first, they considered to be better, because he was better able to combat his fear. But Don Lorenzo, who completely withstood his fear, waiting until the Moors were upon him, was the best knight, in their judgment.

65. An Experiment in Alchemy

My lord, Count Lucanor (Patronio said), there was a man who was a great rogue. Desiring ardently to get rich and abandon the criminal life he led, he heard that a king who was insufficiently cautious was extremely eager to learn alchemy. The rogue took a hundred gold doubloons and filed them down. With the filings, and other materials that he added, he made a hundred pellets, each the weight of a doubloon—plus the weight of the other stuff he had mixed with the doubloon filings.

Going to the town where the king was staying, he dressed up in very respectable clothes, took those pellets, and sold them to an apothecary. The apothecary asked what those pellets were good for, and the rogue said: "For lots of things, and, in particular, no one can practice alchemy without them." And he sold him all hundred pellets for the price of two or three doubloons. The apothecary asked him what those pellets were called, and the rogue said their name was *tabardí*.

The rogue remained in that town for a while, acting like a very respectable man. He kept telling various people, as if it were a secret, that he knew how to practice alchemy. This rumor reached the king, who sent for him and asked him whether he was adept at alchemy. At first the rogue pretended that he wanted to conceal his knowledge, and replied in the negative, but finally he admitted that he *was* an adept. He told the king, however, that his advice was never to trust anyone in the world on that subject, and not to risk much money on it. Nevertheless, if the king so desired, he'd give him a little demonstration to show him what he knew about it. This pleased the king greatly; he thought that a man who spoke that way would never trick him.

Then the rogue requested the necessary materials, all of which were things that were available; and among the other things he asked for a pellet of *tabardí*. Everything he asked for cost no more than two or three silver pennies altogether. After the items had been assembled and melted down, the residue contained fine gold weighing the equivalent of a doubloon. When the king saw that the material which had cost only two or three pennies had produced a doubloon, he was overjoyed and considered himself the luckiest man in the world. And he told the rogue who could do such things (thinking he was an upstanding citizen) to produce more.

The rogue, pretending he knew nothing further on that subject, replied: "Sire, all I knew of this, I have showed you. From here on in, you can do it as well as I can. But you must know one thing: if any of these ingredients is missing, you can't produce gold." Having said this, he took leave of the king and returned to his lodgings.

The king tried to make gold without that instructor. Doubling the ingredients, he produced an amount of gold equivalent to two doubloons. Another time he doubled the amount again, and four doubloons' worth of gold emerged. As he kept increasing the ingredients, he got more and more gold. Seeing he could make as much gold as he wanted, the king ordered enough of every ingredient to make a thousand doubloons. Everything else was located, but not the *tabardí*. Finding that he couldn't make gold because the *tabardí* was lacking, the king summoned the man who had showed him the process, and told him he could no longer make gold as he had done earlier. The man asked whether he was using every item he had prescribed. The king said he was, except that he couldn't find any *tabardí*.

Then the rogue told him that, if any ingredient whatsoever was missing, the gold couldn't be produced, as he had informed him on the very first day. The king asked him whether he knew where to find that *tabardí*, and the rogue said he did. Then the king ordered him, since he knew where it was, to fetch it and bring back enough to make as much gold as he wanted.

The rogue replied that, even though anyone else could do that as well as he, if not better, if it gratified the king, he would fetch it, because there was a lot of it back where he came from. Then the king calculated what he would have to pay for the purchase and the other expenses, and gathered together a hefty sum of money. Once the rogue had got hold of it, he lit out and never returned to the king. And so the king was tricked because he had so little sense.

When the king saw that the man was slower than necessary in getting back, he sent to his house in town to hear if anyone had news of him.

Nothing at all was found in his house except a locked strongbox. Opening it, they discovered a note that read: "Take my word for it: there's no such thing as *tabardí*. Make up your mind that you've been tricked! When I told you I'd make you rich, you should have replied that I should make myself rich first, and then you'd believe me."

A few days later, some men were laughing and joking. They wrote down the names of everyone they knew, and characterized each one of them. They said: "A and B are intelligent, C and D are rich, E and F are prudent," and so on, for all good and bad qualities. When they got up to imprudent people, they put down the king's name.

When the king heard this, he summoned them. Assuring them he wouldn't punish them for their actions, he asked them why they had set him down as imprudent. They replied that it was because he had given so much money to a stranger without taking any precautions.

The king said they were wrong, and that if the man who took the money came back, he wouldn't be considered imprudent. But they said that they wouldn't lose anything by it: if the man did come back, they would take the king's name off the list and put down *his*.

66. A Lesson from the Crows

My lord Count Lucanor (Patronio said), a king had a son, whose education he entrusted to a philosopher in whom he had great confidence. When the king died, his son and successor was still a little boy. The philosopher raised him until he was fifteen. But as soon as he came into young manhood, he began to spurn the counsels of the man who had raised him, and gave heed to other advisers, younger men and such as weren't sufficiently devoted to him to do much to keep him from harm.

As he continued this existence, before long his habits and his health were in the same sad shape as his treasury. Everyone spoke very disparagingly about how that young king was ruining both his body and his fortune. When the situation had gotten so bad, the philosopher who had brought up the king, and who was greatly saddened and grieved for him, didn't know what to do. He had tried many times to set him straight with entreaties and flattery, and even by berating him, but had never accomplished a thing, because his adolescent urges stood in the way. Seeing that he couldn't offer advice in the matter in any other way, the philosopher formulated the following plan.

He began to spread the word gradually in the palace that he was the world's greatest soothsayer. This was repeated by so many people that it reached the ears of the king. Once he heard it, he asked the philosopher if he could really read omens as well as people said. The philosopher pretended at first to deny it, but finally said it was true, but that there was no need for anyone at all to find out about it.

Since young men are impatient to learn and do everything, the king, who was still just a boy, was extremely impatient to see how the philosopher interpreted omens. The longer the philosopher put him off, the more eager the young king grew to find out, and he put so much pressure on the philosopher that he set a date on which they would set out very early in the morning to read omens without anyone else's knowledge.

They arose very early, and the philosopher headed for a valley in which there were many deserted villages. After walking through several, they saw a crow in a tree, cawing. The king pointed it out to the philosopher, who indicated by a gesture that he heard it. Another crow started to caw in another tree, and both crows continued to caw in alternation. After the philosopher listened to them awhile, he started to cry very hard, tearing his clothes and grieving enormously.

Seeing this, the young king was very surprised and asked the philosopher why he was behaving that way. The philosopher pretended to be unwilling to tell. After much prodding, he said he'd rather be dead than alive, because not only human beings, but even the birds, were now aware of how the king, through his imprudence, had ruined his whole kingdom, his treasury, and his health, which he neglected. The young king asked him how that was.

The philosopher said that the two crows had decided to marry off their children, the son of one of them to the daughter of the other. The crow that had spoken first was telling the other one that, since so much time had gone by since the marriage had been arranged, it was high time for their offspring to get married. The second crow had said that it was true that it had been arranged, but now she was much wealthier than the first crow, because, thank God, since the beginning of the present reign, all the villages in that valley had been abandoned. She now found in the empty houses many snakes, lizards, toads, and other such animals that flourish in deserted places, because they had much better things to eat than usual. Therefore the match between bride and bridegroom was no longer equal.

When the first crow had heard this (the philosopher continued), she had started to laugh and had replied that the second crow was speaking foolishly if she wanted to postpone the marriage for that reason. If only God let this king live, she'd soon be richer than the second crow, because very soon the valley where *she* lived would be deserted, too, and it contained ten times as many villages as this one. Therefore there was no reason to postpone the marriage. Finally the two crows had agreed to celebrate the marriage at once.

Hearing this, the young king was very grieved, and began to realize that it was his own fault that his realm was being so impoverished. When the philosopher saw the young king's sorrow and thoughtfulness, and his desire to safeguard his possessions, he gave him much good advice, so that before long his house was completely in order, with regard to both his health and his kingdom.

67. Testing Three Princes

My lord Count Lucanor (Patronio said), a Moorish king had three sons. Because a father can choose as his successor whichever son he wishes, when the king grew old the noblemen in his kingdom asked him humbly to let them know which of the sons he wanted to succeed him. The king said that he would give them his answer in a month.

Eight or ten days later, he said to his eldest son one evening that he wanted to go out riding with him very early the next day. On the following day, the eldest prince came to the king, but not as early as his father, the king, had ordered. When he arrived, the king told him that he wanted to get dressed and that the prince should have his clothes brought. The prince told the chamberlain to bring the clothes, and the chamberlain asked which clothes he wanted. The prince went back to the king and asked him which clothes he wanted. The king said he wanted his long-sleeved coat, and the prince went back to the chamberlain to tell him so. The chamberlain asked him which cape he wanted, and the prince went back to the king to ask him. And so it went for each article of clothing: he kept going back and forth for each question until the king got all the clothes. The chamberlain came and put on his clothes and shoes.

After he was dressed, and had his shoes on, the king ordered the prince to have his horse brought out of the stable. The prince told the keeper of the king's horses to bring the horse, and the keeper asked him which one he should bring. The prince referred this question to the king, and he did the same for the saddle, the bridle, the sword, and the spurs. For everything pertaining to riding he went back and forth to ask the king.

When everything was in readiness, the king told the prince that he was unable to go riding. The prince should ride through the city, paying attention to what he saw, so he could report to the king about it. The prince rode out, escorted by all the distinguished men of the king and the kingdom. Many trumpets, drums, and other instruments made music for them. The prince went through part of the city and, after he returned, the king asked him how he liked what he had seen. The prince said he had liked everything, but that the music had been too noisy for him.

A few days later, the king ordered his second son to come to him the following morning, and that prince did so. The king applied all the tests he had given the eldest prince, this one's brother, and this prince behaved in exactly the same way.

A few days after that, the king ordered his youngest son to join him early the following morning. This prince was up and stirring before the king awoke, and waited until the king was up. As soon as he was, the prince entered his bedroom and prostrated himself with all due reverence. The king ordered him to have his clothes brought. The prince asked him which clothes he wanted, asking him about all his apparel and footwear at one time. Then he went for them and brought them all back. He didn't allow any chamberlain to put on his clothes and shoes, but did it himself, making it clear that he would consider himself fortunate if the king, his father, were pleased or served by anything he could do. Since he was his father, it was only right and proper to offer him as many favors and show him as much submission as possible.

When the king had his clothes and shoes on, he ordered the prince to have his horse brought out. The prince asked him which horse he wanted, and with which saddle, which bridle, which sword, and so on for all the items pertaining to riding. He also asked who he would like to have ride out with him, and so on for everything pertinent. On receiving all the replies, he never asked about anything again, but went and got it and prepared it as the king had ordered.

When everything had been done, the king said that he didn't want to go riding; instead, the prince should ride out and report on what he had seen. The prince rode out, accompanied by all those who had escorted his two brothers. But neither he, nor either of his brothers, nor anyone else at all, knew anything of the king's reasons for doing all this.

When the prince rode out, he ordered his men to show him everything inside the city walls: the streets, the place where the king kept his treasures (asking how much they amounted to), the mosques, and all the noteworthy sights inside the city, and the people who lived there. Then he rode out through the gate, sending for all the king's soldiery, both cavalry and infantry, to come out with him. There he ordered them to take part in war games and show him all their jousts and competitions. He also inspected the city walls, towers, and fortifications. After his tour of inspection he returned to the king, his father.

When he got back it was already very late in the day. The king asked him about what he had seen. The prince replied that, if it didn't upset the king, he would tell him what he thought about it all. The king ordered him, as he valued his paternal blessing, to tell him exactly what he thought. The prince said that, though he was a very honest king, it seemed to him that he wasn't as effective as he could be, because, if he were, with so many valiant subjects and such great power and wealth, it was only his fault if the whole world wasn't his.

The king was very pleased with the reproach the prince had given him. When the time came that he had stipulated to reply to his noblemen, he told them he wanted them to have his youngest son as their king. He had made that decision because of the qualities he had seen in his other sons and those he had seen in him. Though he would have preferred either of the others as his successor, he thought it incorrect to choose them because of what he had seen in them and in his other son.

68. A Vendor of Good Sense

My lord Count (Patronio said), there was a city that was the home of a great teacher, whose only profession and trade consisted in selling good sense. When a certain merchant heard about this one day, he went to see the teacher who sold sense and asked him to sell him some. The teacher asked him how much he was willing to pay, because the sense was sold according to the price paid. The merchant replied that he wanted a *maravedí's* worth of good sense.

The teacher took the *maravedí* and said: "My friend, whenever someone invites you to a meal, if you don't know what dishes are going to be served, fill yourself up on the first one placed before you."

The merchant complained that his statement didn't contain all that much good sense. But the teacher rejoined that he couldn't give him a lot of sense at that price. The merchant then asked him to give him a doubloon's worth of sense, and he did. The teacher told him that whenever he was in a great rage and was about to do something hasty and violent, he shouldn't be too eager or impetuous until he had learned all the relevant facts.

The merchant thought that, if he went on learning such trifling maxims, he could squander all the doubloons he had with him, and he refused to buy more good sense—though he stored away in his mind what he *had* heard. It came about that this merchant made a voyage to a very distant land. He left his wife pregnant when he departed. The merchant remained there on his business until the son whom his wife bore in his absence was over twenty years old.

The young man's mother, who had no other child and who believed that her husband was dead, consoled herself with that son, loving him as a mother should. Because of her great love for his father, she called her son "my husband." He always ate with her and slept in the same bed, as he had done when he was one or two. Thus the woman spent her life very respectably, but very sorrowfully, because she had no news of her husband.

And it came about that the merchant finally sold all his merchandise and returned home in great prosperity. On the day he arrived in the harbor of the city where he lived, he said nothing to anyone, but went secretly to his house and hid in an enclosed spot to see what was going on at home.

Toward evening the good woman's son arrived, and his mother asked him: "Tell me, husband, where are you coming from?"

The merchant, hearing his wife call that young man "husband," was quite irritated, because he thought that he was a man she was sinning with, or, to put the best face on it, that she had married him. Even so, he found her blameworthy, not for having remarried, but for having married such a youngster. He wanted to kill them at once, but, remembering the good sense he had bought for a doubloon, he restrained himself.

After evening had set in, the mother and son sat down to eat. Seeing them together like that, the merchant felt an even greater urge to kill them, but, thanks to the sense he had purchased, he restrained himself again. All the same, that night, when he saw them go to bed, it became too much for him to take, and he advanced toward them intending to kill them. Yet, at the height of his rage, he remembered the good sense he had bought, and stopped in his tracks. Before putting out the candle, the woman, weeping bitterly, said to her son: "Alas, my husband and my son! I've been told that a ship has just arrived in the harbor that came from the country where your father was doing business. For the love of God, go there first thing in the morning. Maybe God will allow us to hear some good news about him."

When the merchant heard that, and remembered that his wife had been pregnant when he left, he realized the young man was his son. You can imagine how very pleased he was. What's more, he thanked God for keeping him from killing them as he had wanted to do. Such a deed would have brought him great misfortune. And he considered well spent the doubloon he had given for the good sense that made him think twice and not act impetuously in his rage.

69. A Spur to Good Deeds

My lord Count (Patronio said), there was a king in Córdoba named Al-Hakam.[3] Though he governed his kingdom well, he didn't strive to perform any honorable or prestigious deed, such as good kings are wont, and obliged, to do. For kings are obliged not only to preserve their realms: those who want to be considered truly great must perform deeds that increase their kingdom lawfully and cause them to be highly praised by people while they live, and remembered honorably after their death for their good works. But this king didn't strive for anything but eating, enjoying himself, and sitting idly at home.

It came about that, while he was being entertained one day, an instrument was played for him that the Moors used to delight in, a type of flute called *albogón*. The king was listening carefully and found that it wasn't producing as good a sound as it should. He took the flute and added another hole to it at its lower end, aligned with the other holes. Ever since then, that kind of flute produces a much better sound than it did till then.

Though that was a notable deed on such a low scale, it still wasn't as great a deed as kings should accomplish, and people started to praise that deed sarcastically. Whenever they praised someone, they'd say: "*Wa hadi*

---

[3]Al-Hakam II, caliph of Córdoba from 961 to 976, did make additions to the famous mosque, but the story of the flute that follows is mere legend.

ziyadat Al-Hakam," which, translated from Arabic, means "It's like Al-Hakam's new addition."

This saying circulated so widely through the realm that it reached the ears of the king, who asked why people were saying that. Though his courtiers tried to conceal it from him, he kept after them until they had to tell. Hearing the explanation, he was very vexed, but, being a very kind king, he wished to do no harm to those who repeated that saying. Still, he resolved to make an addition of another kind, one that would compel people to praise his actions sincerely.

So, because the mosque at Córdoba had not yet been completed, that king funded all the work still remaining, and completed it. It's the largest, most perfect, and noblest mosque that the Moors had in Spain. God be praised, it's now a church called Saint Mary of Córdoba. It was dedicated to the Blessed Virgin by saintly King Ferdinand when he took Córdoba from the Moors.

After King Al-Hakam had completed the mosque with such a noteworthy addition, he said that, whereas he had hitherto been praised sarcastically for his addition to the flute, henceforth he considered himself justifiably praiseworthy for his addition to the Córdoba mosque. And he *was* highly praised for it. The phrase with which he had been praised sarcastically up till then became an expression of genuine praise, and today, when the Moors wish to praise some worthy accomplishment, they say: "It's like Al-Hakam's new addition."

70. The Devil and the Devotee

My lord Count Lucanor (Patronio said), in a certain city there was a very honorable young man, who lived on good terms with his wife, so that there was never any discord between them. Since devils have always been displeased by happy arrangements, this happy couple irritated a certain devil no end, but, though he long planned to break up this couple, he had never been able to manage it.

One day, when this devil was leaving the place where that man and wife lived, very sad because he couldn't sow discord between them, he met a woman who was a religious hypocrite, a false devotee. They struck up an acquaintance, and she asked him why he was so unhappy. He told her he had just left the city where that man and woman lived, and that he had been trying for some time unsuccessfully to create a rift between them. His superior had heard about it and had told him that, since he had tried so long without success, he was no longer in his good graces. That was why he felt so sad.

The woman said that she was amazed at his failure, given his great skill, but that, if he did what she advised, she would guarantee his success. The devil promised to follow her advice if it allowed him to create a rift between that man and his wife.

After the devil and the devotee had made that compact, the woman went to the place where the man and wife lived and gradually, day by day, made the wife's acquaintance, telling her she had been her mother's servant and thus felt an obligation to her. She was determined to enter her service and said she'd serve her to the best of her abilities. The good woman believed this, took her into the house, and entrusted her with everything she had. Her husband did the same.

After living there for some time, and gaining the full confidence of both man and wife, one day she came in great dejection to the woman who trusted her, and said: "My daughter, I'm very sad about something I've just heard. Your husband loves another woman better than you. I urge you to honor and please him as much as you can, so that he will no longer love another woman better than you, because that can bring you greater misfortune than anything else could."

When the good woman heard that, she didn't really believe it; still, she was very hurt by it and became depressed. When the wicked devotee observed her sadness, she went to the place from which the husband was to return. She met him and told him she was very grieved at his actions; he had such a good wife and yet preferred another woman. His wife already knew about it, she said; she was very upset over it, and had told her that, since he was carrying on that way while she was doing so much for him, she herself would look out for some man who'd love her as much as he did, or more. For the love of God, she concluded, he mustn't let his wife know that she had told him all this, or his wife would kill her. Hearing this, the husband didn't really believe it, but he was deeply grieved by it and became very sad.

After the wretched hypocrite had spoken to the husband, she returned to the wife and, with a demonstration of sincere grief, she said: "My daughter, I don't know what great misfortune has made your husband so displeased with you. But, to be convinced that it's really so, just as I'm telling you, notice how unhappy and angry he is when he comes in, unlike his former self."

Leaving her with this trouble in mind, the woman returned to the husband and made the equivalent statement. When he got home and found his wife sad, and when they no longer enjoyed each other's company as before, both of them were care-laden. After the husband withdrew, the evil hypocrite told the good woman that, if she liked, she'd seek out some very wise counselor who'd do something to make her husband shake off his grudge against her.

The woman, who wanted to enjoy her married life again, said that it was all right with her and that she'd be very grateful to her. A few days later, the devotee came back to her, reporting that she had located a very wise man, who had said that, if he had a few hairs from her husband's beard where it grew down his throat, he would prepare a remedy to cure her husband of all his anger against her, and that they'd once again be as happy as before, if not more so. When her husband came home, she was to see to it that he lay down for a nap with his head in her lap. And the wise man had given her a knife, with which the hairs were to be cut.

The good woman, who loved her husband dearly, was deeply grieved at the estrangement that had come between them, and wanted more than anything in the world to return to the happy life they had known. And so she agreed and promised to do as she'd been told. She took the knife that the wicked hypocrite had brought for the purpose.

Then the false devotee returned to the husband, telling him she'd be very unhappy to see him die, and therefore couldn't conceal from him her knowledge that his wife wanted to kill him and run off with her lover. To be convinced that she was telling the truth, and that his wife and her lover were plotting to kill him that way, he should observe that as soon as he got home she would arrange for him to take a nap with his head on her lap; then, when he was asleep, she planned to slit his throat with a knife she had for the purpose.

When he heard this, the husband was very frightened. If he had been suspicious before because of the evil devotee's lying words, what she now told him worried him sick. He resolved to be on his guard and to put her words to the test. And he returned home. As soon as his wife saw him, she greeted him more cordially than on the last few days. She said he was working too hard without taking time off or relaxing. Now he should lie down near her with his head on her lap, and she'd louse him.

When the husband heard that, he firmly believed what the false devotee had said. To be sure of his wife's intentions, he lay down with his head on her lap, and started to pretend he was sleeping. When his wife thought he was fast asleep, she took out the knife to cut off the hairs as the false devotee had instructed. Seeing the knife in her hand near his throat, the man was sure the false devotee had told him the truth. He wrested the knife from his wife's hand and slit her throat with it.

Hearing the racket that was made when she was murdered, the woman's father and brothers came running. When they found her with her throat cut, never having heard her husband or anyone else say a bad word about her, in their great anger they all attacked the husband and killed him. Hearing *that* uproar, the husband's relatives came running and killed the killers of their kinsman. And the whole affair concluded that day with the slaughter of most of the inhabitants of that city.

And all this came about through the lying words of that evil hypocrite. But, because God never allows an evil-doer to escape scot-free, or an evil deed to remain concealed, He brought it to the public's attention that all that misfortune had been caused by the false devotee. She was subjected to many severe tortures and executed in a painful and cruel way.

71. True Spanish Chivalry and Loyalty

My lord Count (Patronio said), Count Rodrigo el Franco[4] was married to the daughter of Don Gil García of Sagra. Though she was a very good woman, the count, her husband, brought false witness against her. Grieved at this, she prayed to God to punish her miraculously if she was guilty, or else to do the same to her husband if he was accusing her falsely.

At the end of her prayer, by a miracle of God the count, her husband, contracted leprosy, and she divorced him. After their separation, the king of Navarre sent envoys to the lady and she married him, becoming queen of Navarre.

The count, finding himself an incurable leper, departed as a pilgrim for the Holy Land, intending to die there. Though he was greatly honored and had many staunch vassals, only three knights went with him: Don Pedro Núñez of Fuente Almejir, Don Ruy González of Cevallos, and Don Gutierre Roy of Blaguiello. They were there so long that the supplies they had brought from home ran out and they fall into such dire poverty that they had nothing to give their lord, the count, to eat. Because of their straitened circumstances, two of them hired themselves out as day laborers every day at the marketplace, while one remained with the count. From what they earned from their hire they supported their lord and themselves. Every night they bathed the count, cleansing his leprous sores.

It came about that, while washing his feet and legs one night, by chance they needed to spit, and did so. The count, seeing them all spitting, thought it was due to their disgust with him. He began to weep and complain of the great sorrow and distress his affliction had occasioned him.

To convince the count that his ailment didn't disgust them, they gathered up handfuls of that water, which was full of the pus and scabs from the count's leprosy sores, and drank a good deal of it. Spending their days with their lord, the count, in that manner, they remained with him until he died.

Because they felt it would be improper to return to Castile without their master, dead or alive, they were unwilling to leave without him. Though they were advised to have his flesh boiled away so they would only need to take along his bones, they likewise refused to let anyone lay a hand on their lord, even dead. So they didn't allow him to be boiled, but buried him and waited for all his flesh to decompose. They put the bones in a small coffer, which they carried on their back, taking turns.

And so they journeyed, begging for their food, carrying their master on their back, but bearing official testimonials to everything that had befallen them. Traveling in such poverty, though healthy, they reached the lands of the count of Tolosa. Arriving in a city there, they came across a multitude

---

[4]The characters in this story are historical figures of the 12th century.

of people who were taking a lady out to be burned because she had been accused by a brother of her husband. An announcement had been made that, unless some knight saved her, her sentence would be carried out, but no knight could be found to champion her.

When Don Pedro Núñez, "the loyal," he of happy memory, heard that the lady was to be executed for lack of a champion, he told his comrades that, if he knew the lady was guiltless, he would save her. He went straight over to the lady and asked her for the true facts. She said that, for a certainty, she had never committed the crime she was accused of, but that she had wanted to do so.

Don Pedro Núñez realized that, since she had desired to do something she shouldn't, it was unavoidable that anyone trying to help her would suffer some harm. Nevertheless, since he had taken the first step, and since he knew that she hadn't actually gone through with the crime she was accused of, he promised to save her.

Though the accusers thought they could get rid of him by affirming that he wasn't a knight, he showed them the testimonials he was carrying, and they couldn't gainsay him. The lady's relatives gave him a horse and armor. Before he entered the lists, he told her relatives that, with God's aid, he would come out with honors and save the lady, but that he would inevitably meet some misfortune because of what the lady had desired to do.

After the combatants entered the lists, God aided Don Pedro Núñez, who won the fight and saved the lady. But he lost an eye in doing so, and thus everything Don Pedro Núñez had said before entering combat came true. The lady and her relatives gave Don Pedro Núñez enough money for him and his comrades to be able to bring home the bones of their lord, the count, with somewhat fewer hardships than before.

When the king of Castile heard the news that those doughty knights were returning with the bones of their lord, the count, and were in such good health, he was very pleased and gave sincere thanks to God because it was subjects of his who had performed such a feat. He sent them orders to come to him on foot, dressed just as poorly as they were. On the day they were to enter his kingdom of Castile, the king went out to greet them before they reached his borders, and he walked some five leagues to do so. He heaped such great honors upon them that the gifts they received from the king are still being handed down from each of their heirs to the next.

The king and everyone with him honored the count, and especially those knights, by escorting the count's bones all the way to Osma, where they were interred. After the interment, the knights returned to their homes.

On the day that Don Ruy González came home, when he sat down at table with his wife and that good lady saw the food in front of her, she raised her hands to God, saying:

"Blessed be the Lord, who has let me see this day! For You know, O

Lord, that ever since Don Ruy González left this land, this is the first meat I've eaten and the first wine I've drunk!"

Don Ruy González was unhappy to hear that, and asked her why she had done it. She said he ought to know why: When he left with the count, he had told her he'd never return without him, and he had asked her to live like an honorable lady, because there would never be a lack of bread and water in her house. Since he had put it that way, and she had no reason to disobey his orders, she had only partaken of bread and water.

Moreover, after Don Pedro Núñez arrived home, and he, his wife, and his relatives were left alone without any company, the good ladies and their kinsmen were so happy to have him back that they burst out laughing. Don Pedro Núñez, thinking they were laughing at him for having lost an eye, covered his head with his cape and went to bed feeling miserable. When the good lady saw how sad he was, she was very upset and kept after him until he admitted he was chagrined by their laughter over his lost eye.

Hearing this, the good lady plunged a needle into her eye, putting it out, and told Don Pedro Núñez she had done this so that, if she were ever to laugh, he would never think she was doing it to make fun of him.

And so God fully rewarded those loyal knights for the loyalty they had shown.

72. A Pact with the Devil

My lord Count (Patronio said), there was a man who had been very wealthy but had become so poor that he had nothing to live on. Because nothing in the world is so disheartening as being in dire straits after once enjoying prosperity, the formerly rich man suffered terribly from the plight he found himself in. One day he was walking alone through a forest, very sad and close to despair, when in his grief he met the Devil.

Though the Devil knows all things past, and was aware of that man's distress, he asked him why he felt so sad. The man asked what was the use of telling him, seeing that he couldn't give him a cure for his sadness. But the Devil said that, if the man followed his instructions, he would show him a way out of his troubles. To convince him of his power to do so, he would tell him what he was worrying about and the reason for his sadness.

Then the Devil told the man his whole story and the reason for his sorrow, because he knew it very well. He added that, if the man followed his instructions, he would rescue him from all his penury and make him wealthier than he, or any of his ancestors, had ever been before, because he was the Devil and had the power to do so.

When the man heard that he was conversing with the Devil, great fear came over him, but, because of his great woes and lack of funds, he told the Devil that, if he showed him how to get rich, he'd do anything he asked.

You may be sure that the Devil always seeks an opportunity to entrap people. When he finds them in some anxiety, through poverty, fear, or the desire to obtain something, he has his way with them to his heart's content. And so he now sought a way to ensnare that man, while he was immersed in sorrow.

Then they agreed to terms, and the man became the Devil's vassal. When the pact was concluded, the Devil told the man that, from that day on, he was to be a burglar. He would never find a door or house, no matter how securely locked, that he couldn't open at once. If, by chance, he ever found himself in a tight spot or was arrested, he should call upon him immediately, saying: "Help me quickly, Don Martín." The Devil would then appear at once and save him from the danger he was in. After the terms were settled, each went his own way.

The man headed for a merchant's house in the dead of night, for those with evil deeds in mind always shun the light. As soon as he reached the door, the Devil opened it for him, and he did the same with the money-boxes, so that he was able to take a large sum out of them right away.

The next day he pulled off another major burglary, and later another one, until he was so rich he no longer remembered his days of poverty. But the wretch, not satisfied with having escaped from want, started to steal even more. He kept at it until he got caught. The moment he was arrested, he called on Don Martín to help him. Don Martín showed up very quickly and freed him from jail. Now that the man saw that Don Martín was keeping his word to him so faithfully, he started to steal just as at the outset. He committed many burglaries, so that he became wealthier and free of money troubles.

During one attempted burglary, he was caught again, and called on Don Martín, but Don Martín didn't come as quickly as he would have liked, and the local magistrates indicted him for that burglary. When things had reached that point, Don Martín arrived, and the man said: "Oh, Don Martín! What a fright you gave me! Why did it take you so long?"

Don Martín replied that he had been tied up with other important business, which delayed him. Then he took him out of prison. The man continued to burglarize homes, and after many break-ins he was caught. At the trial he was found guilty. But after the guilty verdict was pronounced, Don Martín showed up and liberated him.

The man continued his career of burglary because he saw that Don Martín always helped him. Arrested once more, he called on Don Martín, but he didn't come, and he waited until the burglar had been sentenced to death. It was only after the sentencing that Don Martín arrived. The Devil appealed the man's case to the king's court, had him released from prison, and finally got him off.

Again he went back to his burglaries, again he was arrested, and again he called on Don Martín, who didn't arrive until after the man had been sentenced to be hanged and was already at the foot of the gallows. The man said: "Oh, Don Martín! Let me tell you, this was no joke! I assure you I got a bad scare!"

Don Martín said he had brought him five hundred *maravedís* in a purse. If he gave the money to the judge, he'd be set free at once. The judge had already ordered the hanging to begin, but no rope could be found for the purpose. While they were looking for a rope, the burglar called over the judge and gave him the purse with the money. The judge, thinking he was getting five hundred *maravedís*, addressed the bystanders:

"My friends, it's unheard of that a rope for hanging a man should be missing! Without a doubt, this man is not guilty, and God doesn't want him to die. That's why we have no rope. Let's put him back in jail until tomorrow and look into this case further. If he's guilty, he'll still be there tomorrow for justice to be carried out."

The judge was doing this in order to free the man in return for the five hundred *maravedís* he thought he had given him. When all had agreed, the judge withdrew to a private spot and opened the purse. Thinking he'd find the five hundred *maravedís* in it, he found, not the money, but a rope. The moment he saw that, he ordered the man hanged.

When the man was about to be strung up, Don Martín appeared, and the man asked him to rescue him. But Don Martín said that he always helped each of his friends until he brought them to a similar end.

And so that man lost both body and soul by believing and trusting the Devil. You can be sure that no one ever believed and trusted him without coming to a bad end. If you're not convinced, just look at all the soothsayers, fortune tellers, and seers, or the people who draw magic circles, cast spells, and the like, and you'll find that they've always ended up badly. If you don't believe me, remember Álvar Núñez de Castro and Garcilaso de la Vega,[5] who were the world's greatest believers in omens and similar things, and recall how they ended up.

---

[5]Contemporaries, and political enemies, of the author, Juan Manuel.

STORIES 73–77

From *Il Pecorone*
by Giovanni Fiorentino

Among the 14th-century Italian story collections inspired by Boccaccio's rapidly renowned *Decameron* (ca. 1350), *Il Pecorone* is particularly significant, and is often mentioned as a direct source for Shakespeare's *Merchant of Venice*. Yet, aside from that one source story (No. 73), it remains a rare and elusive work.*

Much of our information about the author, date, and title comes from the sonnet that introduces the work (translated here as prose): "One thousand three hundred and seventy-eight was truly the year in which this book was begun, written, and arranged as you see it, by me, *ser* Giovanni. It cost me few pains to baptize it, because a gentleman dear to me gave it its title, and it is called *Pecoron* ["big sheep, ram"; also means "fool; spineless person"] because there are new kinds of dolts in it. And I am the head of that company, I who bleat like a *pecorone* and write books though I don't know the first thing about it. Let's assume that I write this one at such a time and in such a way that it does honor to my name, which will be honored by coarse, boorish people. Don't be surprised at this, reader, because the book is of the same nature as its author."

It is not difficult to read this as humorous self-deprecation by the author, but some scholars have considered the sonnet to be an addition by a disgruntled reader.

In his prose introduction, *ser* Giovanni states that he is a man who has suffered, and now wants to spread joy by way of the stories that follow.

The *Pecorone* has an elaborate frame story (including lyric poems) clearly inspired by the *Decameron*. A well-bred youth named Auretto becomes a friar upon learning that his beloved has entered a convent. They meet in her parlatory, and for twenty-five days each of them tells a story. Of these fifty stories, one is taken from the *Decameron*, and thirty-two are directly based on incidents in the famous history of Florence by Giovanni Villani (ca. 1275–1348). (Probably, this relative lack of originality has kept the *Pecorone* from being widely known in its entirety.)

The stories in the *Pecorone* concern love and adventure. There are tragic and comic ones, realistic and fanciful ones. The style is plain and lucid, and the narra-

---

*No complete edition was available to the translator (if any such edition exists), who was thus unable to supply the original story numbers in his list of sources (with one exception). He found the original text of the stories translated here (and the introductory sonnet) in two rare Italian-language anthologies in his personal library, and derived more background information from large Italian encyclopedias and manuals of literary history.

tive flow is well managed, though typical medieval prolixity can sometimes irritate an impatient modern reader.

Beyond the slightest doubt, No. 73 is the prize of the collection. A comparison with the very similar No. 20, from the *Dolopathos*, is highly instructive. (This is the only instance in this anthology of two versions of the same basic plot being included, though there are many such doublets among the ten story collections represented.) In both stories, the contract calling for a certain amount of flesh to be sacrificed upon default is connected with the wooing of a beautiful noble or royal maiden who outwits her suitors by unfair means. In both stories, the heartless creditor is subdued by that same woman disguised as a man skilled in law. But, in No. 73, the setting of the contract is already Venice, the lady's home is called Belmonte, the debt is contracted by a friend for the suitor's sake, the amount of flesh stipulated is exactly one pound, and the creditor is now a Jew! (The *Gesta Romanorum* has a version that is much closer to No. 20 than to No. 73.)

No. 74 combines several interesting elements. Master Alain's speaking at the papal council from within his abbot's robes is reminiscent of the very widespread folktale motif of the riddle-solver disguised as one of his superiors (the last riddle is always "What am I thinking?" and the answer is "You think you're talking to X, but you're not"). Alain's disappointment with Rome is a distinct echo of the second story of the First Day in the *Decameron*, though in that case the shock caused by the unholy state of the Holy City leads to a very different outcome. (In both stories, the visitor to Rome is coming from Paris!)

No. 75 recounts a medieval vendetta combining brutality and refinement.

No. 76 falls into two separate parts. The first part is a version of the universal folktale motif of the ardent young man who manages to enter a heavily guarded maiden's living quarters (compare "Rapunzel"); in this case there is a strong *Arabian Nights* flavor to the proceedings. The second part reports a pan-European war unrecorded in sober history. Despite the fantasy (certain of the alliances would have been impossible during the real Hundred Years' War of the author's time), there is a certain amount of real observation of history, geography, and heraldry.

No. 77 is another example of the antifeminism that was so fashionable in the Middle Ages.

73. The Pound of Flesh

There was a merchant of the house of the Scali in Florence named Bindo. He had traveled several times to Azov on the Don, to Alexandria, and on all those faraway mercantile routes. This Bindo, who was quite wealthy, had three grown sons. When he felt death approaching, he summoned the two eldest and dictated his will in their presence. He left them heirs to everything he had in the world, leaving nothing to the youngest son. After he made this will, the youngest son, who was called Giannetto, heard about it and went to his bedside, saying: "Father, I'm greatly surprised at what you've done, not remembering me in your will."

His father replied: "My Giannetto, there's not a living being that I care for more than you, and yet I don't want you to remain here after my death;

no, after I'm dead, I want you to go to Venice to your godfather named Master Ansaldo. He has no son, and has sent me a number of letters asking me to send you to him. Let me tell you, he's the wealthiest merchant in Christendom today. So I want you to go to him when I die, and take him this letter. If you act wisely, you'll become a rich man."

His son said: "Father, I'm ready to carry out your orders." Then his father gave him his blessing. He died a few days later, and all his sons mourned him deeply and gave him a fittingly honorable funeral. A few days after that, the two eldest sons summoned Giannetto and said:

"Brother, it's true that our father made a will, in which he left us heirs without mentioning you at all. Nevertheless, you're our brother, and so we feel you're entitled to a share."

Giannetto replied: "Brothers, I thank you for your offer, but as for me, I'm determined to seek my own fortune, wherever that may be. I've made my mind up, so you keep the inheritance, and may it do you good!" His brothers, finding him determined, gave him a horse and money for expenses. Giannetto took leave of them, journeyed to Venice, and arrived at Master Ansaldo's warehouse. He handed him the letter his father had given him before dying.

Reading this letter, Master Ansaldo learned that he had before him the son of his very dear friend Bindo. When he had finished reading, he quickly embraced him, saying: "Welcome, my son, whom I have so longed for!" Right away he asked him about Bindo, and Giannetto reported his death; whereupon the older man shed many tears, hugged and kissed him, and said: "You see, I'm sorely grieved at Bindo's death, because he helped me acquire a large part of what I possess. But I'm so happy to have you here, that my grief is lessened."

He had him led to his home, and instructed his stewards, associates, grooms, and servants, and everyone in the house, to obey and serve Giannetto even better than they served *him*. First, he entrusted him with the keys to all his valuables, saying: "My son, everything here is yours. From now on, dress as you please, invite citizens to dinner, and make yourself known. I leave that up to you, and the finer figure you cut, the more I'll like you."

And so Giannetto began to keep company with the gentlefolk of Venice, offering suppers and dinners, giving charity, keeping liveried servants, buying pedigreed horses, and participating in jousts and similar sports. In all things he was knowledgeable, handy, generous, and courteous, well able to honor and entertain the proper people. He always respected Master Ansaldo more than if he had been his father a hundred times over.

He got along so wisely with all manner of folk that practically the whole city of Venice liked him, finding him so wise, good-natured, and impeccably courteous. So, both women and men were fascinated by him, and he was Master Ansaldo's all-in-all, so greatly did his godfather love his nature and behavior. There was virtually no party in Venice to which Giannetto wasn't invited, he was so well liked by everyone.

Now, it came about that two of his closest friends intended to go to Alexandria on their two ships with their merchandise, as they did every year. They asked Giannetto if he wanted to go along for the pleasure of seeing something of the world, especially Damascus and the adjacent lands. Giannetto replied: "By my faith, I'd really like to, if my father Master Ansaldo gave me permission."

His friends said: "We'll see to it that he lets you go, and that he'll be glad of it." They went at once to Master Ansaldo and said: "We urge you to be so good as to allow Giannetto to come with us to Alexandria this spring. Please furnish him with some vessel or ship, so he can see a little of the world."

Master Ansaldo replied: "It's all right with me if that's what he wants."

They rejoined: "Sir, he really wants to go!" And so, at once Master Ansaldo had a very beautiful ship fitted out for him, loaded with a large quantity of goods, and provided with flags and as much weaponry as necessary. When the ship was ready, Master Ansaldo instructed the captain and crew to obey Giannetto's orders and to take good care of him, because he wasn't sending him with any view toward making a profit, but so he could enjoy himself and see the world.

When Giannetto was ready to set sail, all of Venice assembled to see him off, because it had been a long time since such a beautiful and well-equipped vessel had left Venice. Everyone was sad to see him go. He took leave of Master Ansaldo and all his friends. They put out to sea, hoisted sail, and headed for Alexandria, praying to God and hoping for good fortune.

Now, the three friends were on three separate ships. After they had sailed for several days, it came about that, one morning, before daylight, Giannetto looked out and saw a beautiful harbor in a bay. He asked the captain what it was called. The captain replied: "Sir, that place belongs to a noble widow who has brought many gentlemen to their ruin."

Giannetto asked: "How so?"

The captain said: "Sir, she's a beautiful, charming lady who has established as a law in her territory that any man arriving there must go to bed with her. If he succeeds in copulating with her, he must marry her and become lord of the whole country. If he doesn't, he loses everything he owns."

Giannetto thought this over for a while, then said: "By any means you choose, get me to that harbor!"

The captain said: "Sir, watch what you're saying, because many gentlemen have gone there, and have either lost their property or died."

Giannetto said: "Don't trouble yourself about such things, but do what I tell you!" His order was obeyed: the ship immediately changed course and put in at that harbor before Giannetto's friends on the other ships were aware of a thing. And so, in the morning the news spread that a beautiful ship lay in the harbor. It was so fine a vessel that everyone went to see it. A report was immediately made to the lady, who sent for Giannetto. He came to her at once and greeted her with the greatest respect. She took him by the hand, and asked him his name and land of origin, and whether he was aware of the local custom. Giannetto replied that he *was* aware of it, and had come for no other reason.

The lady said: "Then I welcome you a hundred times over." All that day she entertained him sumptuously, inviting barons, counts, and knights who were her vassals to keep him company. Giannetto's ways pleased all those noblemen, he was so polite, good-natured, and well-spoken. Everyone became quite fond of him. All that day there was dancing and singing, and a party was held in the court in Giannetto's honor. They would all have been glad to have him as their lord.

Now, when night fell, the lady took him by the hand and led him to her bedroom, saying: "I think it's time to go to bed."

Giannetto replied: "Lady, I'm at your beck and call!" When they were in the bedroom, two maids came in, one with wine, the other with sweetmeats.

The lady said: "I know you've grown thirsty, so have a drink." Giannetto ate some tidbits and drank of that wine, which contained a sleeping drug, though he didn't know it. He drank a half-gobletful because he liked the taste. Then he quickly undressed and got into bed. The moment he lay down, he fell asleep. The lady stretched out beside him, but he didn't wake up until after nine in the morning. The lady got up at daybreak and ordered her people to unload the ship, which she found to be full of costly and valuable goods. When the ninth hour had passed, the lady's chambermaids went to the bed where Giannetto was sleeping, made him get up, and told him to be on his way, because he had lost his ship and everything in it. He was ashamed, and felt he had made a big mistake.

The lady had him given a horse and money for expenses. He mounted the horse, miserably unhappy, and set out for Venice. Arriving there, he was too ashamed to dismount at Master Ansaldo's house. At night he went to the home of a friend, who was greatly surprised and said: "Oh, my! Giannetto, what's all this?"

He replied: "One night my ship hit a reef and broke up. Everything got smashed, and the people got separated. I clung to a piece of wood that cast me up on shore; then I got all the way back here by land." He remained for several days in the home of that friend, who paid a visit to Master Ansaldo one day and found him very downhearted. "What's the matter?" he asked. "What makes you so melancholy?"

Master Ansaldo said: "I'm in such great fear that my son may be dead or suffering from some disaster at sea, that I don't know what to do with myself. I won't rest till I see him again, because I love him so very much."

The young man said: "I can give you news of him. He was shipwrecked and lost everything but his life."

Master Ansaldo said: "God be praised! As long as he's alive, I'm happy. I don't care about the possessions he lost. Where is he?"

The young man replied: "He's in my house." At once Master Ansaldo became agitated, and wanted to go and see him. At the first sight of him, he ran over and hugged him, saying:

"My son, there's no need for you to feel ashamed to see me. It's a normal thing for ships to be wrecked at sea, so don't be dismayed, son. I'm so glad that nothing happened to you personally!" He brought him home, comforting him all the while. The news spread through Venice, and everyone was sorry for Giannetto's loss.

Now, it came about shortly thereafter that those friends of his returned from Alexandria with great wealth. On their arrival they asked about Giannetto and were told his story. They ran at once to greet him, saying: "How did you separate from us, and where did you go? We were unable to find out anything about you. We turned back all that day, but we couldn't see you or learn where you had gone. We were so upset over it that we were unable to cheer up again during the entire journey, since we thought you were dead."

Giannetto said: "A wind blew in our teeth when we were in view of some bay, and it carried my ship, head on, onto an offshore reef. I barely escaped with my life, and everything else capsized." That was the excuse Giannetto gave to avoid revealing his error in judgment.

He and his friends celebrated together, thanking God for having at least saved his life. They said: "Next spring, God willing, we'll make up the amount you lost this time, so now let's just enjoy ourselves and not be gloomy." And so they concentrated on fun and good times, as they had been accustomed to do earlier.

And yet, Giannetto's sole thought was of how he could return to that lady. As he mused he said to himself: "I definitely must win her for my wife, or else die there!" He could scarcely cheer up.

And so Master Ansaldo frequently said to him: "Don't be gloomy. We own so much that we can live very easily."

Giannetto replied: "My lord, I'll never be happy if I don't make that journey again." When Master Ansaldo realized how determined he was, at the right season he loaded another ship with much more, and more valuable, merchandise than the first one. They made such an early start that, by departure time, the ship was completely fitted out. Master Ansaldo loaded it with a very large part of his possessions. When Giannetto's friends had furnished their own ships with everything necessary, they and Giannetto put out to sea, spread sail, and commenced their voyage.

While they sailed for a number of days, Giannetto was always on the lookout for that lady's harbor, which was called the Port of the Lady of

Belmonte. Arriving one night at the entrance to that harbor, which was located in that bay, Giannetto recognized it at once. He had the sails and the rudder turned and entered port before his friends on the other ships noticed.

When the lady rose next morning and looked down at the harbor, she saw that ship's flags flapping in the breeze and recognized them on the spot. Summoning one of her maids, she said: "Do you recognize those flags?"

The maid said: "My lady, it looks like the ship of that young man who arrived here a year ago, and left so much valuable merchandise here."

The lady said: "You're certainly right. In truth, this is a rare occasion. He must be in love with me, because I've never seen any other man come back a second time."

The maid said: "I've never seen one more courteous and gracious than he is." The lady sent many pages and servants to meet him. They greeted him heartily, and he was very delighted to see all of them. And so, he ascended to the castle and into the lady's presence. When she saw him, she embraced him heartily and cheerfully, and he very respectfully embraced her. And so they remained all that day in great cheer, because the lady sent invitations to many noblemen and ladies, who came to the court to celebrate Giannetto's return.

Almost all the noblemen were sorry for his misadventure, and would gladly have received him as their lord, because he was so good-natured and courteous. As for the ladies, they were almost all in love with him, seeing how skillfully he led a dance and how cheerful his face always was, making everyone believe he was the son of some great lord.

When it was time to go to bed, the lady took Giannetto by the hand and said: "Let's get some rest." They went to her bedroom and sat down, when two maids brought wine and sweetmeats. They ate and drank, then went to bed. As soon as he lay down, he fell asleep. The lady undressed and stretched out beside him, but, in short, he didn't wake up all night.

In the morning, the lady arose and immediately ordered the ship unloaded. After nine, Giannetto awoke, looked for the lady, but failed to find her. He raised his head and saw that the morning was well advanced. He got up, feeling ashamed. Again, he was given a horse and money for expenses, and told: "On your way!" He departed at once, plunged into melancholy.

He kept going for days and days without stopping, until he reached Venice. At night he went to that same friend's house. When his friend saw him, he was completely amazed, and said: "Oh, my! What's all this?"

Giannetto replied: "Things are bad with me. I curse Fortune for ever bringing me to this city!"

His friend said: "You may very well curse it, because you've ruined Master Ansaldo, who was the greatest and richest merchant in

Christendom. But the disgrace is worse than the loss." Giannetto lay concealed in his friend's house for several days, not knowing what to do or say. He almost decided to return to Florence without telling Master Ansaldo anything, but then he made up his mind to go to him, and he did.

When Master Ansaldo saw him, he stood up, ran over to embrace him, and said: "Welcome, my son!" Giannetto, in tears, embraced him. After hearing the young man's story, Master Ansaldo said: "Do you know what, Giannetto? Don't be dismayed in the least. As long as I've got you back, I'm happy. We've got enough money left to live on modestly. It's the way of the sea to give to some people and take away from others." News of this event spread through Venice. Everyone spoke about Master Ansaldo and regretted the loss he had suffered.

Master Ansaldo had to sell many of his possessions to repay the creditors who had supplied the merchandise. It came about that Giannetto's two friends returned from Alexandria with great wealth. Arriving in Venice and hearing that Giannetto was back after another wreck, in which he had lost everything, they were surprised, and said: "This is the strangest case ever known." They visited Master Ansaldo and Giannetto, whom they greeted warmly, saying to the older man: "Sir, don't be dismayed, because we intend to go out next year and make some money for you. We were practically responsible for your loss, because we were the ones who persuaded Giannetto to come with us at the beginning. And so, have no fear, because, as long as we own some merchandise, you can make use of it as if it were your own." Master Ansaldo thanked them, saying that he still had so much that they could safely remain at home.

Now, it came about that Giannetto, thinking about these things morning and night, was unable to cheer up. When Master Ansaldo asked him what was wrong, he said: "I'll never be happy if I don't recover my losses."

Master Ansaldo said: "My son, I don't want you to make another journey. It's better for us to live modestly on the little we have left than for you to risk it again."

Giannetto replied: "I'm determined to do all I can, because I'd consider myself thoroughly disgraced if I just sat at home like this." And so, seeing how determined he was, Master Ansaldo decided to sell off the rest of what he owned, in order to fit out another ship. He sold every last thing he had, and loaded a beautiful ship with merchandise.

Because he still needed another ten thousand florins, he went to a Jew in Mestre and borrowed the money on the following terms: If he didn't return it by Saint John's Day the following June, the Jew could remove a pound of flesh from any part of his body. Master Ansaldo agreed, and the Jew had a document drawn up with all due solemnity in the presence of witnesses, with all the sureties and formal procedures pertaining to such an arrangement. Then he counted out the ten thousand florins.

With that money Master Ansaldo supplied everything the ship still required. If the first two ships were beautiful, the third one was much cost-lier and better equipped. Giannetto's two friends also fitted out ships, in-tending to give all their profits to Giannetto. When it was time to depart and they were ready to set sail, Master Ansaldo said to Giannetto: "My son, you're going and you see the nature of my indebtedness. I ask you one favor: even if something happens to you, feel free to come and see me. If I can see you before I die, I'll be satisfied." Giannetto promised, and Master Ansaldo gave him his blessing. Then they said good-bye and the three friends set out on their journey.

Giannetto's two friends always kept an eye on his ship, but he was only awaiting the moment when he'd put in at the Belmonte harbor. He arranged with one of the seamen to bring the ship into the lady's harbor one night. When daylight came, his friends on the other two ships looked in every direction and, unable to find Giannetto's ship anywhere, they said: "This definitely means a misfortune for him." And they decided to con-tinue on their way, though they were dumbfounded and amazed.

Now, when Giannetto's ship arrived in port, the whole town came to see it, hearing that Giannetto was back. Very surprised at this, they said: "He must be the son of some great magnate, if he can come here annually with so much merchandise and such beautiful vessels! May God grant that he becomes our lord!" All the townspeople, noblemen, and knights in the city came to see him, and the lady was informed that he was back in port.

She looked out her palace windows, saw the beautiful ship, and recog-nized its flags. Crossing herself, she said: "This is without a doubt a great marvel. This is the man who's made this country rich." She sent for Giannetto and, when he arrived, they greeted each other with many hugs and displays of mutual respect. The whole day was occupied with joy and feasting. In Giannetto's honor a fine joust was held, in which many noble-men and knights took part that day. Giannetto himself participated and performed wonderful feats that day, so well did he wield his weapons and sit his horse. His prowess was so pleasing to all the noblemen that they all desired him to be their ruler.

Now, night fell and it was time for bed. The lady took Giannetto by the hand and said: "Let's get some rest." At the door to the bedroom one of her ladies-in-waiting, who felt sorry for Giannetto, put her lips to his ear and whispered: "Pretend to be drinking, but don't drink anything tonight." Giannetto understood her words and went into the bedroom.

The lady said: "I know you've gotten thirsty, and so I'd like you to have a drink before you go to bed." At once two young women, who resembled two angels, arrived with wine and sweetmeats as usual, and poured Giannetto a drink.

Giannetto said: "Who could refrain from drinking, seeing these two lovely damsels?" This made the lady laugh. Giannetto picked up the gob-let and pretended to drink, but really spilled the wine inside his shirt. The

lady, who thought he had drunk it up, said to herself: "Come back with another ship, because you've lost this one!"

Giannetto lay down on the bed, feeling altogether clear-headed and
ready for action. It felt like an eternity to him before the lady came to bed,
and he said to himself: "I've definitely won her now! 'The roguish customer
has one idea, and the tavernkeeper has another!'" To induce the lady to
come to bed sooner, he began pretending to snore as if he were fast asleep.

And so the lady said: "You're just where I want you!" And she immediately got undressed and lay down alongside Giannetto. He didn't wait a
second; the moment she was between the sheets, he turned to her, embraced her, and said: "Now I have what I've been yearning for all this
time!" Thereupon he inducted her into holy matrimony. She was never
out of his arms all night long. And she was contented.

She arose briskly before daylight the next morning, summoned all her
noblemen and knights, and many other subjects, and announced:
"Giannetto is your liege lord, and so celebrate!" The shout of "Long live
our master, long live our master!" spread rapidly through town. The
church bells rang and bands played, signaling the festivities. Many barons
and counts who were away from the castle were summoned with the
words: "Come and meet your liege lord!" And a great, wonderful celebration began.

When Giannetto left the bedroom, he was knighted and seated on the
throne. The scepter was placed in his hand, and he was named ruler for
life with great triumph and glory. After all the noblemen and ladies had arrived in the court, he married that lady with pomp and joy that can't be described or even imagined. All the noblemen and lords in the country came
to the celebration to make merry, joust, tourney, dance, sing, play music,
and indulge in all the activities that go with such a wedding.

Giannetto generously made them presents of silk textiles and other valuable goods he had brought. He began to assert his manliness, making himself feared and dispensing right and justice to all classes of people. And so
he remained in that euphoric state, forgetting completely about poor
Master Ansaldo, who had pledged his body to that Jew for the ten thousand
florins.

Now, when Sir Giannetto was at the window of his palace with his lady
one day, he saw a group of men passing through the square with small
lighted torches in their hands, on their way to make an offering. Sir
Giannetto said: "What does that mean?"

His wife replied: "They're an association of artisans on their way to make
an offering at the Church of Saint John, because today is his feast day."
Then Sir Giannetto remembered Master Ansaldo. He got up from the window seat, heaved a mighty sigh, and turned pale. He walked to and fro in
the room several times, thinking the matter over. His wife asked him what
was wrong.

When Sir Giannetto said nothing was the matter, his wife started to prod, saying: "Of course something is wrong with you, but you don't want to tell me." She kept on until Sir Giannetto recounted the entire affair, especially how Master Ansaldo had pledged his body for ten thousand florins:

"Today is the deadline," he said, "and so I'm greatly saddened that my father must die for my sake. Because, if he doesn't return the money today, he has to lose a pound of flesh."

His wife said: "My lord, mount a horse at once and go by way of land, which is quicker than the sea route! Take along as many companions as you like, and bring a hundred thousand florins, and don't stop till you reach Venice. If he's not dead, arrange to bring him here." And so he immediately had the trumpets sounded and mounted his horse, taking twenty companions and carrying a large quantity of money. He said good-bye and galloped off in the direction of Venice.

Now, it came about that, the deadline having passed, the Jew had Master Ansaldo seized and kept him in confinement. He then claimed his right to remove a pound of flesh from him. Master Ansaldo begged him to be so kind as to postpone his death for a few days, so he could at least see his Giannetto if he came. The Jew said: "I'm willing to grant your request for the postponement, but, even if he arrives a hundred times, I intend to take a pound of flesh from you, as our contract stipulates." Master Ansaldo replied: "All right."

And so, all of Venice was discussing the affair. It made everyone sad, and many merchants got together and offered to repay the money. But the Jew steadfastly refused, preferring to commit that murder so he could say he had killed the greatest merchant in Christendom.

Now, it came about that, while Sir Giannetto was racing toward Venice, his lady quickly set out behind him, dressed as a judge, and taking along two servants. When Sir Giannetto arrived in Venice, he went to the Jew's house and happily embraced Master Ansaldo. Then he told the Jew he wanted to return the money and add some more on his own account. The Jew replied that he didn't want the money, since he hadn't received it on time, but wanted his pound of flesh.

This led to a general discussion, in which everyone found fault with the Jew. But, since Venice is a law-respecting land, and the Jew had perfectly legal claims and documents, no one dared to stand up against him; they merely pleaded with him. And so, every merchant in Venice came there to plead with the Jew, but he only became increasingly obdurate. Sir Giannetto was ready to give him twenty thousand, but he refused. Then he increased his offer to thirty, forty, and fifty thousand, finally going up to a hundred thousand florins.

Whereupon the Jew said: "Do you want to know where I stand? Even if you gave me more than this city is worth, I wouldn't take it in return for this pleasure. No, I want to abide by the contract!"

When things had reached this pass the lady dressed like a judge arrived in Venice and stopped at an inn. The innkeeper asked one of her servants: "Who is this gentleman?"

The servant, who had been instructed by the lady as to what he should say if questioned about her, replied: "He's a noble judge returning home from the university in Bologna."

Hearing this, the innkeeper welcomed her respectfully. When they were eating, the judge asked the innkeeper: "How is this city of yours governed?"

Her host replied: "By law, sir, and too much so!"

The judge said: "How is that?"

The host said: "Sir, I'll tell you what I mean. A young man named Giannetto came here from Florence to stay with his godfather, Master Ansaldo. He was so charming and well-mannered that both the men and the women of this city were fond of him. No one else ever came here who was equally gracious. Now, on three occasions his godfather fitted out ships for him, each cargo being of enormous value, and each time he met up with disaster, so that after the last ship their money was gone. And so, Master Ansaldo borrowed ten thousand florins from a Jew, pledging to pay it back by Saint John's Day the following June, or else allow the Jew to take a pound of flesh from any part of his body that he wished. Now that blessed young man is back, and has offered a hundred thousand in place of the ten thousand, but the perfidious Jew refuses. He's been pleaded with by all the good men in this city, but nothing does any good."

The judge replied: "This case is easily decided."

The host said: "If you're willing to take the trouble to settle it, so this good man need not die, you'll gain the favor and affection of the most virtuous young man ever born, and those of everyone in this city."

Thereupon the judge issued a proclamation throughout the city, that anyone who had a legal problem to be decided should come to him. Sir Giannetto was informed that a judge had arrived from Bologna who could settle any case. And so, Sir Giannetto said to the Jew: "Let's go to this judge that I hear has arrived."

The Jew said: "Let's go! But, no matter who comes, by law I'll get what I contracted for!" When they came before the judge and paid him due homage, the judge recognized Sir Giannetto at once, but Sir Giannetto didn't recognize his wife, because she had altered her face with certain herbs. Sir Giannetto and the Jew each stated his case, explaining the dispute clearly to the judge.

The judge took the contract and read it, then said to the Jew: "I want you to take the hundred thousand florins and set this good man free, and he'll always be obliged to you for it."

The Jew said: "I'll do nothing of the sort."

The judge said: "It's in your own best interest." But the Jew said he absolutely refused. The judge said: "All right, call him in and take the pound of flesh from wherever you like." The Jew sent for Master Ansaldo. When he arrived, the judge said: "Do your business." The Jew had him stripped naked, picked up a razor he had had made for the purpose, and walked up to him, ready to take hold of him.

But Sir Giannetto turned to the judge, saying: "Your honor, this is not what I was asking you for."

The judge replied: "Don't interfere. Leave it to me, because he hasn't removed the pound of flesh yet." Still, seeing the Jew laying hands on Master Ansaldo, the judge said: "Be careful how you do it! Because, if you take more or less than a pound, I'll have your head cut off. Furthermore I tell you that, if even one drop of blood is spilt, I'll have you executed, because your contract makes no mention of bloodshed. All it says is that you may take a pound of flesh, neither more nor less. And so, if you're wise, behave in the way you consider most advantageous to you."

She immediately summoned the executioner, ordering him to bring the block and the axe, then she said: "The moment I see a drop of blood, I'll have you decapitated."

The Jew began to be afraid, and Sir Giannetto began to take heart. After a further discussion, the Jew said: "Your honor, you've outsmarted me. Let me have the hundred thousand florins and I'll be satisfied."

The judge replied: "I want you to take the pound of flesh stipulated by your contract, and I'm not letting you have a penny. You should have taken the money when I urged you to!" The Jew reduced his demand to ninety thousand, then to eighty thousand, but the judge stood pat.

Sir Giannetto said to the judge: "Let him have what he wants, as long as he releases Master Ansaldo!"

The judge rejoined: "I've asked you to leave it to me!"

Then the Jew said: "Give me fifty thousand."

The judge replied: "I wouldn't give you the most miserable penny you ever owned."

The Jew said: "At least give me back my ten thousand florins, with a curse on land and sky!"

The judge said: "Don't you understand me? I'm not giving you anything. If you want to take the pound of flesh, take it. If not, I'll contest the document and have it nullified."

And so all those present were very happy, and they made fun of the Jew, saying: "The man who tries to cheat others gets cheated himself!" When the Jew realized that he couldn't achieve his purpose, he seized his contract and tore it to bits in his rage. And so Master Ansaldo was set free and brought home in jubilation by Sir Giannetto.

Then Sir Giannetto hastily took the hundred thousand florins and went to the judge's inn, finding "him" in "his" room making ready for departure. Then Sir Giannetto said: "Your honor, you've done me the greatest service

I've ever received, and so I want you to take this money home. You've richly earned it!"

The judge replied: "My good Sir Giannetto, thank you, but I don't need it. Hold onto it, so your wife doesn't say you've squandered it."

Sir Giannetto said: "By my faith, she's so generous, courteous, and noble that, if I spent four times as much, she'd be contented, because she wanted me to take along much more than this."

The judge asked: "Are you happy with her?"

Sir Giannetto replied: "There's not a living being I love better, because she's as wise and beautiful a woman as nature could possibly produce. If you were to do me the great favor of coming to visit her, you'd be amazed at the fine reception you'd get, and you'd see whether I was telling the truth, or even falling short of it."

The judge replied: "I'm unable to accompany you because of other urgent business, but since you say she's so wonderful, greet her for me when you see her."

Sir Giannetto said: "I will! But I want you to take this money."

While he was saying that, the judge saw a ring on his finger, and said: "I don't want any money, but I'd like this ring."

Sir Giannetto said: "All right, but I'm reluctant to give it to you, because it was a gift from my wife, who told me to wear it always for her sake. If she sees me without it, she'll think I've given it to some woman, and she'll get angry with me, imagining that I've fallen in love. And I love her more than I love myself!"

The judge said: "I'm sure that she loves you so much, she'll believe you. Tell her you gave it to *me*. But maybe you wanted to give it to some old flame here?"

Sir Giannetto replied: "I love her so, and I'm so faithful to her, that I wouldn't exchange her for any woman in the world, she's so totally beautiful in every way." He removed the ring from his finger and gave it to the judge. Then they hugged and paid their respects to each other.

The judge said: "Do me a favor."

Sir Giannetto replied: "Just ask it."

The judge said: "Don't stay here. Go back to your wife soon."

Sir Giannetto said: "All the time I don't see her is like an eternity to me." Then they said good-bye. The judge embarked and departed. Sir Giannetto gave supper and dinner parties, made presents of horses and money to his companions, caroused, and held court for several days. Then he took leave of all the Venetians and brought Master Ansaldo along with him. Many of his old friends joined him, as well. Virtually every man and woman wept tenderly at his departure, he had behaved so kindly to everyone all the time he was in Venice. And so he left and returned to Belmonte.

Now, it came about that his wife got there several days before he did. She pretended she had been at the baths. She put on women's clothes again and prepared an elaborate reception, having all the streets covered with sendal and supplying uniforms to many companies of men-at-arms. When Sir Giannetto and Master Ansaldo arrived, all the noblemen and courtiers went out to meet them, crying: "Long live our lord, long live our lord!" When they set foot on the soil, the lady ran to embrace Master Ansaldo, but pretended to be a little angry with Sir Giannetto, whom she really loved better than herself.

A great celebration, with jousts, tourneys, dancing, and song, was made by all the noblemen, ladies, and damsels present. Sir Giannetto, seeing that his wife wasn't as pleased to see him as she usually was, went into their bedroom, sent for her, asked her what was wrong, and tried to hug her. The lady said: "You don't need to caress me. I know that, when you were in Venice, you looked up your old flames."

Sir Giannetto started to defend himself, but his wife said: "Where's the ring I gave you?"

Sir Giannetto replied: "It's happened just as I imagined! I said you'd get the wrong idea! But I swear to you, by my loyalty to God and to you, that I gave the ring to the judge who decided the case in my favor."

His wife said: "And I swear to you, by my loyalty to God and to you, that you gave it to a woman. I know so! Aren't you ashamed to perjure yourself?"

Sir Giannetto said: "I pray to God to remove me from the world if I'm not telling the truth! What's more, I told the judge all this would happen when he asked me for it."

His wife said: "You could have stayed back there and just sent Master Ansaldo here, so you could live it up with your girlfriends. I hear they all cried when you left."

Sir Giannetto began weeping and eating his heart out. He said: "You're swearing to something that's both untrue and impossible."

His wife, seeing him cry, felt as if she had been stabbed in the heart. At once she ran to embrace him, shaking with laughter. She showed him the ring and repeated everything he had said to the judge, because she had been that judge. Sir Giannetto was as surprised as could be, but seeing that it was true all the same, he felt greatly delighted. Leaving the room, he told the story to some of his vassals and friends.

In this way, the love that man and wife had for each other increased and multiplied. Later on, Sir Giannetto summoned the lady-in-waiting who had warned him not to drink the wine that night, and married her to Master Ansaldo. They all lived for years in mirth and delight, enjoying prosperity and good fortune.

74. A Lay Brother at the Pope's Council

Not long ago there lived in Paris two very eminent and capable men who were professors of both civil and canon law. One of them was named

Master Alain, the other Master Jean-Pierre. To tell the truth, there was no one else in Christendom at the time more capable than they were. The two of them took opposite sides on every issue, but Master Alain always won, because he was the greatest rhetorician in the world and pleaded with warmer feeling than Master Jean-Pierre. The latter was practically a heretic, and would have set our religion on its ear more than once, had not Master Alain championed it, rebutting all his opponent's objections.

It came about that Master Alain decided to come to Rome to visit the holy relics there, and to see the pope and his Curia. And so he set out with numerous well-equipped attendants, arrived in Rome, visited the pope, and saw the Curia and how it was governed. He was very surprised— reflecting that the Roman Curia ought to be the foundation of our religion and the support of Christianity—to find it so vice-ridden and a hotbed of simony. For that reason he left Rome and decided to give up secular life and devote himself to serving God.

Leaving Rome and traveling with his attendants, he said to them, when they were near San Chirico di Rosena: "You go ahead and take rooms at the inn, and leave me to myself awhile." The attendants proceeded on- ward, arriving at San Chirico. When Master Alain saw them go, he left the road and headed for the mountains, continuing to ride until finding a shepherd's hut in the evening. Master Alain dismounted, spent the night with the shepherd, and said to him in the morning: "I want to leave you my clothes and horse in exchange for your clothes."

The shepherd thought he was making fun of him, and said: "Sir, I've en- tertained you as best I could. Please don't make fun of me!" Master Alain took off his clothes and asked the shepherd to do the same. He left him his horse and all his belongings, taking the shepherd's clothes, shoes, and small keg. Then he set out at random.

When he failed to show up at the inn, his attendants went out looking for him. Not finding him, and knowing that the road wasn't safe, they sup- posed he had been robbed and killed. They remained where they were for a few days, then departed and returned to Paris.

Now, after Master Alain left the shepherd, he arrived in the evening at an abbey in a fenland. When he begged for some bread, the abbot asked him whether he wanted to stay there. Master Alain said yes. Asked by the abbot what work he could do, Master Alain replied: "My lord, I'll be able to do anything you teach me."

The abbot thought he was a good person. He took him in and sent him out for firewood. Master Alain did such good work that everyone in the abbey liked him: he followed orders cheerfully, never feeling bashful or flinching from hard work or from helping out with whatever needed to be done. Observing his humility, the abbot made him cellarer of the abbey (not knowing who he was) and gave him the name of Benedetto.

So he lived that life, fasting four days out of the week, never undressing, and remaining in prayer a large part of every night. He was never vexed by anything said or done to him, but continually praised Christ. He had determined to serve God in that way. And so, the abbot was very fond of him and held him very dear.

Now, it came about that, when his attendants returned to Paris and reported his death, he was sincerely mourned by all the professionals there, who felt that they had lost the world's greatest legal mind. But when Master Jean-Pierre heard about Master Alain's death, he was overjoyed, and said: "Now I can do what I've wanted to do for so long." He set his affairs in order and set out for Rome, where in the papal Consistory he enunciated a thesis that ran completely counter to our religion, in an attempt to infect God's Church with heresy by means of his wily maneuvers.

And so the pope convoked the college of cardinals, where the decision was made to summon all the knowledgeable men in Italy to a council the pope wished to hold to reply to the thesis that Master Jean-Pierre had enunciated contrary to our religion. And so every bishop, abbot, or other high prelate expert in canon law was summoned to the Curia. Among the others summoned was the abbot who had given shelter to Master Alain. When he was getting ready for the trip to Rome, Master Alain heard why he was going, and asked the abbot to do him the favor of taking him along.

The abbot said: "What do you expect to accomplish there? You don't even know how to read, and that council will be attended by the most learned lawyers in the world, who will converse exclusively in Latin, so you couldn't understand a thing they said!"

Master Alain replied: "My lord, at least I'll see the pope. I've never seen him, and I don't know what he looks like."

Finding him so determined, the abbot said: "It's all right with me if you come, but do you know how to manage a horse?" Master Alain said he did. When he was ready, the abbot set out, taking Master Alain along. In Rome a date was set for the council and it was announced that everyone could go and hear Master Jean-Pierre's thesis. Master Alain asked the abbot, as a favor, to take him along to the council meeting. The abbot said: "Are you crazy? How do you expect me to take you there, with the pope, the cardinals, and all the experts?"

Master Alain said: "I'll hide under your cloak, and no one will see me, because I'm short and slim."

The abbot said: "Take care that the doorkeepers and mace-bearers don't hit you!"

Master Alain said: "Leave it to me."

When the abbot arrived at the council, there was a large crowd at the entrance, and Master Alain deftly ducked under the abbot's cloak, going in with the others. The abbot was seated with the other abbots in the row assigned to them. Master Alain crouched between his legs, under his cloak, looking out through its opening and eagerly awaiting the enunciation of the thesis. Before long, Master Jean-Pierre arrived at the meeting and mounted the dais in the presence of the pope, the cardinals, and all the others there. He stated his thesis, supporting it with cunning and evil proofs.

Master Alain recognized him at once. Seeing that no one stood up to respond or to refute him, no one having the courage to reply, he stuck his head out of the opening of the abbot's cloak and shouted out loud: "*Iube!*" (I request the floor).

The abbot raised his hand, gave him a resounding blow on the head, and said: "Be still, damn you, do you want to shame me?"

Everyone in the vicinity exchanged glances with his neighbor, asking: "Where did that voice come from?"

Almost at once Master Alain stuck his head out again and said, in Latin: "Holy Father, hear me out!" The abbot felt disgraced because everyone was looking at him and saying: "What have you got under there?" The abbot said it was one of his lay brothers who had gone crazy. People began to insult him, saying: "Why bring lunatics to the council?" They called for the mace-bearers to strike Master Alain and throw him out.

He, fearing their blows, emerged from the abbot's cloak, made his way through the bishops, and fell at the pope's feet. This caused loud laughter throughout the room, and the abbot himself came close to being thrown out for having brought him along. Now, when Master Alain was at the pope's feet, he asked his permission to state his opinion on the question, and the pope agreed.

Master Alain climbed onto the dais and refuted everything Master Jean-Pierre had said. Then he settled the problem point for point with lively, natural reasoning. The entire audience was amazed, hearing the polished Latin that issued from his lips and his elegant solution of the controversy. Everyone said: "Truly, this is an angel of God who has appeared among us!"

When the pope heard his eloquence, he thanked God. After Master Alain had confuted Master Jean-Pierre, the latter, dumbfounded at being overcome, said: "Truly, you're the ghost of Master Alain, or some evil spirit!"

Master Alain replied: "I'm the same Alain who shut your mouth for you many a time. If there's an evil spirit here, it's you, since you wanted to infect God's Church with such heresy!"

Master Jean-Pierre rejoined: "If I had thought you were alive, I'd never have come here."

The pope wanted to know who this champion was. Summoning the abbot, he asked him where he had found such a man. The abbot replied: "Holy Father, he's been one of my lay brothers for some time. As for me, I didn't even think he could read. I've never found a man with such great humility, always busy chopping firewood, sweeping out the rooms, making beds, nursing the sick, and tending to the horses. I thought he was a commoner."

The pope, hearing about the holy life he led, observing his virtues, and learning who he had been, wanted to make him a cardinal. Paying him great respect, he said: "If not for you, the Church of God would have gone sadly astray, and so I want to keep you in my Curia."

Master Alain replied: "Holy Father, my desire is to live and die in the contemplative life, and never to return to the worldly life. In fact, I want to return to my abbey with the abbot, to continue the life I've begun, and always remain in the service of God."

The abbot knelt at his feet, begging his forgiveness for not having recognized him, and especially for boxing his ears. Master Alain said: "There's no need for forgiveness, because a father ought to chastise his son."

They took leave of the pope and the cardinals, and returned to the abbey, the abbot together with Master Alain. The abbot treated him with great reverence ever afterward, and he lived a good, holy life there, compiling and writing several fine books about our religion. He persevered in those ways for as long as he lived in this world, and when he died he was rewarded with the glory of eternal life.

75. The Robe with the Silken Seat

Not long ago there lived in Rome a knight whose name was Sir Francesco Orsino of Monte Giordano. He had a wife called Lisabetta, extremely wise, beautiful, and well-mannered, who had lived with him for many years and had presented him with two small sons. It came about that a young man fell in love with this lady, and she with him. Because they were unable to behave discreetly and conceal their love, Sir Francesco was told about it a number of times. He refused to believe the reports, deeming the young man neither handsome, nor well-born, nor wealthy. Besides, the young man pretended to be his good friend and humble servant.

But it came about that one of Sir Francesco's stewards found out about it and informed him. The knight said: "Stand guard till you see him come in, then come and get me, because I want to see it with my own eyes, or I'll never believe it."

The steward said: "I will!" One day Sir Francesco pretended to be journeying to a castle he possessed in the countryside. He and several companions rode away, but at nightfall he returned to Rome and remained in hiding until his steward came to get him. And so, Sir Francesco saw the young man in his bedroom sporting with his wife.

Her lover was saying: "And whose is this little mouth?" Then he kissed her. His wife replied: "It's all yours." "And these thieving eyes?" "Yours!" "And these cheeks?" "Yours!" "And this beautiful throat?" "Yours!" "And these beautiful breasts?" "Yours!" With each question, he touched the corresponding places on her body, and each time she replied they were his. But when it came to her behind, she said that *that* was her husband's and the two of them laughed uncontrollably.

Sir Francesco saw all that they did and heard all that they said. He said to himself: "God be praised for leaving me some part of her!" After he had heard and seen enough, and more than enough, he left quietly and returned to his castle, where he stayed as long as he pleased. Back home, he had a robe made for his wife completely out of coarse cloth, except that the seat was made of samite and lined with ermine. He ordered a splendid dinner prepared at his castle, inviting that young man, two of the young man's brothers, and several of his relatives and kinsmen, as well as several of his wife's relations.

The time of the invitation was a Sunday noon. Sir Francesco asked his wife to put on that robe, sending it to her in Rome, and ordering her to come to the castle to dine in that company. All this was done. When they were about to go to the table, Sir Francesco seated his wife beside that young man, whose name was Rinaldo, then assigned seats to their brothers and relatives. That noon he had them served a copious and excellent meal.

Everyone who saw his wife dressed that way on that occasion was surprised, especially all her relatives and Rinaldo's. They said to themselves: "This is something strange!" Rinaldo was terrified. After dinner, Sir Francesco said: "I'm now about to have the fruit served." He stood up and handed everyone at the table a heavy stick. Then he went into one of his private rooms, where he had posted eight of his servants, each one carrying a stick. They were equal in number to those at the table. He had them come out and surround the table.

To those seated at the table he said: "Defend yourselves!" To his stick-carrying servants he said: "The fruit course is coming!" The servants overturned the table, as they had been instructed to do, and they started beating the seated guests with their sticks. It was a lively brawl, in which blows were exchanged, because when those at the table felt the servants laying on with a heavy hand, they returned tit for tat "by the rules." But, finally, the servants who had come out of that room got the upper hand and vanquished those at the table, who were all killed in that great hall. (His wife was permitted to live.)

Then Sir Francesco had them pick up young Rinaldo's body and place it on a cross, arms outspread, in a bedroom. He had all the other bodies brought to their own homes at night. And so there was a great outcry all through Rome at the death of so many distinguished people. But no one dared make a peep in view of the perpetrator's rank in Roman society. Sir Francesco had his wife taken and tied to Rinaldo's body every night, so that she embraced it all night long. When day came, he had her untied, but she was fed only two slices of bread and a glass of water every day, to increase her hardship. She was treated that way for several days.

Every day she sent word to her husband, Sir Francesco, to have mercy on her, but he never paid her any mind. Seeing that her death was inevitable and that she had no way of escape, she asked, as a favor, to be permitted to see her sons before she died. So her two little boys were brought to her. She took them in her arms and said, weeping copiously: "My dear baby boys, I leave you with God's blessing and mine, and I declare that you are legitimate sons of Sir Francesco, born in lawful wedlock. Though my name is no longer worthy to be remembered because of the crime I committed, nevertheless it was the anger of a chambermaid that brought me to this pass. Even though that's not a sufficient excuse, I leave to God and to you, my sons, the task of avenging your unhappy and unlucky mother."

Unable to kiss them as much as she would have liked because of the haste imposed on her, she made the sign of the cross over them and gave them her blessing. Then she gave them back to their nurse, saying: "I charge you, by God and on your soul, to tell them about my death when they're old enough—especially this younger one." (He was crying and wouldn't let go of her neck.) After handing them back, and certifying that they were legitimate and not bastards, she commended her soul to God, and never spoke another word in this life. Not long afterward, she died. The bodies were taken up and carried away. This cruelty was praised by some, blamed by others.

Now, it came about that, when the time came, the nurse told the story to the two sons. This drove Sir Francesco mad, and he went around insane for a long time, always at odds with his sons, especially the younger one. He used to roam the woods and sleep there like a savage, doing all the odd things that madmen do. And that, they say, is how his wife got her revenge.

76. A War Fought for Love

The king of Aragon had a daughter named Lena, as young, beautiful, charming, well-mannered, and wise as Nature could have made her. The repute of that noble being shone throughout the land, and many valiant lords sought her hand. But her father rejected everyone, refusing to give her away. Now, when the son of the Holy Roman Emperor, a young man named Heinrich, heard about her beauty, he fell in love with her, and all his thoughts were bent on winning her for his wife. Finally, he conceived a lofty, noble plan.

He summoned a goldsmith, the greatest master that could be found, and had him fashion a beautiful golden eagle big enough to conceal a man inside it. When the eagle was completed, as beautifully and skillfully as words can tell, he gave it to the master who had fashioned it, and said: "Take this eagle to Aragon, and set up a residence and workshop in the square opposite the palace in which the king's daughter lives. Bring out the eagle every day and display it on your counter, saying that you want to sell it. I'll be there at the same time. Do what I tell you, and don't worry about the rest."

The goldsmith took his handiwork and a large sum of money, and departed for Aragon. As ordered, he set up shop opposite the palace in which the king's daughter lived, and began working at his craft. Certain days every week he displayed the eagle outside. All the townspeople came to view that marvel, it was so wonderfully and artistically made. One day the king's daughter looked out the window and saw the eagle. She sent word to her father that she wanted it for her collection of valuables. The king made overtures to buy it. By this time, Heinrich had arrived and was living secretly in the goldsmith's house. The artisan told him about the king's offer.

Heinrich said to the goldsmith: "Tell him you don't want to sell it, but that, if he likes, you'll make him a gift of it."

The goldsmith went to the king and said: "Your Majesty, I don't want to sell it, but if you like it, take it; I make you a gift of it."

The king replied: "Have it brought up here, and then we'll reach a full agreement."

The artisan said: "It shall be done!" He returned to Heinrich and told him that the king wished to see the eagle. At once Heinrich concealed himself in the bird, taking along a little food to keep him alive and well. The bird had been so constructed on the inside that he could open and close it at will. Then he had it brought before the king, who, at the sight of that lovely object, gave it to his daughter as a gift. The goldsmith went to set it up in the young woman's bedroom, near her bed.

After doing so, he said: "My lady, don't put any cover over it, because the gold is of a sort that would turn black if it were covered, and it wouldn't gleam anymore." Then he said: "My lady, I'll be back frequently to take a look at it." The young woman said that she had no objections. The goldsmith returned to the king and reported that his daughter was very pleased with the bird. Then he added: "And I'll soon have something she'll like even more: I'm working on a crown for that bird to wear on its head."

The king was very pleased. He sent for a large sum of money and said: "Master, take as much as you think suitable."

The goldsmith replied: "Your Majesty, your good graces are payment enough." They had a long discussion, but the king was unable to make him accept any money; he kept saying: "I have payment enough."

It came about that, when Lena was asleep in bed one night, Heinrich came out of the bird and quietly walked over to the bed in which the woman he loved more than his own self was lying. Quietly he kissed her peaches-and-cream cheek. The young lady awoke and was greatly startled. She started praying a Salve Regina. Trembling, she called one of her maids, and Heinrich immediately returned to the bird. The maid got up and said: "What is your wish?"

The princess said: "I heard someone beside me who touched my face." The maid searched the whole room, but couldn't see or hear a thing. Failing to find anything, she went back to bed, saying: "I'm sure she was dreaming!" After a while Heinrich walked softly back to the bed and kissed the princess very gently, saying quietly: "Darling, don't be afraid!"

The princess woke up and gave a piercing shriek. All her maids woke up and said: "What's wrong? Why do you keep on dreaming?" Indeed, Heinrich had run back to the bird, while they paid attention to the door and the windows. Finding them locked, and seeing nothing, they started to reproach her, saying: "If you make another peep, we'll tell your tutoress about it! Well! What madness is this, not allowing us to get our rest? A fine way to behave, yelling at night! Now see that you don't say another word! Try to sleep, and let *us* sleep!"

The poor girl was scared. After a while, when Heinrich thought enough time had elapsed, he came out of the bird, went up to her bed, and said: "Lena dear, don't scream and don't be afraid."

She said: "Who are you?"

Heinrich replied: "I'm the son of the emperor."

She said: "How did you get in here?"

Heinrich answered: "Most noble lady, I'll tell you. For a long time now I've been in love with you, after hearing how beautiful you are, and I came with the purpose of seeing you frequently, but I could never manage to. So I had this eagle made, and I came here inside it, just to be able to speak with you. I beg you, deign to pity me, because I care for nothing in the world but you. See! I'm risking death for your sake."

Hearing the tender words Heinrich had addressed to her, the princess turned to him, embraced him, and said: "Considering what you've gone through for my sake, it would be terribly mean of me not to give you something in return. So I will gladly let you do whatever you want with me. But first I want to see what you look like. So, go back to your hiding place and have no fear. Tomorrow I'll pretend I want to sleep late. Then I'll lock the door to the room and stay here alone, so we can take a look at each other. Then we'll be able to speak at greater length."

Heinrich replied: "My lady, even if I were to die now, I'd be content, seeing that you've accepted me as your servant. But please give me one kiss to seal the bargain!" The princess gave him a tender kiss, because she already felt the flames of ardent love in her heart. And Heinrich went back to the bird.

The next morning, the princess announced that she wanted to sleep late—she was on tenterhooks to see Heinrich again—and, dismissing her maids and locking the door, she went up to the bird. Heinrich came out at once and knelt at her feet. When she saw how blithe and handsome he was, she immediately flung her arms around him. He nimbly caught her in his arms and said: "I'm the happiest man in the world, because I have the joy I've yearned for all this time!"

He told her his entire lineage, and who he was, in words so soft and gentle they were like fragrant violets, mingled with delicious kisses. No one could describe the love that was rekindled between them. They remained that way for several days and nights. The princess fed him on superlative food and wine.

The goldsmith came frequently to inspect the bird and to ask Heinrich whether he needed anything. The answer was always no. It came about that, on one occasion, Heinrich said to the princess: "I want us to go to my home in Germany."

She replied: "Heinrich dear, whatever you like is all right with me."

Heinrich said: "I'll leave and come back with a ship. I'll dock it by the king's seashore castle. I'll be there on such-and-such a night. Tell your father you want to make an excursion to the seashore, and wait for me in that castle. I'll come one night and put you on the ship, and we'll sail away." The princess approved his plan.

She sent for the goldsmith and said: "Take away this bird, and make the crown for it that you told us about. I'd like it to be ready when I get back."

The artisan said: "If it's all right with the king, it's all right with me."

The princess replied: "Do as I say." The goldsmith had the bird brought back to his shop. At the proper time, Heinrich came out. Taking leave of the artisan, he returned secretly to his own country, where he had a fine ship fitted out, together with some armed galleys to protect it. Then he set sail and docked beside that castle belonging to the king of Aragon, according to plan.

In the meanwhile, the princess had said to her father: "My lord, I want to go to the harbor to visit the seashore and stay in your castle there for a few days." Her father consented, and sent along a large number of older and younger women to help her enjoy herself. The princess and the other ladies went to that castle, where she joyfully awaited Heinrich, praying to God to let him come soon. All day long she looked out to sea in search of a sight of him.

One night, at the hour he had mentioned, Heinrich came to the foot of the castle. The princess went down to meet him at once, and embraced him. Swiftly they got on board, set sail, and departed. Heinrich took her to his own country. In the morning, when she proved to be missing, there was a great uproar, and it was reported to the king that pirates had come to his castle and abducted his daughter.

The king was grief-stricken, sure that he had lost her. Unaware of the true facts, he sent for his son, who was an extremely robust man, and said: "I order you, as you value your life, not to come back before you've found out where she is and who kidnapped her." The prince followed Heinrich's ship at sea, and learned that it was the emperor's son who had abducted her. When he was sure, he returned to his father and reported that the emperor's son had come to Aragon in person and had carried her off.

Thereupon the king made great preparations to wage war against him, even if it meant invading Germany. He called upon the kings of France, England, Navarre, Majorca, Scotland, Castile, and Portugal, and many other lords and barons of western Europe. Hearing about these warlike preparations being made against him, the emperor acted accordingly, inviting and summoning the kings of Hungary and Bohemia, and many other German margraves, counts, and barons. On both sides huge armies were assembled for the fray, in the manner that will be described.

It came about that, after assembling his army, the king of Aragon set out and came to the emperor's domains in Germany. When the emperor learned of his arrival, he marched against him, coming to a city called Vienna with a mighty army. When the two armies were camped close together, the king of Aragon held a council and determined to challenge the emperor to fight. This was done: quickly he sent a herald with a blood-soaked glove on a thorn branch.

Heinrich, who was battle commander, accepted the challenge graciously. An agreement was reached as to the day for a pitched battle. On the night before, the king of Aragon assigned twelve marshals, all men of great prowess and courage. In his first unit were three thousand good soldiers, all dressed in black, mainly cavalry with golden spurs, calling themselves the Knights of Death. At their head he placed his son, who was named Sir Princivale, and said: "My son, today is the day on which we shall recoup your sister's honor. And so, please be valiant and vigorous! Extinguish every bit of fear in you, so that you would rather be cut to pieces than turn tail." He gave him a standard depicting a golden lion, on a blue field, with a sword in its paw.

The second unit was led by the Duke of Burgundy, commanding three thousand Burgundian and French troops, all on horseback and well-armed. His standard that day was golden fleur-de-lis on a blue field.

The third unit was led by the Duke of Lancaster, commanding three thousand brave Englishmen who were expert fighters, all in armor, with skirts of tasses (armored kilts), breastplates, and gleaming helmets, and all aligned beneath a standard depicting three golden leopards on a field of gules.

The fourth unit was led by the kings of Castile and Scotland, with four thousand men, all on horseback and well armed. They bore two banners, one depicting a white castle on a field of gules, and the other a green dragon, on a field of gules, with a blue bar in the center.

The fifth unit was led and directed by the kings of Majorca and Navarre, with two thousand good fighting men. Their coats-of-arms that day appeared on two banners: one bore a black she-wolf on a white field, and the other three red squares, on a white field, with a red stripe in the center.

The sixth unit was led by Count Novello of "Sansogna,"[1] with fifteen hundred men of Provence. The coat-of-arms on his pennant depicted three red roses on a white field.

The seventh and last unit was led by the valiant king of Aragon and four of his nephews, with five thousand Aragonese equipped with good armor and weapons and riding on heavy chargers covered with both plate and mail armor. His banner that day depicted an angel wielding a sword. Surrounding that unit were two thousand archers on foot. The twelve marshals of the army kept on dressing and aligning the ranks, and so many trumpets and fifes were blowing that it sounded like a real thunderstorm.

On his side, the emperor deployed his forces. That morning he knighted his son, Sir Heinrich of Swabia, creating him a count at the same time. He gave him a unit of three thousand barons and knights, all distinguished noblemen, and assigned him an imperial standard depicting a black eagle on a golden field. Moreover, that day Sir Heinrich carried a shield depicting a maiden with a palm branch in her hand. The shield was given to him by the woman the battle was being fought over. After giving him that unit and that standard, the emperor said: "My son, this affair is yours, so I say no more."

The second unit was led by a nephew of the king of Hungary, with five thousand well-equipped Hungarians. The coat-of-arms on his standard depicted golden fleur-de-lis on a blue field, with white and red stripes.

The third unit was led by the elderly king of Bohemia, with six thousand cavalrymen well armed and well mounted, and eager for the fray. His standard depicted a white lion with two tails on a field of gules.

The fourth unit was led by the "seri della Lipa,"[2] duke of Austria, with seven thousand extremely bold horsemen experienced in weaponry and accustomed to warfare. This unit carried two pennants, one depicting a two-headed white eagle on a field of gules with white dots, and the other a white mountain on a blue field, with a sword planted in the mountain.

The fifth unit was led by the count of Savoy and Count Wilhelm of Luxemburg, with thirty-five hundred horsemen, all valiant, sturdy, and fearless. One of their two pennants depicted a bear in natural colors on a yellow field, the other was quartered in white and red.

The sixth unit was led by the Patriarch of Aquileia, with fourteen hundred counts, barons, and knights with golden spurs. Their standard depicted a bishop's mitre between two white crosiers on a field of gules.

The seventh and last unit was led by the emperor himself, with four thousand Germans, all tried and true, who looked as if they had been born in armor. That day his unit bore the standard that an angel had brought to

---

[1]The translator has been unable to identify this term with any place in France. In some medieval Spanish texts, "Sansoña" is said to stand for Saxony, but that is very improbable here.   [2]A mysterious term. The Hapsburg dukes of Austria in the 14th century were named either Albert, Rudolph, Leopold, or Frederick.

Charlemagne: the oriflamme, which is a burning flame on a golden field. Truly, that final unit was accompanied by many brave and dexterous men of war. Each unit had four seneschals, who kept riding around their units so no one could break ranks, and so there would be no unlucky accident or slip-up.

When the ranks were deployed on both sides, and the ground-clearers had gone ahead to cut down hedges and trees and fill in ditches, at daybreak the sun's rays began to be reflected from the gleaming armor of both armies, and the standards, pennants, and banners were seen to be flapping in the wind. The neighing of the horses and the sound of the fifes and trumpets could be heard on both sides. The world seemed full of lightning and thunder. Never before had so many flourishing noblemen been gathered on a single field, or so many brave, wise, and good fighting men on both sides, as there were on that beautiful battleground.

If any army was ever skillfully led and directed, it was that army of the brave king of Aragon. At daybreak, when the men could see and recognize one another, he went around encouraging his units, instructing them in martial deeds, and urging them to behave well and bravely, because that day, with sword in hand, they were going to wrest the title of emperor from the Germans, acquiring it for themselves with great glory and triumph, as in the days of good King Charlemagne. Therefore, he said, he wanted each of them to be a paladin; they should reflect on how famous their names would be perpetually among their descendants for their achievement on this blessed day of victory, on which God and blessed Saint George would help them conquer.

"And so," he concluded, "see that your swords bite deep. Take no prisoners—a dead man doesn't return to the war. Whoever thinks he won't cut a good figure in this day's attempt to win such noble and glorious fame, should resign himself to dying. Because we're on their territory and we have no place to hide in. All we have for us is our swords, so we just have to be brave."

Then he ordered that, if any of his people turned their backs to run away, they should be the first to be killed. All his units were impatient to join battle, because they believed they had the right on their side.

The emperor and Sir Heinrich did the same for their own people, reminding them that German blood was the noblest and bravest in the world. "Not without reason," they said, "did we acquire the holy imperial crown, possessing it for centuries. And so, be brave and vigorous in quelling the pridefulness and audacity of these Gauls from across the hills, who have invaded our land in their pride to devour us. Remember our ancestors, who were always skillful in warfare, and eager to win fame for their country, such as the good and valorous Otto of Saxony, the first emperor, and the very bold first Heinrich and first Conrad, and the third and fourth Heinrich, and the first Friedrich, that good Barbarossa, and

Heinrich the fifth of Swabia, and Otto the fourth of Saxony, and so many more!"

Likewise, the Patriarch of Aquileia walked through the ranks, giving the men his blessing and absolving them of their sins. He urged them all to fight bravely, for they would emerge victorious.

When both armies had been lined up face to face, and the patron saints of the battle had been named, Saint Paul by the emperor and Saint George by the king of Aragon, the first two units readied for attack. Couching their lances, they moved forward briskly and assailed one another bravely and fearlessly. When their lances were broken, they drew their swords, giving and receiving tremendous blows on their gleaming helmets, from which sparks flew up to the sky, so eagerly did both sides thrust and cut.

It came about that Sir Heinrich's horse was killed under him, so that he fell. But he stood right up again, and cut his way through the enemy with his sword. Many of the Knights of Death surrounded him, but no one could capture him. Sir Princivale, racing down the field, chanced to come up to him, and they recognized each other. Sir Princivale berated him, saying: "Traitor, you're a dead man!"

Sir Heinrich replied: "For your sister's sake, please don't kill me."

Sir Princivale retorted: "God forbid I should show you any consideration, for you showed none to me." He raised his sword and struck him, and, had it not been for the good, tried-and-true armor he was wearing, he would certainly have died that day. His shield was badly sliced. But the nephew of the king of Hungary came to his aid with the entire Hungarian unit. Rapidly he was given another mount and cut his way through the throng, sword in hand.

Then the opposing army began to fall back because of the tremendous numbers pressing down on them. And so the duke of Burgundy attacked with his unit, and there was fierce fighting and great bloodshed. Nevertheless, the Hungarians pulled aside and plied their bows to such deadly effect that their arrows nearly formed a solid mass. They kept on wounding and killing many men with their volleys, so that their enemies had no choice but to fall back. Seeing this, the duke of Lancaster and his brave and robust English cavalry went into action. Like an unchained lion he plunged into the midst of the Hungarians, shouting "Death!" The Hungarians fled from their attack like sheep.

In the course of the action the duke came face to face with the nephew of the king of Hungary. Couching his lance, he charged at him, and threw him a lance's length from his horse. Immediately his enemies were on and around him. Because he was of royal blood, they didn't want to kill him, but took him prisoner. When the Hungarians saw that their leader had been captured, they hastily retreated. The king of Bohemia, seeing this, gallantly moved forward with his unit, shouting to the enemy: "Blood! Blood!" And there was an extremely hard and rugged fight. In the same way, the other units were brought into action by the kings of Castile and Scotland and the duke of Austria.

When these units clashed, the noise, shouting, and clattering of their armor were so loud that both earth and sky seemed to tremble. Racing across the field, the king of Scotland met the duke of Austria and they attacked each other with great hardihood. Their lances broken, they drew their swords, and the duke wounded the king of Scotland with a thrust to his arm, so that the king could no longer wield his sword. The duke seized him and took him prisoner. His men, seeing their liege lord captured, turned his way, closed ranks, hedged in the duke, and rescued the king by force of arms.

Furious at this, the duke plunged into their midst with such frenzy that anyone who could escape his attack was a lucky man. His impetus was so unbridled that he broke through into the fifth unit, where the kings of Navarre and Majorca were prudently moving into battle. Meeting him, the king of Majorca lowered his lance, struck him in the breast, and pierced him through and through, so that the brave duke of Austria fell to the ground and died.

Now that the men of that unit had tasted such victory right after joining battle, they became even bolder and valiantly attacked the unit led by the counts of Savoy and Luxemburg. The fight was hard and rugged, but the two counts' banners were thrown down, and they were all but defeated. Seeing this, the Patriarch of Aquileia quickly moved his unit against the frenzied king of Majorca. He was so well mounted and led such good men that he was able to break through. He raced furiously to the place where the valiant Sir Princivale was fighting. Princivale met his onslaught smartly, wounding him with his lance in such a way that part of the lance's butt remained in his chest. But he was so strong that he was still able to ride away.

Badly wounded as he was, he was still able to inflict serious damage on the enemy, but he was losing so much blood that his sight began to fail. Racing across the field, he met up with Sir Heinrich, who recognized him. Seeing his serious wound, he said: "Oh, no! My lord, what's this?"

The Patriarch replied: "My son, undo my armor, for I'm dying." He did so at once, and the Patriarch said: "I can hardly see, so plug up and bind up this wound very carefully, and then lead me into the thick of the battle, for I'm sure that, before I die, many another man will die at my hands." Sir Heinrich tended to his wound. After it was bandaged, the Patriarch kissed Sir Heinrich, blessed him, and said: "My son, don't be dismayed at my death, but take an example from me, and continue fighting, because this is no time to stand around talking." He plunged into the fray, holding his sword in both hands, and woe to anyone that came too close to him! He kept going for a while, then died.

It came about that Sir Heinrich, seeing the count of Sansogna's unit approaching, attacked it with his men, who had had a breather. He desperately assailed the count, who, seeing him attack that way, raced toward him very boldly. Sir Heinrich struck him in the breast with his lance so hard that he ran him through. And so the brave count fell from his horse and soon died. His body was retrieved by his own men and carried to their camp.

When the king of Aragon saw that the good count of Sansogna was dead, he couldn't hold back his tears. Then he grasped his lance and said: "Men, if you love me, follow me!" He moved out like a storm, dealing sword cuts to all who stood their ground against him. He raced across the field like a dragon, while everyone fled before him.

When the emperor saw this, he angrily led his unit against the king of Aragon. When the two units clashed, they resembled demons from Hell, such was the tempest raised by both sides, cutting and thrusting with tremendous blows. The king of Aragon slung his shield behind his back, gripped his sword with both hands, and slashed at all who stood their ground against him, so that everyone fled before him, unable to withstand his mighty blows. Many barons and counts were killed by his hand. The battle was now a mêlée, in which mighty blows were given and received; armor, hands, and arms were slashed; and much blood was shed all over the field. Yet, the emperor and his unit inflicted severe losses on the enemy.

It came about that the king of Aragon came to a fountain at which Sir Heinrich had removed his helmet to take a drink. The king of Aragon dismounted, recognized Sir Heinrich by his coat-of-arms, and, saying not a word, dealt Sir Heinrich a heavy back-handed sword blow across the face, saying: "Take this as a down payment on my daughter's dowry!" He mounted again, and said to Sir Heinrich: "Put your armor back on, for this is the day on which you must die at my hands by this fountain."

Sir Heinrich replied: "It's not chivalrous to fight with someone who has a nasty wound like mine."

The king said: "Bind up your wound and get on your horse, because I intend to see whether you're as doughty as I've heard." While they were engaged in this discussion, Count Wilhelm of Luxemburg and some of his barons came to the fountain for a drink. Recognizing the king of Aragon and Sir Heinrich, and hearing their dispute, the count turned to the king and told him he wished to settle it. Both the king and Sir Heinrich consented.

The count said: "Your Majesty, I want an end put to this battle today. Meanwhile Sir Heinrich will receive medical treatment. As soon as he's fit to fight again, the two of you can meet on the field and decide this issue between you, so that all these good men don't have to die on account of a woman. For, by my faith, I've never seen a bloodier battle than this one!"

The king agreed, and so did Sir Heinrich. They shook hands and

pledged to fight each other. Then they departed and returned to the battlefield, where they had the trumpets sound recall. It was very difficult to
break up that fierce combat. After both armies had returned to camp in the
evening, the king of Aragon assembled all the kings, counts, and barons,
and informed them of the promise he had given. Almost all of them approved of it, except Sir Princivale, who said: "My lord, I think I should be
the one to fight him, because I'm of the same age, and all day long today
I was searching for him on the field, but could never find him."

His father said: "My son, let him get well, and then do as you like."

It came about that the pope heard about the enormous armies that had
been assembled on both sides, and sent two cardinals to make peace.
Finding the leaders unwilling, they had several meetings with the emperor
and the king of Aragon, who was particularly set against making peace. But
their vassals urged them to it very insistently, and the cardinals ordered
them to do so in the pope's name, on penalty of excommunication, so that,
as God willed, they reached an accord.

With great joy and celebration Sir Heinrich married the daughter of the
king of Aragon, and Sir Princivale married the daughter of the emperor,
Sir Heinrich's sister. They forgave each other, made peace, and became
kinsmen, thanks to the two cardinals. Then they parted with great comfort
and happiness, each man returning to his own land and enjoying good
fortune.

77. Hell Hath No Fury

There once lived in Romagna a very wealthy gentleman whose son was
skilled in language arts and adorned with all virtues. After his mother's
death, his father had remarried and had begotten another son, who was by
now twelve years old, the elder son being twenty-two. His stepmother,
more beautiful than virtuous, had cast her eyes on her stepson's beauty and
had fallen deeply in love with him. She kept her love under control at the
outset, while she was still strong enough to do so; but after she felt her heart
ignited by that detestable fire, she was compelled to surrender to her
passion.

Pretending to be ill, she concealed the wound in her mind, and said she
was suffering from a hidden fever. Finally, urged on by her ardent
thoughts, she had a maid summon her stepson. The true facts were the far-
thest thing from his mind. He entered her bedroom and, with a pleasant
smile, asked her the cause of her illness. Then the lady, thinking that his
question suited her purpose, grew a little bolder. Covering her face with
her sheet to indicate modesty, and accompanying her words with a flood
of tears, she began to address him as follows:

"The cause and origin of my present illness and my great sorrow, and
also my cure and my salvation, is you yourself. Your eyes, whose radiance

has entered mine and penetrated to the fibers of my heart, have kindled such a fire in my unhappy breast that I can't abide it. And so, have pity on a woman who's dying on account of you! Don't be put off by our kinship and your duty to your father, because you'll be doing a service to a poor woman who can no longer stay alive without your help. In you I see his image, and I love my husband, and deservedly so, in your guise. Our being alone together here offers us the desirable security and convenience. When a thing is done without anyone's knowledge, it's almost as if it had never happened."

The well-bred young man was stupefied at that abominable request. Abhorring such a terrible sin so greatly that he wanted to turn his back on her without replying, nevertheless he thought better of it, and decided not to exasperate her with a brutal refusal. He deemed it wiser to put her off by requesting a delay, so he could try to rid her mind of such a bizarre and filthy idea. And so he told her to concentrate on getting well, and to be of good cheer, because he promised to reward her suitably for her love. With these words he calmed her for the moment.

The youth considered that a disaster of that order called for wise counsel, and decided to refer the matter to an elderly sage who had guided him in his boyhood to great advantage, and was now steering him through the tortuous course of young manhood. The old man, well acquainted with the power an enraged woman could wield, advised him to run away as fast as he could from the impending storm that cruel Fortune had in store for him. But, before the prudent advice could be put into effect, the impatient young woman, to whom a day seemed like a year, continued planning how to achieve her unspeakable desire.

Persuading her husband that it was a good idea for him to visit some of his estates, because she had heard that things were going to rack and ruin there, she got him out of the house for an indeterminate number of days. With her husband gone, she prodded the young man hourly to keep his promise. He made a variety of excuses, doing his best to put off her desire with fine words until he could take a long trip and get out of her sight.

The lady, who had been made more than usually impatient by her high hopes, and who gathered from his feeble excuses that the more promises he made, the farther he got from satisfying her in any way, became enraged. Her criminal love was suddenly transformed into a much more criminal hatred, and she took counsel with one of her servants, whom she trusted greatly, as to the way in which she should take revenge on the man who refused to keep his promise. Finally they decided to take the poor boy's life by poison.

The scoundrelly servant made no delay in realizing their plan. He left the house and returned late that night with a potion in a glass. Mixing it with wine in the lady's bedroom, he put it in a cupboard in which edibles were kept, intending to serve it to the wretched youth at dinnertime at noon of the following day. But, as Fortune would have it, when that evil woman's own son, who, as mentioned, was twelve years old, came back from school the next morning and had a snack, he got thirsty. Finding that glass of poisoned wine, which had carelessly been left in the unlocked cupboard, he drank it all, and before long fell to the floor as if dead.

When the servants became aware of this, they raised a cry, and his mother came running. He was judged to have been poisoned. His mother and the servant who had bought the potion withdrew to a private place and conversed in secret. They hit on the plan of laying the blame on the elder son. And so the servant announced in public that he was sure that the elder son had committed the crime, because a few days earlier he had promised him fifty *scudi* for killing the boy. When he, the servant, refused, he had threatened him with death if he breathed a word of it to anyone.

The lady immediately summoned the police, and had her stepson thrown in jail on the basis of the servant's testimony. Then she sent a messenger to her husband, informing him of these events. Her husband returned at once, and she had the servant repeat to him the testimony he had already given. Then she added that her stepson had done this because she had refused to yield to his shameless lust. Furthermore, he had threatened to kill her.

The unhappy father was deeply grieved, seeing his young boy carried to the grave, and his elder son about to be condemned to death for the murder. Deceived by his wife's false lamenting, he became more and more furious with his son by the hour. Right after the funeral, the wretched old man left the gravesite and returned to his palace just as he was, his face streaked with tears. There, sunk in tears and prayers, he occupied himself with hastening the death of the son that remained to him, calling him incestuous because he had tried to stain his father's bed, a murderer because he had killed his brother, and an assassin because he had threatened to kill his stepmother.

His words had brought people's minds to such a pitch of indignation that they were all clamoring that no time should be lost in a formal prosecution and defense, but that the sin should be publicly punished by stoning. But the official judges said that they wanted the case tried legally in accordance with long-standing custom. They wouldn't allow such a cruel precedent to be set, executing a man because of public indignation without conclusive proof of his crime.

And so the law was observed. The criminal was indicted and the case turned over to the prosecution. The father of the accused testified that his elder son had poisoned his younger brother, and that he had solid evidence of this, because a few days earlier he had tried to get a servant to kill him, promising him fifty *scudi*. When the accused was questioned, he denied everything.

After hearing all the testimony, the judges weren't satisfied. They felt they had heard only conjectures and suspicions, and no real proof or truth. And so they insisted on hearing the servant himself. And so that gallows-bait was led before the judges, maintaining perfect composure, and said the same thing he had told the boys' father. Furthermore, he was ready to undergo torture along with the accused to uphold the truth of his story. Not one of the judges was so kindly inclined to the accused that he didn't think the lad should be subjected to the strappado first, and the servant after him, in case the boy persisted in denying the crime even under torture.

At that point a physician of great integrity and authority in the city stood up and said: "I'm happy to state that up to now I have enjoyed a good repute, and I cannot stand by and see this innocent boy unjustly tortured or killed. But what will be the result of my being the only one to refute someone else's testimony? I am the man you know and esteem, whereas he is a scoundrelly servant who deserves to be hanged not once, but a thousand times. I know that my conscience isn't deceiving me, and so listen to the real facts of the case. This scoundrel came to me asking me to sell him a fast-acting poison and offering me fifty gold ducats for it. He said he needed it to give it to a sick man who was tortured day and night by an incurable dropsy and by a thousand other pains, and wanted to escape all that suffering by putting an end to himself. Seeing this criminal hunting for words while inventing those deceitful excuses, I began to suspect that he wanted it for some nefarious purpose, and I was about to show him the door. But, reflecting that, if I didn't give it to him, he would go to someone else less wide awake than I am, and would receive it, I thought it was a good idea to give him a potion (as I did), but one of such a nature as I shall describe. Being certain that this matter would be investigated in the course of time, I didn't want to take the sum he had offered me right away. Instead, I said to him: 'Because I suspect that there may be counterfeit or clipped ducats among them, put them in this bag, seal the bag with your ring, and some other day, when we have more time, we'll go to the bank and show them.' Fooling him that way, I had him seal the bag with his seal. Now, having sent my own servant for it, I show it to all of you. Let him look and acknowledge that the seal is his, and then let him tell us that he wants to accuse this innocent boy of giving the poison to his brother, seeing that he himself bought it!"

While the worthy man was saying this, that evil servant, looking like a disinterred body, was trembling, and sweat poured from him in beads as cold as ice. Shuffling his feet back and forth, and tossing his head to and fro, he started to pucker his lips and utter such inanities that no one could reasonably consider him innocent. Nevertheless, the bold scoundrel soon worked up enough nerve to overcome his fear. Dispelling all fear, he resumed his audacity and began inventing his customary shrewd alibis. With the same quickness of wits he accused the physician of lying and denied all his accusations.

But the well-esteemed physician, in order not to soil his limpid fame in his old age, strove in every way to prove the truth of the matter. And so, requesting one of the bailiffs to take the ring off the servant's finger, he compared it with the seal on the bag, and it was found to be identical, which gave the judges sufficient reason to have him tortured. After several jerks of the strappado, he still denied everything categorically.

Then the physician said to the judges: "I have yet to inform you that, when this criminal asked me to furnish him with the poison, as I've stated, I felt it unbecoming a good doctor to be the cause of anyone's death (for I knew that the medical art had been given to man by God for the good, and not for the harm, of humanity). And, since I feared, as I've also said, that he might go to someone else whose greed for money might have made him give the fellow what he wanted, I gave him, not poison, but a mandrake potion. This medicine makes you sleep so deeply that, while its effects last, the man who has drunk it resembles a dead man. And so, if that child drank the potion I mixed for him, he's still alive, and merely sleeping peacefully. As soon as the vigor of his constitution shakes off the dense fog of that slumber, he will see daylight again as well as he did before. If he's really dead, seek the cause for it elsewhere."

After this statement by the doctor, everyone agreed that it was necessary not to lose any time, but to go to the child's burial place and clear up the matter. And so, locking up the servant and the elder son in jail, the others went to the gravesite. Arriving there, the boy's father insisted on lifting the stone from the tomb with his own hands. No further aid was needed, because Nature had already shaken off the darkness of slumber, and the boy had returned from the realm of Pluto.

His father embraced him with all the warmth you can imagine, having no words sufficient to express the joy he felt. In silence he drew him out of the tomb and presented him, dressed in his shroud as he was, to the mayor of the city.

When the servant saw that the boy was alive, he thought he would be set free because there had been no death. For that reason, and to avoid further torture, he confessed to everything. And so, the lady was arrested and brought before the judges. A little torture induced her to confess, as well. The verdict was that, for having carried out the crime, even though death hadn't ensued, the servant should be hanged. At the entreaties of the woman's husband and son, her life was spared, but she was sent into perpetual banishment. By common consent, the doctor was allowed to keep the money he had received from the servant for the sleeping potion.

And so the father who had been in danger of losing both his sons, sacrificing them to his miserable wife, got them back alive and cleared of all crimes.

STORIES 78–90

From *Il Trecentonovelle*
by Franco Sacchetti

The author of this story collection, the most important one in post-*Decameron* 14th-century Italian literature, was born shortly before 1335, perhaps in Ragusa (today Dubrovnik in Croatia), where his father, a Florentine, resided as a merchant. Franco settled in Florence, the city he served as a politician and diplomat, through good times and bad, from the 1360s until his death in 1400. (His political career also took him to other Italian cities; it was the custom for certain high civic offices, like the position of *podestà*, to be filled by nonresidents for fixed periods.)

Sacchetti somehow found time for an extensive literary production as well, including numerous lyric poems and the *Sposizioni di Vangeli* (Reflections on the Gospels), keyed to the Church services for the different days of Lent (the miscellaneous reflections contain a number of *exempla*, or illustrative stories, and apologues).

His masterpiece, the *Trecentonovelle* (Book of Three Hundred Stories), was the fruit of his very late years, ca. 1389–1397. In his preface he states the twofold purpose of affording pleasure in exceedingly troublous times, and of emulating his famous contemporary Boccaccio, whose *Decameron*, Sacchetti notes, had already been translated (at least partially) into French and English. He goes on to say that both old and recent events, including personal experiences of the author, will be found in the stories, and that the emphasis will be on his beloved city of Florence.

Despite the title, manuscripts are defective and fewer than the titular three hundred stories are extant. The last remaining story bears the original number 258 and, even up through that number, thirty-six stories are lost and seven are incomplete. There never was a frame story or a clearly discernible principle of organization.

Among the many historical Florentine figures, great and small, represented are such titans as Giotto (No. 80) and Dante (No. 84). In addition to a pervasive Boccaccian flavor, some favorite characters from the *Decameron* reappear here (see the comments that follow on Nos. 82, 86, and 89). Jollity and wit underlie all the narratives.

Sacchetti is fond of tagging philosophical reflections onto the ends of his stories. Some of these are so "politically incorrect" to modern ears (see Nos. 81 and 83) that they unintentionally read like black humor.

No. 78 is a good satire on courtiers and their highfalutin speech.

No. 79, though the plot details are altogether different, is reminiscent, because of its naïve hero and his unforeseen misadventures that end well, of the famous story of Andreuccio in the *Decameron* (fifth story of Day Two).

The doings of the officials called *priori*, in No. 81, were perfectly familiar to Sacchetti, who once served as a *priore* himself.

No. 82 is in the European tradition of the *fabliau* (misadventures, often risqué, in the life of commoners). The painter Calandrino mentioned in the story was a favorite Florentine laughingstock. He appears in four *Decameron* stories (the one in which he is beaten by his wife Tessa is the fifth story of Day Nine) and in three other *Trecentonovelle* stories.

No. 83 is an example of the extremely widespread "taming of a shrew" folktale motif. This particular version was not a direct source for Shakespeare, being much less subtle (and even savagely amoral when the hero wishes for the death of two innocent people).

No. 84, a reflection of Dante's reputation for cantankerousness, is in part a purely legendary explanation of his exile.

No. 85, a slapstick farce about Florentine eccentrics and incompetent officials, affords priceless glimpses of everyday street life and market activity, including the grain-market building Orsanmichele, which had been purpose-built in 1337, and in which Andrea Orcagna's world-famous tabernacle had been installed between 1349 and 1359. Bucephalus and Bayard, whose names are satirically applied to the hero's nag, were two legendary horses, belonging, respectively, to Alexander the Great and to the titular hero of the 12th-century French epic *Renaud de Montauban*. The *Distichs of Cato* were maxims in Latin couplets written in the first Christian millennium and falsely attributed to the Roman statesman and sage of the 3rd and 2nd centuries B.C.

The witty painter Bonamico, or Buffalmacco (1262–1340), who appears in Nos. 86 and 89, was another local favorite. He participates in five *Decameron* stories and six *Trecentonovelle* stories. The Guelphs and Ghibellines mentioned in No. 86 were the two major opposing parties in the Italian politics of the 13th and early 14th centuries. Roughly speaking (there were many nuances and contradictions), the Guelphs were loyal to the popes in their opposition to the interference of the (German) Holy Roman Emperors in Italian affairs, whereas the Ghibellines supported the emperors.

No. 90, another *fabliau*, is a knockabout bawdy farce. The humorously applied quotation in the final paragraph is from Canto XXXIII of the "Inferno" in Dante's *Divine Comedy*. In Dante, the words refer to Ugolino, who in Hell gnaws eternally on the skull of the man who tormented him and his children on earth.

78. Rewarded for Vilification

Old King Edward of England[1] was a king of great prowess and fame, and the present tale will show how wise he was. Well, in his days there was a grain winnower from Linari, in the Valdensa area of the Florentine countryside, and his name was Parcittadino. He got the urge to abandon his winnowing altogether and to become a courtier. He learned quite a lot

---

[1]There had been three Edwards of England by the time of writing, but scholars believe Sacchetti means Edward I (reigned 1272 to 1307).

about this new profession, and as he continued to try his hand at the courtly art, he conceived a great desire to visit the aforesaid King Edward. Not without a good reason, either, for he had heard a great deal about his magnanimity, especially toward his courtiers.

With this in mind, he set out one morning and didn't stop till he reached the city of London in England, where the king resided. Arriving at the royal palace, in which this king lived, he went from door to door until reaching the great hall in which the king spent most of his time. He found him absorbed in a game of chess with his majordomo. When Parcittadino came before the king, knelt down, and uttered words of homage, the king gave him no more notice or attention than if he weren't there, and so Parcittadino remained kneeling there for some time. Seeing that the king made no acknowledgment of his presence, he stood up and began to say:

"Blessings on the hour and moment that led me here, where I have always wished to be, so I could see the most noble, prudent, and valorous king in Christianity! I count myself more fortunate than any of my peers, now that I am here, where I can see the flower of kings. Oh, what great glory Fortune has granted me! If I were to die now, I could face it without much sorrow, because I am standing before that most serene crown, which, just as a magnet attracts iron, attracts all men with its prowess, making them desirous of viewing its dignity."

Parcittadino had barely reached this point in his tirade when the king arose from his game, grabbed hold of him, threw him to the floor, and showered so many punches and kicks on him that Parcittadino was all black and blue. Then the king immediately returned to his chess game. Parcittadino, quite wretched, stood up, but hardly knew where he was. He considered his long journey and his praises of the king ill spent, as he stood there sheepishly, not knowing what to do. Taking heart a little, he decided to try and see whether he'd do better by addressing the king in the opposite way, seeing that his praises had brought him such an ill reward. And so he said:

"Curses on the hour and day that brought me to this place! I thought I had come to see a noble king, as public opinion has it, but instead I see an ungrateful, unappreciative king. I thought I had come to see a virtuous king, but I see one filled with vices. I thought I had come to see a wise and honest king, but I see a wicked, evil one. I thought I had come to see a holy, just crown, but I see a man who returns bad for good. The proof is ready to hand, because when I, a lowly being, lauded and honored him, he beat me so badly that I don't know whether I can ever go back to winnowing, in case I need to take up my old trade again!"

The king got up again, more furious than the first time, stepped over to a door, and called for one of his courtiers. There's no need to ask how Parcittadino felt when he saw that. He resembled a corpse, except for his trembling, and he was sure the king would have him killed. When he heard the king calling for that nobleman, he thought he was calling an executioner to have him crucified. When the nobleman who had been summoned by the king arrived, the king said to him: "Go and give such-and-such a robe of mine to this fellow to reward him for his true words, because I myself gave him a rich reward for his lies!"

The nobleman left at once and brought Parcittadino a royal robe, one of the most ornate the king owned, with so many pearl buttons and gems that, deducting the punches and kicks he had received, it was worth three hundred gold florins or more. Parcittadino, still suspecting that the robe might be a serpent or basilisk that would bite him, took it in a gingerly fashion. Then, reassured, he put it on, reappeared before the king, and said: "Your Majesty, if you always reward me this way for my lies, I'll seldom tell the truth." And he realized that the king lived up to his reputation, and the king was more pleased with *him*.

Then, after this good experience, he took his leave and parted from the king, making his way through Lombardy. He sought out all the local lords and recounted this incident, which brought him in more than another three hundred florins. Back in Tuscany, he showed all his wealth to his fellow winnowers in Linari, who were so poor and covered with dust from their work. As they marveled, Parcittadino said to them: "They kicked and punched and threw me to the ground, and yet in England this reward I found." He helped out many of them financially, then left in quest of his fortunes.

This was one of the nicest things a king can do. How many people are there who, if they were praised as highly as this king was, wouldn't have puffed out their cheeks with pride? But he, knowing that he deserved the praise, wanted to indicate that it wasn't true, proving himself so clever in the final analysis. Many ignorant people, when lauded to their face by flatterers, tend to take them at their word, but this king, who was truly meritorious, wanted people to think the opposite.

79. The Vicissitudes of Fortune

In the city of Florence there was once a citizen named Piero Brandani, who spent all his time in lawsuits. He had a son aged eighteen. One morning Piero was obliged to go to the palace of the podestà, or chief magistrate, to answer a complaint against him. He had given certain papers to his son, telling him to set out ahead of him with the papers and to wait for him beside the Badìa, or abbey church, of Florence. In obedience to his father's instructions, he went there and, with the papers, awaited his father's arrival. All this was in the month of May.

It came about that, while the lad was waiting, a torrential rain came down. A farm woman, or she may have been a peddler, came by with a basket of cherries on her head. The basket fell and the cherries were scattered all over the street. Whenever it rains, the gutter in that street rises until it's like a brook. The lad, always greedy for a treat, as those of his age are, started scurrying here and there along with others to pick up the cherries, and they even ran into the gutter after them.

It came about that, after the cherries were consumed and the lad returned to the place where he had been standing, he no longer found the papers under his arm, because they had fallen into that water, which had rapidly carried them into the Arno. He hadn't noticed it. Now he ran back and forth, asking everyone if they had seen them, but his words went for nothing: the papers were sailing toward Pisa and the sea.

The youth was in great distress and decided to run away out of fear of his father. His first stop on the way, the usual one for vagabonds and runaways, was in Prato. There he went to an inn, where several merchants arrived after sunset. They didn't intend to spend the night there, but to rest awhile and then continue their journey to Ponte Agliana. When these merchants saw how downhearted the youth was, they asked him what was wrong and where he was from. He told them, and they asked him whether he wanted to join their party and travel with them.

The lad, consenting, thought it was taking them forever to set out again, but they finally did. At two in the morning they reached Ponte Agliana and knocked at an inn door. The innkeeper, who had already gone to bed, came to the window and called: "Who's there?"

"Open the door for us, we want a room."

The innkeeper grumbled: "Don't you know this area is full of highwaymen? I'm amazed that you weren't captured!" He was telling the truth, because a numerous gang of bandits was terrorizing the countryside.

They pleaded with the innkeeper until he opened the door. When they were inside and their horses had been tended to, they said they were ready for supper, but their host said: "I don't even have a mouthful of bread."

The merchants said: "What are we going to do?"

The host said: "I see only one solution. This boy of yours must put on some ragged clothing, so he looks like a beggar, and go down this slope, where he'll find a church. There he must call Master Cione, who's the priest there, and tell him from me to lend me twelve loaves of bread. I say this because, if those criminals find a poorly dressed youngster, they won't do anything to him."

The lad was shown the way, but didn't relish the walk, since it was nighttime and he couldn't see clearly. As frightened as you would imagine, he groped his way back and forth and never found that church. Entering a small wood, he saw on one side a little light reflected on a wall. He decided to head in that direction, thinking it was the church. He arrived at a large threshing floor, which he took for the forecourt of the church. But it was really a farmer's house. He came up to the door and started to knock. When the farmer heard him, he shouted out: "Who's there?"

The lad said: "Open up, Master Cione, because the innkeeper at Ponte Agliana has sent me here to ask you to lend him twelve loaves of bread."

The farmer said: "What bread, you thief? You're in cahoots with those highwaymen! If I go out there, I'll catch you and send you to Pistoia, where they'll hang you!"

Hearing this, the youth didn't know what to do. Beside himself, and turning every which way to find a path to a safer harbor, he heard a wolf howling close by at the edge of the wood. Looking around, he saw on one side of the threshing floor a wine cask standing upright, with its top stove in. He ran to it at once and got in, fearfully awaiting the outcome that Fortune had in store for him.

While he was in that situation, the wolf, who was mangy, perhaps with age, came up to the cask and started rubbing up against it. As he did so, he lifted his tail, which entered the bung hole. When the lad inside felt the tail touching him, he was scared stiff, but, once he realized what was going on, he decided in his fright to grab hold of the tail and not to let go of it, if he could help it, until he saw what was to become of him.

The wolf, feeling himself caught by the tail, began to tug, but the lad held on tight and tugged back. As they both tugged, the cask fell over and started rolling. The lad held tight and the wolf tugged. The more he did so, the more bumps he got from the cask. It went on rolling for some two hours, and struck the wolf so many times that he died. The lad himself was badly injured, but Fortune favored him: the harder he had gripped the tail, the less harm he had done to himself, and the more to the wolf. Though the wolf was now dead, the lad didn't dare to get out of the cask, or even loose his hold on the tail, all night long.

In the morning, when the farmer at whose door the lad had knocked got up, he went out to inspect his farm, and caught sight of the cask at the foot of a ravine. He started to ponder over this, saying to himself: "These devils who go around at night do nothing but mischief. This time they've taken my cask, which was on the threshing floor, and rolled it all the way down there." He went down after it and found the wolf, who didn't seem to be dead, lying next to the cask. He started yelling: "Wolf, wolf, wolf!" He stayed there, and when his neighbors came running to see what the racket was about, they found the wolf dead and the lad inside the cask.

They crossed themselves repeatedly and asked the youth: "Who are you? What is all this?"

The lad, more dead than alive, and scarcely able to catch his breath, said: "I beg you for the love of God to hear me out and do me no harm!" The farmers listened, to hear the why and wherefore of such an odd occurrence. He told them everything that had befallen him, from the loss of the legal papers down to that moment. The farmers felt very sorry for him, and said:

"Son, you've been extremely unlucky, but things won't be as bad for you as you think. In Pistoia there's an ordinance stating that whoever kills a wolf and brings it to the city hall will receive fifty *lire*."

Some of the life that had been knocked out of the boy came back to him when they offered him their company and their assistance in carrying the dead wolf. He accepted. He and a number of those men, carrying the wolf, arrived at the Ponte Agliana inn, from which the boy had set out. The innkeeper was amazed by those events, as you may well imagine, and reported that the merchants had left. They and he, after waiting and waiting for the boy, thought he had either been eaten by the wolves or captured by the highwaymen.

Finally the boy presented the wolf at the Pistoia city hall, and, when his story was heard, received the fifty *lire*. Of these, he spent five *lire* entertaining the party that had come with him. The other forty-five, after he had made his adieux, he brought back to his father, begging his forgiveness and reporting all that had occurred. He gave the forty-five *lire* to his father, who, being a poor man, was glad to get them and forgave him. He used some of the money to obtain copies of those papers, and with the rest he went on energetically with his lawsuit.

And so, no one should ever despair, because frequently Fortune gives as much as she takes, and takes as much as she gives. Who would have imagined that the papers lost in the water would be restored by a wolf who stuck his tail through the bung hole of a wine cask, and got caught in that unusual way? Certainly this is a case that teaches us, not only not to despair, but never to be distressed or melancholy over anything that happens to us.

80. Giotto's Unwelcome Client

Everyone must have heard who Giotto was, and how he surpassed all others as a painter. An artisan of low degree, who needed to have a shield painted with his coat of arms, perhaps because he was to be made governor of a castle, went at once to Giotto's workshop with a man behind him carrying the shield. On arriving and finding Giotto in, he said: "God save you, master. I'd like you to paint my arms on this shield."

Giotto, observing the man and his manners, merely said: "When do you want it?" When the man told him, Giotto said: "Leave it to me."

The man left. Giotto remained where he was, thinking to himself: "What's the meaning of this? Did someone send me this fellow as a practical joke? However that may be, I've never been commissioned to paint a shield. Besides, the man who brought it is a little nobody, and yet wants me to paint his arms as though he belonged to the French royal family. I definitely have to create an unheard-of coat of arms for him!"

With these thoughts in mind, he took his stand in front of that shield, drew the outlines of the coat of arms he deemed suitable, and told a pupil to paint it in. The pupil did so. The painting depicted a helmet, a gorget, a pair of brassarts, a pair of iron gauntlets, a pair of breastplates, a pair of cuisses and jambs, a sword, a dagger, and a lance.

When the fine fellow, who barely knew his own name, came back, he stepped forward and said: "Master, is my shield painted?"

Giotto said: "Yes, it is; go get it."

The shield was brought, and that would-be gentleman started to look at it. Then he said to Giotto: "What is this mess that you've painted?"

Giotto replied: "You'll really think it's a mess when you pay me for it!"

The man said: "I wouldn't give four cents for it!"

Giotto said: "What did you tell me to paint?"

The man replied: "My arms."

"Well," Giotto rejoined, "aren't your arms and armor all here? Is anything missing?"

The man replied: "It's good."

Giotto said: "No, it's bad, and may God give you times just as bad, because you must be a real idiot. I bet that if someone asked you who you were, you'd have a terrible time answering. You come here and say 'Paint my arms.' If you were one of the financiers of the Bardi family, that would have been all right. But what arms do *you* bear? What family are *you* from? Who were your ancestors? You ought to be ashamed! Make a name for yourself in the world before you come and talk about arms as if you were the knight Namo of Bavaria, right out of a novel of chivalry! I painted all sorts of arms and armor on your shield. If there are other kinds, tell me, and I'll paint them."

The man said: "You're insulting me after ruining a shield for me!" He left, went to the magistrate in charge of contracts, and laid a complaint against Giotto. Giotto appeared before the magistrate with a complaint of his own, demanding two florins for the painting. Meanwhile the man was seeking damages from Giotto. When the officials had heard their statements, Giotto having made a much better one, their judgment was that the man should take his shield, painted as it was, and should give six *lire* to Giotto, who had the law on his side.

And so, the man had to accept the shield and pay for it in order to be let off. Failing to take due measure of himself, he had others take his true measure. Because every nobody wants to acquire a coat of arms and establish a lineage, including some people whose fathers came from foundling homes.

81. Strange Doings of City Councilmen

Marco del Rosso of the Strozzi clan, Tommaso Federighi, Tommaso Baronci, and others served as Florentine priors—guild heads and rotating city councilmen—in their day.[2] It came about, as it often does, that this Marco and Tommaso Federighi wanted to play a joke on one of their

---

[2]Between 1358 and 1363. The councilmen clubbed together in official quarters during their two-month term.

friends, and they decided that Tommaso Baronci was the one who'd provide the best entertainment. He was the president of the council at the time.

One night he went to bed, leaving at his bedside a pair of large pointed shoes, and his friends turned them inside out. In the morning, when he got up and quickly rang the bell for a council meeting, he put on his shoes in the dark. He went to the meeting in great haste, took his seat, and waited a long time for all his colleagues to assemble.

Marco, looking at Baronci's feet, said: "What's this, Mr. President? Are you going hunting in those shoes?"

Baronci looked at them and said: "What! What ill fortune is this? They don't look like mine, though I can't see them well without my glasses." He took out his glasses, put them on, and bent over as far as he could, leaning toward the window. Everyone looked to see what was the matter with his shoes. Baronci said: "They're not mine. Mine had points, and these don't."

Finally he went to his room, took them off, and stared at them over and over. His attendant Toso, who was there, said: "Tommaso, those shoes have been turned inside out." He showed him the points, which were inside.

Baronci said: "Toso, you're right, but what could have happened?"

Toso replied: "I don't know. The best thing to do is turn them the right way again." He and Baronci, working together, had their work cut out to turn the shoes right side out. It took them until nine in the morning. But Baronci got through it all without getting too upset.

That same day, Marco and Federighi played a second trick. They made a hole in the glass urinal hanging at the foot of Baronci's bed, the one into which he urinated at night, standing up straight in bed. Then they put it back where it belonged. That evening at supper there were many roast capons on the table. Baronci, as president, gave a capon to Toso, saying: "Go and put it in my chest. Tomorrow morning take it to Lapa" (Baronci's wife).

Toso put away the capon, and Marco and Federighi saw him. After supper they secretly got hold of one of the female cats in the house, took the capon out of the chest, and put the cat in, then locked it. With the urinal and the cat in place, they awaited the time when their well-laid plans would bear the fruit they desired.

After all the gentlemen had gone to bed, around midnight Baronci stood up in bed, seized the urinal, and performed his customary function. Marco, who was awake, said: "Mr. President, you wake us up every night when you urinate." Baronci, who was dripping on the bed, turned a deaf ear. When he hung the urinal up again, he saw that everything had gone on the bed. Lying down again, he barely found any dry place.

When he got up in the morning and Toso came to help him dress, Baronci said: "Toso, I've been put to shame, and I don't know what to do about it." He described what had happened: "The urinal seems to be broken. Last night, when I urinated into it as usual, all the urine got onto the bed. If my colleagues see it, they'll say I pissed myself."

Toso said: "I've often told you that it would be better to get a little away from the bed, because glass frequently cracks, especially with urine in it, and then the contents spill out."

Baronci said: "I'm going to keep doing what I've always done! Why should I have the urinal if I have to get out of bed?"

Toso said: "I think you've done too much this time!" He spread out the blanket. "All right, I'll take the sheets to your house and ask them to give me another pair."

Baronci said: "Don't. If Lapa saw them filthy like this, she would never let me rest. Do as I say: take them to *your* house and give them to a maid there. Tell her to wash them in cold water and dry them, but don't say whose they are. Then you'll take them to my house. But see to it that they get cleaned today, and then you'll take them. At the same time, I want you to take the capon."

Toso followed orders. He took the sheets, had them washed, and immediately hung them out to dry. When they were dry, he brought them back to Baronci, who commended him for his diligence in doing laundry without heating water. Then he said: "Come here. Let's go get that capon, because Lapa is a capricious woman. If she has anything to say about the sheets, she'll calm down a little when she sees the capon."

While Baronci and Toso were still saying this, they reached the bedroom and Baronci opened the chest in which he had put the capon. The cat darted out and struck his breast. In his alarm, he let the lid fall and dashed out, so confused that he almost lost his mind. Marco and Federighi were walking his way to see how things would turn out. When they reached Baronci, they said: "What was wrong, that made you dash out of the bedroom?"

Baronci said: "I think it was the Enemy of God. And he was probably the one who turned my shoes inside out."

Toso said: "It looked like a cat to me."

Baronci said: "A tomcat, maybe. It seemed to me three times the size of a female."

Toso said: "Let's go to the chest, and give me the capon to take." They opened it again, but when it was open, there was nothing on the tray inside it.

Baronci said: "Oh, no! Toso was probably right: it was a cat, and she ate the capon!"

Marco and his confederate said: "How did the cat get in? Does the chest have an entrance for cats?"

Baronci pulled out all the fittings, studied them, and said: "I don't see any door for cats, or any other hole."

Federighi said: "I had a similar experience once when I was one of the council of *signori*. To make a long story short, when I sent my attendant to put the tray back in the chest, a cat was asleep in it. He didn't notice it, and it ate up everything on the tray, and then escaped in the same way this one did."

"What bad luck, because such a strange thing never happened to me before! I think that ever since yesterday I've been having an inauspicious day. Now I don't think I'll ever get through this term of office and get back home to my Lapa (when I'm with her, I never have any fears). From now on, I'll be awfully afraid living in these quarters, because I think there's something uncanny and accursed in these rooms. You keep on saying it was the cat, but did the cat turn my shoes inside out, or do something else that was even worse?"

Marco said: "You may be right. Prayers and litanies are good for this sort of thing. Get advice from masters of divinity."

For three days Baronci summoned learned divines, who advised him to pray and recite the Lord's Prayer for a week from four o'clock until matins. This advice had been concocted by the two confederates. And so Baronci, sick with fear, had practically no sleep for a week, protecting himself with many Lord's Prayers so the Devil wouldn't get into the chest again. By the time his term of office was over, he had lost forty pounds. Then he went home to Lapa, in whose arms he felt very safe. He told her he didn't want to sit on the council of priors ever again, because the Devil was in those rooms and had done the above-mentioned things to him (he narrated them in detail). He firmly believed it as long as he lived, which wasn't very long.

Clever men are often tempted by the ingenuousness of many of their fellows to do stunts to pass away the time. Even though these clever men may be city councilmen, it seems not unfitting for them to act that way, because they are often burdened with troubles and need something to cheer themselves up.

82. The Living Crucifix

In Siena there once was a painter named Mino, who had a very frivolous, and very beautiful, wife. A man of Siena had courted her a long time and had even enjoyed her favors. One of Mino's relatives had told him about it several times, but he didn't believe it. It came about, one day, that, while Mino was out of the house, and even out of the city gates for the purpose of looking at some art commission, night overtook him before he was back in town. His wife's lover, learning this, went to the painter's home in the evening to have his will of her.

When Mino's relative, who had posted lookouts, found out, he decided to convince Mino once and for all. He immediately left the city to locate Mino. Saying that he had to leave town for something, but needed to get

back in, he sent for someone with the keys to the city gate. Then this relative left town, leaving the man with the keys to wait for him. He found
Mino, who was in a church near Siena, and, on arriving, said: "Mino, I've
told you several times about the shame your wife is heaping on you and
our whole family, but you would never believe me. But, if you want to see
it with your own eyes, come with me right now and you'll find the man in
your house."

Mino was persuaded at once and returned to Siena through the gate.
His relative said: "Go home and make a careful search, because, when her
lover hears you, he'll hide, as you may well imagine."

Mino agreed, saying to his relative: "Please come with me. If you don't
want to come in, stay outside." And his relative consented.

This Mino specialized in painting crucifixes, particularly ones with relief carving, and in his house there were always four or six to be found, either finished or not. As painters usually do, he kept them standing on a
table, a very long banqueting table, in his workshop, leaning up against the
wall in a row, each one covered with a big cloth. At the moment there were
six, four with carving and two simply painted on the flat surface. All of
them were standing on a very tall table, lined up against the wall. Each was
covered by a large linen cloth of some type.

Mino arrived at his house door and knocked. His wife and her young
lover, who were awake, heard the knock and immediately suspected what
was happening. His wife, neither opening the window nor replying, went
over silently to a small, permanently open peephole to see who was there.
Discovering that it was her husband, she went back to her lover and said:
"I'm as good as dead! What should we do? The best thing is for you to
hide." They didn't see a good place—and he was in his shirt only—until
they hit upon the workshop where those crucifixes were.

The woman said: "You know what to do? Climb up on this table, and
place yourself up against one of these flat crucifixes. Spread out your arms
crosswise, the way these others are, and I'll cover you with the same linen
cloth that that one is covered with. Then let him come looking to his
heart's content! I don't think he'll find you all night. I'll make a little bundle of your clothes and put them in some chest until daylight. Then some
saint will help us."

The lover, unable to think straight, climbed onto the table, lifted the
cloth, and flattened himself against the plain crucifix, so that he resembled
one of the carved ones. The woman took the linen cloth and covered him
exactly the way the others were covered. Then she went to tidy up the bed
a little so it wouldn't look slept in, except by her. She picked up her love's
breeches, shoes, doublet, tunic, and other clothes, and rapidly made a
small, tight bundle of them, which she placed among other linens. Then
she went to the window and said: "Who's there?"

Her husband replied: "Open up, it's Mino."

She said: "At this time of night?" And she hurried to open the door.

When the door was open, Mino said: "You sure kept me waiting—showing how glad you were that I was back!"

She said: "If you waited too long, blame it on sleep, because I was sleeping and I didn't hear you."

Her husband said: "All right, let it rest." He picked up a candle and started looking all around the bed, and under it.

His wife said: "What are you looking for?"

Mino said: "You're pretending to be ignorant, but you'll find out."

She rejoined: "I don't know what you're talking about. You'll find out, too."

As he continued searching the whole house, he came to the workshop, where the crucifixes were. When the living crucifix heard him there, just imagine how he felt! But he had to stand still just like the wooden ones, even though he was scared to death. Fortune came to his aid, because neither Mino nor anyone else would ever have thought that someone was hiding there that way. After spending a little while in the workshop without finding anything, Mino left it.

This workshop had a door leading to the street that locked from the outside. A young assistant of Mino's used to open it every morning, the way other doors are unlocked. Where the workshop adjoined the living quarters, there was a little door through which Mino himself would come in. When he left the workshop for the family rooms, he would lock this door. And so the living crucifix couldn't have got out, even if he had wanted to.

After Mino had gone to and fro for a third of the night, finding nothing, his wife went to bed, saying: "Go on with your lunacy as long as you like. If you want to come to bed, come. If not, roam around the house like a cat as much as you want to."

Mino said: "When I'm good and ready, I'll show you clearly that I'm not a cat, you filthy sow. I curse the day you came here!"

His wife said: "I could say the same thing. Is it white or red wine that's talking out of you?"

"I'll let you know before too long!"

She said: "Come on to bed, it's best for you, or at least let me sleep."

Weariness put an end to their troubles for that night. The woman fell asleep, and Mino went to bed, too. His relative, who was waiting outside to see what would happen, stood there until after the bells rang, then went home, saying: "I'm sure that, when I left town to get Mino, the lover returned home."

Mino got up very early the next morning and made another search in every nook and cranny. Finally, when he was fed up, he opened the little door to the workshop and went in. His assistant opened the street door to the workshop. Meanwhile, Mino, looking at his crucifixes, noticed two toes of the hidden man's foot.

Mino said to himself: "I'm sure that's her lover!" Rummaging among the tools with which he smoothed and carved those crucifixes, he found none more suited to his purpose than a hatchet that was lying there. He took the hatchet and approached the table, ready to climb up to the living crucifix and cut off the main thing that had brought the lover there. When the man became aware of this, he leaped up, saying: "Don't fool around with hatchets!"

He ran outdoors through the open door, with Mino only a few steps behind him shouting: "Stop thief! Stop thief!" The man got away. Mino's wife, who had heard the whole thing, was met at her door by a lay brother from the Dominican friary, who was making his rounds with a basket, collecting alms for the friars. After he had come up the house stairs, as they sometimes do, she said: "Brother Puccio, give me your basket and I'll put some bread in it for you."

He handed it over. The woman took out the bread that was in it, and put in the bundle of her lover's clothes. On top of that, she put back the bread the friar had come with and four of her own loaves, saying: "Brother Puccio, for the sake of a woman who brought this bundle here from the public baths, where it seems Master So-and-so went yesterday evening, I've placed it underneath the bread in your basket, so no one would get the wrong ideas about it. I've given you four loaves. I beg of you, because the man lives near your church, to give it to him on your way. You'll find him at home. Tell him that the woman from the bathhouse is returning his clothes."

Brother Puccio said: "Not another word! Leave it to me." And he took his leave. Arriving at the lover's door, he pretended to be begging for bread, and asked: "Is Master So-and-so in?"

The man was on the ground floor. Hearing his name, he came to the door and said: "Who is it?"

The friar went up to him, gave him the clothes, and said: "The woman from the bathhouse sends you these." The man gave him two loaves of bread, and he left. The lover thought the whole thing over carefully and departed for the city center, the Piazza del Campo, being one of the first ones there that morning. There he went about his business as if his adventure had never occurred.

As for Mino, after much huffing and puffing, he found that he had been outdone by the living crucifix, who had escaped. He went over to his wife, saying: "You filthy whore, you call me a cat, you accuse me of drinking white and red wine, and you hide your lovers on crucifixes! Your mother has got to hear about this!"

. The woman said: "Are you talking to *me*?"

Mino said: "No, I'm talking to the donkey's shit."

"Well, have a good conversation with it," his wife said.

Mino continued: "And your face isn't red, and you're not ashamed? I can hardly restrain myself from sticking a hot coal up your you-know-what!"

His wife said: "You wouldn't dare, because I've given you no reason. By God's Cross, if you lay hands on me, it'll be the most dangerous thing you've ever done!"

He said: "Disgusting pig, you made a crucifix out of your lover! How I wish I had cut off the part of him that I wanted to before he got away!"

His wife rejoined: "I don't know what you're whining about. What crucifix was ever able to run away? Aren't they nailed down with sharp nails a span long? If that one wasn't nailed down, you should suffer the loss if he got away. Because it's your fault, not mine."

Mino dashed over to his wife and started battering her. "So you heaped shame on me, and now you're making fun of me?" Feeling the blows, the woman, who was much more robust than Mino, began to hit him back. What with one blow and another, Mino was soon down on the floor with his wife on top of him, giving him a good hiding.

She said: "What are you talking about? Take it any way you like. You get drunk in this place and that, then you come home and call me a whore. I'll beat you harder than Tessa beat her husband Calandrino the painter in Boccaccio's story. A curse on the man who first married off a woman to any painter! You're all fantastics and lunatics, always getting drunk and feeling no shame."

Finding himself getting the worst of it, Mino asked his wife to let him get up and to stop yelling, so the neighbors wouldn't hear the noise, run in to help, and find his wife straddling him. Hearing this, his wife said: "I'd like the whole neighborhood to be here!" She got up, allowing Mino to do the same. His face was all bruised. To quiet things down, he asked his wife to forgive him, because scandalmongers had led him to believe things that weren't true. In fact, he said, that crucifix had run away because it wasn't nailed down.

When Mino next walked through town, he was asked by the relative who had gotten him into his fix: "What happened? How did it go?"

Mino told him that he had searched the whole house without finding anyone. As he was looking among the crucifixes, he said, one of them had fallen on his face and bruised him as could now be seen. Similarly, to everyone in Siena who asked what had happened to his face, he replied that a crucifix had fallen on it.

Now it came about that, for his own good, he did no more about the matter, saying to himself: "What a fool I am! I had six crucifixes and I still have six. I had a wife, and I still have one, though I wish I didn't! If I stir up trouble, I'll only add to the harm that came to me this time. If she's determined to be a slut, no one in the world can make her mend her ways."[3]

---

[3]Here the translation omits a few words that refer to the story that follows in Sacchetti's collection, but is not included in this volume.

83. Taming a Shrew

About thirty years ago there was a man in Imola called Brother Michele Porcello. He was called Brother Michele, not because he was a friar, but because he was a lay member of the so-called Third Order of Franciscans. He was married, and he was a malicious, evil man, very hot-tempered. He used to travel through Romagna and Tuscany as a merchant. He would then return to Imola, when it was convenient for him.

As he was heading back to Imola one time, he arrived at Tosignano one evening and stopped at an inn kept by a man called Ugolino Castrone. This Ugolino had a very unpleasant, shrewish wife named Giovanna. When Brother Michele had dismounted, and was tidying himself up, he said to the innkeeper: "Make me a good supper. Do you have decent wine?"

"Yes, sir, you'll get a fine meal."

Brother Michele said: "Please prepare me a salad."

Ugolino said to his wife: "Giovanna, go pick a lettuce for the salad."

Giovanna made a face and said: "Go get it yourself."

Her husband said: "Please go and do it."

She replied: "I don't feel like it."

When Brother Michele observed her behavior, he ate himself up with vexation. Then, when Brother Michele wanted something to drink, the innkeeper said to his wife: "Please get such-and-such a wine." And he held out the jug.

Giovanna said: "You go! You'll get back faster, you're holding the jug, and you know the right cask better than I do."

Brother Michele, seeing how unpleasant she was in so many ways, said to the innkeeper: "Ugolino Castrone, you really are a *castrone*, a castrated ram. In fact, you're a sheep! Believe me, if I were in your place, I'd make your wife do whatever I told her."

Ugolino said: "Brother Michele, if you were in my place, you'd do just what *I'm* doing."

Brother Michele was boiling with rage at the loathsome behavior of Ugolino's wife. He said to himself: "Lord God, if You were so kind as to have my wife die, and Ugolino die, it would certainly be a good idea for me to marry this woman and knock her foolishness out of her." Brother Michele got through the night the best way he was able, and proceeded to Imola in the morning.

It came about that, the following year, there was an epidemic in Romagna that carried off Ugolino Castrone and Brother Michele's wife. Several months later, when the plague had passed, Brother Michele used every means possible to marry Giovanna, and his wish finally came true. After the wedding ceremony Giovanna went to bed, expecting to be treated the way new brides generally are, but Brother Michele, who had not yet digested that Tosignano salad, treated her to a cudgel. Without pausing, he battered her until she was a wreck. The woman's screams did her no good, because he really let her have it, and then went to sleep.

Two evenings later, Brother Michele asked her to put water up to boil, because he wanted to wash his feet. His wife didn't tell him to do it himself. She obeyed. When she took it off the fire and poured it into the basin, it was so hot that Brother Michele scalded his feet all over. When he felt it, he didn't say: "What's going on here?" He poured the water back into the pitcher, put it back on the fire, and brought it to a boil again. Then he poured the water back into the basin and said to his wife: "Come sit down. I want to wash *your* feet." She refused, but finally, fearing something worse might happen, she had to consent. He washed her with boiling water, and she squealed in pain and pulled away her feet. Brother Michele shoved them back into the water, punched her, and said: "Hold your feet still."

His wife said: "Woe is me, I'm being completely boiled!"

Brother Michele said: "There's a saying: Take a wife and she'll boil you. Now, I've taken you to boil *you* before I let *you* boil *me*." In short, he scalded her so badly that she was practically unable to walk for over two weeks, she was so thoroughly flayed.

On another day Brother Michele told her: "Go get the wine." His wife, who could hardly stand on her feet, took the carafe and hobbled away as best she could. When she reached the head of the stairs, Brother Michele gave her a punch from behind, saying: "Make it snappy!" And he threw her down the stairs. Then he added: "Do you think I'm Ugolino Castrone, who told you to go for the wine, and you told him to go himself?"

And so, Giovanna, scalded, battered, and bruised, had to do what she had refused to do when she was in perfect health.

It came about one day that Brother Michele Porcello locked the house doors, intending to celebrate an eight-day festival of wife-bashing. When she realized what he had in mind, she ran upstairs, climbed onto the roof through a window, and leaped from roof to roof until she reached the home of a woman who lived nearby. This woman took pity on her and kept her in her house. Then, when various neighbors, male and female, came to ask Brother Michele to take his wife back, and treat her as a husband should, he answered that she should come back by the same route. If she had departed over the rooftops, she should return that way, and no other. Otherwise, she should never expect to come back to his house.

The neighbors, acquainted with Brother Michele's nature, convinced the woman to return to that slaughterhouse by way of the roofs, like a cat. When she was back, Brother Michele started his drumming practice again. Emaciated and tortured, the woman said to her husband: "I beg you to kill me rather than torture me like this every day without telling me why."

Brother Michele said: "Since you still don't know why I'm doing this, I'll tell you. Do you remember the time I came to the inn at Tosignano one evening, when you were married to Ugolino Castrone? And do you remember how, when he told you to pick a lettuce for me, you told him to go get it himself?" At that point he gave her a terrific punch; then he continued: "And when he told you to get a certain wine, you said you didn't feel like it." Another punch. "I got so furious then that I prayed God to kill Ugolino Castrone and the woman I was then married to, so I could marry you. Granting my request in His mercy, He did away with them, and He has made you my wife so I can give you the correction that your Castrone failed to give you. And so, everything I've done up to now was to punish you for your faults, for your disgusting behavior when you were his wife. Now, being my wife from here on in, imagine what I'll do if you insist on acting that way. I assure you, everything I've done so far will seem like milk and honey to you. So, it's now up to you whether you want to keep testing me. I'll be there with the sticks and fists if I have to."

The woman said: "Husband, if I behaved improperly in the past, you've given me ample punishment for it. May God assist me in His grace to behave in such a way from now on that you'll be satisfied! For my part, I'll do my best, with God's help!"

Brother Michele said: "Master Stick has shown you the light. Now it's up to you."

The good woman changed her ways so completely, she seemed like another person. Without Brother Michele having to beat her, or even scold her, she divined his wishes and flew, not walked, through the house to carry them out. She became a model wife.

For my part, as I've indicated, I believe that it's almost entirely the husband's behavior that makes his wife good or bad. Here we've seen that Porcello accomplished what Castrone had been unable to. Though a proverb states that both good and bad wives need a taste of the stick, I, for one, believe that bad wives need the stick but good wives don't. Because if beatings are administered in order to change bad habits into good ones, bad women need them so they'll change their evil habits; whereas good women don't need them: if they gave up their good habits, they might acquire bad ones, just as it often happens that, when good horses are beaten and maltreated, they become fractious.

84. Dante, the Good Neighbor

Dante Alighieri of Florence, that most excellent Italian-language poet whose fame will never diminish, lived near the Adimari family in Florence. On one occasion a young knight of that family got on the wrong side of the law for some crime or other, and was about to be condemned by a special judge empowered by the Ordinances of Justice (which allowed control over the nobility). Now, this judge seems to have been a friend of Dante's. So, the young knight asked Dante to put in a good word for him with the judge.

Dante said he was glad to do so. After dining, he left home and set out on that errand. Passing by Porta San Piero, he came across a blacksmith who was beating iron on his anvil while singing a setting of poetry by Dante in the manner of a popular ballad singer. He was mixing up the words, skipping one here and adding one there, and Dante took it as a terrible insult.

He said not a word, but marched up to the smith's workplace, where there were many tools of the man's trade. Dante picked up the hammer and threw it into the street. He picked up the tongs and threw them into the street. He picked up the scales and threw them into the street. In the same way, he tossed out many of the tools. The blacksmith turned around violently and said: "What the devil are you doing? Have you gone crazy?"

Dante said, "Well, what are *you* doing?"

"I'm working at my trade," the blacksmith said, "and you're ruining my equipment, throwing it in the street that way."

Dante said: "If you don't want me to ruin *your* things, don't ruin mine."

The blacksmith asked: "What of yours am I ruining?"

Dante said: "You're singing my poetry, and not performing it as I wrote it. That's my only trade, and you're ruining it."

The blacksmith, furious, had nothing to say in return. He picked up his belongings and went back to work. If he felt like singing, he chose ballads about Tristan and Lancelot, and left Dante's poetry alone.

Dante continued on his errand to the judge's place. Arriving there, he recalled that the Adimari knight who had asked that favor of him was a haughty, impolite young man. Whenever he went through town, especially on horseback, he spread his legs so wide that he monopolized the street, unless it was a very wide one, making every passer-by polish the pointed toes of his shoes. Dante, who observed everything, had always disliked that sort of behavior.

Now Dante said to the judge: "You have this knight up before you for his crime. I'm putting in a good word for him, even though his behavior is such as to deserve an even greater penalty. I think that making wrongful use of public property is a tremendous crime."

Dante wasn't preaching to the deaf, because the judge asked what public property the man was making wrongful use of. Dante replied: "The thoroughfares: when he rides through town, he spreads his legs out so wide that everyone coming his way has to turn back and can't continue on his regular path."

The judge said: "And do you consider that a joke? It's a worse crime than the other one."

Dante said: "Well, you see, I'm his neighbor, and I'm putting in a good word for him." He went back home, where the knight asked him how things stood.

Dante said: "He gave me a favorable answer."

One day, men came to where the knight was and asked him to go and respond to the charges against him. He appeared in court, where, after the first charge was read aloud, the judge had the second one read, the one about his selfish way of riding. The knight, hearing that an additional penalty would be inflicted, said to himself: "I really improved matters! I thought that Dante's visit would get me off, and here I am with a double sentence!"

After responding to the charges, the knight went home. He looked up Dante and said: "You've really and truly done me a great service! Before you got there, the judge wanted to convict me of a single crime. After your visit, he decided to convict me of two." In his great annoyance with Dante, he went on: "If he convicts me, I have plenty of money to pay the fine, and when the time comes, I'll pay back the person responsible."

Dante said: "I gave you such a good recommendation that I couldn't have done better if you were my son. I'm not to blame if the judge made another decision."

The knight went home, shaking his head. A few days later, he was fined a thousand *lire* for the first offense and another thousand for his selfish way of riding. He was never able to forget his grudge, neither he nor the rest of the house of Adimari.

And so, Dante, as the principal cause of this, was exiled from Florence not long afterward as a member of the White faction. He later died in exile, in the city of Ravenna, to the great shame of his native city.

85. A Runaway Horse

Not long ago in the city of Florence there was a citizen very old in years, but highly novel in his ways. His name was Rinuccio di Nello, a man of great ancestry, and he lived near the church of Santa Maria Maggiore. He always kept a riding horse that was even older than he was. I don't know the breed of all those horses he kept in the course of his life, but each one seemed more ungainly than the last.

He had one horse toward the very end of his life that looked like a camel. Its back was like the hill at Pinza di Monte near Prato, it had a mandrake's head, and its hindquarters were like those of an emaciated ox. Whenever he spurred it, it moved all of a piece, as if made out of wood, raising its muzzle to the sky; and it always seemed to be asleep, except when it had seen some broken-down mare. Then it would raise its tail, whinny a bit, and fart. It was no wonder that this horse had digestive troubles, because Rinuccio often gave it vine runners instead of straw, and acorns instead of barley.

It came about by chance one day that this Rinuccio wanted to take a ride, and had tied up this horse out in the street. A mare came to the square where the lumber market was held, almost directly opposite his house.

Breaking herself loose from a hook, the mare started running down the street where Rinuccio's horse was tied. Hearing the mare behind him, he pulled his head up so sharply that he broke his very strong bridle. Rinuccio had had this bridle made on purpose, to show everyone that the horse was so strong as to be barely manageable. Now the horse pulled back his head, with all his bodily strength behind it, and snapped the bridle. Turning toward the mare, which was heading toward Santa Maria Maggiore, he followed her in a frenzy, as stallions usually do.

Rinuccio, all ready to step outside and mount his horse, heard an enormous racket. Everyone was running to see this unusual incident. Coming to the door, he saw no sign of his horse, and he asked where it had gone. A cobbler told him: "Rinuccio, your horse is pursuing a mare with his member standing, and I thought I saw him covering her in Santa Maria Maggiore Square. Go help him, because he could very well get hurt!"

Not even taking the time for an exclamation of surprise, Rinuccio started running, and frequently came close to tripping over his spurs. Taking new streets in his pursuit of his nag, he came to the Old Market. There he found his horse covering the mare. Seeing this, he began to yell: "Saint George! Saint George!"

The junk dealers, thinking this was the announcement of a riot, started locking up their stands. The two horses got among the butcher stalls, which were in the open air at the time, in the middle of the square. Reaching the counter of a butcher named Giano, who sold veal, the mare jumped onto that counter, with the stallion behind her as you'd expect. Giano was dumbfounded and nearly died. The pieces of milk-fed veal displayed on the counter were all trampled and turned into pieces of mud-fed veal. And Giano, nearly out of his mind, escaped into an apothecary's shop. Rinuccio, beside himself, kept shouting: "Saint George!" For his part, Giano was shouting: "Oh, Lord, I'm ruined!"

The owner of the mare was still pursuing the horses with a stick. In an attempt to mitigate their carnal desires, he dealt out hard blows, now to the stallion, now to the mare. A number of times, when he was beating the stallion, Rinuccio jumped on him, saying: "By Saint Eligius, the protector of horses, if you hit my horse, I'll hit you!"

And so they, and all their hubbub, reached Via Calimala, where all the cloth vendors began to toss their fabrics into their shops and lock them up. One person said: "What's going on?" Another said: "What's this all about?" Others were just stupefied. Many followed the horses, which had turned down the narrow lane that leads to Orsanmichele. Now the horses got among the grain sellers and the tubs of grain that they sell outside the building with the great chapel. Here the horses trampled a lot of grain.

And the blind men, who were always stationed there in great numbers by the Pilaster, heard the racket and got shoved and trampled. Not knowing the reason for the uproar, they were lashing out with their staffs, hitting people at random. Most of those getting hit attacked the blind men, unaware of their condition. Others, knowing they were blind, noisily reproached their attackers, and were attacked in turn. And so, everyone started beating someone else with his staff, on this side and that, in one way or another. There were numerous scuffles on all sides.

At the same time those damned horses left Orsanmichele, the stallion's amorous animal ardor not yet having cooled down, but in fact having increased. With perhaps some punches delivered to Rinuccio and the owner of the mare, the whole group, fighting and raising a racket, reached the Piazza dei Priori. The priors, and everyone else in their official building, seeing such a noisy mob arriving from all directions, were sure it was an uprising. They locked the building and armed their attendants, as well as those of the city captain and the chief of police. The square was filled with people, some fighting one another, others chasing "Bucephalus" and Rinuccio, who was by now exhausted and in need of help.

As Fortune wished, the stallion and the mare almost simultaneously entered the little courtyard of the chief of police. He, terrified and ignorant of the true state of affairs, imagined that the populace was furious with him for wanting to execute a prisoner of his, though public opinion was strongly against it. He escaped behind the bed of one of his notaries, and then crawled under it, though he was already wearing half his armor.

The mob was still mainly fighting with their fists, but was almost ready to resort to weapons, when suddenly the gate of the chief of police, which is never locked, did get locked, and the stallion and mare were laboriously captured. The two horses were dripping with sweat, and Rinuccio di Nello was more dead than alive. He wasn't sweating because he was so dried up at his age. The wheels of his spurs had slipped down and had pierced the soles of his feet; the area beneath his heels was all torn up.

When the *signori*, who had observed all this, were reassured, they sent out commanders and soldiers to quell the brawls and racket. It took all their proclamations and issuing of orders to quiet the mob down.

Finally, when a period of calm had set in, the people started to disperse, but hundreds of them still followed Rinuccio and his "Bayard." They considered Rinuccio a real crackpot. The owner of the mare returned with her to Via Venezia, all bruised and battered. There he rested up until he was more or less himself again, though he swore that he'd never keep a mare again as long as he lived (and he kept his word).

When the podestà and the captain, who had put on their armor, heard that all danger had passed—having learned the cause of the commotion and of the subsequent calm—they mounted their horses and entered the square with their two brigades at nearly the same time. Those few who had remained there made fun of them, as having obeyed the philosophy of the *Distichs of Cato*: "Shun commotions." The soldiers stayed there awhile, saying: "Where have they all gone to?" Then they finally left.

One citizen, who had gone for the chief of police (who had hidden), said to the chief's financial officer: "What's the chief doing? Sleeping?"

The man replied: "When the racket started, I saw him putting on his armor, but since then I haven't seen him."

The citizen rejoined: "He must have hidden in some latrine. He has certainly brought honor both on himself and on me, since I was sent to get him! Did our other authorities do the same?"

As they spoke, they went to his building, where the citizen inquired after the chief. Everyone shrugged their shoulders; he was nowhere to be found. Finally his closest associate, who knew where he had run off to, entered the bedroom where he was hiding under the bed, and said: "Come out, it's nothing."

He came out, covered with straw and cobwebs. Entering the main room, he met the citizen, who said to him: "Ho, Chief, where are you coming from? Do you think it's honorable not to have gone outside today?"

The chief replied: "It's been so long since I've put on armor that I couldn't find any good enough. It took me over an hour to put on the gorget, because the clasps that attach it were broken. It's still not right! But, my friend, do you think I should still go out to the square?"

"Go as fast as you can!"

"Go find my horse, and let's move out!" Then he went to put on a helmet; when he took hold of it, a nestful of mice swarmed out of the lining. When the chief saw that, he started to cross himself and step backwards, saying: "My God, this is my unlucky day!" Turning to an attendant, he said: "Where did you keep this helmet, may Christ and His Mother confound you!"

Nevertheless, just as it was, he put it on his head. Mounting his horse with a surcoat full of cobwebs and trimmed with straw, he sallied forth into the square, where nothing had been going on for two hours. Those who saw him said: "Bravo! Bravo! A fine time! He must be crazy!" Others said: "Where the devil is he coming from? To me he looks as if he's coming from Nepi." Still others said: "He's coming from some stable, where he must have hidden when he got scared."

And so he halted where the quintain is planted to be tilted at. Looking all around, he said: "Where are all the rioters? Just watch me massacre them!"

Some people came up to him and said: "Chief, go home, it's all over!" Others said: "Go tell your men to give you a good shaking and then come back, because you're covered with cobwebs!"

At that moment he was turning toward the windows of the Palazzo Vecchio, signaling to learn whether his superiors wanted him to do anything. The priors sent word to him to go and take his armor off; the honors were his, because he had remained master of the battlefield. The chief left, feeling as if he had been shamed in actuality. After taking off his armor, he planned a way to remove that shame.

The next day he set in motion a trial, charging Rinuccio di Nello with disturbing the peace. Rinuccio went to the *signori* for help, begging them for mercy, so he wouldn't be ruined on account of a lustful, lively horse. The priors, who had been amused by a number of his previous scrapes, sent for the chief. It took them four days to break down his opposition, because he insisted that he'd either convict Rinuccio or resign.

Finally, he was "satisfied with the facts," as Dante says. The chief thought he had regained his honor, though he grumbled for over a month at not having been able to see justice done. And that's where the matter ended.

Now, let rulers of governments stop to think how easy it is to start mobs rioting! Certainly, anyone pondering this seriously would live in greater fear, the higher he thought his station in society was. Since this has already occurred in many places, you, too, reader, stop to think whom you should trust if you want to live in peace!

86. Adventures of a Florentine Painter

There have always been eccentrics among painters. One such, from what I've heard, was a Florentine painter named Bonamico, who was nicknamed Buffalmacco. He was a contemporary of Giotto's, and an eminent master. Since he was so highly esteemed in his profession, he was commissioned by Bishop Guido of Arezzo to paint a chapel when that bishop was lord of Arezzo. And so, Bonamico visited the bishop, and they agreed on terms. When the subject matter and the deadline had been arranged, Bonamico began working.

At the beginning he painted several saints, then he left off work toward Saturday evening. A monkey, not to say a big ape, belonging to the bishop had watched the painter's movements and gestures while he was on his scaffold, and had seen him mix his colors, handle the pots of paint and add egg to them, pick up his brushes, and apply them to the wall. The monkey had studied the whole process well enough to botch it up, as they always do. Furthermore, being a mean, destructive creature, it had a wooden ball tied to one foot, by the bishop's orders.

All the same, on Sunday, while the people were at their midday meal, this monkey went to the chapel, climbed up one of the supports of the painter's scaffold, and jumped onto the scaffold. When it was there, it picked up the paint pots, upsetting the contents of one into another, and squashed and spilled the eggs. Then it took the brushes, smelled them, dipped them into the paint, and smeared them across the figures of the saints. It was all the work of a moment. And so, before very long, the figures were all painted over, and the paints and their containers turned upside down, spilled, and ruined.

When Bonamico returned to his workplace on Monday morning to complete the painting he had begun, he found some of his paint pots on their sides and the rest upside down, his brushes scattered all over, and his painted saints all smeared over and spoiled. His first thought was that someone in Arezzo had done it out of envy or for some other reason. He went to the bishop and told him that what he had already painted was destroyed.

The bishop was infuriated, and said: "Bonamico, go back and redo the ruined part When you've redone it, I'll assign six soldiers with falchions to you. They'll stand guard with you, hidden somewhere. Whoever comes, they are to show him no mercy, but cut him to pieces."

Bonamico said: "I'll go and restore the figures as quickly as I can. When that's done, I'll come and let you know, and you can do what you said." With that understanding, Bonamico painted the same figures over again. When he finished, he told the bishop where things stood. Immediately the bishop summoned six soldiers armed with falchions and ordered them to remain with Bonamico, hidden in a certain spot near the fresco. If anyone came to disfigure it, they were to let him taste their steel at once. And so it was done: Bonamico and the six falchion-bearing soldiers waited in ambush to see who would come and spoil the painting.

After remaining there awhile, they heard someone prowling in the church, and at once they knew it was the people who had come to disfigure the saints. The rolling sound they heard was made by the wooden ball tied to the monkey's foot. Immediately the monkey came up to the scaffold support and climbed onto the scaffold where Bonamico worked. Knocking over all the paint pots, mixing up their contents, taking the eggs and spilling and smelling them, it picked up the brushes and rubbed them against the wall one by one until it had smeared it all up.

When Bonamico saw this, he laughed and burst with rage at one and the same time. Turning to the soldiers with the falchions, he said: "We don't need falchions, you can go with God's blessing. The case is solved, because the bishop's monkey paints one way, and the bishop wants the painting to be done a different way. Go take off your armor."

When they left their hiding place and approached the scaffold, where the monkey was, the monkey immediately started to lose its temper. Scaring them by thrusting out its muzzle, it began to run away and finally left. Bonamico and his retainers went to the bishop, to whom he said: "Father, you have no need to send to Florence for a painter, because your monkey wants the paintings done his way. Besides, it knows how to paint so well that it has corrected *my* paintings twice. So, if I'm due anything for my labors, please give it to me, and I'll go back to the city I came from."

When the bishop heard this, he was sorry that his painting commission was taking that turn, but, all the same, he burst out laughing at this unusual occurrence, and he said: "Bonamico, though you've already redone these figures, I want you to do them one more time. The worst way I can punish that monkey is to have it put in a cage close to where you're work-ing. It will see you paint, and it won't be able to ruin your work. I'll keep it there until several days after the painting is finished and the scaffolding has been removed."

Bonamico agreed to that, and it took no time for work to resume, while a makeshift cage was constructed and the monkey was placed in it. When the monkey saw the artist at work, you wouldn't believe the grimaces and gestures it made, but it had to face up to the reality of its situation. A few days later, when the painting was done and the scaffold was gone, the mon-key was released from prison. It returned to the chapel for several days to see if it could smear up the wall again, but, no longer finding the platform or any other way to climb up, it had to turn its attention elsewhere.

The bishop and Bonamico laughed over this odd incident for several days more. In order to make amends to Bonamico, the bishop called him aside and asked him to paint an eagle, the symbol of the Ghibellines, in his palace. It was to resemble a living eagle standing on a lion (symbol of the Guelphs and of Florence), which it had killed.

Bonamico said: "My lord bishop, I'll do it, but when I work I must be enclosed all around by reed mats, so no one can see me."

The bishop said: "No, not with mats: I'll have you shut in with paneling in such a way that no one can watch you at work." And it was done. When Bonamico had assembled his paint pots, paints, and all his other gear, he entered the church he was to decorate. There he began to paint the ani-mals the bishop had commissioned, but just the other way around: a large, fierce lion stood on an eagle it had torn to shreds. When he was done, he locked up the enclosure in which he had worked, and told the bishop that he was lacking certain colors, and that it was necessary to lock up his en-closed workplace with several different locks until he went to Florence and came back.

When the bishop heard this, he gave orders to lock up the place with lock and key and with a bolt until Bonamico was back from Florence. And so, Bonamico left Arezzo and arrived in Florence. The bishop waited one day after another, but Bonamico didn't return; he had finished the paint-ing and departed with no intention of ever coming back. After the bishop had waited in vain several days for Bonamico to return, he ordered some of his servants to go and break down the paneling that enclosed the scaf-fold and to see what Bonamico had painted.

Some men went there, opened the place up, and looked at the painting. Then they returned to the bishop and said: "The painting shows clearly that the artist did just the opposite of what you wanted."

"How is that?"

And they told him. Wanting to make sure, he went to see it. Once he had seen it, he flew into such a rage that he proclaimed the painter's prop-erty and person forfeit in Arezzo, and even sent threats to him in Florence.

To those who threatened him with action by the bishop Bonamico replied: "Tell the bishop to do his worst. If he wants me, he'll have to send me either a bishop's mitre or the mitre worn by people sentenced to the pillory!"

After observing Bonamico's character, and after condemning him, the bishop, who was after all a wise ruler, thought things over, and decided that Bonamico had acted properly and wisely. He revoked the proclamation against him and made friends with him again. Sending for him many times, he treated him as an intimate and a faithful servant as long as he lived. And so it happens many a time that lesser men overcome their superiors by various shrewd actions, and win their good favors when they most expect their enmity.

87. A Shower of Ink

In the parish of San Pancrazio in Florence there was once a notary named Master Buonavere. He was a tall, portly man, with very yellow skin, as if he suffered from jaundice, and his shape was so odd, he seemed to have been rough-hewn with a pickaxe. He was enamored of lawsuits, and was always in court with some rightful or wrongful case. On top of that, he was careless; in the writing case he wore there was never any inkpot, quill, or ink. Whenever he was stopped by someone in the street with the request to draw up a contract, he would rummage through his writing case and say he had forgotten his inkpot and quill at home. And he would tell the people to go to the apothecary's for ink and paper.

It came about by chance that a rich man in that neighborhood was dying after a long illness. He wished to make his will at once, and his relatives were afraid he might be overtaken by death before he could make it. One of them looked out the window and saw this Master Buonavere coming down the street. He called to him to come up, and met him halfway up the stairs, begging him for the love of God to draw up this will, because it was high time.

Master Buonavere rummaged through his writing case and announced that he didn't have his inkpot. He said he'd go for it at once, and he did. Back home, it took him a good hour of hard searching to find the inkpot and a quill. When the sick man's relatives, who were eager for him to make his will before he died, saw that it was taking Master Buonavere so long, they were afraid the patient would die on their hands and sent right away for Master Nigi da Santo Donato.[4] They had *him* draw up the will.

After leaving home again, Master Buonavere, who had had a lot of trouble and had spent a lot of time liquefying the surface of the dried-up ink in his pot, arrived to draw up the will. He was told that he had taken so long

---

[4]A historical figure, shown by a document to be still living in the year 1403. Other real contemporaries of Sacchetti are mentioned later in the story.

that the task had been assigned to Master Nigi. So he went back home in disgrace. Lamenting greatly to himself for the loss he seemed to have suffered, he determined to lay in a long-lasting supply of ink, paper, and quills, and to go around with a well-stocked writing case, so that such a thing would never happen again.

He visited an apothecary and bought a quantity of paper. Binding the sheets tightly, he put them in his bag (which resembled a gamebag). Buying a small bottle and filling it with ink, he attached it to his belt. Then he purchased not one quill, but a bundle of quills, and he labored for a full day to sharpen a large number of them. He hung them at his side in a little leather bag of the kind you keep medicinal drugs in. Thus equipped, he said: "Now let's see whether I'm as ready to draw up a will as Master Nigi is!"

When Master Buonavere's supplies were all at hand, he happened to go to the podestà's office that very day to draw up a document impugning the competence of a judge. He was to do this for an assistant judge of a podestà, who had come there from Monte Falco. This assistant judge was an old man, who wore a cap trimmed all around with entire squirrel bellies, and a pink robe. As he sat at his bench, Master Buonavere arrived, with the ink bottle hanging at his side and the document in his hand. Making his way through the big crowd there, he came face to face with the judge. The counsellor for the other party was Master Cristofano de' Ricci, and Master Giovanni Fantoni was his attorney. These two, on seeing Master Buonavere with the document, made their way into the crowd, pushed through, and came before the judge. When both they and Master Buonavere had the judge's attention, Master Cristofano said: "What's this about an impugnment and crap like that? This business will get settled by axes!"

Just then, as they brushed up against one another, Master Buonavere's ink bottle broke, and most of the ink found its way onto the assistant judge's cape, while some splashed the counsellor's. The assistant judge, seeing this and lifting up the edge of his cape, was nonplussed and started looking all around and ordering court attendants to lock the door to the building, so the source of the ink could be located.

Master Buonavere, seeing and hearing this, put his hand to his belt in search of the ink bottle. He found it shattered, with a lot of the ink all over him, too. He immediately made his way through the crowd and disappeared. The assistant judge, wet almost from head to foot, and Master Cristofano, spattered, looked at each other, dumbfounded. The judge looked up at the vaulted ceiling to see if the ink had come from up there; then he looked at the walls. Seeing no source of the ink there, he turned back to the bench, studying the top of it, then, leaning over, the bottom of it. Next, he walked down the bench steps, looking at each one. Finally, after inspecting everything, he started to cross himself so hard he nearly went out of his senses.

Master Cristofano and Master Giovanni, to get the judge on their side, kept saying: "Your honor, don't touch it! Let it dry!"

Other people said: "That robe of yours is ruined."

Others said: "It looks like those ash-colored clothes people used to wear."

While everyone was staring and making remarks, the judge started getting suspicious. Looking at the crowd, he said: "Does anyone know who it was that disgraced me this way?"

One person gave one answer, another gave another. Finally the judge, beside himself, told the police sergeant to ask the supervisor of sanitation to file an official report of this crime, which fell under his jurisdiction.

The sergeant, nearly laughing, said: "To whom should he charge it, if you, on whose person it was committed, don't know who? The best thing you can do is see that no one brings ink up to your bench. Have your robe, which is black at the bottom, shortened. If it's shorter, that will be no harm, because you'll look halfway like a man-at-arms."

The judge, hearing such talk and being all but mocked on every side, accepted the sergeant's advice, and was the loser in that affair. For a good two months he inspected everyone who approached his bench, thinking that more ink would be thrown at him. From the part of his robe that he cut off at the bottom he made socks and gloves, as well as he could.

On the other hand, right after the splashing incident occurred, Master Cristofano came down the bench steps, lifted the skirts of his robe, puckered up his lips in amazement, and he and Master Giovanni Fantoni said, in Latin: "By the Gospels of Christ, this is a great miracle!"

And so several people were stupefied in the course of a single morning, not counting the fact that Master Buonavere possessed only one pair of white hose, and, when he got home, he found them all ink-spattered and resembling the slate on which children write their ABC's. Each of the victims washed up and reduced the ink stains as best he could, but the best medicine for them was to calm down again and forget about it.

It would have been better if Master Buonavere had never become a notary, or, since he *was* one, if he had more forethought and went about better equipped for his profession, as his wiser colleagues did. If he had been prepared, he would have drawn up that will, which was a very profitable job. He wouldn't have ruined the judge's robe or Master Cristofano's, and wouldn't have driven the judge and the others there out of their wits. He wouldn't have spilled the ink on his own tunic, or on the hose, which cost him more. Finally, he wouldn't have lost the money he spent on the broken ink bottle and the ink it contained—though Fortune was largely on his side, because, if that judge had identified him as the culprit, he would have had to pay for the ruined robes, and might have received even worse punishment.

That's where matters rested, proving the proverb that says: "In a hundred years and a hundred months, water returns to its source." That's how it was with Master Buonavere: after a long drought without ink, he hung so much of it on his belt that he flooded a podestà's courtroom with it.

88. Dreams of Glory

If, in the preceding story, Master Buonavere lost his income and lived in poverty because he was careless and didn't suspend his writing implements from his belt, as notaries generally do, in the story that follows I wish to show how a Florentine became very rich in a single night and reverted to an impoverished condition the next morning.

And so, my story goes that, in the days after Gian Galeazzo Visconti, also known as the Count of Vertus, murdered his uncle Bernabò, lord of Milan,[5] there was much talk of this in the city of Florence. It came about by chance that a man named Riccio Cederni, a very pleasant-natured fellow, was involved in a lawsuit in the course of which his life had been threatened. He always went around wearing a skirt of tasses, or armored kilt, and a helmet.

One day he heard a lot of gossip about the quantity of money and jewels the new count of Milan had taken possession of. Going to bed that night, he took off his helmet and placed it upside down on a strongbox, so the sweat on it could dry. When asleep in bed, he began to dream. In one of his dreams he arrived in Milan, and Bernabò and Gian Galeazzo welcomed him with honors. They led him to one of their huge palaces, and, after he had been treated like the Holy Roman Emperor for a while, they had him seated between them. Sending for enormous containers of gold and silver, full of freshly minted ducats and florins, they made him a gift of them. In addition, they offered him their entire domain. In his sleep this Riccio[6] had become either a lion or a peregrine falcon!

After this slumber and these dreams of glory, Riccio awoke toward dawn. He was nearly beside himself because, now that he was awake, he realized he had reverted from the loftiest rank and wealth to his state of poverty. He knew he was back in his great distress, and started to lament the awful misfortune of seeing his wishes go up in smoke. Then, nearly out of his wits with sorrow, he got out of bed and got dressed to go out. His mind still clouded by his fancies, he went down the stairs with great difficulty, not sure whether he was asleep or awake.

Reaching his doorway on his way out, and reflecting on the wealth he considered he had lost, he raised his hand to scratch his head, as gloomy people often do, and found he was still wearing the nightcap he had slept in that night. In his mingled absentmindedness and melancholy, he turned

---

[5]This occurred in 1385. Vertus, near Champagne, was the dowry brought to Gian Galeazzo by his royal French bride.   [6]Among the meanings of this name is "hedgehog."

around and went right back to his bedroom. Tossing the nightcap onto the bed, he headed straight for the strongbox on which he had left his helmet in its cloth hood. He picked it up briskly and put it on his head, when he felt trickling down his temples and cheeks an abundance of smelly filth. During the night a cat had defecated copiously into that helmet. When Riccio felt himself so well bedaubed, he took off the helmet at once—its lining was soaked through—and called his maid, while he cursed his luck.

He told her his dream and said: "How unlucky I am! In my dream last night I had all that wealth and prosperity, and now I find myself covered with filth!" The maid, not thinking straight, wanted to wash him with cold water, but Riccio started yelling at her to light a fire and put up some lye to boil. She did so. Riccio remained bareheaded the whole time it took for the lye to boil. When it was hot, he went into a small courtyard, where the disgusting water from his washing could drain off into a sewage channel. For about four hours he laboriously washed his head.

After his head was washed (but not so thoroughly that it didn't smell for another few days), he told his maid to bring the helmet. It was so well filled all around that neither one of them felt like touching it. There was a small tub in the courtyard, which he decided to fill with water. When it was full, he flung the helmet into it, saying: "Stay there till you're good and clean!" Then he put on his head the warmest hood he owned. But, warm as it was, because he wasn't wearing the helmet he got a toothache on top of everything else, and he had to stay at home several days. His maid was kept in, too: she removed the helmet lining and scrubbed it for two days as if she were cleaning tripe.

Riccio was sad when he recalled his dream of wealth, the reality he had woken up to, and his toothache. Finally, after much grumbling, he sent for an artisan to make him a new lining. When his toothache had abated, he went outdoors and headed for the Canto de' Tre Mugghi, where his shop was located. There he regaled many people with sad tales of that incident and his bad luck in general. Now that the loss of his nocturnal gold had been compensated for by the cat's dung, he was forced to accept the facts.

It's that way very often with dreams. There are lots of men and women who believe in them as firmly as they would in a real thing. They'll avoid passing by a place on the day after dreaming they met misfortune there. One woman will say to another: "I dreamed a snake bit me." Then, if she breaks a drinking glass that day, she'll say: "That's what the snake in my dream meant." Another woman may have dreamed she was drowning. An oil lamp will fall, and she'll say: "That was my dream last night." Yet another woman will dream of falling into the fire. The next day she'll have a fight with her maid for doing something wrong, and she'll say: "That was the dream last night." And Riccio's dream can be interpreted that way, too: at night he was surrounded with gold and money, and in the morning he was covered with cat dung.

89. The Demon Cockroaches

When a man living in this world has many odd, amusing, and varied adventures, the entire course of his life can't be recounted in a single short story. Therefore, I'll now tell yet another one about a character I've introduced in a number of the preceding stories: the painter Bonamico, who tried to sleep at night, unlike Gian Sega in the last story I told,[7] who attempted just the opposite.

When Bonamico was young, he was the pupil of a painter named Tafo[8] and spent nights in his house, in a bedroom separated from Tafo's by a partition. Master painters are accustomed to wake up their pupils at the hour of matins to start painting, especially in winter, when nights are long. For half a winter now, Tafo, following this custom, had continually awakened Bonamico while it was still dark. Bonamico was getting fed up with the situation, since he much preferred sleeping to painting, and he pondered over ways and means to break that pattern. Reflecting that Tafo was getting on in years, he hit on a clever trick to stop him from awakening him at night, so he could get some more sleep.

And so, one day he went down to an ill-swept cellar, where he caught about thirty cockroaches. Somehow getting hold of some small, thin pins and some wax candle stumps, he placed everything in a little box in his room. Waiting one night for Tafo to get up to call him, and hearing him sit up in bed, he took the cockroaches one by one, planted the pins in their backs and stuck the lighted candle stumps onto the pins. Then he sent them through the opening under his door, into Tafo's bedroom.

When Tafo spotted the first one, and then the others, with their lights all over his room, he began to shake like a twig. Covering his face with his blanket (his sight was bad, and limited to one eye), he commended himself to God, reciting prayers to the Blessed Virgin and penitential psalms. He remained in fear that way until daybreak, really believing they were demons from Hell. Then, getting out of bed as if possessed, he called Bonamico, saying: "Did you see what I saw last night?"

Bonamico replied: "I didn't see a thing, because I was sleeping and had my eyes closed. I'm surprised that you didn't wake me up as usual."

Tafo said: "Wake you up? I saw a hundred demons in this room and got the worst scare I ever had! This past night, not only did I not think about painting: I didn't know whether I was coming or going! And so, my friend Bonamico, I beg you for the love of God, find some other house we can rent. Let's get out of this one, because I don't intend to stay here. I'm an old man, and if I have three nights like the one I've just spent, I won't live till the fourth one."

Hearing his master speak that way, Bonamico said: "I find it odd that,

---

[7]Not included in this selection.   [8]Or Tafi, aka Andrea Ricci. Still living in 1320.

sleeping in the very next room to you, as I do, I didn't hear or become aware of any of this. It often happens that someone thinks he sees something during the night that doesn't really exist. And many times people have dreams that seem to be true, but are merely dreams. And so, don't hasten to change houses so impetuously. Try this one another night or two. I'm right beside you and I'll be alert, so that, if anything happens, I'll take care of everything."

Bonamico reassured Tafo at such great length that he reluctantly agreed to remain. When he got home in the evening, he kept staring at the floor like a man possessed. After going to bed, he was on guard all night without sleeping, raising his head and laying it down again. It never entered his mind to wake up Bonamico so he could start painting. Rather, he was ready to call upon his assistance, in case he saw what he had seen the night before.

Bonamico was aware of the whole situation. Still afraid of being awakened too early, he sent three cockroaches, with their customary light fixtures, through the opening. The moment Tafo saw them, he wrapped himself up in the blanket, commending himself to God, making vows, and saying numerous prayers. He didn't have the courage to call Bonamico, who, his joke over, went back to sleep, wondering what Tafo would say to him in the morning.

When morning came, Tafo ventured out of his blanket, sensing that day had broken. He got up feeling dull-witted and called Bonamico in a shaky voice. Bonamico, pretending he had just awakened, said: "What time is it?"

Tafo said: "I heard every hour rung last night, because I didn't shut an eye."

Bonamico asked: "Why?"

Tafo replied: "On account of those devils—though there weren't as many as the night before. You won't persuade me again to stay! Let's get out of here, because I'll never set foot in this house again!"

No matter how many times Bonamico urged him to stay at least one more night, only one argument did the trick: he made him believe that, if an ordained priest were to sleep in Tafo's house, the demons would no longer have the power to remain there. And so, Tafo went to his parish priest and begged him to have supper and spend the night with him. He told him why, and, while they were discussing the matter, they met Bonamico and all three went to the house.

The priest, seeing Tafo almost beside himself with fear, said: "Don't be afraid, because I know so many prayers that, even if the house were full of them, I'd drive them all out."

Bonamico said: "I've always heard that the demons were God's worst enemies. If that's so, they must be great enemies of painters, since they paint God and His saints, and through their work they strengthen the Christian faith, which would seriously flag if our paintings didn't make people devout. And so, this being the case, when the demons, whose power is greater at night, hear us getting up at that time to paint things that cause them great anger and grief, they come in great force to hinder us from doing it. I don't guarantee the truth of this; but it seems quite evident to me that it may be so."

The priest said: "As I hope for God's grace, this reasoning is very convincing! But things proven are more trustworthy." Turning to Tafo, he said: "Your need to make money isn't so great that, if what Bonamico says is really true, you can't give up painting at night. Try it for a few nights while I sleep here: don't get up and don't paint, and let's see what happens."

They were convinced of this after the priest had slept there a few nights, during which no cockroach-demons were seen. Then they believed firmly that Bonamico's theory was self-evident and true. For two weeks Tafo slept soundly, and didn't awaken Bonamico. After this reassurance, Tafo, who needed money, started calling out to Bonamico one night, because he had to finish a panel painting for the abbot of Bonsolazzo. Bonamico, seeing the whole business starting over again, caught more cockroaches. The following night he set them loose in Tafo's room again at the usual hour.

When Tafo saw them, he ducked under the blanket and said sadly to himself: "All right, Tafo, work at night now that the priest isn't here! Mother of God, help me!" He added much more, dying of fear until daybreak. When he and Bonamico got up, Tafo told his pupil that the demons had reappeared.

Bonamico replied: "It's clear that what I said when the priest was here is true."

Tafo said: "Let's go see the priest."

They visited him and told him what had occurred. And so, the priest declared that Bonamico's theory was correct, and announced it to his parishioners as the gospel truth. The result was that not only Tafo, but the other painters, too, were afraid to work at night for long afterward. The news spread abroad, crowding out all other topics of conversation. People deemed that Bonamico, a man of saintly life, had been vouchsafed, either through divine inspiration or through revelation, the reason why those demons had appeared in Tafo's house. From that time on, his reputation soared, and from a pupil he became a master.

He left Tafo's house and, a few days later, set up shop on his own, determined to be a free man and sleep as long as he liked. For the years Tafo had yet to live, he found a different house, where he vowed that he would never again paint at night, so he wouldn't fall into the hands of the cockroaches.

And so it often happens that, when a master looks out for his own profit and cares nothing about his pupil's comfort, the pupil racks his brains to keep within the schedule that nature requires. When all other means fail, he devises a novel way to trick his master, as Bonamico did, enabling himself to sleep as much as he wanted for some time thereafter—until, on another occasion, a woman kept waking him up with her spinning-wheel, as the next story will tell.[9]

90. The Crab's Revenge

The following is a novel story about a husband and wife, possibly more unusual than any other you'll ever hear. In the city of Cittanuova in the Marches, near the seacoast, there once lived a shallow-water fisherman, who used hooks, lines, and small nets. A young man, he was named Mauro. He had a young wife called Peruccia. It came about by chance one day that Mauro, who had gone out to fish, caught some sea crabs, which, since they're very hard to handle, he had placed in a net bag. If you've ever seen crabs of that type, and how big their pincers are, you can imagine how pleasant it is to be seized by one.

When Mauro came home with his catch toward evening, dying for some food and drink, as people in his trade generally are after a day's work, he said to Peruccia: "Prepare me some supper." Then he put down the bag of crabs on the foot end of the bed. Pretty soon the food was ready, and husband and wife sat down to eat. After supper, they both felt tired and went to bed, forgetting to take away the bag.

And so, shortly after they had fallen asleep, one of the crabs, which are always restless, looking for holes through which it could get out and get back to the sea, escaped through the opening of the bag and crept between the sheets. It came up to the woman where her "mouth without teeth" was located, perhaps seeking a hiding place. When the woman felt it, she got scared and touched it to find out what it was. The crab, feeling itself touched, tensed up, the way they do, seized one lip of the woman's nether "mouth," and squeezed. Peruccia couldn't help emitting a loud shriek.

The sound awakened her husband, Mauro, who said: "What's wrong?"

She replied: "Husband, some creature or other has grabbed me you-know-where!"

Her husband got up at once, went for a candle, and said: "Where is it? Where is it?" as if he were drawing near a fire.

Continuing to scream, the woman pulled down the blanket, saying: "My God! Look what's covered me with shame!" And she was close to fainting away.

Mauro, seeing how and where the crab had taken hold of her, said: "By the Virgin of Oreno! One of the sea crabs I caught today has come out of the bag I put on the bed, and has grappled you this way!" Trying with his hands to seize now this leg, now that one, he tugged at the crab to separate

---

[9]Not included in this selection.

it from the woman. But the crab, as their nature is, clamped down and held on harder, the harder it was pulled. With its other pincer it tried to catch the hands of the man pulling it. The women, yelling, was in tremendous pain.

Then the man hit on a different tactic, a very simple one: he bent his head down toward that part of his wife's anatomy, planning to bite off the pincer that was giving her so much grief. As he thrust forward his mouth to bite down on the crab's occupied claw, its free claw seized him by the lip. He immediately started to yell. His wife was yelling and tugging, and he was yelling and tugging.

Mauro's yells were very loud, because they reechoed within his wife's body. The harder they pulled, the harder the crab pinched. The noise attracted the others in the house, who yelled: "What's going on?" And it attracted the neighbors, who entered and stopped at the bedroom door. The room was locked, but the door was small and weak. They knocked it down and came in. When they asked the couple what was wrong, they heard the story, though it was very hard for Mauro to tell it with his lip caught in the crab's claw.

In her shame, on top of her other suffering, his wife had pulled up the blanket. Her husband was yelling because, besides his pain, he was suffocating under the blanket. The more adventurous members of the household said: "We've got to see this!" They pulled away the blanket and, amazed to see the married couple caught by a sea crab in two such different places, they crossed themselves. Mauro lamented and, as well as he was able, asked them to help him.

Among the assembled group was a strong blacksmith, who ordered an apprentice of his to go to his smithy for a pair of pliers. The lad quickly made the round trip, and the blacksmith quickly cut through the crab's pincers. Peruccia and Mauro were very frightened at those pliers, not to mention their shame, which was as great as their fear.

And so, the shame-laden couple were freed from the sea crab by the blacksmith. The crab had left them with such bad and painful wounds that the husband went around for a few days with a little ointment on his lip; while his wife probably medicated herself as well, because for some time she walked with her legs wide apart.

The locals found the incident a rich source of laughs and gossip for long afterward. But that wasn't the last of it: the blacksmith demanded payment and Mauro refused, claiming that blacksmiths were paid for putting on horseshoes, not for removing them. The blacksmith retorted:

"What! Shouldn't I get paid when I give medicine to a horse and save it from danger of death or some other misfortune? Or if a mad dog (and that crab was very similar) sank its teeth into a horse and wouldn't let go, and I got it to let go and then cured the horse, wouldn't I be entitled to payment?" And, giving many more good reasons, he finally got them to give him twenty *soldi,* as if he had shoed a horse.

Things like that happen frequently to people who are careless, or, better yet, absentminded. This man came from the sea with crabs, put them on his bed, and got what he deserved for being so foolish; because, even though he had caught the crab in the sea, the crab avenged itself by catching him and his wife in such a way that, when the crab was removed by the blacksmith, Dante's lines were applicable to the situation: "He raised his mouth from his bloodthirsty meal," and so on. And so, in this life men get caught in various predicaments so numerous that no one could imagine them all. Therefore, no one should trust in Fortune, because many a time the bite of a tiny spider has killed a powerful man.

STORIES 91–99

From *Les cent nouvelles nouvelles*

This work, usually characterized as the earliest French-language story collection, in the modern sense of the term, is the product of an extremely sophisticated milieu of the very late Middle Ages. It was compiled in the years just preceding 1467, when the ruler to whom it was dedicated died. This was Duke Philip the Good of Burgundy, who was born in 1396 and began to rule in 1419. In his day, Burgundy, whose capital remained Dijon, became a small empire, with territories forming an arc in a northwesterly direction through what is now eastern and northern France, into parts of the Low Countries (the latter bringing in the richest revenues). This empire was unwieldy and precarious, and began to fall apart under the very next duke; but while it lasted, Burgundy was one of the most highly cultured areas of Europe, a trendsetter in fashion, the fine arts, and music.

The *Cent nouvelles nouvelles* reflect a pleasure-loving, frivolous court. Their unknown compiler collected and retold in a uniform style a hundred stories (without a frame story) that he attributed to thirty-six people: the duke himself and his courtiers and friends in Dijon. The stories included in this anthology have the following attributions:

No. 91: Monseigneur de la Roche (Philippe Pot).

Nos. 92 and 93: Philippe de Loan, the duke's equerry, or master of the horse.

Nos. 94 and 97: Michault de Chaugy (or, Chauzy), gentleman of the chamber.

No. 95: Monseigneur de Quiévrain.

No. 96: Monseigneur de Thalemas.

No. 98: Anonymous.

No. 99: The compiler (several people have been suggested, but there is no agreement).

The dedication to Duke Philip states that the collection is being called "A Hundred New Stories" because it is meant as a local counterpart to Boccaccio's *Decameron*, which was then generally referred to in French as the *Cent nouvelles* (Hundred Stories). "The contents, style, and fashion of these [new stories]," the dedication concludes, "are quite fresh in our memory and present a very new countenance."

The stories are of the sort that might once have been told in a regimental officers' mess, or after dinner over the port and cigars. They are almost all humorous, and a very large number of them are risqué, or "Gallic." This was perfectly to the taste of Duke Philip, who was a sexual adventurer. It is said that a study of the archives and judicial records of the time makes even the wilder stories seem true-to-life and not mere wish-fulfillment fantasies.

Many of the stories are inspired by early medieval *fabliaux*, by Boccaccio (naturally), and by the scabrous Latin-language anecdotes called the *Facetiae* (Jokes), written ca. 1450 by the Italian humanist Poggio Bracciolini. The style of the *Cent nouvelles nouvelles* is conversational, like that of a good storyteller — jaunty, frothy, full of irony, uninhibited.

No. 91 bears an uncanny resemblance, in its theme of a miller's sexual revenge on a magnate, to Pedro de Alarcón's novella *El sombrero de tres picos* (The Three-Cornered Hat; 1874), though in the Victorian-era Spanish story neither adultery is actually consummated. (Alarcón was the source for Hugo Wolf's opera *Der Corregidor* of 1895 and Manuel de Falla's ballet of 1919, produced by Diaghilev as *Le tricorne*.)

No. 92 is a reminiscence of very recent military history, and indicates how rapidly witty sayings and doings become attributed to historical characters.

No. 93 is especially memorable for the phrase "the beast with two backs," which reappears in Rabelais in the 16th century and in Act I, Scene i of Shakespeare's *Othello*.

The double-entendre tirade ostensibly addressed to the dog at the end of No. 94 puts one in mind of the end of Marcel Pagnol's 1939 film *La femme du boulanger* (The Baker's Wife; based on material by the novelist Jean Giono), in which the baker refrains from upbraiding his runaway wife, but delivers a scathing tirade against their house cat, just back from a night on the tiles.

Nos. 95 and 97 have typical *fabliau* plots.

The voluntary capture, and especially the mode of rescue, in No. 96 cannot fail to remind readers of English of certain ballads about Robin Hood.

The basic plot of No. 98 occurs in earlier literature, but this telling is outstanding.

No. 99 is a rarity for this collection: a thoroughly tragic story. The unforeseeable, senseless brutality that comes out of nowhere to destroy all plans is a plot element very familiar to readers at the end of the unnerving 20th century.

91. Tamping and Fishing

Not long ago in the duchy of Burgundy there was a noble knight whose name will not be stated in the present story. He was married to a beautiful, charming lady. Quite near the castle where this knight resided there dwelt a miller, who was also married to a beautiful and charming young woman. It came about on one occasion that the knight was riding around his home to pass the time of day in pleasure. Alongside the stream on which both his home and that miller's mill were situated (at the time, the miller wasn't in, having gone to Dijon or Beaune) he caught sight of the miller's wife, who was carrying two pitchers, on her way back from fetching water at the stream.

He rode toward her and greeted her pleasantly. She, being both polite and well-mannered, paid him due respect, curtseying. Our knight, observing the beauty and fine figure of the miller's wife, and noticing that brains weren't her strong point, came up to her good-naturedly and said: "My good woman, I can see for a fact that you're ill and in grave danger."

Hearing this, the miller's wife came nearer, saying: "Alas, my lord, what's wrong with me?"

"Truly, my good woman, I see clearly that, if you keep on walking ever so little, your privates are in very great danger of falling off. I dare say that they'll fall off before very long, if I'm any judge."

The naïve miller's wife was amazed and upset at the gentleman's words: amazed at his power to predict that disaster, and upset to hear she would lose the best part of her body, which both she and her husband made the most use of. So she replied: "Alas, my lord, what's this you tell me? By what signs do you recognize that my privates are in danger of falling off? I have the feeling they're quite firmly attached."

"Come now, my good woman," the gentleman replied, "my word should be enough for you. You may be sure I'm telling you the truth. Nor would you be the first woman that it happened to."

"Alas, my lord," she said, "now I'm a ruined, dishonored, and lost woman! And what will my husband say, by Our Lady, when he learns of this disaster? He'll have no more regard for me."

"Don't be dismayed too soon," the gentleman said. "It hasn't happened yet, and, besides, there are reliable cures for it."

When the miller's young wife heard that there was a possible cure for her case, the blood began returning to her cheeks. To the best of her ability she begged the gentleman, for God's sake, to be so good as to teach her what to do to keep those poor privates from falling off.

The gentleman, who was very courteous and gracious, said: "My dear, since you're a beautiful and good girl, and I'm fond of your husband, I have pity and compassion for your case. And so I'll teach you how you can keep your privates."

"So, what must I do, my lord?"

"My dear," he said, "the way to keep your privates from falling off is to tamp them down again as soon, and as often, as possible."

"Tamp them down, my lord? Who knows how to do that? Whom should I speak to to get the job done properly?"

"I'll tell you, my dear," the gentleman replied. "Now that I've warned you about your disaster, which was imminent and very serious, and informed you of the necessary means to avoid the distress that might result from your condition (for which I'm sure you'll be grateful to me), it pleases me, in order to cement our good relations, to tamp down your privates personally. I'll restore them to such a good state that you'll be able to carry them around anywhere without fear or apprehension that they might ever fall off. And this I guarantee."

There's no need to say or ask whether our miller's wife was overjoyed. She strained the little sense she had in thanking the gentleman sufficiently. The two of them walked up to the mill, and it was no time before they set their hand to their task. For, the gentleman in his courtesy produced a tool with which in a brief period he tamped down the privates of the miller's wife three or four times, making her quite happy and contented.

After their labors were at an end, after they had had a long conversation, and after a day had been set for more work on those privates, the gentleman departed and rode back home smartly. On the prearranged day the gentleman visited the miller's wife and, to the best of his ability, using the same method, he labored to tamp down those privates. Over a period of time he had done so much good work that the privates were out of danger, and were very solidly attached.

During the time when our knight was tamping down and plugging up the privates of the miller's wife, the miller returned from his business trip. He and his wife greeted each other effusively. After discussing their business and duties, the oh-so-clever wife said to her husband: "By my faith, husband, we're greatly obliged to the lord of this manor."

"Really, dear?" the miller said. "In what way?"

"It's only right for me to tell you, so you can thank him yourself, because you really ought to. While you were away, he passed in front of our house once when I was going to the stream with two pitchers. He greeted me, and I returned his greeting. While I was walking, he noticed (who knows how?) that my privates were very loosely attached and might fall off any minute. He graciously told me about it, and I was amazed, God knows, and just as upset as if the world were coming to an end. The kind gentleman, seeing me lamenting so, took great pity on me. And so he taught me a fine cure to escape that danger. He did even more for me, something he wouldn't have done for any other woman—because he himself performed the cure he told me about, which was to tamp down and plug up my privates to keep them from falling off. It was hard work for him, and he sweated at it on several occasions, because my case required a number of visits. What more can I tell you? He did the job so well that we'll never be able to repay him. By my faith, one day this week he tamped me down three or four times, another day twice, another day three times. He never abandoned me before I was all cured. And he's restored me to such a condition that right now my privates are as solidly attached as those of any woman in our village."

The good miller, hearing this adventure, gave no outward sign of what was in his heart. Instead, as if he were tickled pink, he said to his wife: "Well, well, dear! I'm very glad that the lord did us this favor. If God wills, whenever it's possible I'll do as much for him, if I can. But, all the same, since your case involved a part of the body that's not respectable, take care not to tell anyone about it. Furthermore, since you're cured, there's no need for you to put the gentleman to further trouble."

"Rest assured," his wife said, "that I'll never say a word about it, because the gentleman forbade it, too."

Our miller, who was a jolly rogue, often recalled the favor his master had done for him, but behaved so well and discreetly that the gentleman never noticed that he suspected the trick he had played on him, and was confident that he knew nothing of it. But, alas, he did, and all his desires, study, and thoughts were bent on a revenge, if possible, that would match the lord's deception of his wife. His mind was never at rest, and finally he came up with a plan whereby, if he could accomplish it, he would surely give his master tit for tat.

Some time afterward, the knight had some business to attend to. He mounted his horse and took leave of his lady for a month. Our miller felt no little joy in learning this. One day, the lady of the manor felt like bathing. She had water drawn and heated for a bath in her bedroom. Our miller was aware of this, because he was accustomed to come and go there. He hit on the idea of taking a fine pike that swam in his pond and making a gift of it to the lady in her castle.

Some of the lady's maids wanted to take the pike and bring it to her, saying it was a gift from the miller, but he wouldn't let them, insisting on presenting it to the lady in person. Otherwise he'd take it away again. Finally, because he was a familiar figure and a merry fellow, the lady sent for him while she was in her bath. The gracious miller offered her the fish, for which she thanked him, sending it to the kitchen to be prepared for supper.

While the lady was chatting with the miller, he noticed on the rim of her tub a beautiful, large diamond that she had taken off her finger, fearing that the water might damage it. He filched it so deftly that nobody noticed. At an opportune moment, he said farewell to the lady and her attendants, and returned to his mill, thinking about what still remained to be done.

The lady, enjoying herself with her women, saw that it was late and already time for supper. She left her bath and lay down on her bed. Looking at her arms and hands, she didn't see her diamond. She called her maids and asked them about it, inquiring as to which one she had entrusted it to. They all said: "It wasn't me." They searched high and low, in the tub, on the tub, everywhere. It was no use: it was nowhere to be found.

The search for the diamond continued for some time, but there was no trace of it, and the lady felt awful about it, because the jewel was unfortunately lost, and lost in her own room. Besides, her husband had given it to her on their wedding day, so it was all the dearer to her. There was no one to suspect, and no one to ask about it, so that great sorrow reigned in the castle.

One of the maids thought things over, and said: "Not a soul came in except us here and the miller, so I think you should send for him." He was sent for and he arrived. The lady, as upset and chagrined as possible, asked the miller whether he'd seen her diamond. He, as good a fibber as any man, if truth be told, defended himself up and down, even going so far as to ask the lady whether she thought he was a thief.

She replied gently: "Certainly not, miller. Besides, it wouldn't be theft if you had taken my diamond as a joke."

"My lady," said the miller, "I tell you on my faith that I know nothing of your diamond." So, the group of women was downcast, especially the lady, who was so chagrined that she couldn't refrain from shedding copious tears, she missed that ring so badly. The sorrowful group had a consultation about what to do. One woman said the diamond must be in the room, and another said she had searched everywhere, and it couldn't be there without being found, since it was very conspicuous. The miller asked the lady whether she had it before entering the bath, and she said yes.

"If that's the case, my lady, in view of the great diligence with which the search was made, and its lack of success, this is definitely an odd occurrence. All the same, it seems to me that, if there's anyone on this manor who could help you recover it, it's me. But, because I don't want my powers to be revealed or generally known, I think it opportune to speak to you in private."

"I have no objection," the lady said. She sent away her attendants. As they left, Jeanne, Isabeau, and Katherine said: "Ah, miller, how kind it will be of you if you make the diamond come back!"

"I don't guarantee it," said the miller, "but I'll say this: If it's at all possible to locate it, I'll find out how." Seeing himself alone with the lady, he told her that he strongly suspected, and was pretty sure, that, since she had had the diamond just before bathing, it had slipped off her finger, fallen into the water, and lodged in her body, unless someone was withholding it from her.

He made another careful search, then told the lady to go to bed. She would surely have refused, except that it was part of the procedure. After uncovering the front of her body, he pretended to scrutinize it all over, and said: "My lady, there's no doubt that the diamond has entered your body."

"And you say you've seen it, miller?"

"Yes, indeed."

"Alas!" she said. "How can it be removed?"

"Very easily, my lady. I'm confident I can manage it, if you let me."

"As I value God's aid, there's nothing I wouldn't do to get it back," the lady said. "Go to it, good miller!"

The lady, still lying on her bed, was positioned by the miller in just the way that the gentleman had positioned his wife while tamping down her privates, and he used the same tool as a probe for locating and fishing out the diamond. In the pauses after the first and second soundings in the miller's search for the diamond, the lady asked whether he had felt it. He said yes, so that she cheered up and asked him to continue until he located it.

To make a long story short, the good miller kept at it until he gave the lady back her beautiful diamond, and great joy pervaded the castle. Never

.uler receive as many honors and preferments as the lady and her at-
.ants showered on him. The good miller, to whom the lady was exceedingly grateful after the long-desired accomplishment of his master
plan, left the castle and returned home, without boasting to his wife about
his new adventure, which made him happier than if he had won the whole
world.

Shortly thereafter, with God's aid, the lord returned home, where he was
pleasantly welcomed and humbly greeted by his lady. After a little pillow
talk, she told him about her wonderful adventure with the diamond, how
the miller had retrieved it from her person. In short, she described every
detail of the procedure and the precise way in which the miller had located the gem.

Her husband wasn't very happy about it, and he realized that the miller
had put one over on him. The very next time he met the good miller again,
he greeted him loftily, saying: "May God keep, may God keep this good
diamond fisher!"

To which the good miller replied: "May God keep, may God keep this
vagina tamper!"

"By Our Lady, you're right!" said the gentleman. "If you keep quiet
about me, I'll do the same for you." The miller agreed and never spoke of
the matter again. Neither did the gentleman, so far as I know.

92. Anecdotes about Talbot in France

Lord Talbot,[1] may God have mercy on his soul, that English captain so
well remembered for his prowess, valor, and success in war, delivered two
judgments during his life that are worthy of being recounted and forever
retained in the minds of those who hear them. In order that this will actually be the case for these two incidents, I shall narrate them briefly in this,
my own first story,[2] but the fifth in this book.

During the time of the accursed and pestilential war between France
and England, which is not yet over, a French soldier was made prisoner by
some Englishman, as frequently occurs. After the amount of his ransom
was set, he was given a safe-conduct by Talbot and sent back to his own
commander to receive the sum, which he would then send or bring to his
captor. While on his way, he met another Englishman on the field, who,
seeing he was French, immediately asked him where he was coming from
and where he was going. The Frenchman told him the truth.

"And where's your pass?" asked the Englishman.

"Not far away," replied the Frenchman. Then he drew a small box from
his belt, containing his pass, and handed it to the Englishman, who

---

[1] John Talbot, first earl of Shrewsbury (1388?–1453), was a daring warrior, one of the principals on the
English side in the last phase of the Hundred Years' War in France. [2] The first one in the collection that
was allegedly told by Philippe de Loan.

perused it from end to end. Since it's general practice to include in all letters of safe-conduct the clause, "The bearer is forbidden to wear armor or
carry weapons of war," the Englishman noticed those words, and observed
that the Frenchman's doublet still had hanging from it the iron-tipped
cords used for attaching armor.

The Englishman decided that the Frenchman had violated the terms of
his safe-conduct, those cords being "habiliments of war," and he said:
"Friend, I'm taking you prisoner because you've broken your agreement."

"By my faith, I've done no such thing, saving your grace," the
Frenchman replied. "You see how I'm dressed."

"No, no," said the Englishman, "by Saint John, your safe-conduct has
been disobeyed. Surrender, or I'll kill you." The poor Frenchman, who
had only his page with him and was completely unarmed, whereas his opponent was in armor and had three or four archers to subdue him, surren-
dered. The Englishman led him to a spot very close by and threw him in
the guardhouse. The Frenchman, finding himself in this predicament,
rapidly sent word of his plight to his commander, who was dumbfounded
on learning what had befallen his man.

The commander immediately wrote a letter to Talbot and sent it by a
herald, who was well instructed and informed of the account that the imprisoned soldier had submitted to his commander at length: how one of
Talbot's men had detained one of his own who was traveling under Talbot's
safe-conduct. This herald, carefully instructed as to what he should say and
do, left his master and presented the letter to Talbot.

Talbot read it, and had his secretary read it aloud to several knights,
squires, and others of his entourage. I'll have you know that he immediately got on his high horse, because he was hotheaded and irascible, and
got very unhappy whenever his orders weren't carried out just so, especially
in wartime. Learning that a safe-conduct he had issued had been dis-
avowed, he was beside himself with rage.

To make a long story short, he called for the Englishman and the
Frenchman, and told the Frenchman to state his case. The man told how
he had been taken prisoner by one of Talbot's people, and that a sum had
been fixed for his ransom. "And under your safe-conduct, my lord, I was
proceeding toward my companions to obtain the sum when I met this gentleman here, who is also one of your men. He asked me where I was going,
and whether I had a pass. I said I did, and I showed it to him. After reading it, he told me I had violated it. I replied that I hadn't and that he
couldn't prove any such thing. In short, he wouldn't listen, and I was compelled to surrender, if I didn't want to be killed on the spot. I know no
reason why he needed to detain me, and I ask you for justice."

Talbot was very uneasy as he listened to the Frenchman. Nevertheless,
when the prisoner finished, he said to the Englishman: "What have you
got to say in reply?"

"My lord," the man said, "it's true what he says, that I met him and asked to see his pass, which I read every word of. And I saw at once that he had violated its terms. Otherwise I wouldn't have arrested him."

"In what way did he violate them?" Talbot asked. "Tell me at once."

"My lord, it was because his pass states that he's forbidden to wear habiliments of war, and he was wearing (and still is) his armor attachments, which constitute habiliments of war, because without them you can't put on your armor."

"And so," Talbot said, "armor attachments are really habiliments of war? Do you know anything further he did to violate the terms of his pass?"

"Nothing at all, my lord," the Englishman replied.

"And so, peasant," Talbot cried, "by the devil that's in you, you've detained a gentleman traveling under my safe-conduct because of his armor attachments? By Saint George, I'll show you whether they're habiliments of war or not!" Then, completely riled up and shaking with anger, he dashed over to the Frenchman, pulled two of those cords off his doublet, and gave them to the Englishman. He had the Frenchman handed a good sword, then drew his own excellent sword from its scabbard, and said to the Englishman: "Defend yourself with your so-called habiliments of war, if you can!" Then he said to the Frenchman: "Strike this peasant, who detained you without rhyme or reason. We'll see how he defends himself with your habiliments of war! If you spare him, I'll bring down *my* sword on your head, by Saint George!"

So, the Frenchman, willy-nilly, was compelled to strike the Englishman with the drawn sword he was holding. The poor Englishman ran around the room as nimbly as he could. Talbot followed them, constantly forcing the Frenchman to strike the other man, to whom Talbot shouted: "Peasant, defend yourself with your habiliments of war!" Truly, the Englishman was hurt so badly, he nearly died. He begged mercy of Talbot and the Frenchman, who in this way was set free, and released from his obligation to pay ransom, by Talbot. In addition, Talbot had the Frenchman's horse and trappings, and all the gear he possessed on the day he was captured, returned to him. That was the first of the above-mentioned judgments delivered by the good lord Talbot.

There remains to narrate the second, which was as follows: He learned that one of his men had stolen from a church the ciborium in which the consecrated wafers are kept, and had sold it for a hefty sum. I don't know exactly how much he got for it, but it was big and beautiful, made of gilded silver and elegantly enameled. Though Talbot was fierce and cruel, and savage in wartime, he always held the Church in great reverence, and wouldn't allow anyone to burn or plunder any monastery. Whenever he heard that someone had done so, he severely punished those who had disobeyed his orders in that regard.

Now he sent for the man who had stolen the ciborium from the church.

When the man came before him, God alone knows what a welcome Talbot gave him! He insisted on executing him, but those around him pleaded with him to spare the man's life. All the same, he wanted him to be punished, and said to him: "Villain and scoundrel, how did you dare to rob the church despite my orders forbidding it?"

"Ah!" cried the poor thief. "For God's sake, my lord, mercy! I cry you mercy! I'll never do it again."

"Come forward, villain!" Talbot said. The man came up to Talbot as willingly as if he were going to his doom. Talbot raised his fist, which was big and heavy, and brought it down on the good pilgrim's head, saying: "Ha, you thief, you robbed a church!"

The man yelled: "My lord, I cry you mercy! I'll never do it again."

"Will you ever do it?"

"No, my lord!"

"Now, villain, swear that you'll never set foot in any church again!"

"I swear, my lord," the man said.

The others present, hearing him swear never to enter another church, had a good laugh, though they pitied the thief, who was thus forbidden by Talbot to attend church, and made to swear that he would never set foot in one. Believe me, Talbot thought he was doing the right thing, and his intentions were honorable.

Now you have heard Talbot's two judgments.

93. The Virgin Husband

It's nothing new that in the lands of the count of Champagne there's always been a bumper crop of dullards, strange as that may seem to some, considering that they're such near neighbors to wickedly shrewd customers. Plenty of stories could be told on the subject to demonstrate the thickheadedness of the people of Champagne. But for the present the following story must suffice.

In that district, not long ago, there was a young orphan who had been left quite rich and powerful after the death of his father and mother. Though he was dull-witted, ignorant, and rather ill-natured to boot, he was industrious at holding onto his property and conducting his business as a merchant. Because of this, many people, including people of quality, would gladly have given him their daughters' hand.

One of these girls found special favor with the friends and relatives of our man of Champagne for her goodness, beauty, and fortune. They told him it was time to get married, and that he just couldn't carry on his business all alone. "Besides," they said, "you're already twenty-four, and just the right age for marriage. If you want to listen to us, we've looked around and picked out a beautiful, good-natured girl who we feel is just right for you. Her name is So-and-so; you know her quite well." And they stated her name.

Our hero, who didn't care what he did, whether it was getting married or anything else, as long as it didn't cost him any money, agreed to do what they asked. "Since you find it's to my benefit, handle the matter the best way you can, and I'll abide by your advice and orders."

"That's the right spirit," those good people said. "We'll watch out for you, and do your thinking for you, as if you were one of us or one of our children."

To make a long story short, pretty soon our man of Champagne was joined to that girl in holy wedlock. But on his first night in bed with his wife, inasmuch as he had never mounted a human steed, he immediately turned his back on her after giving her a few simple kisses, and nothing further. The bride was very dissatisfied, if any woman ever was, though she didn't let it show.

This barbarous proceeding took place on more than ten nights, and would have gone on and on, if the bride's mother hadn't come up with a remedy. I mustn't conceal from you that our hero, a tyro in social graces and in marriage, had been held on a very tight rein while his father and mother were alive. Above all, he had been forbidden to do the business of the beast with two backs, since they were afraid that, if he took a liking to it, he might squander his fortune. It seemed to them, with good reason, that he wasn't a man who would be loved just for his good looks. He, being a man who would never have upset his parents, and wasn't particularly amorous, was still a virgin. His wife would gladly have changed this in the usual pleasant way, if she had only known how to go about it.

One day the bride's mother visited her and asked her about her husband, his nature, his character, their marriage, and the hundred thousand other things women talk about. On each point our bride gave her mother a very satisfactory answer, assuring her that he was a kind man and that she had no doubt he was treating her well. This pleased her mother, but, since she was well aware from her own experience that in marriage something more is required than just getting enough to eat and drink, she said to her daughter: "Now, come over here and tell me, on your faith, how is he at those nighttime things?"

When the poor girl heard her mention those nighttime things, her heart nearly gave out, she was so vexed and grieved. Her eyes showed what her tongue didn't dare say: she started to shed a flood of tears. Her mother immediately grasped the meaning of those tears, and said: "Daughter, don't cry anymore, but speak to me straight out. I'm your mother, from whom you should have no secrets, and with whom you shouldn't feel ashamed. Hasn't he touched you yet?"

The poor girl, recovering from her near-faint and somewhat reassured and comforted by her mother's words, dried up the high tide of tears, but still didn't have the strength or presence of mind to reply. Her mother questioned her again, saying: "Give me a plain answer and stop crying. Has he touched you yet?"

In low tones and a voice choked with tears, the girl replied: "By my faith, mother, he has never touched me. As for the rest, he *is* a good and gentle man, by my faith!"

"Now, tell me," her mother said, "do you know whether he's missing any parts? Speak up if you know!"

"Saint John! He's perfectly healthy," her daughter replied. "Several times I've happened to feel his organs, while I was turning over and over in our bed, unable to sleep."

"That's enough," her mother said. "Leave the rest to me. Here's what you must do. Tomorrow morning you've got to pretend that you're very ill, and that you feel so bad, your soul is about to leave your body. Your husband will either visit me or send for me, I'm sure, and I'll play my part so well that you'll be deflowered before you know it, because I'm going to take your urine to a doctor who'll give the prescription *I* tell him to."

No sooner said than done: the next morning, at the first peep of day, our lovelorn heroine, in bed with her husband, began to moan and groan, counterfeiting an ailment so expertly, you would have thought a perpetual fever was gnawing at her body and soul. Our dunce, her husband, was extremely surprised and upset, not knowing what to do or say. He sent at once for his mother-in-law, who didn't keep him waiting. As soon as he saw her, he cried: "Alas, mother-in-law, your daughter is dying!"

"My daughter!" she said. "And what's wrong with her?" Then, continuing their conversation, they walked to the patient's room. The minute the lady caught sight of her daughter, she asked her how she felt. Carefully instructed, the girl didn't answer right off, but after a while she said: "Mother, I'm dying!"

"God forbid! Don't, daughter! Buck up! But how did this illness come upon you so suddenly?"

"I don't know, I don't know," the girl replied. "You're driving me frantic with your questions!" Her mother took her hand, felt her pulse, body, and head, then said to her son-in-law: "By my faith, take my word for it, she's sick! She's burning up! We have to find a cure. Is there any of her urine here?"

"Her urine from midnight is still around," said one of the maids.

"Let me have it," the lady said. Receiving the urine, she then asked for a urinal and poured the liquid into the vessel. Then she told her son-in-law to take it and show it to a doctor to learn what could be done for her daughter, and whether any help was possible. "For God's sake, let's spare no expense!" she said. "I still have some money, which I don't love as much as I love my daughter."

"Spare expenses!" shouted the dunce. "Believe me, if she can be helped out for money, I won't fail her!"

"Now get going!" the lady said. "While she rests a little, I'll go home, but I'll come back whenever I'm needed."

Now, I must inform you that, the day before, when our good mother had
left her daughter, she had primed the doctor, who knew exactly what prescription to give. Here's our ninny arriving at the doctor's with his wife's
urine. After paying his respects, he told him that his wife was suffering
from an ailment—in fact, she was extremely ill. "Here, I've brought her
urine so you can diagnose her illness better, and give me better advice."

The doctor took the urinal and lifted it, shaking up the urine inside.
Then he said: "Your wife has been severely attacked by a fever and is in
mortal danger unless she's tended to at once. Her urine here shows it
clearly."

"Oh, doctor, for the love of God, please tell me (and I'll pay you handsomely!), what can be done to make her well again? Do you think she can
survive?"

"She can survive if you do what I tell you," the doctor said. "But if there's
any delay, all the gold in the world couldn't save her."

"For the love of God," our hero said, "tell me and I'll do it!"

The doctor said: "She must lie with a man, or she's dead."

"Lie with a man?" the ninny said. "What do you mean by that?"

"It means," the doctor said, "that you must climb on top of her and give
her a good screwing three or four times very quickly. The more often you
can do it the first time around, the better it will be. Otherwise the great
heat that's drying her up and killing her can't be cooled down."

"Really?" the man asked. "Would that be good?"

"She's a dead woman beyond a doubt," the doctor said, "unless you do
it, and quickly, at that."

"Saint John!" the man said. "I'll do my level best!" He left and returned
home, where he found his wife loudly moaning and groaning. "How do
you feel, dear?" he asked.

"I'm dying, husband," she replied.

"No such thing, God willing!" he said. "I spoke to the doctor, who told
me a method of curing you." While speaking, he undressed and got in bed
next to his wife. As he approached her clumsily to follow the doctor's advice, she said: "What are you doing? Are you trying to kill me altogether?"

"No, I'll cure you," he said. "The doctor told me." Saying this, following
the dictates of Nature, and aided by the patient, he serviced her vigorously
two or three times. While he was resting, quite surprised at his experience,
he asked his wife how she was feeling.

"I'm a little better than before," she said.

"Thank God!" he said. "I hope you're out of danger, and that the doctor
was right." Then he resumed with renewed strength.

To make a long story short, he applied himself so well that his wife regained her health in just a few days, which made him very happy. So was
his mother-in-law when she found out. After this introduction to the battlefield, our man of Champagne became a jollier companion than he had

been previously. Since his wife was maintaining her good health, he got the idea of inviting his friends and relatives, along with her parents, to dinner one day. He did so, and dished up a grand feast in his rustic fashion, at which everyone was very merry. They toasted him, and he toasted them. He was amazingly sociable. But listen to what befell him:

At the height of the dinner party's merriment, he suddenly started to cry very hard, as if all his friends, if not the whole world, had died. There was no one at the table who wasn't wondering what those sudden tears were all about. Several people asked him what was wrong, but he could hardly answer, he was so hampered by that crying jag.

Finally he was able to speak, and said: "I have good reason to cry!"

"By my faith, you do not," his mother-in-law said. "What are you lacking? You're rich and powerful, you have a good home and good friends, and—don't forget—you have a beautiful, good-natured wife, whose health God has restored after she had one foot in the grave. I think you should be happy and carefree."

"Alas, I'm not!" he said. "It's my fault that my parents, who loved me so, and left me all this wealth that they had amassed for me, are no longer living. Because both of them died of a violent fever, and if I had given them the same good screwing when they were sick that I gave my wife, they'd still be with us today."

When he said that, there was no one at the table who wasn't itching to laugh, but they managed to contain themselves. The tables were removed, and everyone departed. The good man of Champagne remained there with his wife, who, to keep healthy, was frequently serviced by him.

94. An Exasperating Greyhound

If the incident I wish to recount had occurred in the days of the famous and eloquent Boccaccio, and had come to his ears or cognizance, I'm sure he would have added it to his volume of accounts of celebrated men who met with ill fortune.[3] Because I don't believe any nobleman ever suffered a more intolerable misfortune than the good lord whose story I'll tell you (and may God have mercy on his soul)! I let all my listeners be the judge whether his misfortune doesn't deserve to be in Boccaccio's book.

In his day, the good nobleman of whom I speak was one of the principal figures in the kingdom he lived in, endowed and gifted with every praiseworthy quality a nobleman should possess. Among his other qualities was that of surpassing all other men in his good relations with women.

Now, it came about that, while this reputation and happy destiny of his were flourishing, and he was the topic of every conversation, Love, who bestows his favors wherever he likes, threw him together with a young woman

---

[3]*De casibus virorum illustrium*, one of the Latin reference works Boccaccio wrote later in his life.

who was beautiful, charming, gracious, and shapely, and who enjoyed like
no other woman in her day a reputation for matchless beauty and praiseworthy and virtuous behavior. Nor was it any disadvantage that she was also
so well liked by the queen of the country that she shared her bed on nights
when the queen wasn't sleeping with the king.

This romance I'm speaking of had progressed so far that only the time
and place were still lacking for both parties to be able to do what they desired most in the world. On many occasions they met to decide on a place
suitable to their purpose. Finally the young lady, who desired her sweetheart's welfare no less than the salvation of her soul, hit on a good idea,
which she immediately communicated to him, in the following terms:

"My most faithful friend, you know that I sleep with the queen and that,
if I don't want to ruin all my chances, there's no way for me to give up that
honor and preferment, which the wealthiest woman in the kingdom would
be happy and honored to have; though, by my faith, I want to requite your
love and give you as much pleasure and affection as I give her. I'll prove
the truth of this to you, but without giving up the woman who shows me
the greatest honor in the world, and can do even more to advance me. I
don't think that you would want me to act otherwise, either?"

"No, by my faith, darling," the good nobleman replied, "but, all the
same, I beg of you, that while serving your mistress you don't neglect the
good that you can do for your own loyal servitor, who thinks so highly of
you that he'd rather win you than gain everything else in the world."

"Here's what I'll do for you, my lord," she said. "As you know, the queen
has a female greyhound she's very fond of. She lets it sleep in her bedroom.
Tonight I'll find a way to shut it out of the room without her knowledge.
When everyone else has left, I'll dash into the adjacent dressing room, un-
lock its door, and leave it open. When you think the queen is in bed, come
by very quietly, go into that room, and shut the door. There you'll find the
greyhound, which knows you and will let you get near it. Pick it up by the
ears so it gives a good, loud yelp. When the queen hears it, she'll recognize
its voice at once, and I'm sure she'll ask me to get up that very moment and
let it into the bedroom. When I do so, I'll join you. Don't fail if you ever
want to speak to me again!"

"Ah," the nobleman said, "my dear, faithful sweetheart, I thank you all
I can! You can be sure I won't fail you!" He took his leave and departed, as
did his lady, each of them planning and desiring to carry out their purpose.
Why waste a lot of words? When the time came, the greyhound expected
to enter its mistress's bedroom as usual, but the woman who had determined to keep it out forced it into the adjoining room. The queen went to
bed without noticing this, and very shortly afterward she was joined by her
good lady-in-waiting, whose thoughts were fixed on hearing the yelp, the
signal for amorous battle.

Before very long the nobleman prepared for action, and made his way into the room where the greyhound was sleeping. Groping around with hands and feet, he finally located the dog; then, picking it up by the ears, he made it give two or three sharp yelps. When the queen heard it, she recognized her greyhound at once, and thought it wanted to be let in. Calling her lady-in-waiting, she said: "My dear, my greyhound is crying outside. Please get up and let her in."

"Gladly, Your Majesty," said the lady-in-waiting. Though she was awaiting a battle, the day and hour for which she had herself arranged, the only armor she put on was her shift. Then she went to the door and opened it. At once she was met by the man who had been waiting for her. He was so happy and overcome at seeing his sweetheart's beauty and shapeliness that he lost his strength, wits, and presence of mind, and it was totally beyond his powers to draw his dagger and try to cut open her armor with it. There was plenty of kissing, hugging, fondling breasts, and what have you, but not a sign of the main event!

And so, the charming young lady had to withdraw without having left with him that which could never be his if he didn't win it by force of arms. As she turned to go, he tried to hold her back with force and fine words, but she was afraid to stay any longer. She shut the door in his face and returned to the queen, who asked her if she had let her greyhound in. She said she hadn't, because she hadn't been able to find it yet, though she had looked very hard.

"Well," said the queen, "we'll get her yet! Come back to bed." At that time, the poor lover was very unhappy, God knows, finding himself dishonored and enfeebled in that way. In the past he had been so confident in his powers that, in less time than he had just spent with his sweetheart, he could have taken on three just like her and conquered them with honor. Finally, he took heart again and said to himself: "If I'm ever so lucky as to find my lady in such a favorable situation again, she won't leave me the way she did this time!"

And so, inspirited and spurred by shame and desire, he picked up the greyhound by the ears again, pulling them so hard in his great vexation that he made the dog yelp much louder than the first time. At that outcry the queen awakened her lady-in-waiting, who once again came and opened the door. But she returned to her mistress without obtaining either more or less than she had done before.

Now she returned for the third time, and that poor nobleman did all in his power to service her as he wished, but the devil take him if he was ever able to break a lance on that girl, who wanted nothing better and stood her ground valiantly, awaiting him! When she realized he wasn't going to make holes in her basket, and that he was merely capable of holding his lance at rest, no matter how good an opening she offered him, she knew she had been unsuccessful in the joust and she thought all the less of her opponent.

She didn't wish or dare to remain there any longer, no matter what she might accomplish. But when she turned back to the bedroom, her lover kept her back by force, saying: "Alas, darling, stay a little longer, I beg you!"

"I can't," she said, "I can't. Let me go! I've been here too long, for all I've got out of it." She began to return to the bedroom with the man at her heels, trying to hold her back. Seeing this, in order to get even with him and to please the queen, she said out loud: "Go away, go away, you filthy hound! By God, you're not coming in here now, mean animal that you are!" And, as she said this, she shut the door behind her.

The queen, hearing this, asked: "Who are you talking to, dear?"

"To that dirty dog, Your Majesty, which gave me so much trouble looking for it. It had squeezed under a bench in here and hidden, flat on its belly and its muzzle on the floor, so that I was unable to find it. When I did, it refused to lift itself up, no matter how I coaxed it. I'd gladly have pushed it inside, but it never wanted to lift its head, and I got so annoyed, I left it outside and shut the door in its face."

"You did the right thing, dear," the queen said. "Come to bed, come to bed, and let's sleep."

As you've heard, the nobleman was most unfortunate. Because he couldn't respond when his lady was all ready, I for one believe that, later on, when he had his weapons under control, she was the one no longer interested.

95. The Devil from the Latrine

Not long ago, in the Picardy border country there was a gentleman (and I think he's still living there today) who was so deeply in love with the wife of one of his neighbors, a knight, that he couldn't enjoy a day or hour without being near her, or at least hearing news of her. And he was equally dear to her, which is no small thing. But their sorrow was that they couldn't find any way to be alone together in private, so they could have sufficient time to reveal what they felt in their heart—things that they'd never say in the presence of others, no matter how friendly those others might be.

Finally, after so many bad nights and painful days, Love, who aids and abets his faithful servants when he feels like it, arranged a happy day for them on which her vexatious husband, the most jealous man on earth, was compelled to leave his house to attend to a business deal of enormous importance to him. If he weren't there in person, he stood to lose a substantial sum, which he could gain if he were present. He did go, and in winning that sum, he made a better profit than he did by adding the name of cuckold to that of jealous man which was already his.

For, the minute he was out of his house, that gentleman, who wasn't barking after any other prey, arrived and made his way inside. (Without much delay he carried out his mission, receiving from his lady all that a loving servant dares, or is able, to ask—all this with as much pleasure and leisure as anyone could wish. They had no fear of being surprised by her husband, and didn't worry about such things at all. They intended to complete, that night, what they had begun during that jolly day, which had been much too short for them. They were sure that her damned husband couldn't be back before noon of the next day, at the earliest.

But it turned out differently, because the Devil brought him back home, managing somehow or other (and I really don't care how) to speed up his business. Suffice it to say that he returned that evening, at which those in his house—that is, the two lovers—were greatly amazed. They were so surprised, not having expected that unfortunate return, that the poor gentleman had no other recourse than to hide in the latrine adjoining the bedroom, from which he hoped to emerge whenever his lady love found a way, before the knight set foot there.

But things turned out quite differently, for the knight, who had covered fifteen or sixteen leagues on horseback during the day, was so tired that he couldn't drag himself around. He insisted on having supper in the bedroom, where he had removed his hose. He had a table set there instead of in the great hall. You may well imagine that our amorous gentleman was now regretting all the fun he'd had that day, because he was dying of hunger, cold, and fear.

What's more, to drive him even crazier and make his suffering worse, he was seized by a coughing fit, amazingly severe and awful, so that each of his coughs could almost be heard in the bedroom where the knight, his wife, and their servants were assembled. The lady, whose eyes and ears were constantly attentive to her lover, happened to hear him coughing, and became very frightened, thinking her husband might hear him, too. Right after supper she found a way to sneak into the latrine alone. There she urged her lover for God's sake to refrain from coughing like that.

"Alas, dear," he said, "I can't help it! God knows what punishment I'm suffering! For the love of God, think of a way to get me out of here!"

"I will," she said, and she left. The good man resumed his melodious coughing, and now so loudly that he would have been heard clearly in the bedroom, were if not for the conversations that the lady kept setting in motion. Finding himself unable to stop coughing, the good man knew no other way to keep from being heard than to stick his head into the opening of the latrine, where he was properly perfumed, God knows, by the preserves inside. All the same, he found that preferable to being heard.

To make a long story short, he remained for quite a while with his head in the latrine, spitting, clearing his nose, and coughing. He felt as if he was going to spend the rest of his life that way. Nevertheless, after that clever idea, the cough was gone, and he intended to pull his head out. But he was unable to do so, because he was so far in that he was stuck. Imagine how good he felt!

In short, he didn't know how to get out, no matter how hard he tried. His neck was all skinned and his ears were cut up. Finally, with God's help, he made such an effort that he detached the seat of the latrine, which was now encircling his neck. It was quite beyond his powers to get it off. Though it was cumbersome, it was better than his previous situation.

At that point, the lady came to see him. She was quite amazed, but couldn't help him. All she could say to comfort him was that she had no way of getting him out of that room.

"Is that how it is?" he said. "Hey, hey, by God's death, I'm wearing enough armor to fight someone, if I only had a sword in my hand." And the woman quickly brought him a very good one. Seeing the state he was in, despite her great fear she couldn't help laughing. Nor could the gentleman himself. "Well," he then said, "I commend myself to God, and I'm going to try to make my way out. But first blacken my face as much as you can." She did, and she prayed to God to help him.

And so, our merry companion, the toilet seat around his neck, a drawn sword in his hand, and his face blacker than coal, stepped forth into the bedroom. As chance would have it, the first person he met was the vexatious husband, who was so frightened at the sight of him, thinking he was a devil, that he collapsed on the floor, nearly breaking his neck, and remained there in a near-faint for some time.

His wife, hearing her husband just then, came forward, pretending to be much more frightened than she actually was. She grasped his arms and asked him what was wrong. Coming to his senses after a while, he said, in a pitiful, shaky voice: "Didn't you see the devil I met?"

"Of course, I did," she replied. "I almost died with the great fright I got, seeing him."

"How did he get in here?" he asked. "And who sent him to us? I'll never have an easy moment this year or next, I got such a scare!"

"By God, the same with me!" said his devoted wife. "Take my word for it, it means something. May God keep and guard us from all misfortune! I'm completely upset over this apparition!"

Then everyone in the house told his own version of the devil's visitation; they all thought it had really happened. But the good lady knew the truth of the matter, and was very glad that the others were deluded. Afterward, she and that devil had further sessions of everyone's favorite pastime, without the knowledge of her husband or anyone else, except for a chambermaid who was privy to their secret.

96. A Daring Rescue

At the time of the war between the Burgundian and Armagnac factions,[4] there occurred at Troyes in Champagne a very entertaining incident that

---

[4]First third of the 15th century.

is well worth telling, and including here. The city of Troyes, formerly on the Burgundian side, had become an Armagnac stronghold. There had formerly dwelt there a half-mad fellow—not that he had entirely lost his reason, but, rather, he was closer to Lady Folly than to Dame Reason, despite the fact that sometimes he said and did a number of things that a saner man couldn't have accomplished.

To come to the point, this gay blade was now garrisoned with the Burgundians at Sainte-Menehould. One day, in a conversation with his companions, he said that, if they were willing to trust him, he'd show them how to capture a large army of those skirt-chasers from Troyes. To tell the truth, he hated the people of Troyes mortally, and they had no love lost for him, but were always threatening to hang him if they could catch him.

He said: "I'm going to Troyes. I'll make my way into the outskirts, pretending to spy out the city and try out the moat with my lance. I'll come so close to town that I'll get captured. I'm sure that, the minute the judge sees me, he'll condemn me to be hanged, and no one in town will take my part against him, because they all hate me. And so, early in the morning I'll be led to the gallows, while you're lying in ambush in the closest woods. As soon as you hear them coming with me, attack the group, seize and capture as many as you like, and release me from their hands."

All his comrades in the garrison agreed and said that, if he was foolhardy enough to undertake that enterprise, they'd help him see it through. To make a long story short, the brave madcap approached Troyes, as he had said, and intentionally let himself be captured. The news of this event quickly spread throughout the city. Everyone there wanted to see him strung up. The judge, too, the moment he saw him, swore by Heaven that he'd hang by the neck.

"Alas, your honor," he said, "I beg for mercy! I've done nothing wrong."

"You're lying, scoundrel!" said the judge. "You've led the Burgundians to this area, and you've made accusations against the good citizens and merchants of the town. You'll pay for that, because you'll be hanged on the gallows!"

"Ah, for the love of God, your honor," said our jolly rogue, "since I must die, at least be good enough to make it early in the morning, so that, in this city where I've been familiar or acquainted with so many people, my execution isn't too public."

"All right, all right," said the judge, "I'll think it over." The next morning, at daybreak, the executioner was outside the prison with his tumbril. He had been there no time at all before the judge came riding up with his police officers and a large number of other attendants. Our hero was placed on the tumbril, trussed and tied. While he held onto his bagpipe, which he kept playing, he was led to the place of execution, where despite the early hour, there were more spectators than for many another hanging, so much was he hated in the city.

Now, I need to tell you that his comrades from the garrison in Sainte-

Menehould hadn't forgotten to wait in ambush in the woods near the gallows. They had been there since midnight, not only to rescue their friend, though he was none of the wisest, but also to take prisoners they could ransom, and whatever else they could. After arriving there, they deployed their forces on a war footing, and stationed a man in a tree to keep a lookout and tell them when the people in Troyes were about to proceed with the execution. This lookout, on his lofty perch, promised to do faithful duty.

By then the justicers had arrived in front of the gallows, and, making the ceremony as brief as possible, the judge ordered the dispatching of our poor madcap, who wondered where his comrades were, and why they weren't attacking these scoundrelly Armagnacs. He was extremely nervous, and kept looking all around, especially at the woods. But he couldn't hear or see a thing. He stretched out his Confession for as long as he could. Finally, he was taken away from the priest and he climbed the ladder to the gallows.

Reaching the platform, he was dumbfounded, God knows, and kept looking toward the woods, but in vain—because the lookout whose duty it was to rouse his rescuers had fallen asleep in the tree! And so, our poor hero didn't know what to say or do, except to reflect that his last hour had come. Before long, the executioner made his preparations to tie the noose around his neck and dispatch him. Seeing this, the prisoner had an idea that saved his life. He said:

"Your honor, I beg of you, for the love of God, that, before anyone else lays a hand on me, I may be permitted to play a song on my bagpipe. I ask nothing more. After that I'll be ready to die, and I'll forgive you and everyone else for taking my life."

His request was granted, and his bagpipe was brought up to him. When he received it, he started to play it, taking all his time about it. He played a song that was very familiar to his comrades in the ambush. Part of the song lyric said: "You're waiting too long, Robin, you're waiting too long!"

At the sound of the bagpipe the lookout awoke, so frightened that he fell right out of the tree, saying: "Our friend is being hanged! Forward, forward, and double time!" His comrades were all ready. They sounded a trumpet and emerged from the woods, assailing the judge and everyone else that was standing around the gallows. The executioner was so startled, bewildered, and amazed that it never occurred to him to tie the noose and hurl the prisoner down. Instead, he asked the prisoner to spare his life. The madcap would gladly have done so, but it was no longer in his power.

But he did something else even better. Standing on the gallows ladder, he shouted to his comrades: "Capture this one, capture that one! This one is rich, that one is a rat!" In short, the Burgundians killed a great number as they attacked the men of Troyes, and they took numerous prisoners. They rescued their comrade in the way that you've heard. He told them that never in his life had he suffered such anguish as at that hour.

97. A New Way to Recover Lost Property

In the good province of the Bourbonnais, where people are glad to work hard and do good, there lived very recently a physician, who shall remain nameless. Never did Hippocrates or Galen practice the art as well as he did. Because, instead of syrups, potions, doses, electuaries, and the hundred thousand other medicines that doctors generally prescribe, either to keep people healthy or cure them when they've lost their health, he used one method and one alone: enemas. All the same, he was so successful at what he did that everyone was pleased with him, and he cured every patient. And so his reputation grew and increased until he was sent for by everyone, being called to the homes of rulers and lords, as well as to large abbeys and big cities.

Aristotle and Galen were never as highly regarded as this good doctor was, especially among the common folk. His fame spread so far and wide that his advice was sought on every subject, and he was so incessantly clamored for that he didn't know what to attend to first. If a woman had a coarse, brutal, and malicious husband, she came to this good doctor for a remedy. In short, no matter what kind of advice people wanted, they looked up our hero.

It came about one day that a simple countryman had lost his donkey. After seeking it for some time, he got the idea of calling on this doctor, who was so wise. When he got to his house, he found the doctor so surrounded by people that he didn't know whose turn was next. Nevertheless, this good man pushed his way through the crowd, and, even though the doctor was addressing and answering several people at the same time, he described his case to him, reporting the loss of his donkey. He begged him, for the love of God, to prescribe and give him something by means of which he could get it back.

The doctor was paying more attention to others than to him. When the murmur of his speech came to an end (the doctor hadn't taken any of it in), the doctor turned to him, thinking he had some ailment. To get rid of him quickly, he told his assistants: "Give him an enema." Having said this, he turned back to the others.

The simple fellow who had lost the donkey, not knowing what the doctor had said, was seized by the doctor's assistants, who immediately followed orders and gave him an enema. This surprised him no end, because he didn't know what it was. Once the liquid was in his bowels, he spurred his horse and departed, asking no further about his donkey, because he was now sure he'd find it. Before he had gone very far, his belly rumbled and grumbled so hard that he was compelled to dash into an old, tumbledown hovel to make way for the enema, which was demanding its freedom.

His bowel movement made so much noise that the poor fellow's donkey, which was walking nearby, having strayed and come there merely by chance, began to bray. The good fellow got up and marched out, chanting a *Te Deum*. He located his donkey, and firmly believed that the enema the doctor had given him had made it all possible. And so, the doctor's reputation grew by leaps and bounds. He was considered an expert recoverer of lost objects, and a preeminent professor of all knowledge, though all this fame derived from a single enema.

And now you have heard how a donkey was found by means of an enema, which is an obvious and frequently occurring event.

98. The Dog's Legacy

Now, if you will, hear what happened recently to a wealthy but naïve village priest, whose simplicity made him pay his bishop a fine amounting to fifty gold crowns. This good priest had a dog that he had raised from a pup. The dog outdid all the others in the area in his skill at fetching a stick thrown into the river, or a hat that his master had either forgotten or left behind somewhere on purpose. In short, he was a star at all accomplishments pertaining to a good, well-trained dog. For this his master loved him so much that it would be hard to tell just how crazy he was about him.

And yet, it came about, I don't know why—whether he got too hot or too cold, or whether he ate something that disagreed with him—that the dog got very sick and died of that ailment, going straight from this life to dogs' paradise. What did the good priest do? His house—that is, the presbytery—adjoined the cemetery. When he saw that his dog had departed this life, it seemed to him that such a good and well-trained animal shouldn't be deprived of a proper burial. So he dug a hole very close to his house door, which faced the cemetery, as I said, and there he buried him. I don't know if he set up a stone for him and had an epitaph engraved on it, so I'll say no more on that subject.

It wasn't long before the death of the priest's good dog was generally known in the village and neighboring hamlets. The news spread till it reached the ears of the local bishop, along with a report of the solemn burial the dog's master had given him. So the bishop sent for the priest with a summons, which a bailiff brought to him. "Alas," the priest said to the bailiff, "what have I done to receive an official summons? I'm totally surprised by this call from the bishop's court."

"As for me," the man said, "I don't know what it's about, unless it's for having buried your dog in consecrated ground where the bodies of Christians are placed."

"Ah," the priest thought to himself, "it's for that?" Now for the first time it occurred to him that he had done wrong, and he realized that there was trouble in store for him. If he were locked up, he'd be fleeced, because the bishop, thank God, was the greediest prelate in this kingdom, and had people around him who knew how to turn everything to his profit, by God knows what means. "Now I have no choice but to lose some money, so it's better to do it sooner than later."

He arrived for his appointment, and headed straight for the bishop. The moment the bishop saw him, he delivered a long harangue about the holy burial he had given his dog, putting his deed in such a bad light that you'd have thought the priest's sin was worse than renouncing God. After the lengthy speech, he ordered the priest to be led to prison.

When the priest found himself about to be put behind bars, he asked to be allowed to state his case, and the bishop granted this. I must tell you that this inquest was attended by a great number of bigwigs, such as the ecclesiastical judge, the representatives of the secular arm, the scribes, notaries, counsellors, and prosecutors, all of whom were greatly amused by the unusual case of this unfortunate priest who had buried his dog in consecrated ground.

The priest spoke briefly in his own defense, saying: "Truly, my lord bishop, if you had known my good dog as well as I did (may God have mercy on him), you wouldn't be as surprised as you are at the burial I arranged for him. For he never had his like, and never will have." Then he told some of the wonderful things he had done. "And if he was good and obedient while he was alive, he was as much so, if not more, when he died. Because he left a very fine will. And, since he knew how needy and hard up you were, he left you fifty gold crowns, which I've brought for you."

He took the purse out of his shirt front and handed it to the bishop, who was glad to get it. Then the bishop praised the wonderful dog's good sense, and gave his authorization for the burial the priest had given him.

99. A Disastrous Elopement

On the French borderlands there lived a wealthy and powerful knight, noble not only for the ancient nobility of his ancestors, but also for his own noble and virtuous deeds. His wife had borne him one daughter only, a very beautiful and clever maiden of about sixteen or seventeen. This good, noble knight, finding that his daughter had attained an age appropriate for marriage, desired greatly to bestow her on a knight who was a neighbor of his, a very wealthy man, but not so rich in noble lineage as in temporal possessions and power. Moreover, this man was somewhere between sixty and eighty years old.

This desire gnawed away at the father's mind, giving him no rest until the match and the betrothal had been arranged between the girl's parents and that knight, who was promised the girl's hand. She herself knew nothing about these meetings, promises, and contracts, and never thought about such a marriage.

Very close to the home of the girl's father there lived another knight, young, adroit, valiant, but only moderately wealthy, not nearly as much so as that elderly man. This ardent young man was deeply in love with the girl, and she was very much taken with him because of his reputation for virtue and nobility. Though it was very difficult for them to speak to each other, because the girl's father suspected they were in love and did all he could to deprive them of opportunities to meet, nevertheless he couldn't make them abandon the wholehearted, faithful love that mutually joined and ignited their hearts.

Whenever Fortune favored them to the extent that they could converse, their only topic of conversation was the ways and means to accomplish their paramount desire by legitimate marriage. Now, the time was approaching when the girl was due to be given to that elderly nobleman, and her father disclosed the deal and contract to her, and set a day for the wedding. She was tremendously upset, but she felt confident of finding some way out.

She sent a message to her dear sweetheart, the young knight, asking him to visit her clandestinely as soon as he could. When he arrived, she informed him that she had been betrothed to the elderly knight, and she asked him his advice about overturning the arrangement, because she wanted to be *his* bride and nobody else's.

The young knight answered: "Darling, since, in your goodness, you're willing to humble yourself by offering me what I wouldn't dare request without feeling very immodest, I thank you. If you are ready to be constant in your kindness, I know what we must do. We'll set a date for me to come to this city accompanied by many friends and servants, and at a given hour you'll proceed to a place, which you'll tell me now, where I can find you alone. You'll get on my horse, and I'll take you to my castle. Then, if we can reconcile your parents, we'll proceed with the consummation of our betrothal."

The girl thought it was a good plan, and said that she knew how to carry it out properly. She told him to come to a certain place at a certain time on a certain day, and he'd find her there, so they could go on with their plan.

The agreed-upon day came. The good young knight showed up in the designated place, where he found his lady. She got up on his horse behind him, then they galloped away till they were far from that spot. When they were some distance away, the good knight, afraid of tiring out his sweetheart, slackened his horse's pace and sent all his attendants out on different paths to see whether anyone was following them. Then he rode across country, as gently and easily as he could, following no road or path. He ordered his people to reassemble in a big village that he mentioned, where he intended to rest and have a bite to eat.

That village was quite far removed from the highroad taken by horsemen and wayfarers. The lovers kept riding until they reached that village alone. There, a public festival was being celebrated, which had attracted crowds of all sorts of people. The lovers entered the best inn there, and immediately asked for food and drink, because it was well after the time for the midday meal, and the girl was exhausted.

They had a good fire made, and a good meal prepared for the knight's attendants, who had not yet arrived. They had hardly been in the hostelry any time at all, when four lumbering plowmen, or even coarser oxherds, appeared on the scene, and boldly entered the inn, asking rudely where the slut was that some lecher had just brought riding behind him on his horse. They said they had to have a drink with her and then have a tumble with her, one by one.

The innkeeper, who was well acquainted with the young knight, was quite sure that the situation was not the one those scoundrels had described. He replied courteously that the girl wasn't the sort they thought she was.

"No shilly-shallying!" they said. "If you don't hand her over to us this minute, we'll break down the doors and carry her off by force, in spite of all that you two can do!"

When the good host heard this and saw how rough and ready they were, not liable to be swayed by gentle words, he told them the name of the young knight, whose standing was very high in that border country, but whose name was little known to the populace at large, because he had long been out of the region, winning honor and glorious renown in the wars and on distant journeys. The innkeeper also told the intruders that the woman was a young maiden related to the knight, and that she was born of a great family and a noble lineage.

"Alas, gentlemen," he said, "without danger to yourselves or others, you can cool your hot desires with several other women who have come to the village for this festival with no other view in mind than entertaining you and those like you. For God's sake, leave this noble girl in peace, and try to imagine the great dangers you're risking! Don't be so foolhardy as to think the knight will let you take her without defending her. Stop and think about how unreasonable your purpose is, and what a great crime you intend to commit for no good reason."

"Enough sermonizing!" the lustful men said, as they burned with the flames of carnal concupiscence. "Give us a way to have her, or else we'll heap shame and blame on you: we'll drag her out in public here, and each of us four will have his will of her."

When they finished speaking, the good host went upstairs to the room where the knight and the girl were resting. He called the knight aside, and told him what those four maddened peasants intended to do. The knight, hearing him out completely without showing any signs of disturbance, went downstairs, wearing his sword, to talk to the four scoundrels. He asked them very calmly what their pleasure was.

They, coarse and surly as they were, replied that they wanted to have the slut he was keeping locked up in his room, and that, if he didn't hand her over nicely, they'd seize her and ravish her in a way he'd regret.

"My good gentlemen," the knight said, "if you knew me better, you wouldn't take me for a man who takes women of the type you mean across country. I've never done anything that crazy, thank God! Even if the notion took me, God forbid, I'd never do it in this border country, where I and all my family were born. My noble birth and the purity of my heart would never allow me to behave that way. This woman is a young maiden, a close cousin of mine, of a noble household. I've come here for some amusement and a quiet good time, bringing her with me and accompanied by my people, who aren't here yet but will come soon. I'm waiting for them. Don't imagine in your minds that I'm such a coward that I'd let her be manhandled, or allow her to suffer even the slightest insult. No! I'll defend her staunchly as long as I have a breath in my body—to the death!"

Before the knight finished speaking, the dirty peasants interrupted him. First, they denied that he was the person he said he was, because he was all alone, and the knight he had named never rode out without many attendants. Therefore they advised him to hand over the woman, if he was smart, or they'd take her by force, no matter what the consequences might be.

Alas! When the brave and valiant knight realized that his soft answers did no good, and that it was an occasion for severity and boldness, his heart became steadfast, and he resolved that the peasants would never have their way with the girl, or else he'd die defending her. In short, one of the four stepped forward to bang on the bedroom door with his staff, and the others followed. They were bravely repulsed by the knight. And so the battle began, lasting a long, long time.

Though the two sides were unequal in numbers, the good knight overcame and repulsed the four scoundrels. While he was pursuing them, trying to get the upper hand, one of them, who had a javelin, made a sudden about face and thrust it into the knight's stomach, running him through. The blow killed him on the spot, which delighted them. Then they forced the innkeeper to bury him in the garden of the inn, without making an uproar, or they'd kill him.

After killing the knight, they battered the girl's door (she was very upset by her lover's long absence) and broke it down. The moment she saw those churls come in, she knew at once that the knight must be dead, and she said: "Alas, where's my protector? Where is my sole refuge? What's become of him? How is it that he's left me alone like this?"

The scoundrels, seeing the troubled state she was in, thought to deceive her with soft words. They said that the knight was in another house in the village, and had sent word to her to go there in their company. He'd be better able to protect her there. But she didn't believe a word, because her heart kept assuring her that they had murdered him. She began to lament and weep more bitterly than before.

"What's this?" they said. "Why are you acting so strangely with us? Do you think we don't know you? If you suspect your lover man is dead, you're not mistaken. We've rid the countryside of him. So, rest assured that all four of us are going to enjoy your company!"

After they said this, one of them stepped forward and grabbed her as rudely as possible, saying he'd have his way with her before she got away from him, whether she liked it or not. The poor girl, finding herself under such pressure, which her soft words did nothing to abate, said to them: "Alas, gentlemen, since your minds are set on this crime, and humble prayers are powerless to soften or bend them, at least be as decent as this: Since I must surrender my body to you, let it be with one man at a time, while the others wait outside."

They granted her request, albeit very unwillingly. Then they made her choose the one among the four who was to stay with her first. She chose the one she thought was most kindhearted and gentle, but he was actually the worst of them all. The room was locked, and immediately the good maiden fell at the scoundrel's feet, pleading with him piteously and begging him to show her mercy. But he persevered in his evil purpose, and said he would enjoy her favors.

When she saw that he remained unmoved and obdurate, and wouldn't grant her humble prayer, she said: "All right, since it must be, I'm satisfied. But I beseech you to shut the windows, so we can have more privacy." He did so, very much against his will. While he was shutting them, the maiden took the little knife that hung from her belt, cut her own throat, and breathed her last.

When the scoundrel saw her lying on the floor dead, he ran away with his companions. Presumably they were punished as their heinous crimes deserved.

Such was the end of those two faithful lovers, one following on the other's heels. Neither of them tasted any of the happy pleasures they expected to enjoy all their lives in wedded bliss.

STORIES 100–108

From *Dil Ulenspiegel*

Various nations have had a national prankster with whose name all sorts of funny stories about practical jokes are associated. In Germany this figure is Till Eulenspiegel, who may have been a historical person who died about 1350. His legend grew and grew, and in the 19th century still inspired such works as the novel *Légende de Ulenspiegel* (short form of the title!) by the Belgian writer Charles De Coster (1867), in which Till symbolizes the immortal Flemish love of liberty; and the great tone poem *Till Eulenspiegels lustige Streiche* (T. E.'s Merry Pranks) by Richard Strauss (1895).

Till is a North (or Low) German pet name for Dietrich. His surname is ostensibly a combination of *Eule* (owl) and *Spiegel* (mirror), sometimes Englished as Owl-glass,* and Eulenspiegel is attested as a 14th-century family name, but it has also been considered to be derived from dialect words of quite different meanings (the interpretation "wipe-behind" has been suggested!).

Many commentators have seen Till as a peasant's son deliberately out to confound burghers, noblemen, and royals. Others see him as totally asocial and a lone wolf delighting in his own wits.

At any rate, Till doesn't put in an appearance in extant literature until 1515, when the publisher Johannes Grieninger (or Grüninger) in Strasbourg issued the book titled *Ein kurtzweilig lesen von Dil Ulenspiegel geboren uß dem Land zu Brunßwick. Wie er sein leben volbracht hatt. xcvi seiner geschichten* (An Entertaining Book About Till Eulenspiegel, Born in the Brunswick [Braunschweig] Region. How He Spent His Life. 96 Stories About Him [there are actually only 95, the one numbered 42 being missing]).

The anonymous preface to the 1515 edition states that the author, or compiler, was requested in the year 1500 to gather all the Till stories that he could find. He adds that he included a few from various non-Till sources (see comments on Nos. 101 and 102, below). Internal evidence and other clues have led some scholars to identify the author as Hermann Bote (ca. 1450–1525), a Brunswick poet and chronicler; Bote, they say, wrote a Low German version, which was somewhat hastily and carelessly translated into High German for the 1515 edition. The actual settings and details of the stories are said to reflect 15th-century conditions.

Though the 1515 volume really breaks down into separate stories of diverse origins, its stories fall into clear groupings by content, and they are arranged so as to

---

*He is shown holding an owl and a mirror in the 1515 title-page illustration.

simulate a complete biography of the prankster from birth to death. German scholars speak of this *Dil Ulenspiegel* as a *Schwankroman* (a merry-tale novel).

Two features of the book are intentionally not well represented in the selection
made here: Till's predilection for deceiving people by willfully misinterpreting
their instructions (usually taking them unbelievably literally), and the compiler's
predilection for scatology (the book as a whole reeks of excrement).

An important aspect of German society in the years immediately preceding the
Reformation can also be detected here: disillusionment with the priesthood and
the Church of Rome (see stories 100, 105, and 107, and more especially 103 and
104).

The book's style is rough-and-ready, but forthright and vital, and its satire is
sometimes very sharp.

No. 100 is fascinating for its depiction of a traditional Latin-language Easter play
being performed in a lowly village church, with such props as the sepulcher, the
angel's wings, and Christ's banner. (The original 1515 illustration shows that the
sepulcher is a complete small structure, something like a large doghouse.) The visit
of the three Marys to the tomb, with the same Latin opening words as here, was
performed in churches as early as the 10th century.

Nos. 101 and 102 were adapted by the original compiler from episodes in *Der
Pfaffe Amis*, a humorous narrative poem by the German author known as Der
Stricker (first half of the 13th century). The plot of No. 101 is very widespread.
The plot of No. 102 (which is successfully developed here, blossoming out into
a very witty satire on genealogy and nobility) is also found in *El Conde Lucanor*
(exemplum 32), in which the charlatans pretend to weave a tapestry. The theme
is very similar to that of Hans Christian Andersen's "The Emperor's New
Clothes."

No. 107 shows clear signs of not having originally been a story about Till. For
one thing, he is the *victim* of the old woman's equivocation; for another, the sexual
double-entendres at the end are not part of the (more scatological than risqué) Till
tradition.

No. 108 calls to mind the story that some critics consider to be Arthur
Schnitzler's greatest, "Der blinde Geronimo und sein Bruder" (Blind Geronimo
and His Brother; 1912), in which an analogous trick played on the blind—making
them believe that a companion of theirs has received money for them—takes on a
tragic turn before the final resolution.

→ janitor for church 100. A Violent Easter Play

Now that Easter was approaching, the priest who had hired Eulenspiegel
as his sacristan said to him: "There's a custom here that, on the night before Easter, the peasants always put on an Easter play, acting out Our
Lord's resurrection from the grave. You've got to help out, because it's only
right for sacristans to arrange and direct such plays."

Then Eulenspiegel spoke up, asking how the peasants were able to put
on a religious play. He told the priest: "Now, after all, there's no peasant
around here with any education. You must lend me your servant woman
for the purpose. She knows how to read and write."

The priest said: "Yes, yes, take anyone who can give you a hand. Besides, my maid has attended many such performances."

The housekeeper liked the idea. She wanted to play the angel at the sepulcher, because she knew his lines by heart. Then Eulenspiegel sought out two peasants to join him as actors. The three of them would portray the three Marys at the tomb. Eulenspiegel coached the peasant with a speaking part in his Latin lines. The priest was to play Our Lord rising from the grave.

When the play was put on, and Eulenspiegel and his peasants came to the grave dressed as the Marys, the housekeeper playing the angel spoke her line in Latin: "*Quem queritis?* (Whom seek ye here?)"

Then the peasant playing the first Mary gave the reply that Eulenspiegel had taught him: "We seek a priest's whore who's old and has only one eye."

When she heard herself being mocked for being one-eyed, she became furious with Eulenspiegel. She leaped out of the sepulcher and aimed for his face with her fists. Lashing out uncontrollably, she hit one of the peasants and gave him a black eye. When the other peasant saw that, he joined the fray and hit the housekeeper on the head so hard that her angel's wings fell off.

Seeing all this, the priest dropped Christ's banner of victory and came to the aid of his housekeeper. He grabbed one of the peasants by the hair, and the two of them tussled behind the sepulcher. When the peasants in the church audience saw this, they came running and there was a tremendous commotion. The priest and his housekeeper got the worst of it, but the two peasant Marys were also hard pressed, and the other peasants had to separate the combatants by sheer force.

But Eulenspiegel, who had paid careful attention to the course of events, escaped in time. He ran out of the church, departed from the village, and never returned.

Only God knows where they found a new sacristan.

101. The Miracle Cure

On one occasion, Eulenspiegel came to Nuremberg, where he posted large notices on the church doors and the city hall, proclaiming that he was a good doctor who could cure any disease. There were numerous patients in the city's new hospital,[1] where the holy lance that pierced Christ's side is kept, along with other noteworthy objects. The director of the hospital would have been very pleased to get those patients off his hands, and sincerely wished them good health.

And so, he visited "Doctor" Eulenspiegel and asked him whether he really could help his patients as he had stated in the notice he had posted.

[1]The Heilig-Geist-Hospital, founded in the 14th century.

He would be well rewarded if he could. Eulenspiegel replied that he would cure many of his patients if he promised to pay him two hundred guilders. The hospital director promised him the money if he helped his patients. In return, Eulenspiegel pledged that, if he didn't cure the patients, he wouldn't take a penny. The hospital director was very pleased by that, and gave him a down payment of twenty guilders.

So, Eulenspiegel went to the hospital, taking two assistants along. He asked each of the patients what he was suffering from. At the end of each such interview, Eulenspiegel implored the patient as follows: "What I'm going to reveal to you now, you must keep completely to yourself, and not breathe a word of it to anyone else!" Each patient solemnly promised Eulenspiegel to obey him.

Then he said to each of them separately: "If I'm to cure the lot of you and get you back on your feet, the only way I can possibly do it is to burn one of you to ashes and mix the ashes into a medicine for all the rest to drink. I've got to do that. And so I'll take the sickest one among you, one who can't walk, and burn him to ashes, so I can cure all the rest of you with them. To rouse you all up, I'm going to call the hospital director, stand in the doorway of the hospital, and shout: 'If you're no longer ill, come out!' Don't miss that opportunity!"

In that way he told each patient individually that the last one out had to pay the piper. Each of them paid close attention to the communication. On the day that had been announced, they hurried out on their sick, crippled legs, since no one wanted to be the last. When Eulenspiegel summoned them in the prearranged way, they immediately started running, though some of them hadn't been out of bed for ten years. When the hospital was empty, Eulenspiegel asked the hospital director for his pay, saying he had urgent business elsewhere. The man gave him the money and many thanks, and Eulenspiegel rode away on his horse.

But, three days later, all the patients returned, complaining about their various ailments. The hospital director asked: "How can that be? I sent the great expert to you, who clearly cured you, because you all walked away on your own power."

Then they told the hospital director what Eulenspiegel had said to them in confidence: the last one out the door when he called would be burned to ashes. Then the hospital director caught on to Eulenspiegel's trick. But he was gone, and nothing could be done to him. So the patients returned to the hospital and the money was lost.

102. Invisible Murals

Eulenspiegel had wild adventures in Hessen. After roaming throughout Old Saxony and becoming so well known there that he could no longer support himself with his rascally tricks, he entered Hessen and came to the landgrave's court in Marburg. The landgrave asked him what he could do. He replied: "My lord, I'm an artist." The landgrave was pleased because he thought the art he referred to was alchemy and the magic arts, which he himself was greatly addicted to. So he asked him whether he was an alchemist.

"No, my lord, I'm a painter, one whose like is not to be found in many a land, because my work far surpasses that of others."

The landgrave said: "Let's see a sample."

Eulenspiegel said: "Of course, my lord." He had with him some canvases and art objects that he had bought in Flanders. He took them out of a bag and showed them to the landgrave, who liked them very much, and said:

"Dear master, what fee would you ask for painting our great hall? I'd want you to depict the origins of the landgraves of Hessen, how they became friends with the king of Hungary and other rulers and lords, and how long our government has lasted. And I'd like you to do this in the most elaborate way."

Eulenspiegel replied: "My lord, what you suggest would cost about four hundred guilders."

The landgrave said: "Master, just do a good job, and we'll give you proper compensation."

So Eulenspiegel accepted the commission, but the landgrave had to advance him a hundred guilders to buy paints and hire assistants. When Eulenspiegel and his three journeymen were ready to begin work, he made a request of the landgrave that no one but his assistants should be permitted to enter the great hall while his work was proceeding, so he wouldn't be hampered in his artistic endeavors. The landgrave consented.

Then Eulenspiegel conferred with his assistants and made a deal with them: they would keep quiet and let him do what he wanted. They'd get their pay even though they did nothing. Their main work would be to play board games. The journeymen agreed to accept pay for sitting idle.

After about four weeks, the landgrave asked how the master and his assistants were getting on, and whether the finished job would be as good as the sample. He said to Eulenspiegel: "Dear master, I'm extremely eager to see your work. Please allow us to go into the great hall with you and take a look at your painting."

Eulenspiegel said: "Of course, my lord, but there's one thing I must tell you. If someone comes in with you to look at the painting who was born out of wedlock, he won't be able to see it."

The landgrave said: "Master, that would be a remarkable thing!" They entered the hall, where Eulenspiegel had spread a long linen cloth close to the wall that he was supposed to be painting. Shoving the cloth away a little, Eulenspiegel touched the wall with a white pointer, and said: "As you can see, my lord, this man is the first landgrave of Hessen. He was of the Colonna family of Rome, and was married to a duchess of Bavaria, a daughter of the magnanimous Justinian, who later became emperor. Look over here, my lord: that first landgrave begat Adolph. Adolph begat William the Black. William begat Louis the Pious. And so on, and so on, down to your lordship. I know for a fact that no one can find fault with my work, which is so artistic and brightly colored."

The landgrave saw nothing but the whitewashed wall, and thought to himself: "Was my mother really a whore? — because all I can see is a plain white wall!" But, for decency's sake, he said: "Dear master, we're satisfied, though we confess we can't take it all in." And he left the room.

When the landgrave came to see his lady, she asked: "My lord, what is your free-lance artist painting? You've gone to see it; how do you like his work? I don't trust him very much; he looks like a swindler."

The landgrave said: "My lady, I'm fairly well satisfied with his work, so do him a little justice."

"My lord," she said, "can't I see it, too?"

"Yes, if the master allows it."

She sent for Eulenspiegel and asked whether she could see the painting, too. Eulenspiegel told her what he had told her husband: no one born out of wedlock would have the power to see his work. She went to the great hall with eight ladies-in-waiting and a female jester. Eulenspiegel drew aside the cloth, as before, and told the countess the same story about the earliest landgraves, one by one. But the countess and her ladies-in-waiting spoke not a word. None of them had any praise or blame for the painting. They were all unhappy over being illegitimate, whether it was their fathers or their mothers who were at fault. Finally the female jester spoke up: "Dear master, I tell you I can't see a thing, even if that means I'm to be called a whore's child all my life!"

Then Eulenspiegel thought: "No good will come of this! When fools tell the truth, it's time for me to make tracks." But he made a joke out of her declaration.

Meanwhile, the countess returned to her husband, who asked her how she liked the painting. She replied: "My lord, I like it as much as you do. But our jester doesn't like it; she says she can't see anything. The same goes for my ladies-in-waiting, and I'm afraid there's some swindling going on."

The landgrave took this to heart and began wondering whether he'd been tricked. But he sent word to Eulenspiegel to keep on working. He said he wanted all his courtiers to look at his work. The landgrave would thus learn which of his vassals was legitimate or not. The domains of the illegitimate ones would revert to him. *born out of wedlock*

Then Eulenspiegel went to his journeymen and discharged them. Next, he asked the treasurer for another hundred guilders. When he received the money, he lit out. The next day, the landgrave inquired after his painter and was told he was gone.

The day after that, the landgrave went to the great hall with all his courtiers, to learn whether anyone could see any painting. But no one could truthfully say he did. Since they all remained silent, the landgrave said: "Now we see that we've been rooked. I never wanted to have anything to do with Eulenspiegel, but *he* came to *us*. We'll take the loss of the two hundred guilders in our stride, but it's to be made publicly known that he's a confidence man, and he has to keep out of our territory."

And so Eulenspiegel left Marburg and never accepted another painting commission.

103. A Village Without Cuckolds

Eulenspiegel had made a name for himself in every region with his wicked ways. In every place he had previously visited he was *persona non grata*, so he had to disguise himself and remain incognito. Finally it became clear to him that he could no longer expect to feed himself by going idle, though he had been a merry fellow since childhood and had made plenty of money through all sorts of swindles. But now that his roguery was a byword everywhere, and his means of support were letting him down, he pondered over what activity to pursue that would let him make a living doing nothing. He decided to pretend he was a dealer in relics, and to peddle such items all through the area.

With the help of a student, he dressed up like a priest. He acquired a human skull and had it mounted in silver. Then he traveled to the province of Pomerania, where priests are more interested in boozing than in preaching. Whenever he came to a village where a fair, a wedding, or some other local gathering was taking place, he visited the parish priest and told him that he wanted to deliver a sermon and tell the peasants about his relic, so they would let him touch them with it. Whatever offerings he got, he would split with him fifty-fifty. This always satisfied those uneducated priests, who only cared about money.

On one occasion, when the church was full, he climbed into the pulpit and said something about the Old Testament, and dragged in the New Testament, as well, with the Ark of the Covenant and the golden container of the heavenly manna, which he said was the greatest of all relics. As he went on, he mentioned the head of Saint Brendan, who had been a holy man. That head he had with him, and he had been ordered by his superiors to use it to collect money with which to build a new church. He had been ordered to do this with great regard to purity: by no means was he to accept any offering made by an adulteress. If there were any such in his audience, they should remain seated:

"If women guilty of adultery offer me anything, I won't take it, and they'll be shamed in front of me. Act accordingly!" He held out the skull for the people to kiss. It may have been a blacksmith's head that he had taken from a cemetery. He blessed the peasants and their wives, left the pulpit, and stood in front of the altar. The parish priest began to chant and ring his handbell.

Then the wives, both good and bad, brought their offerings to the altar, groaning under the loads they were carrying. Those with a bad reputation (and there were some present) wanted to be the first with their offering. He accepted the offerings of good and bad alike, and didn't turn anyone down.

The simple women believed so implicitly in his cunning, roguish words that they thought that any woman who remained seated wasn't truly pious. Any woman that had no money with her gave him a gold or silver ring. Each one observed all the others to see if they were making an offering. And each one who made an offering felt that she had vindicated her honor and expunged her bad reputation. There were even some who made an offering two or three times, so their neighbors would see this and stop talking about them.

Eulenspiegel collected the most generous offering ever heard of. After he had taken it away, he commanded everyone who had made an offering never to commit sins thenceforth, on pain of excommunication, because for now they had proved they were completely free of sin. If there had been any adulteresses there, he wouldn't have accepted any offering from them. This made all the women happy.

Whenever Eulenspiegel went, he preached that way. And it made him rich. People considered him to be a pious preacher, because he was so well able to cover up women's failings.

104. A Papal Interview

Eulenspiegel was gifted with consummate roguery. After he had tried out all forms of it, he recalled the old proverb: "Go to Rome as a pious man, and return home a good-for-nothing." So, he traveled to Rome. There he hit on new confidence schemes, and took up lodgings in a widow's home. She saw that Eulenspiegel was a handsome man, and asked him where he was from. He said he was from Saxony, and was an Easterner, and that he had come to Rome because he wanted to speak with the pope.

The lady said: "My friend, you may very well get to *see* the pope, but I don't know about speaking with him. I was born and raised here, and my ancestry is of the highest, but I've never been able to converse with him. How do you expect to manage that so soon? I'd give a hundred ducats for a chance to speak with him."

Eulenspiegel said: "My dear landlady, if I find an opportunity to bring you to the pope, so you can speak with him, will you give me the hundred ducats?"

The lady was eager, and promised him the hundred ducats on her honor if he succeeded in arranging that meeting. But she didn't think he'd be able to, because she was well aware of the great effort and trouble involved.

Eulenspiegel said: "My dear landlady, if I do manage it, I want the hundred ducats."

She said yes, but she thought: "You're not in the pope's presence yet!"

Eulenspiegel waited, knowing that every four weeks the pope read a Mass in the Jerusalem Chapel in Saint John Lateran. (Or should it be called *Latronum*: "Saint John of the Highway Robbers"?) On the first occasion, after the pope had read the Mass aloud, Eulenspiegel pushed his way into the chapel, and got as close to the pope as he could. When the pope continued with the whispered portion of the Mass (from the Sanctus to the Lord's Prayer), Eulenspiegel turned his back to the Communion wafers. The cardinals saw this. When the pope spoke the blessing over the Communion cup, Eulenspiegel turned around again.

When the Mass was over, the cardinals told the pope that a certain person, a handsome man who had attended the Mass, had turned his back to the altar during the preparations for Communion. The pope said: "He must be found, because that was an insult to Holy Church. If blasphemy went unpunished, it would be an affront to God. If the man really did that, it's to be feared that he's an unbeliever and not a good Christian." And he ordered him brought into his presence.

They came after Eulenspiegel and told him he had to see the pope. Eulenspiegel immediately followed them into the pope's presence. The pope asked him what sort of man he was. Eulenspiegel replied that he was a good Christian. Then the pope asked what the articles of his faith were. Eulenspiegel replied that he had the same beliefs as his landlady. He mentioned her name, which was well known at the time. And so, the pope had the lady brought before him.

The pope asked the lady to describe her religious beliefs. She replied that she believed in Christianity, and in what the Holy Christian Church bade and forbade her to do, and that those were her only beliefs. Eulenspiegel, who was standing there, began to twist his mouth into a sarcastic expression, and said: "All-merciful Father, servant of the servants of God, my faith is just the same. I'm a good Christian."

The pope said: "Then why did you turn your back to the altar during the whispered Mass?"

Eulenspiegel said: "Most holy Father, I'm a great sinner, and my sins reproached me, telling me I was unworthy to participate in that mystery before making Confession."

That satisfied the pope, who dismissed Eulenspiegel and returned to his palace. Eulenspiegel went to his lodgings and told his landlady she must now give him the hundred ducats. He remained the same old Eulenspiegel, and his trip to Rome didn't do much to improve him.

105. Eulenspiegel's Dying Confession

Eulenspiegel didn't shy away from malicious roguery in the village Kissen-brück, near Wolfenbüttel in the Asseburg jurisdiction. A parish priest lived there who had a very beautiful housekeeper and a neat, lively little horse. The priest was fond of both of them, his horse and his servant. At the time, the duke of Brunswick was in Kissenbrück, and sent people to ask the priest to be good enough to sell him the horse, for which he'd give him a satisfactory amount. The priest kept telling the duke that he had no inten-tion of selling the horse. Nor could the duke seize the horse by a judicial procedure, because the village court was answerable to the Brunswick city council.

Eulenspiegel, to whose attention the whole matter had come, said to the duke: "My lord, what present will you make me if I get the parish priest of Kissenbrück to give up the horse?"

"If you can do it," the duke said, "I'll give you the coat I'm now wear-ing." It was made of camel's hair and embroidered with pearls.

Eulenspiegel accepted, and rode from Wolfenbüttel to the village, where he took up lodgings with the priest. Eulenspiegel was a familiar fig-ure in the priest's house, because he had often stayed with him in the past, and was a welcome guest. After living there three days on this occasion, he pretended to be ill. He groaned loudly and went to bed.

The priest and his housekeeper were grieved at this, but were perplexed as to how to help. Finally, Eulenspiegel was apparently so sick that the priest had a talk with him, urging him to make Confession and take Communion. Eulenspiegel was willing, but he insisted that the priest him-self should hear his Confession and interrogate him thoroughly. He said he was worried about his soul, because he had done many misdeeds in his lifetime, and wasn't sure that God would forgive his sins.

Eulenspiegel feigned serious illness as he spoke. After recounting nu-merous sins, he told the priest that he recalled only one further sin that he had committed, but didn't dare confess it to him. He asked him to call in another priest to hear that particular sin, because, if he disclosed it to his host, he was afraid it would make him angry.

When the priest heard this, he suspected it was some deep secret, and he wanted to learn that, too. He said: "Eulenspiegel, he lives far away. I can't get hold of the other priest so soon. If you were to die in the mean-time, both you and I would be blamed by God for your failure to confess. Tell it to me now; it can't be so grave a sin that I can't absolve you of it. Besides, what good would it do me to get angry, since I can't repeat your Confession to anyone else?"

Eulenspiegel said: "In that case, I'll confess it." It wasn't such a grave sin, he said; it was just that he felt bad about angering the priest, because it con-cerned him.

Then the priest insisted all the more on hearing it. If Eulenspiegel had stolen something from him or done him some harm, or whatever it was, he must confess it. He'd forgive him for it and never hate him.

"Oh, my good friend," Eulenspiegel said, "I know it'll make you angry. But I feel, and I fear, that my time is nearly up. I'll tell you, even if you get really furious. It's this, my friend: I slept with your housekeeper."

The priest asked how often it had happened.

Eulenspiegel replied: "Only five times."

The priest made a mental note to give her five beatings as a penalty, and he absolved Eulenspiegel. Then he went to his bedroom, sent for his housekeeper, and asked her whether she had slept with Eulenspiegel. The housekeeper said no, it was a lie. The priest said he had told him so during his Confession, and he believed it. She said no, he said yes and grabbed hold of a stick, with which he beat her black and blue.

Eulenspiegel was lying in bed and laughing, thinking to himself: "Now things are beginning to get good." With his promised gift in mind, he spent the rest of the day in bed. During the night his illness left him. In the morning he got up and announced that he was better. He had to travel to another area, he said, and he wanted the priest to give him a bill for what he had consumed. The priest settled up with him, but was so confused that he didn't know what he was doing. He wasn't really aware of how much he was charging Eulenspiegel, because he was so glad to be getting him off his hands. So was the housekeeper, who had suffered a beating on his account.

Well, Eulenspiegel was ready and all set to go. "My friend," he said, "let me remind you that you disclosed my Confession. I'm on my way to the bishop in Halberstadt, where I intend to report you."

The priest forgot his anger when he heard that Eulenspiegel wanted to get him in trouble. He begged him earnestly to remain silent. It had happened in a fit of rage. He'd give him twenty guilders not to inform on him.

Eulenspiegel said: "No, I wouldn't take a hundred guilders not to talk. I'm on my way to report this, as is only proper."

The priest turned to his housekeeper with tears in his eyes, begging her to ask Eulenspiegel how much he wanted the priest to give him, and whether he'd accept it from her. Finally, Eulenspiegel said that, if the priest gave him his horse, he'd keep quiet and wouldn't report him. The only thing he'd accept was the horse. The priest, who loved the horse dearly, would rather have given him all his ready money, if only he'd leave him the horse. But he had to give it up against his will, because necessity compelled him to.

He gave Eulenspiegel the horse and let him ride away with it. So Eulenspiegel rode to Wolfenbüttel with the priest's horse. When he arrived at the city moat, the duke was on the drawbridge, and he saw Eulenspiegel trotting nearer with the horse. At once the duke took off his coat, which he had promised to Eulenspiegel, walked up to him, and said: "Look, my good Eulenspiegel, here's the coat I promised you."

Eulenspiegel dismounted and said: "My lord, here's your horse." The duke thanked him and made him tell how he had acquired the horse from the priest. The duke laughed at the story and, in his great glee, gave Eulenspiegel another horse in addition to the coat. But the priest missed his horse sorely, and frequently gave his housekeeper a good drubbing for her part in his misfortune, so that the housekeeper finally left. And so he had lost both of them.

106. The Tailors' Convention

Eulenspiegel sent out letters summoning all tailors to a general trade council. He sent the summons to the Wendish cities of the Hanseatic League, to Saxony, Holstein, Pomerania, Stettin, and Mecklenburg, as well as to Lübeck, Hamburg, Stralsund, and Wismar. In the announcement, he assured them of his best wishes, and ordered them to assemble at Rostock, where he then was. He wanted to teach them a technique that would profit them and their descendants forever after, as long as the world existed.

The tailors in the cities, towns, and villages corresponded with one another to arrive at a consensus regarding the announcement. They all wrote saying they'd be in Rostock on the date set. They held local meetings, each one asking the others what Eulenspiegel intended to tell them, and what technique he'd teach them after sending such urgent letters.

They all arrived in Rostock together according to plan, so that many people wondered what all those tailors were doing there. When Eulenspiegel heard that the tailors had obeyed his summons, he called them together, waiting until everyone was present. Then the tailors told Eulenspiegel that they had come in obedience to his summons, in which he had promised to teach them a technique that would profit them and their descendants. They requested him to promote their interests by disclosing that technique, and they promised him a gift in return.

Eulenspiegel said: "Yes, I want you to assemble in a place where you can all hear me." They assembled on a broad open area. Eulenspiegel went into a house there, looked out the window, and said: "Honored followers of the tailor's trade! I'd like you to note and understand that, when you have a pair of shears, an ell measure, thread, a thimble, and a needle, you have all the tools you need for your trade. There's no difficulty in acquiring them, and they're absolutely necessary if you are to practice your trade. But now hear this bit of technical advice from me, and think of me every time you follow it: Whenever you thread your needle, don't forget to make a knot at one end of the thread, or you'll take many a stitch for nothing. But, my way, the thread won't be able to slip out of the needle."

The tailors exchanged glances and said to one another: "We're all acquainted with that technique, and with everything he's told us." They asked him whether he had anything to add, because that nonsense wasn't worth a journey of forty or fifty miles and the trouble of sending one another messages. Tailors had been acquainted with that technique for over a thousand years.

Eulenspiegel replied: "No one could possibly remember something that goes back a thousand years." He added that, if they didn't appreciate his information and weren't grateful to him for it, they could just lump it. They could go back where they came from.

At that, the tailors, who had made such a long trip to hear him, were furious with him. They'd have liked to lay their hands on him, but they couldn't get at him. And so the tailors dispersed. Some of them were angry, cursed, and sulked, because they had come such a long way for nothing, while the local residents laughed at them and made fun of them for letting themselves be tricked that way. They said the tailors themselves were to blame, because they had believed and obeyed the national jester and wag. They should have known all along what sort of dizzy fellow Eulenspiegel was.

107. The Old Woman's Subterfuge

Long ago, in the village of Gerdau in the Lüneburg district, there lived an elderly couple, who had been joined in wedlock for fifty years. They had grown children, who helped them with advice and material support. Now, at the time the parish priest was a sly fellow who was excessively fond of eating and drinking. He had an arrangement with his parishioners whereby every peasant had to invite him at least once a year, and entertain him and his housekeeper with good meals for a day or two.

Now, for many years that elderly couple hadn't had any celebration, baptism, or other festivity at which the priest could indulge his gluttony. This vexed him, and he thought of a way to get those peasants to offer him a meal. He sent the husband a messenger, asking how long he and his wife had been married. The peasant answered: "Your reverence, it's been so long that I've forgotten."

The priest rejoined: "That's a situation dangerous to your spiritual welfare. If you've been together for fifty years, the marriage vows you made have expired, just like a monk's vows in a monastery. Talk this over with your wife, then come back and report to me, so I can advise you about the salvation of your soul. I have that duty toward you and all my parishioners."

The peasant followed his instructions and discussed the matter with his wife, but still couldn't tell the priest exactly how long they'd been married. The two of them visited the priest, very eager to receive his advice concerning their ungodly state, living in sin.

The priest said: "Since you can't give me any exact figure, and you're worried about your spiritual welfare, next Sunday I'll renew your marriage vows, so that, in case you're not in a state of holy wedlock at the moment, you will be again. And so, kill a good ox, sheep, and pig, and invite your children and friends to a real feast, and I'll join you, too."

"Yes, your reverence, I will! I'm not going to neglect that for the sake of a flock of hens! If we've been together so long that we're no longer properly married, that's terrible!" Then the peasant went home and prepared for the party. The priest invited several prelates and other priests of his acquaintance. Among them was the provost of Ebstorf, who always kept a fine horse or two, and didn't mind the sight of food.

Eulenspiegel had spent some time with this provost, who now said to him: "Mount my young stallion and come along. You'll be made welcome." Eulenspiegel did so. When they arrived, they ate, drank, and made merry. The old woman who was to be the bride sat at the head of the table, as is the custom for brides, but she was tired and grew faint. So she was excused. She walked behind her farmyard to the Gerdau stream and cooled her feet in the water.

Meanwhile, the provost and Eulenspiegel rode by on their way back to Ebstorf. Eulenspiegel entertained the bride by making the stallion rear and curvet. As he did so, his belt and pouch fell from his side (they were of the kind that men wore at the time). When the good old woman saw that, she stood up, picked up the pouch, and sat down on it beside the stream.

After Eulenspiegel had ridden the length of a field, he noticed that his pouch was missing, and he galloped right back to Gerdau, and asked the good old peasant woman whether she had spotted or found a rough old leather pouch. The old woman said: "Yes, friend, on my wedding day I got a rough pouch, which I still have, and which I sit on. Is that the one you mean?"

"Oho, that was long ago!" Eulenspiegel said. "If you got it as a bride, it must now be an old, mildewed pouch. I don't want your old pouch!" But, mischievous and cunning as Eulenspiegel was, he was still fooled by the old peasant woman, and had to go without his pouch. The women in Gerdau still have that same rough bridal pouch. I think the elderly widows there have it in their keeping. If you're interested in it, you can go ask them.

108. Charity to the Blind

While Eulenspiegel was wandering through the various regions of Germany, he once came to Hanover, where he played many unusual tricks. On one occasion, he rode a field's length out of the city gate for pleasure, and met twelve blind men. As he came up to them, he said: "Where are you coming from, blind men?"

The blind men halted. They could hear very well that he was riding a horse, so they thought he was a respectable man, took off their hats and hoods, and said: "Your honor, we were in the city on the occasion of a rich man's death. There was a Mass for his soul, and they gave alms."

It was a terribly cold day, and Eulenspiegel said to the blind men: "It's very cold, and I'm afraid you might freeze to death. Look, here are twelve guilders. Go back to town. I've just come from an inn there." (He told them the name of it.) "Live there on these twelve guilders and think of me till the winter is over, and you can resume your wandering safely."

The blind men bowed and thanked him effusively. Each of them thought that one of his companions had the money: the first one thought the second one had it, the second thought it was the third, the third thought it was the fourth, and so on down the line, with the twelfth man thinking the first one had it. So they reentered the city and went to the inn that Eulenspiegel had told them about.

When they arrived at the inn, all the blind men said that a generous man had ridden by them and had charitably given them twelve guilders, which they were to spend in remembrance of him till the winter was over. The innkeeper was greedy for the money, and welcomed them as guests. It never occurred to him to inquire and see which of them had the twelve guilders on him. He said: "Yes, dear brothers, I'll entertain you handsomely!"

He slaughtered and prepared animals, cooked for the blind men, and continued to feed and lodge them until he thought they had had twelve guilders' worth. Then he said: "Dear brothers, if you stop to calculate, you'll find that you've used up the twelve guilders."

The blind men agreed, and each one told the companion who he thought had the money, to pay the innkeeper. The first man didn't have the money, nor the second, third, fourth, nor any of them. The blind men scratched their heads, saying they had been tricked, and the innkeeper did the same.

Their host sat and reflected: "If you get rid of the blind men now, your expenses won't be paid, and if you keep them, they'll gobble and guzzle even more. And if they still have no money by that time, your loss is doubled." He drove them into the pigsty behind the inn, locked them in, and threw down straw and hay in front of them.

Eulenspiegel reckoned that the time must have come for the blind men to have incurred expenses amounting to twelve guilders. He disguised himself, rode into town, and went to the inn owned by that man. When he entered the innyard and wanted to tie up his horse in the stable, he saw the blind men lying in the pigsty. He went into the house and said to the innkeeper: "Landlord, what's the idea of locking up the blind men in the pigsty? Don't you pity them for having to eat stuff that's bad for them?"

The innkeeper replied: "I wish they were in blazes, as long as I had the money they owe me." And he told Eulenspiegel the whole story of his disappointment with the blind men.

Eulenspiegel said: "What, landlord, can't you find anyone to be a guarantor for them?" The innkeeper thought to himself: "If I only had one!" He said aloud: "Friend, if I could find a guarantor I could trust, I'd accept his security and let the poor blind men go."

Eulenspiegel said: "Good, I'll go through town trying to locate a guarantor for you." Then he went to the parish priest and said: "Your reverence, do you want to be a good friend? There's this innkeeper whose guest I am; tonight he became possessed by an evil spirit, and he begs you to exorcise it for him."

The priest assented, but he said he had to wait a day or two, because such matters can't be rushed. Eulenspiegel said: "I'll go get his wife, so you can tell her that yourself."

The priest said: "Fine, let her come." Eulenspiegel returned to his host and said: "I've found a guarantor for you, your parish priest, who's ready to pledge that he'll make good your losses. So, let your wife go to him with me, and he'll give her full assurance."

The innkeeper was glad and willing, and he sent his wife along with Eulenspiegel to the priest. Eulenspiegel began: "Your reverence, here's the lady. Now tell her yourself what you told and promised me."

The priest said: "Yes, dear lady, in just a day or two I'll help him out." The lady said everything was all right. She went back home with Eulenspiegel and told her husband what the priest had said. He was happy. He released the blind men and told them to forget what they owed him. Eulenspiegel left the premises for good.

Two days later, the innkeeper's wife went to ask the preacher for the twelve guilders that the blind men had chalked up. The priest said: "Dear lady, did your husband give you that message?" She said yes. The priest said: "It's typical of evil spirits to ask for money."

The woman said: "He isn't an evil spirit; pay the reckoning!"

The priest replied: "I've been told that your husband is possessed by an evil spirit. Bring him here, and I'll relieve him, God willing."

The woman said: "That's the way swindlers are: they tell lies instead of paying up. You'll find out before the day is over whether or not my husband is possessed by an evil spirit!" She ran home and told the innkeeper what the priest had said. The innkeeper provided himself with javelins and halberds, and dashed over to the presbytery. When the priest saw him coming, he called to his neighbors to help him. Crossing himself, he said:

"Come and help me, dear neighbors. Look! This man is possessed by an evil spirit!"

The innkeeper said: "Priest, make up your mind to pay me!"

The priest stood there, crossing himself. As the innkeeper was about to strike the priest, the neighbors intervened and separated them with great difficulty. As long as the innkeeper and the priest lived, the innkeeper dunned the priest for that tab, and the priest maintained that he owed him nothing, but that the innkeeper was possessed with an evil spirit, from which he was willing to release him. That situation continued for the rest of their days.

A CATALOG OF SELECTED
DOVER BOOKS
IN ALL FIELDS OF INTEREST

A CATALOG OF SELECTED DOVER
BOOKS IN ALL FIELDS OF INTEREST

CONCERNING THE SPIRITUAL IN ART, Wassily Kandinsky. Pioneering work by father of abstract art. Thoughts on color theory, nature of art. Analysis of earlier masters. 12 illustrations. 80pp. of text. 5⅜ x 8½.   23411-8 Pa. $4.95

ANIMALS: 1,419 Copyright-Free Illustrations of Mammals, Birds, Fish, Insects, etc., Jim Harter (ed.). Clear wood engravings present, in extremely lifelike poses, over 1,000 species of animals. One of the most extensive pictorial sourcebooks of its kind. Captions. Index. 284pp. 9 x 12.   23766-4 Pa. $14.95

CELTIC ART: The Methods of Construction, George Bain. Simple geometric techniques for making Celtic interlacements, spirals, Kells-type initials, animals, humans, etc. Over 500 illustrations. 160pp. 9 x 12. (Available in U.S. only.)   22923-8 Pa. $9.95

AN ATLAS OF ANATOMY FOR ARTISTS, Fritz Schider. Most thorough reference work on art anatomy in the world. Hundreds of illustrations, including selections from works by Vesalius, Leonardo, Goya, Ingres, Michelangelo, others. 593 illustrations. 192pp. 7⅛ x 10¼.   20241-0 Pa. $9.95

CELTIC HAND STROKE-BY-STROKE (Irish Half-Uncial from "The Book of Kells"): An Arthur Baker Calligraphy Manual, Arthur Baker. Complete guide to creating each letter of the alphabet in distinctive Celtic manner. Covers hand position, strokes, pens, inks, paper, more. Illustrated. 48pp. 8¼ x 11.   24336-2 Pa. $3.95

EASY ORIGAMI, John Montroll. Charming collection of 32 projects (hat, cup, pelican, piano, swan, many more) specially designed for the novice origami hobbyist. Clearly illustrated easy-to-follow instructions insure that even beginning papercrafters will achieve successful results. 48pp. 8¼ x 11.   27298-2 Pa. $3.50

THE COMPLETE BOOK OF BIRDHOUSE CONSTRUCTION FOR WOODWORKERS, Scott D. Campbell. Detailed instructions, illustrations, tables. Also data on bird habitat and instinct patterns. Bibliography. 3 tables. 63 illustrations in 15 figures. 48pp. 5¼ x 8½.   24407-5 Pa. $2.50

BLOOMINGDALE'S ILLUSTRATED 1886 CATALOG: Fashions, Dry Goods and Housewares, Bloomingdale Brothers. Famed merchants' extremely rare catalog depicting about 1,700 products: clothing, housewares, firearms, dry goods, jewelry, more. Invaluable for dating, identifying vintage items. Also, copyright-free graphics for artists, designers. Co-published with Henry Ford Museum & Greenfield Village. 160pp. 8¼ x 11.   25780-0 Pa. $10.95

HISTORIC COSTUME IN PICTURES, Braun & Schneider. Over 1,450 costumed figures in clearly detailed engravings–from dawn of civilization to end of 19th century. Captions. Many folk costumes. 256pp. 8⅜ x 11¾.   23150-X Pa. $12.95

FRANK LLOYD WRIGHT'S DANA HOUSE, Donald Hoffmann. Pictorial essay of residential masterpiece with over 160 interior and exterior photos, plans, elevations, sketches and studies. 128pp. 9¼ x 10¾. 29120-0 Pa. $12.95

THE MALE AND FEMALE FIGURE IN MOTION: 60 Classic Photographic Sequences, Eadweard Muybridge. 60 true-action photographs of men and women walking, running, climbing, bending, turning, etc., reproduced from rare 19th-century masterpiece. vi + 121pp. 9 x 12. 24745-7 Pa. $12.95

1001 QUESTIONS ANSWERED ABOUT THE SEASHORE, N. J. Berrill and Jacquelyn Berrill. Queries answered about dolphins, sea snails, sponges, starfish, fishes, shore birds, many others. Covers appearance, breeding, growth, feeding, much more. 305pp. 5¼ x 8¼. 23366-9 Pa. $9.95

ATTRACTING BIRDS TO YOUR YARD, William J. Weber. Easy-to-follow guide offers advice on how to attract the greatest diversity of birds: birdhouses, feeders, water and waterers, much more. 96pp. 5 3/16 x 8¼. 28927-3 Pa. $2.50

MEDICINAL AND OTHER USES OF NORTH AMERICAN PLANTS: A Historical Survey with Special Reference to the Eastern Indian Tribes, Charlotte Erichsen-Brown. Chronological historical citations document 500 years of usage of plants, trees, shrubs native to eastern Canada, northeastern U.S. Also complete identifying information. 343 illustrations. 544pp. 6½ x 9¼. 25951-X Pa. $12.95

STORYBOOK MAZES, Dave Phillips. 23 stories and mazes on two-page spreads: Wizard of Oz, Treasure Island, Robin Hood, etc. Solutions. 64pp. 8¼ x 11. 23628-5 Pa. $2.95

AMERICAN NEGRO SONGS: 230 Folk Songs and Spirituals, Religious and Secular, John W. Work. This authoritative study traces the African influences of songs sung and played by black Americans at work, in church, and as entertainment. The author discusses the lyric significance of such songs as "Swing Low, Sweet Chariot," "John Henry," and others and offers the words and music for 230 songs. Bibliography. Index of Song Titles. 272pp. 6½ x 9¼. 40271-1 Pa. $9.95

MOVIE-STAR PORTRAITS OF THE FORTIES, John Kobal (ed.). 163 glamor, studio photos of 106 stars of the 1940s: Rita Hayworth, Ava Gardner, Marlon Brando, Clark Gable, many more. 176pp. 8⅜ x 11¼. 23546-7 Pa. $14.95

BENCHLEY LOST AND FOUND, Robert Benchley. Finest humor from early 30s, about pet peeves, child psychologists, post office and others. Mostly unavailable elsewhere. 73 illustrations by Peter Arno and others. 183pp. 5⅜ x 8½. 22410-4 Pa. $6.95

YEKL and THE IMPORTED BRIDEGROOM AND OTHER STORIES OF YIDDISH NEW YORK, Abraham Cahan. Film Hester Street based on *Yekl* (1896). Novel, other stories among first about Jewish immigrants on N.Y.'s East Side. 240pp. 5⅜ x 8½. 22427-9 Pa. $7.95

SELECTED POEMS, Walt Whitman. Generous sampling from *Leaves of Grass*. Twenty-four poems include "I Hear America Singing," "Song of the Open Road," "I Sing the Body Electric," "When Lilacs Last in the Dooryard Bloom'd," "O Captain! My Captain!"–all reprinted from an authoritative edition. Lists of titles and first lines. 128pp. 5 3/16 x 8¼. 26878-0 Pa. $1.00

THE BEST TALES OF HOFFMANN, E. T. A. Hoffmann. 10 of Hoffmann's most important stories: "Nutcracker and the King of Mice," "The Golden Flowerpot," etc. 458pp. 5⅜ x 8½. 21793-0 Pa. $9.95

FROM FETISH TO GOD IN ANCIENT EGYPT, E. A. Wallis Budge. Rich detailed survey of Egyptian conception of "God" and gods, magic, cult of animals, Osiris, more. Also, superb English translations of hymns and legends. 240 illustrations. 545pp. 5⅜ x 8½. 25803-3 Pa. $13.95

FRENCH STORIES/CONTES FRANÇAIS: A Dual-Language Book, Wallace Fowlie. Ten stories by French masters, Voltaire to Camus: "Micromegas" by Voltaire; "The Atheist's Mass" by Balzac; "Minuet" by de Maupassant; "The Guest" by Camus, six more. Excellent English translations on facing pages. Also French-English vocabulary list, exercises, more. 352pp. 5⅜ x 8½. 26443-2 Pa. $9.95

CHICAGO AT THE TURN OF THE CENTURY IN PHOTOGRAPHS: 122 Historic Views from the Collections of the Chicago Historical Society, Larry A. Viskochil. Rare large-format prints offer detailed views of City Hall, State Street, the Loop, Hull House, Union Station, many other landmarks, circa 1904-1913. Introduction. Captions. Maps. 144pp. 9⅜ x 12¼. 24656-6 Pa. $12.95

OLD BROOKLYN IN EARLY PHOTOGRAPHS, 1865-1929, William Lee Younger. Luna Park, Gravesend race track, construction of Grand Army Plaza, moving of Hotel Brighton, etc. 157 previously unpublished photographs. 165pp. 8⅞ x 11¾. 23587-4 Pa. $13.95

THE MYTHS OF THE NORTH AMERICAN INDIANS, Lewis Spence. Rich anthology of the myths and legends of the Algonquins, Iroquois, Pawnees and Sioux, prefaced by an extensive historical and ethnological commentary. 36 illustrations. 480pp. 5⅜ x 8½. 25967-6 Pa. $10.95

AN ENCYCLOPEDIA OF BATTLES: Accounts of Over 1,560 Battles from 1479 B.C. to the Present, David Eggenberger. Essential details of every major battle in recorded history from the first battle of Megiddo in 1479 B.C. to Grenada in 1984. List of Battle Maps. New Appendix covering the years 1967-1984. Index. 99 illustrations. 544pp. 6½ x 9¼. 24913-1 Pa. $16.95

SAILING ALONE AROUND THE WORLD, Captain Joshua Slocum. First man to sail around the world, alone, in small boat. One of great feats of seamanship told in delightful manner. 67 illustrations. 294pp. 5⅜ x 8½. 20326-3 Pa. $6.95

ANARCHISM AND OTHER ESSAYS, Emma Goldman. Powerful, penetrating, prophetic essays on direct action, role of minorities, prison reform, puritan hypocrisy, violence, etc. 271pp. 5⅜ x 8½. 22484-8 Pa. $7.95

MYTHS OF THE HINDUS AND BUDDHISTS, Ananda K. Coomaraswamy and Sister Nivedita. Great stories of the epics; deeds of Krishna, Shiva, taken from puranas, Vedas, folk tales; etc. 32 illustrations. 400pp. 5⅜ x 8½. 21759-0 Pa. $12.95

THE TRAUMA OF BIRTH, Otto Rank. Rank's controversial thesis that anxiety neurosis is caused by profound psychological trauma which occurs at birth. 256pp. 5⅜ x 8½. 27974-X Pa. $7.95

A THEOLOGICO-POLITICAL TREATISE, Benedict Spinoza. Also contains unfinished Political Treatise. Great classic on religious liberty, theory of government on common consent. R. Elwes translation. Total of 421pp. 5⅜ x 8½. 20249-6 Pa. $10.95

PERSPECTIVE FOR ARTISTS, Rex Vicat Cole. Depth, perspective of sky and sea, shadows, much more, not usually covered. 391 diagrams, 81 reproductions of drawings and paintings. 279pp. 5⅜ x 8½. 22487-2 Pa. $9.95

DRAWING THE LIVING FIGURE, Joseph Sheppard. Innovative approach to artistic anatomy focuses on specifics of surface anatomy, rather than muscles and bones. Over 170 drawings of live models in front, back and side views, and in widely varying poses. Accompanying diagrams. 177 illustrations. Introduction. Index. 144pp. 8⅜ x11¼. 26723-7 Pa. $9.95

GOTHIC AND OLD ENGLISH ALPHABETS: 100 Complete Fonts, Dan X. Solo. Add power, elegance to posters, signs, other graphics with 100 stunning copyright-free alphabets: Blackstone, Dolbey, Germania, 97 more–including many lower-case, numerals, punctuation marks. 104pp. 8⅛ x 11. 24695-7 Pa. $8.95

HOW TO DO BEADWORK, Mary White. Fundamental book on craft from simple projects to five-bead chains and woven works. 106 illustrations. 142pp. 5⅜ x 8. 20697-1 Pa. $5.95

THE BOOK OF WOOD CARVING, Charles Marshall Sayers. Finest book for beginners discusses fundamentals and offers 34 designs. "Absolutely first rate . . . well thought out and well executed."–E. J. Tangerman. 118pp. 7¾ x 10⅝. 23654-4 Pa. $7.95

ILLUSTRATED CATALOG OF CIVIL WAR MILITARY GOODS: Union Army Weapons, Insignia, Uniform Accessories, and Other Equipment, Schuyler, Hartley, and Graham. Rare, profusely illustrated 1846 catalog includes Union Army uniform and dress regulations, arms and ammunition, coats, insignia, flags, swords, rifles, etc. 226 illustrations. 160pp. 9 x 12. 24939-5 Pa. $10.95

WOMEN'S FASHIONS OF THE EARLY 1900s: An Unabridged Republication of "New York Fashions, 1909," National Cloak & Suit Co. Rare catalog of mail-order fashions documents women's and children's clothing styles shortly after the turn of the century. Captions offer full descriptions, prices. Invaluable resource for fashion, costume historians. Approximately 725 illustrations. 128pp. 8⅜ x 11¼. 27276-1 Pa. $11.95

THE 1912 AND 1915 GUSTAV STICKLEY FURNITURE CATALOGS, Gustav Stickley. With over 200 detailed illustrations and descriptions, these two catalogs are essential reading and reference materials and identification guides for Stickley furniture. Captions cite materials, dimensions and prices. 112pp. 6½ x 9¼. 26676-1 Pa. $9.95

EARLY AMERICAN LOCOMOTIVES, John H. White, Jr. Finest locomotive engravings from early 19th century: historical (1804–74), main-line (after 1870), special, foreign, etc. 147 plates. 142pp. 11⅜ x 8¼. 22772-3 Pa. $12.95

THE TALL SHIPS OF TODAY IN PHOTOGRAPHS, Frank O. Braynard. Lavishly illustrated tribute to nearly 100 majestic contemporary sailing vessels: Amerigo Vespucci, Clearwater, Constitution, Eagle, Mayflower, Sea Cloud, Victory, many more. Authoritative captions provide statistics, background on each ship. 190 black-and-white photographs and illustrations. Introduction. 128pp. 8⅞ x 11¾. 27163-3 Pa. $14.95

ANATOMY: A Complete Guide for Artists, Joseph Sheppard. A master of figure drawing shows artists how to render human anatomy convincingly. Over 460 illustrations. 224pp. 8⅜ x 11¼. 27279-6 Pa. $11.95

MEDIEVAL CALLIGRAPHY: Its History and Technique, Marc Drogin. Spirited history, comprehensive instruction manual covers 13 styles (ca. 4th century through 15th). Excellent photographs; directions for duplicating medieval techniques with modern tools. 224pp. 8⅜ x 11¼. 26142-5 Pa. $12.95

DRIED FLOWERS: How to Prepare Them, Sarah Whitlock and Martha Rankin. Complete instructions on how to use silica gel, meal and borax, perlite aggregate, sand and borax, glycerine and water to create attractive permanent flower arrangements. 12 illustrations. 32pp. 5⅜ x 8½. 21802-3 Pa. $1.00

EASY-TO-MAKE BIRD FEEDERS FOR WOODWORKERS, Scott D. Campbell. Detailed, simple-to-use guide for designing, constructing, caring for and using feeders. Text, illustrations for 12 classic and contemporary designs. 96pp. 5⅜ x 8½. 25847-5 Pa. $3.95

SCOTTISH WONDER TALES FROM MYTH AND LEGEND, Donald A. Mackenzie. 16 lively tales tell of giants rumbling down mountainsides, of a magic wand that turns stone pillars into warriors, of gods and goddesses, evil hags, powerful forces and more. 240pp. 5⅜ x 8½. 29677-6 Pa. $6.95

THE HISTORY OF UNDERCLOTHES, C. Willett Cunnington and Phyllis Cunnington. Fascinating, well-documented survey covering six centuries of English undergarments, enhanced with over 100 illustrations: 12th-century laced-up bodice, footed long drawers (1795), 19th-century bustles, 19th-century corsets for men, Victorian "bust improvers," much more. 272pp. 5⅜ x 8¼. 27124-2 Pa. $9.95

ARTS AND CRAFTS FURNITURE: The Complete Brooks Catalog of 1912, Brooks Manufacturing Co. Photos and detailed descriptions of more than 150 now very collectible furniture designs from the Arts and Crafts movement depict davenports, settees, buffets, desks, tables, chairs, bedsteads, dressers and more, all built of solid, quarter-sawed oak. Invaluable for students and enthusiasts of antiques, Americana and the decorative arts. 80pp. 6½ x 9¼. 27471-3 Pa. $8.95

WILBUR AND ORVILLE: A Biography of the Wright Brothers, Fred Howard. Definitive, crisply written study tells the full story of the brothers' lives and work. A vividly written biography, unparalleled in scope and color, that also captures the spirit of an extraordinary era. 560pp. 6⅛ x 9¼. 40297-5 Pa. $17.95

THE ARTS OF THE SAILOR: Knotting, Splicing and Ropework, Hervey Garrett Smith. Indispensable shipboard reference covers tools, basic knots and useful hitches; handsewing and canvas work, more. Over 100 illustrations. Delightful reading for sea lovers. 256pp. 5⅜ x 8½. 26440-8 Pa. $8.95

FRANK LLOYD WRIGHT'S FALLINGWATER: The House and Its History, Second, Revised Edition, Donald Hoffmann. A total revision–both in text and illustrations–of the standard document on Fallingwater, the boldest, most personal architectural statement of Wright's mature years, updated with valuable new material from the recently opened Frank Lloyd Wright Archives. "Fascinating"–*The New York Times*. 116 illustrations. 128pp. 9¼ x 10¾. 27430-6 Pa. $12.95

THE INFLUENCE OF SEA POWER UPON HISTORY, 1660–1783, A. T. Mahan. Influential classic of naval history and tactics still used as text in war colleges. First paperback edition. 4 maps. 24 battle plans. 640pp. 5⅜ x 8½. 25509-3 Pa. $14.95

THE STORY OF THE TITANIC AS TOLD BY ITS SURVIVORS, Jack Winocour (ed.). What it was really like. Panic, despair, shocking inefficiency, and a little heroism. More thrilling than any fictional account. 26 illustrations. 320pp. 5⅜ x 8½. 20610-6 Pa. $8.95

FAIRY AND FOLK TALES OF THE IRISH PEASANTRY, William Butler Yeats (ed.). Treasury of 64 tales from the twilight world of Celtic myth and legend: "The Soul Cages," "The Kildare Pooka," "King O'Toole and his Goose," many more. Introduction and Notes by W. B. Yeats. 352pp. 5⅜ x 8½. 26941-8 Pa. $8.95

BUDDHIST MAHAYANA TEXTS, E. B. Cowell and others (eds.). Superb, accurate translations of basic documents in Mahayana Buddhism, highly important in history of religions. The Buddha-karita of Asvaghosha, Larger Sukhavativyuha, more. 448pp. 5⅜ x 8½. 25552-2 Pa. $12.95

ONE TWO THREE . . . INFINITY: Facts and Speculations of Science, George Gamow. Great physicist's fascinating, readable overview of contemporary science: number theory, relativity, fourth dimension, entropy, genes, atomic structure, much more. 128 illustrations. Index. 352pp. 5⅜ x 8½. 25664-2 Pa. $9.95

EXPERIMENTATION AND MEASUREMENT, W. J. Youden. Introductory manual explains laws of measurement in simple terms and offers tips for achieving accuracy and minimizing errors. Mathematics of measurement, use of instruments, experimenting with machines. 1994 edition. Foreword. Preface. Introduction. Epilogue. Selected Readings. Glossary. Index. Tables and figures. 128pp. 5³/₈ x 8¹/₂. 40451-X Pa. $6.95

DALÍ ON MODERN ART: The Cuckolds of Antiquated Modern Art, Salvador Dalí. Influential painter skewers modern art and its practitioners. Outrageous evaluations of Picasso, Cézanne, Turner, more. 15 renderings of paintings discussed. 44 calligraphic decorations by Dalí. 96pp. 5⅜ x 8½. (Available in U.S. only.) 29220-7 Pa. $5.95

ANTIQUE PLAYING CARDS: A Pictorial History, Henry René D'Allemagne. Over 900 elaborate, decorative images from rare playing cards (14th–20th centuries): Bacchus, death, dancing dogs, hunting scenes, royal coats of arms, players cheating, much more. 96pp. 9¼ x 12¼. 29265-7 Pa. $12.95

MAKING FURNITURE MASTERPIECES: 30 Projects with Measured Drawings, Franklin H. Gottshall. Step-by-step instructions, illustrations for constructing handsome, useful pieces, among them a Sheraton desk, Chippendale chair, Spanish desk, Queen Anne table and a William and Mary dressing mirror. 224pp. 8¼ x 11¼. 29338-6 Pa. $13.95

THE FOSSIL BOOK: A Record of Prehistoric Life, Patricia V. Rich et al. Profusely illustrated definitive guide covers everything from single-celled organisms and dinosaurs to birds and mammals and the interplay between climate and man. Over 1,500 illustrations. 760pp. 7½ x 10⅛. 29371-8 Pa. $29.95

Prices subject to change without notice.

Available at your book dealer or write for free catalog to Dept. GI, Dover Publications, Inc., 31 East 2nd St., Mineola, N.Y. 11501. Dover publishes more than 500 books each year on science, elementary and advanced mathematics, biology, music, art, literary history, social sciences and other areas.